By Paul H. Rosenfeld

Gravity Drive - Key to the Cosmos

Gravity Drive 2 - Jason's Ark

Gravity Drive 3 - The Scattering
December 2023

Gravity Drive 2

Jason's Ark

-

Paul H. Rosenfeld

Gravity Drive 2 - Jason's Ark is a work of fiction. People's names are fictitious and purely products of the author's imagination or coincidental, except for historical or public figures. With the exception of generally accepted and documented historical events, the incidents in this book are also fictitious and for the sake of our planet, let's hope they stay that way.

First Edition

Cover images Courtesy NASA/JPL-Caltech

For those peaceful environmentalists

working tirelessly to

Save Mother Earth

"For most of history, man has had to fight nature to survive;
in this century he is beginning to realize that, in order to survive,
he must protect it."

— Jacques-Yves Cousteau

Preface

Thank you for coming back for the sequel to *Gravity Drive - Key to the Cosmos*. In the first book this is where we talked about acceleration from gravity. Didn't really want to trouble you with that whole thing again, so I'll just let you get on with reading the exciting sequel, *Jason's Ark*.

However, if you really found it useful or fun to refer back to the graph showing the velocity and distance traveled at 1 G, rest assured you can still find it at the back of the book. In other words, the original preface is not gone, just retired.

I hope you enjoy reading this sequel as much as I enjoyed writing it. Thank you for buying my book. It demonstrates you have excellent taste in Science Fiction and authors.

Prologue

The Big Bang wasn't an orderly and evenly distributed affair. Along with the countless small particles that streamed out in all three dimensions, some rather large lumps of various sizes were left over and even these didn't distribute themselves uniformly. So as the expansion during the first billion years slowed, these lumps began to pull together and form larger lumps. The influence of their gravity wells reached further and further as they grew. The original lumps began to collapse from the force of their own gravity, and draw themselves back into extremely dense matter; the first of the black holes.

Enormous clouds of dust and gas along with already formed stars were caught in the gravity well of the black holes and began to orbit. The first galaxies were formed. Our Milky Way was among one of those early galaxies, though she was much smaller then, turning slowly while gliding through the mostly empty vastness of space and time.

For billions of years she continued to gather stars from the stray groups that occasionally crossed her path. Eventually her strong gravity well extended far enough to capture the stars from other galaxies that passed too close. Through these billions of years, she collected a wide variety of stars. Some were so large and bright, they burned themselves out during just a few rotations, sharing themselves in vast bursts of energy; forming wide spread dustings to provide the raw materials for new stars to form. Others were so small they barely gained enough gravitational pressure to ignite, and burning slowly they've lived among her since the beginning. About a tenth of all the stars were between these two extremes. These mid-sized, yellow stars were far more stable than the larger ones, and provided superior conditions for the extended evolution of life on the planets that formed in their systems. This was especially true of the those systems which formed far from the crowded center of the galaxy. Far from the deep gravity wells, super novas, and unpredictable orbits which constantly rained destruction on life.

In the quieter outer regions, among those yellow stars life flourished on virtually every planet. The diversity of these life forms was immense given the brilliant design of the base DNA strands which populated the galaxy and spread among all the planets. This flexibility allowed life to evolve in virtually any imaginable environment: from hot rocks, to cold turbulent gases, to deep oceans. The formation of water molecules from the raw materials of stars was one of the great gifts of the physics and chemistry of stellar evolution, and it's abundance further enhanced the ability of life to thrive.

The Universe however is as cruel as it is kind. What it gives to allow life to form, it also takes away. From one perspective this seems utter cruelty when a billion years of evolving life is suddenly wiped out by the arrival of a single large rock.

Regardless of the great variety of life forms, they all have one thing in common; They all evolve in environments of delicately balanced ecosystems, each organism depending on something from another organism or specific chemical reaction to survive. So when that one rock comes barreling into it's environment with the speed and inertia provided by the planet's own gravity well, it's energy will alter the environment where it impacts the planet, and change the conditions under which life survives. We've seen fossil records of these occurrences many times on Earth. The most well known is the one which exterminated the great dinosaurs. For at least 165 million years the dinosaurs evolved and thrived, creating a splendid diversity of their kind. The balance within the ecology during those millions of years must have been nearly perfect, for life to have stayed in such a stable condition. If that rock hadn't impacted Earth, it's quite likely humans would never have even had a chance to start. So from the perspective of humans, that impact was a good thing.

Humans think of themselves as a successful species, yet our time of existence is so short compared to those dinosaurs, it's statistically insignificant. We see ourselves as masters of our destiny, though one little rock could so easily teach us otherwise. The dinosaurs, as successful as they seemed, didn't even see one complete revolution of our *Milky Way* galaxy, which astronomers and physicists calculate to take between 230-250 million years. Do we know what awaits us as the galaxy turns? What caused that one rock to enter our system and wipe out the dinosaurs after so many millions of years? What changed?

The collisions between galaxies are not tidy affairs with a place for every star, and every star in it's place. Astronomers tell us that even when two large galaxies collide, almost no stars actually make contact. This seems reasonable considering the unimaginably vast distances between them. However, don't let this deceive you into thinking there are no residual effects. Consider our small star and it's average solar system. The gravity well produced by our Sun is vast enough to maintain planets in stable orbits, including our eighth planet, Neptune, which is almost three billion miles distant and roughly 17 times the mass of Earth. Strong enough to maintain the Oort Cloud which some estimates place at between one quarter, to one half the distance to the closest star. A distance approaching two light years. So now when you think of two galaxies colliding, think about those vast gravitational wells all interacting. It's easy to see how disruptive this can be to the stable orbits of planets and those countless billions of rocks and comets waiting to be knocked out of the Oort cloud towards the inner system, and a planet teaming with life.

Many billions of years in the past, a massive dwarf galaxy we refer to as *Gaia*, passed closely enough to the *Milky Way* to lose all it's stars. We see evidence of it's sharing among the groups of clusters left behind and the thickening of our own disk. But what happened to it's central core, it's black hole? Is it still out there circling our galaxy perhaps faster than the outer rim, effecting the orbits of stars or causing asteroids and comets to collide with planets? Was it this orphaned black hole that four billion years ago came close enough to stop the dynamo at the heart of the fourth planet of our system; the dynamo that powered it's protective magnetic shield? When the shield collapsed, the atmosphere and oceans were ripped away by the stellar winds. Was Mars just beginning to come to life when this happened? What awaits Earth in the unknown future? It would appear that Earth and it's life has been very lucky.....so far.

Part One

RECOVERY

Chapter 1

Earth Date: 8,409

Pelagic Recovery Program – Deep Water Research Facility
Cocos Island, Costa Rica

Delphini was born underwater. Her mother, Balaena, was one of many in a long line to use the tank since it's installation over a hundred years ago. The clear sided birthing tank was attached to the primary diving platform so it could rise and fall with the changing tides. The local marine population was aware of it's purpose, so it attracted quite a lot of attention. The seawater in the tank was carefully filtered to remove any potential parasites, and warmed to 97 degrees Fahrenheit. Two underwater birthing specialists assisted Balaena through the process to ensure a safe delivery, and also a brief opportunity for two of her adopted aunts to witness the birth and have a quick peek and ping at the newborn. Her aunts were a pair of older female Spotted Dolphins who were permanent residents in the waters surrounding Cocos Island. Also in witness from the ocean side, and peering through the tank with his snorkel gear barely clearing the surface was Ben, Delphini's father. The aunts were playfully nudging Ben to the side and seemed to enjoy that he was physically separated from the birth, though they were well aware of his role in this miracle.

As Delphini emerged from her mother's womb, she stretched her body, enjoying the sudden freedom and added space. Moving from one warm and wet environment into another created little stress and she instinctively continued to rely on her umbilical cord for oxygen. She also recognized the sounds and feelings of the pings from her two aunts, who contrary to Delphini were quite excited and closely watching from the other side of the tank, their rostrums pressed tightly against the transparent titanium siding. The two birthing specialists nodded their heads at Balaena indicating that all was well, so she reached down and raised Delphini slowly to the surface and lifted her above the water for her aquatic friends to witness. As expected the dolphins breached the surface in celebration, and Dad popped out of the water with his mask off for a better look, while Mom gently hugged her daughter for the first time. The specialists moved quickly and with experience as one tied off the umbilical cord while the other administered prophylactic eye and ear drops to prevent any possible infection from the underwater environment. The first nursing would take care of the rest.

Throughout her pregnancy, Balaena and Ben had continued their work as marine restoration biologists, stationed at the Deep Water Research Facility located one mile off the west side of Cocos Island. The location was originally chosen almost 6,000 years ago during the first stage of the ocean life restoration project following the arrival of the Octopod's artificial intelligence ambassador known simply as Jason. His arrival sparked the beginning of the restoration of terrestrial Earth and it's oceans back to their unspoiled state, prior to human contamination. Even before the intervention of the Octopods on behalf of life on Earth, the Costa Rican government had taken a very serious stand on protecting the island, ocean, and sea life which utilized the waters off Cocos Island as the ancient gathering and breeding grounds for virtually every major Pacific Ocean pelagic species of both fish and Cetaceans. Among these was a resident pod of Spotted Dolphins. Resident in the sense they didn't migrate long distances to breed or feed, though they often disappeared for weeks chasing schools of fish or simply enjoying their freedom and the clean deep waters of the Pacific. Two of the alpha females in this pod took a serious interest in Balaena from her first week of pregnancy. Balaena would smile as she thought about how they knew, before she or Ben did. Balaena could feel their gentle sonic pings as they inspected the growing fetus. As the baby grew inside her, she also knew that it could feel the pings since it always kicked or stretched in response. She wondered how this would effect her baby's eventual relationship with the aunts. They would often accompany her and Ben on their daily dive inspections, instinctively providing protection to a pregnant member of their extended pod.

Raising a child on a research facility located in the middle of the Pacific Ocean was going to be a challenge for both the parents, and their daughter. Though they were in good company with many families that have been here, and done that. The facility itself was enormous. This wasn't your typical research station from the 20th century. The facility was designed with the idea that it would be a large, self sustaining, and permanent community of researchers and their families. So in addition to the usual laboratories and sub-marine observatories, there were family homes, gathering places for social events and entertainment, massive exercise zones for running track and playing outdoor sports, and of course schools. Each researcher at the facility was required to allocate at least a portion of their time to teaching at the school, in the hopes of providing a variety of world views from each of the distinctive personalities that worked and lived there, in addition to the minutiae of their unique research specialties. At the time of Delphini's birth there were 18 families with 28 children ranging from infants to college age adults. Delphini would have at least two other children her age to grow up with and explore places to get in trouble.

With all these facilities and options at their disposal, there was no denying these children would grow up with more fins and gills than the average human. So it was not an exaggeration to say that most of them learned to swim in the ocean, before they learned to walk. Which also meant that around the age most kids were learning to drive, these would already be comfortable in the advanced stages of underwater SCUBA diving. This was one area that had seen a great deal of technical improvement. The diving equipment of this era consisted of self contained re-breathing units that were also capable of pulling oxygen from the ocean in emergencies. Very small computer controlled high pressure tanks with various gases were part of the streamlined backpack, which fed air to the diver's full face mask. This arrangement allowed an unobstructed full view of the diver's surroundings, while permitting voice communications. However, like many technical advancements, the ability to communicate underwater had the disadvantage of sometimes being annoying, especially if you were diving with someone who tended to talk or mumble to themselves. So the general rule was to practice "silent diving," and save the chatter for emergencies, unless of course you were conducting research with your dive partner.

The computerized air mixers allowed extended deep water diving with the reduced chance for nitrogen narcosis and the bends. The computer also kept track of the individuals tissue gas state, and alerted them when it was necessary to begin the decompression portion of their dives. However, even with all these advanced safety features, humans were still humans, and their bodies were still susceptible to damage from improper use of the equipment or unsafe surfacing practices. Therefore, just like in the days of old, each person had to go through a course of instruction for the safe use of the equipment. In the case of living and working in an ocean research facility, this meant the training proceeded to the level of becoming pure muscle memory, and second nature. The risks in these deep and turbulent waters was just too great to allow anything less.

Today was certification day for Delphini and her two friends, Tris and Murena, to advance from Basic Level 1, to Mid-Level Cert. For this test, parents were never allowed to be involved. It was important to confirm a student's skill level wasn't dependant on parental support. Old Ben was the examiner today, and all three students liked him for his easy going approach and gentle corrections when they made a mistake. The residents at the facility had adopted the new social trend of not using last names. This had the desired side effect of making the overall environment less formal. There was however the occasional conflict of first names, which is why everyone called him Old Ben, so as not to confuse any reference to Delphini's father.

Old Ben watched his three students closely as they changed into their dive gear, making sure they performed all pre-dive gear safety checks. The gear room was situated on the lowest level above water, and immediately adjacent to the dive platform. The platform was mounted to a large vertical cylinder with a massive internal float, allowing the platform to rise and fall with the tides. A secondary platform, much like an open elevator provided flexible access to the ever moving dive platform. With all four participants now on the diving platform, Old Ben watched silently again as the three students made the final safety check of each other's gear. When everyone was ready, all he said was, "Good. Water's rough so use a roll entry. The tide is also strong today so descend immediately to 45 feet and group up. Remember, Silent Diving! Go." The three students, their backs to the ocean, rolled into the water and descended, with Old Ben close behind.

They met up at 45 feet and Old Ben was happy to see them all checking their internal gauges. The heads-up displays on the face masks made the old fashioned dangling gauges obsolete, and the information could be easily read from both sides; an additional safety feature. The instructor swam slowly around the small group, waiting to see who would notice their 5th companion first. It was a sunny day above, so when the shadow slowly passed overhead, all three students looked up at the same time. The manta ray was a familiar resident and she showed no fear of the four divers. Again, all Old Ben said was "OK" and the three students adjusted their buoyancy compensators and rose slowly to gently scratch the underbelly of the ray. Cleaning stations were common underwater sights all around the island, and the small fish who performed these tasks were far better at their jobs then the three girls. For some reason however, the ray seemed to enjoy the human interaction and the feelings were mutual. From the human side, this was likely a substitute for the unfortunate policy that dogs were not allowed at the facility. Previous experiences had made it impractical, and people definitely suffered for that type of company. But the policy was for the benefit of the dogs, not the people, so everyone grudgingly accepted it.

The ray was eventually satisfied and glided off into the deep waters. No matter how many times he saw this, it just never grew old; even moving against the strong current, the ray moved with slow powerful strokes that appeared almost effortless, and soon faded into the deeper, darker waters. He looked up to see his three students had returned so he began, again gradually swimming around them like a predator, "Today is all about confidence and muscle memory. It's been drilled into your heads that Panic is the one thing that most often kills a diver. Even with our advanced gear, accidents can happen, and when they do it's usually unexpected. If you don't believe me, just ask Delphini here." And with that, he reached over and yanked her face mask and breathing gear completely off her head. He chose her to go first with this skill since he'd witnessed her use it once before. They were on their first student night dive in the shallows. Delphini saw something on the bottom and swam over slowly to investigate. The stingray exploded off the bottom with no warning, and smacked her right in the face, knocking her mask clear off. Old Ben was almost more shocked at the suddenness then Delphini. He instinctively started to move towards her but stopped when he realized she hadn't panicked. She sat there for a moment with her eyes closed, and reached up slowly to retrieve her mask, pull it over her face and tip the bottom open to blow out the water. Students are made to practice this technique repeatedly, but it's always different the first time you need to do it in open water. After clearing her mask she calmly looked over at Old Ben, and gave him the OK sign by tapping the top of her head.

She did the same thing now, only Old Ben saw something he hadn't noticed the other time. With her mask off, while she sat there calmly for a moment, a small smile appeared on her mouth, and with her eyes closed she tipped he head up slightly as if she was enjoying the physical contact of her face with the salty water. She moved much slower this time and seemed to drag the whole process out. Perhaps she was just trying to show him she wasn't scared and in no rush, but he didn't think so. The other two students performed the skill equally as well, though without the obvious enjoyment Delphini displayed.

The next test was far more dangerous, and the instructor had to be prepared to act quickly if needed. "OK everyone, I want you to turn off your auto gas regulators, and switch to standard air mode, manual over-ride. As you know, this will simulate a gas mix computer failure, and force you to use your self awareness training to survive. Everyone look down. There's a small group of sharks and rays, sleeping in the current down there among the rocks. I want you to take your time headed down and join them." Without another word, the group descended slowly towards the sleeping assemblage. What Old Ben hadn't said, was the bottom here was at 140 feet. Just deep enough for nitrogen narcosis to set in within a couple minutes, or less. Each person was different for how quickly it hit them, and how they reacted. This was the part he had to be closely on watch for, even though he trusted this group of students, and they wouldn't be here today if he hadn't. Many years ago, he'd been diving a blue hole with a group that was supposed to be all highly advanced. One of the coral specialists however had gotten too wrapped up in studying one of the deeper species, gradually descended below 160 feet, and disappeared around an insert in the wall. If the Dive-master hadn't been paying attention, and shot down after him, the biologist would have been lost. It's a visual he'll never forget, watching that man disappear around the wall, and he couldn't help but have that in the back of his mind today.

Thankfully his fears quickly dissipated as the three girls silently communicated with the appropriate hand signals indicating they had noticed the depth, and the dreamy, wavy feeling of narcosis setting in. They all joined in the thumbs up signal to ascend and stopped at 80 feet as their heads cleared. They checked their own computers and each others for their gas tissue status, and without a word, elected to ascend gradually to 50 feet for their first stop in decompression. He would have no problem with this group. Growing up in this environment gave them a level of comfort with their skills that couldn't be taught. They would all be promoted to Mid-Level Cert., allowing them the freedom to dive the local waters in unsupervised groups of at least three; a practical and hard learned upgrade from the old two-person buddy system.

Open water diving wasn't the only form of learning kids growing up on the platform were exposed to. Sometimes it even came down to that old fashioned class room concept from thousands of years ago. The big difference here, for both the student and the instructors, is the people wanted to be here. They enjoyed their life, and the children inherited that love of the ocean from the entire environment they grew up in. So today, the class discussions were rather lively, and touched deeply on some of the painful lessons humanity had to endure in the distant past. The instructors all agreed that the understanding of these past lessons, no matter how distant in time, were important to avoid humanity from making the same mistakes all over again. So when today's instructor had one of her students ask what this island was like 6,000 years ago, when Jason first arrived, she saw her opening.

"The ocean environment you've all grown up in, being lucky enough to live on this research facility, was so different those thousands of years ago, you would be shocked if transported back to that time," the instructor began. "You've all read about how bad things were, and the root causes, so let's focus on how we got from there to here."

"During the thousands of years of ocean restoration, the populations of all species increased dramatically until roughly 1,000 years ago when they stabilized into a healthy balance. It was a major undertaking and required a complete U-turn with regards to human's use of the oceans. The first step was locating and removing as much of the "trash" as possible. Simultaneously, it was no longer permitted to use the ocean as a convenient place for dumping. This included any factories or sites of human activity on the major rivers that fed eventually into the oceans. In the short term, this part proved to be significantly easier then the cleanup. With the introduction of new manufacturing techniques provided by the Octopods, along with improved recycling systems, the amount of global waste was reduced to almost zero."

"The next part proved to be the hardest to accomplish. Since humans first learned to fish, they felt entitled to anything in the ocean that was available for the taking. That was no longer allowed, per direct mandate from the Octopods. Initially the removal of anything from the ocean was strictly forbidden, allowing fish populations to recover. Eventually, a return to the taking of certain species of fish was allowed, but only for the direct and conservative consumption of nutrients, as we all experience here at this facility. Gone were the days of using fish products for terrestrial fertilizers, decorations, or voodoo medicines. Practices such as shark finning were strictly forbidden and the punishments were severe. Of course the key to this success wasn't just stopping people from taking, it was learning how to stop the demand for these products. Where there's no demand, the process of removal automatically stops." "With regards to the struggling Cetacean populations, in addition to the prohibition against any hunting or capturing of these distant human cousins, there were also penalties against harassment of any kind, which included close approach by sightseers. In areas where these mammals were common, the use of prop driven boats was strictly forbidden. Though this last point was minor since improved drive systems had converted most power boats to thrust propulsion. Finally, all nations were no longer allowed the use of any type of underwater sonar systems, and these were methodically stripped from all ocean going vessels including submarines, which substituted the use of tight beam, non-reflective lasers for scannering."

"As a direct result of the virtual elimination of pollutants spewed into both the air and water systems, combined with advanced transportation systems that didn't produce unburned hydrocarbons, the global temperature slowly fell, and a return of the ice caps and glaciers proceeded. This led to a return of the healthy breeding grounds for the massive quantities of basic life forms such as krill that fed the growing populations of polar feeding whales, among others. The major ocean currents had also stabilized providing a more balanced and consistent environment for the fish populations as well as a return to more predictable weather patterns with fewer extreme events."

"Right here at this very station, we see the benefits of all these global improvements. Virtually every pelagic species in the Pacific Ocean passes through these waters surrounding Cocos Island. They pass through here on their way to feed or breed. They come here to gather in large numbers taking advantage of the vast cleaning stations provided by the resident fish populations, before moving on. And you've all been fortunate to witness many of these gatherings. People who go recreational diving in places like Hawaii might talk about how beautiful that one green parrot fish was. Here, you've seen that same green parrot fish school in the thousands! It's the main reason we're here; we monitor the health of these pelagic species as they visit and pass. You're very fortunate to have the privilege of growing up in this environment and enjoying the results of 6,000 years of cleanup efforts."

"But that's just how we stopped polluting, and cleaned up the mess we made," one of the students commented, "but how did we actually get all the fish and marine mammals to recover?"

"That's a really great question, Bruce," the teacher responded, "and the answer is probably the most important thing you'll learn today. First of all, it's important to understand that we all live in a physical world. In other words, life is subject to the exact same forces as inorganic matter all the way up to level of planets, solar systems, and galaxies. A good example is a pendulum, like the kind you've seen used in grandfather clocks or on the films you've watched of the Foucault Pendulum at the Smithsonian Museum. You could say, that a pendulum is the perfect example for the balance of life in any ecosystem. The pendulum doesn't sit still at the bottom of it's swing, it forever moves back and forth through that center spot. When the tick and the tock are equally spaced in time and pace, the clock is in perfect balance. For example, the relationship between prey and predator swings back and forth through time. When the predators over hunt the prey's ability to recover, the predator's own population suffers for lack of food, until the prey recovers. The numbers swing back and forth until a balance is reached, though it's never exactly static, just like the pendulum. Another way of looking at it is by realizing that everything moves in waves. You're used to seeing waves displayed on your monitors horizontally. Or I suppose, living on this facility it's the ocean's waves you see, though they're also horizontal. If you tilt your head and watch the pendulum swing back and forth you realize it's transcribing the same crest and trough of a wave form. So the same analogy applies. If the crest and trough are the same height and depth, the wave is balanced."

"So now we introduce humans into the environment. Some researcher from the distant past notices an imbalance and decides they want to correct it. A good example was back in the mid 1900's when marine biologists saw a huge upswing in the sea star populations. They felt these slow moving predators were over hunting other marine life, like the sea urchins, so they decided to kill as many sea stars as they could. Their intentions were good, but they didn't see the whole picture, mainly because the picture is so huge and complex. What happened as a result of removing the sea stars was the urchin population exploded. Urchins eat the root structures of kelp, so suddenly we had mass die offs of kelp. The kelp formed both shelter and food sources for many sea creatures in the shallows so suddenly the entire ecosystem was thrown out of balance. And yet prior to this attempt, the system was mostly in balance, it was just swinging to one side, like our pendulum. Of course, it's even more complicated then that, since one of the other disturbances humans caused was by the hunting of sea otters, who loved nothing better than swimming to the bottom of the kelp bed and grabbing a nice sea urchin lunch. So as you begin to see, this gets more and more complicated. At some point, you'll realize that just about everything you do disrupts the environment in some fashion, at some level."

"We can simplify this by going back to our pendulum. If we equate our attempt to change something in the environment to giving the pendulum a good shove, what happens? The pendulum swings wildly, completely loosing it's balance, and depending on how hard we shoved it, it might even break entirely. Which is pretty close to what we did. So you could equate all our cleanup efforts to the repair of the pendulum. The cleanup was basically just humanity getting out of the way of nature. Nature does a pretty good job of balancing itself. It took thousands of years to recover, but eventually it did, as we've seen for ourselves. And the lesson here, is that the best thing we can do is LEAVE IT ALONE. So that became our motto as a species, as we moved forward. The best thing we can do to heal and maintain our environment in it's pristine and balanced state, is to do Nothing to disturb it."

"But doesn't the grandfather clock depend on it's weights to keep moving?" Bruce asked. "So aren't humans sort of the weights in that analogy? Aren't we needed to keep things moving?"

"That's another great observation, Bruce, and very representative of how easy it is to get it wrong. No offense intended, and you're not the first to think of that. It was a common mistake in the past. The simple answer is, No, we're not the weights, we're the child running past and bumping the clock. The difference is between open and closed systems. The clock exists in a very closed system, and yes it does depend on humans to move the weights back up. But we're not the weights. The environment of the Earth however, is an open system, so there are many factors effecting the balance. But if we're focused on the weights, then the best analogy is that our Sun, is like the weights. It's the main source of energy for the planet. Same as the weights are the energy for the pendulum."

Delphini enjoyed these topside classes since they got her thoughts rolling and gave her a chance to explore new ideas. Something about today's discussions made her feel melancholy though and she wasn't sure why. Whenever she felt this way it always seemed to help clear her mind if she just put on her dive gear and sat on the bottom of the ocean. Fortunately her two close friends, Tris and Murena, felt the same way so the three of them gathered their gear and made an after school dive under the facility. They had an agreement at times like this to stay close enough to each other in case of an emergency, but just far enough apart to allow some solitude.

A short time later, Delphini was sitting cross-legged on the sandy bottom directly under the main construct of the facility. She loved to just stare at the support structures and colonies of life that grew there; complete ecosystems in miniature. They were built that way on purpose, to attract life and serve as anchors for the colonies. These were miniatures of the massive 300 foot tall posts made from recycled ocean trash that formed the open water artificial reefs and atolls surrounding many of the ocean research facilities dedicated to studying non-pelagic species. Her studies included many detailed holographic videos of these vast constructs and the permanent underwater living facilities for the researchers and their families. The housing and research labs were vast acres of single story structures anchored to the ocean bedrock. The structures were kept low to reduce the upward stress from the massive amounts of water they displaced. Tall structures were just too difficult to anchor, and essentially unnecessary. With only a few exceptions the "roofs" of these structures were mostly covered with the same colonies as the tall poles, giving the entire facility the look of a giant underwater forest. Exceptions were made for the clear transparent titanium view ports used for research. And of course each separate family housing had a relatively small (about 10%) section set aside for viewing, to prevent claustrophobia and enhance the living conditions for the families. She imagined what it would be like to live and work in that environment; an environment so different than the open ocean air, sunshine, and high sea waves of the powerful storms that swept the area where she lived.

Delphini closed her eyes, slowed her breathing, and let her mind go blank the way she'd been taught when trying to search her deepest feelings. Time passed in an unpredictable fashion when she was in this state of mind, so she wasn't sure how long it had been, when the feeling came to her. At first it was like a very gentle knock at the door of her awareness. It grew slowly. She had the distinct feeling she was being watched, so when she opened her eyes she wasn't surprised to see one of her dolphin aunts hovering motionless in the water 10 feet away. Her mind was still in a relaxed and empty state so she was open to the strong feelings coming from the dolphin. She knew all about how they communicated with clicks and sonar, sounds that were words in their own language, and even body language. But there was something else here now. Something that people studying dolphins missed. It was the thing that prevented humans and dolphins from communicating beyond the simplest of ideas. It was the thing that was hardest to quantify because even in our language there were no words for it. It was the exchange of feelings that completed the array of other forms of communication and brought them all together. She was feeling it now, and it brought an understanding to her conscious level. The message from the dolphin was clear and simple and it felt something like, "what the heck are you still doing here?"

When she surfaced from this dive, she went straight to her mom and dad, and announced that she was 18 years old now, and it was time to move on to something different. Time for new experiences. Time to study ocean life from the other side.

Chapter 2

Earth Date: 8,409

Clavius Base – Earth's Moon

The speed rover was sliding sideways as it rounded the sand pit just inside the boundary warning marker. As the driver brought his rover around the far side of the pit, the rover he was chasing overcorrected and spun directly into the pit, logging itself in the sand. Now he had an open track straight back towards the second marker and victory if he could only pass this last speeder who's dust he was currently eating. He slammed the accelerator to the floor and tried passing on the rough surface at the innermost portion of the lane but his tire caught something and jerked to the right, sending him right into the other speeders path. The crash sent the second speeder flying through the air off the other side of the track, and right into the Administrator for Clavius Base, Arnold Speck. Arnold managed to survive the encounter with the hologram recording saying only, "this is the type of crap we have to put up with now that the tourism industry has basically taken over Clavius Base! Lights."

When the lights came back up in the conference room, Arnold was standing over his edge of the great round table that housed the holoprojector and central processing displays for the 5 other members of the Base's management team: Flight, Recycle, Engineering, Agriculture, and Tourism. "Some of you have been with me since I came here over 25 years ago," he continued. "Back then, we completed the water extraction processing having utilized all the raw materials available in the region. In fact, all the major undertakings over the past several thousand years

Paul H. Rosenfeld

25

planned for Clavius Base have been completed and now we're expected to just switch into long term maintenance mode."

"Humans are creatures of conflict. For whatever genetic reason, we evolved with the need to be constantly challenged. The moment we let our guard down, the moment we find ourselves idle, we start looking for ways to stay busy or get ourselves in trouble. As our ancestors proved for our entire history, the simplest way to achieve that was through war. So much easier to throw a rock at your neighbor than to sit down and figure out ways to improve your relationship. When we stop progressing, our lives and our science languishes. We rot. Our lives are a sorry affair unless each generation has something to investigate or something to create. That's why we're here today. I'll be damn if we're just going into maintenance mode on my watch. So we're going to sit here until we come up with some good ideas for what we can do next. I want to hear from each of you so get your coffee warmed up. I'll start."

"Before the days of GASA and the first gravity drive vehicles, this base broke ground with a ridiculously limited budget and the idea of providing a permanent base on the Moon primarily as an efficient jumping off point for deep space travel and eventual colonization. Then along came our alien friends and we got a major upgrade in our finances. At first we all thought the gravity drive would eliminate the need for a jump off point, but it turned out to be just the opposite."

"The main focus back on Earth was cleaning the place up, so undertaking major space exploration projects didn't quite fit in. Better to do it someplace else. Also, with the gravity drive, we now had a cheap and easy way to pack up all that old trash, and send it to the Moon where we could make it into something useful. We got pretty good at doing just that, and combined with the good luck of finding enough water here to survive, we created all these Lunar research bases, orbiting residences, and hotels for our idiot tourists, like the guy that just ran into me a few minutes ago. We still haven't figured out a healthy way for people to permanently live on the surface in 1/6 G, and maybe we won't until we can either come up with some efficient way to create gravity on a house by house basis, or until we evolve our DNA to live for long periods of time in minimal gravity."

"Off Moon, our brothers and sisters on Mars wouldn't have even survived their first couple years up there, and they'd still be eating just potatoes and ketchup, if we hadn't developed the techniques for off-Earth farming and terraforming in a high radiation environment. They still depend on us as the middle-person brokers for all the supplies they can't wrangle for themselves out there. All in all, we're in a pretty sweet spot right now and I intend to make that even better. I remind you of all this history as a way of getting your minds back on track towards creating a new future for all of us up here living in Lunar orbit. So, your turns now. Give us a quick update of where you are and any ideas we can brainstorm for moving forward. Flight, let's start with you Gracie."

Gracie Armstrong was a GASA lifer, who chose this position on the Moon because it was getting too boring down in Houston. Flight's job down there wasn't much different then directing an old fashioned shipyard loading dock, except when you lifted something up to load, it just kept going up and up. Besides, the view was much nicer up here since all the residents had clear and unobstructed views of Earth and the Moon, given the stepladder high polar orbits dictated by GASA. Maybe we were actually learning a few lessons from our past mistakes of filling Earth's orbit with every conceivable piece of junk.

"Well, starting with ground base operations," Gracie began, "the amount of traffic we're seeing from shipping and receiving, between Earth and Mars, and the number of tourist flights each week, we're pretty much maxed out. We had to have a supply ship sit in orbit for over an hour last week waiting for an opening. So my first item would be to add at least 3-4 more complete bases with drop elevators for the ships, as well as all the connecting tunnels. That would be a good 10-15 year project if you want to keep people busy. And speaking of which, I think we have enough traffic to finally warrant a dedicated space port, at least for people traffic and maybe some light goods and food. That would ease using the bases for moving stuff up and down, and free up another dock or two. That's another 10 year project for your list. Then we've got the bus station for inter-base transport and tourist buses. Same overcrowding is starting to happen there. Personally, I'd like to have a completely separate facility for the tourist buses so we don't have to worry about overexpansion in any one region. Moving the tourists off site would be a heck of a lot cheaper than moving cargo transports. That's a 50 year project for you. How long do you plan to live Chief? I can keep going."

"That's a pretty good start, Gracie," Arnold responded, while recording everything into the automated budgeting proposal system. "OK Recycle, let's move to you John before Gracie takes the whole Lunar budget."

John Fish, was the new guy of the group, and came up from private industry. He'd worked for one of the rare companies that started thousands of years ago collecting and recycling both land based and ocean trash. They were a unusual company that wasn't concerned primarily about profit, and were motivated largely by the opportunity to help clean up the planet. They were also the company that came up with the chemistry for turning just about any trash into functional, high strength building materials. The end result of their processes were providing materials for everything from corrosion proof deep sea construction to the space stations in orbit around Earth, Mars, and the Moon. They even invented the process for making transparent titanium from trash. This brought the company to the head of the list when it was time for GASA to take the Moon project seriously. John wasn't actually bored with his work on Earth and wasn't sure how well he'd adjust to the environment here. His main reason for taking the "promotion" as they called it, was the wife and kids. For some reason they all wanted to live on the Moon so what's a dad to say?

"Sounds like we're in about the same situation as Gracie. Our supply of water is stable enough for now, and adequate to meet the needs for current consumption including all the Ag farms. That includes the waste recyclers ability to keep up with current loads. But if we plan to do any growing, we're going to need more resources, especially for water. Our evaporation rates are the lowest we've had since the new seals went in last decade, but we're still losing water. I don't even want to think about asking Earth for any since the last time we did that there were riots down there from the ocean rights protesters at the desalination plants. They felt providing water to the Moon, Mars, and all the space stations was eventually going to have an impact on ocean levels, and put us back to the short sighted thinking of 6,000 years ago. That's when they came up with that slogan, *Let them drink rainwater*. And we all know they weren't talking about Earth. So my first item would be to increase our hunt for more Moon based sources. The obstacles are the same as always though; the water's there, it's just damn hard and expensive to get to. I'd say a good 5-10 years to develop the new fields and start production. Unless of course you want to start hauling comets in from the Oort cloud. As for mineral mining, there's not much change there. The demand for what we have is pretty low and steady, so no need to expand. Besides, it looks like Mars is going to start mining the asteroid belt more aggressively and that will likely eliminate almost all demand from them. In fact, if that's successful, they'll probably want to start shipping stuff downhill through us but that's a concern for Flight I suppose. Sorry Gracie."

"OK, thanks John. That's about where we figured to be, especially on water," Arnold said. "Pretty much a no-brainer to move ahead there. Engineering. Sundar, you're up."

Sundar Narayen had been here since before Arnold and people figured he was getting ready to retire, though he just kept going. Everyone had to admit that Engineering pretty much stood for *Everything and Anything that wasn't covered by another department*. That could really wear on a person, but Sundar seemed to enjoy the challenge and was about the best multi-tasker Arnold had ever known. Probably helped that he was single and a major introvert.

"I'm happy to hear about all the new and expanded projects that everyone wants," Sundar groaned. "No seriously, I'm not being nearly as sarcastic as I probably sound. There's a ton of engineers and workers Earth-side that would enjoy the opportunity to get paid for coming to the Moon, and it sounds like we're going to need thousands more. Besides Arnold, I totally agree with you that there could be nothing more boring than just going into maintenance mode. The only thing I'd like to add to what's been said so far, is the next Space Station we build should be ten times the size of our largest. Area wise, the cost is much lower, and the engineering stresses are far less. I'd say make that one the upgraded residential station and tourist arrival port, and convert one of the older ones to dedicated materials transport. Unless of course we have an unlimited budget?"

"Hahaha," Arnold chuckled. "I was worried we might not have the enthusiasm to keep growing but it looks like the real roadblock will be money. As always. Agriculture, you're up Amol."

No one really seemed to know how long Amol Luciano had been Moonside. He just seemed to have always been here which was ridiculous of course. Somewhere along the way HR lost his

Gravity Drive 2 - Jason's Ark

records, or they got hacked. That was pretty much ignored though since Agriculture was doing a great job of feeding everyone, and the quality of the fresh food just kept improving. He had a green thumb for the job and passed it on to his field workers. Technically Agriculture was in charge of not just growing, but processing and storage of all Lunar food production as well as the import and export of food products. They also handled all the personal items people need like soaps, clothing, hygiene, etc.. Amol however almost never got involved in anything but managing the greenhouses. He hired other people to handle all the rest, though he did keep in touch well so he knew what was going on.

"This all just feels like a giant expanding spiral to me. Everything you're all saying points back to the need for more food and personal items. Just make sure that for every 500 people you add to permanent residence, tack on the budget to build another full size greenhouse to feed them, and the water, raw fertilizer, and amendment materials we're going to need to get them running. Otherwise, I see no problems on our end keeping up with demand."

"Thanks Amol," Arnold said. "So really Amol, how long have you been here?"

Amol just looked back at Arnold and said, "I grew up here. I was born in Station 3 and it's not my fault they lost my records or someone in IT deleted them. Never really cared. And don't ask me how old I am because they deleted that too, and I don't remember or care."

"Good evasion Amol. Well that just leaves my favorite department, Tourism. Jane do I even want to ask what you're thinking?"

Jane Kong was also born in Lunar orbit, but they hadn't lost her records, though she seemed a lot younger than what HR showed. She was your basic 100% people person. Attended every social and sporting event possible, as well as any meetings involving residential housing since that was one of her primary duties as well. There was originally a bit of concern that her moving into this position was the result of a bit of nepotism, though no one really complained since it wasn't exactly the kind of job people were pounding down doors to get. Besides, she was doing such a good job of bringing much needed funding to the Lunar budget, no one wanted to disturb the money tree.

"Arnold why is it every time we meet like this you conveniently leave Housing out of your introduction?" Jane asked. Before he could respond she continued, "The permanent housing issue seems to have already been addressed. It obviously boils down to whatever we need to grow. I do agree with Sundar, that the next orbital station should be as big as possible. Everyone loves the slower rotation of the bigger stations since it gives a much longer view. Also, that's a great excuse to update furnishings and add some additional orbital attractions."

"It's a bit surprising how many visitors are attracted here by the physical activities, rather than the idea of being on the Moon. Low gravity golf brings more rich visitors than just about anything else, even though they have to use balls that are 6 times the mass as the ones on Earth. The two mile long zip lines, long distance running, and even ping pong are still big attractions. The crowds for our local sporting events keep filling the stadiums. Especially basketball. Nothing like watching a short engineer stuff a ball into a 19' high basket. The exploration adventures with scientific groups were never a big draw but we need to keep those running for the educational groups and students. Same for the historical sites like Apollo 11 and *Gravitas-1*, though we are having some problems at the *Gravitas-1* site since we noticed the bottom of the "termite mound" was getting narrower. People taking samples home. We've roped that off now, and figure we lost about 50 Earth pounds of dust. It's amusing to look at the sites on Earth that pawn moon rocks. Apparently if you total it all up there's about a ton of *genuine Gravitas-1* termite dust for sale."

"OK kidding aside, the bottom line for my department is simple. The more tourists we can bring up, the more money goes into the local economy. Expanding these rec sites would be a good use of funds since they're starting to get a bit crowded, and they're big money makers. Unfortunately, we do have to put up with the occasional morons like the one that ran into Arnold earlier, but the good news is nobody was seriously injured so there won't be any lawsuits."

"That's always good to hear, Jane," Arnold said. "Thank you and sorry about the Housing oversight. You just do such a great job with that and the services it all feels seamless. So, it looks like I'll need to crack out the old spreadsheet later and try to add all this up. If we did everything we've discussed today, we're probably going to need another 10,000 permanent bodies up here, and Jane only knows how many tourist accommodations. I'll be calling each of you to go over the details in the next few weeks. And look at that, it's almost dinner time. Amazing planning on my part." That was the traditional Arnold way of closing a meeting and the hint for everyone to go home.

Moondust

The conference room was in the lowest step orbit of the stations, with Arnold's home in the next one up. He left the stations in higher orbits to the workers and tourists. There were over two million full time residents in orbit counting all the families, and almost that many available hotel spaces for visitors. Each station had several schools and most tended to specialize in various trades and useful disciplines. In Lunar orbit, going off to college often meant moving to a different station. Anything to get away from the folks. The colleges even had dorms to complete the experience. For those with different interests, Earth colleges were always an option. Arnold's home wasn't much different than any of the other residents. He didn't want it to seem like he was somehow deserving of more than someone who toiled on the Lunar surface, or risked their lives working on construction and maintenance in the cold vacuum and high radiation of space.

His wife Angie, and their two kids Wendy and Peter, who were both born in orbit, were waiting for his pod to arrive so they could start dinner. This was one area where Arnold was predictable and punctual. He enjoyed having his meals at set times, mainly so it was easy for the family to be together. That worked great when the kids were young, but now they were teenagers. At meal time it felt like the gravity in the station had reversed as the kids couldn't wait to finish, pop out of their seats and fly out the door to go hangout with friends. They'd just started to eat when Arnold's emergency phone chimed. "Darn it, Arnold," Angie complained, annoyed at the inevitable interruptions at meal time, "do they have to call you every time someone's toilet backs up?"

Arnold ignored the outburst, knowing she was right, but also knowing they didn't call him on that line unless it really was something important. After answering, he stood quietly and listened, with the whole family watching. "OK, I'll be right down. Send the exact coordinates to my pod's nav." He grabbed his personal comm-link and headed directly towards the garage door. "A tour bus got caught in Moondust. I need to get down there. I'll keep you posted." And with that he was in his pod and on the way down. There was just enough space in his personal pod to change into his environment suit for the surface. By the time the pod's automatic navigation system had him over the site, he was ready.

The tour bus was a ground type, setup for people who wanted the whole 1/6 G bumpy ride experience to go along with their site seeing. The routes are carefully laid out with electronic markers buried along the roads to keep the buses exactly inside the well established safe zones. This shouldn't have happened. The bus was smack in the middle of a road that's been used for generations. The engineers do safety scans of these roads on a yearly basis. But there was no denying that big bus sitting out there half sunk in Moondust, held up only by it's emergency floatation ring. These devices have been installed on every vehicle that works on the Lunar surface, since the beginnings of colonization. Astronomers had predicted the existence of these Lunar traps, that resembled dry versions of quicksand on Earth. The dust was so light and fluid it flowed like water. Anything, or anyone, who's displacement weighed more than the dust, would quickly sink with no sign left above for searchers. So every ring was specifically designed for each type of vehicle to displace at least twice their weight in dust as a safety margin. It was the same concept that allowed the gigantic ocean going vessels to stay afloat. Thousands of years ago, during early colonization, these types of events were common, which led to the development of the safety devices. Like the Apollo astronauts who didn't like to think of their friends who died in Apollo one, Arnold didn't like to remember those unfortunate early discoverers of these traps. You gave your thanks, learned your lessons, promised never to forget and moved on. Nowadays falling into one of these traps was rare since scanners had been developed to spot these areas in advance. The fact that this happened in the middle of a well known safe spot, made Arnold realize immediately there was something else going on here.

Before touching down he saw the rescue shuttle lifting off from the bus. "Good, they got here quickly, before any panic could set in among the tourists," he thought to himself. "But where's the crane? Why were the engineers leaving the bus alone and walking around it's perimeter in their personal inflators and scanning the ground?" He used his pod's link to call Jane Kong who answered quickly. "Jane, in case you haven't heard, one of your buses hit a dust trap. The safety ring kept the bus afloat, and they got everyone off quickly, but you probably have some tourism-type damage control to attend to. I just arrived on-site so I'll call again if there's anything else you need to know. Out." He hung up quickly, not wanting to get trapped in a conversation about tourists. The instant he landed he vented the pod and popped the door, inflating his own safety boots as he exited.

Sundar Narayen was already on site directing the engineers in what looked like a search. "Sundar," Arnold started as he walked up, "did we lose someone? What's going on?"

"No, we got everyone off quick but there's obviously something strange going on. This shouldn't have happened here." Sundar started walking towards the bus and Arnold followed closely. "Look at the dust directly around the float ring. See anything unusual?"

Arnold tried to see what Sundar was talking about and then noticed what looked like a shadow under the ring, was too large given the location of the sun. "Is that moisture?"

"Yes! Free water. It doesn't seem to be trapped in any type of minerals. It's seeping up from right under the bus, which is why we're not going to move that thing till we figure out what's happening. My best guess is the water's always been here under a heavy layer of compressed sand and rock. We've been driving over this area for so many centuries, I think the bus finally broke through some upper layer. The scans show it's just a small crack, and there's no pressure forcing it up so we may have ourselves an actual underground lake here. Maybe an ancient impact site for a comet that buried itself quickly."

As they were talking one of the engineers came up and pointed to his portable scanner screen, turning it so both his bosses could see the readout. There was a rough line across the top representing the Lunar surface and a small rectangle barely visible that was the bus. Underneath the entire bottom of the screen was a very light blue color which the scanner represented as water. "Sir, it looks like we have a large lake here. The scanners still can't pick it up from above. This came from one of the probes we stuck through the crack under the bus. There's something about the rock here that's shielding the water scanners. Sir, I think we should get the fabrication guys out here pronto and seal that crack as soon as we pull the bus off, or we'll risk losing this water to space."

"Well," Arnold said, "looks like we won't have to worry about our water supply for a while, and at least I have a good excuse for letting my dinner get cold, this time."

Chapter 3

Earth Date: 8,409

Sebangau National Park
Central Kalimantan - Borneo

The small family of Orangutans were perched quietly in the Ironwood trees just above the two humans who'd waded into their territory. They'd seen humans many times, and despite their instinctive feelings, they knew these two posed no threat; they had the look and smell of creatures that lived in the peat swamp forest. Unlike those pale skinned humans that stumbled and splashed, and jammered without stop, disturbing the peaceful nature of their home, these two were standing very still over one of the *bad-smell* plants that were to be avoided.

The small skink had climbed up the stem of the tall plant slowly stocking the beetle he was hoping would be an easy meal. The skink was young and inexperienced with the abundant variety of deadly plants that populated his limited hunting ground. The smell should have been a warning but the beetle was too tempting and had his full attention. This Nepenthes rajah was almost a full 5 feet tall, and with a pitcher that could hold up to three quarts of a sweet smelling digestive fluid, it was the largest carnivorous plant on Earth. The plant was so large, the lizard thought it was climbing a tree, still not paying attention. The beetle was almost to the opening of the pitcher and hesitated. The skink leaped the last 6 inches at the beetle, grabbing it firmly in it's mouth, it's momentum carrying them both over the lip and into the pitcher.

"Ahhhh, disgusting. Poor lizard," Ismail said to his companion, as they both stood almost hip deep in the marshy peat of the forest. "I just don't get what you find so attractive about these gross plants. With all the amazing insects and other animals that live in our country, you choose to study….. these."

"Ismail my dear old friend, and almost cousin," Farah said, "at least the things I study don't crawl into your bed at night or drop into your soup. These plants are beautiful miracles of evolution. There's nothing like them anywhere else in the whole world, and they're right here in our backyard. And best of all, I get paid to study them."

"Granted, Farah, they're miracles all right but why? Why did all these plants evolve into carnivores? And don't start in with the *how*. It's always the *how*. I know how they evolved with their defense mechanism genes changing into digestive attack mode but *why* did they evolve to eat meat?"

"It's just their way of surviving in areas where the soil doesn't have enough nutrients."

"That's just more *how*, Farah. Look, you're a plant, living happily in the dirt. Your roots go down for water and nutrients and your leaves look up for the sun to power the whole food making process. If you're already growing in this place, then the soil must have enough nutrients. It's not like they pickup and move someplace else only to discover the soil sucks. If the soil is nutrient poor, what the hell are they doing growing here in the first place?"

"OK Ismail, it's a fair enough question. We do know a lot more about the *how*, then the *why*. There's a lot of different possibilities and some of them go back millions of years. But you have to realize it's not just here. It's not just these plants that we grew up with. The same thing happened all over the world, completely independent of each other. There's carnivorous plants everywhere. And they don't all work exactly the same way. So there must be a very good *why* sometime deep in the past. Maybe it happens anytime plant life becomes too dense in areas, which triggers the activation of the defensive mechanism of one of the plants, and it starts digesting anything around it, including insects and lizards. Or maybe plants were carnivorous way way back in the beginning of life on Earth and they evolved in the other direction when they figured out it was easier to just eat dirt. Or maybe the supply of fresh meat ran out. There just aren't good enough fossil records to give us more of the *why*, so we have to theorize."

Ismail was looking down into the pitcher. The lizard had stopped moving. He never got to enjoy his beetle. The beetle had actually escaped the lizard's grasp and was making a better show of trying to escape. They were just naturally tougher creatures than lizards, but it was hopeless none the less. "Well, if I ever forget to water one of my plants, I hope it doesn't suddenly decide to eat me."

Farah's communicator beeped. It was the Center, so she answered, "OK, we're finishing up and we'll head back in a few. Thanks. We need to head back Ismail."

They turned up river towards the dryer land and left the poor lizard and beetle to their fate, and the Orangutans watching from the trees, to return to the research center where they worked. Farah Rinong, and Ismail Jugah had grown up together in these forests, and spent endless days exploring the rich ecosystem and sometimes just playing as kids do everywhere. They were lucky not to have lived in the time when these forests were practically stripped clean and left to die by the endless logging operations and natural resource strip miners that practically destroyed their entire country. But that was 6,000 years ago, and long before they were born. Thanks to the efforts of their ancestors, these forests were restored, and life came back to the land as it had once been. Even the village they grew up in, which had gone from being a primitive society into an almost extinct culture, had rebounded and repopulated these forests, living as they once had before the encroachment of uncivilized civilization. In many ways their village was a single family sharing their rich culture and preserving some of the old ways. At the same time, they enjoyed the modern conveniences of clean homes, electricity, plumbing, organically maintained septics for sewage treatment, modern medicine, and full connection to the outside world. It was a good mix of old and new, and the people went back to being another member of the ecology, instead of being at odds with it.

Like most of the children in their expanded village, Farah and Ismail, climbed trees to pick the many varieties of fruit that grew wild once again, and learned to fish and even hunt in the tradition of their tribes. They went to the local school, and had full access to all the accumulated knowledge of the human species at their fingertips, the same as anywhere in the world. Learning about life in other places gave them a deep appreciation for the uniqueness of their country, and even as they left for college, and the possibility of careers outside of Borneo, they both seemed to know their lives would bring them back home someday. Maybe it was the teachings of their village elders, which was part of their education, that spoke of the Dayak way where family is forever. Or maybe it was something much simpler. Regardless, as they both went off to continue their higher education, Farah as a botanist, and Ismail as an entomologist, they never fully left their homes. In their individual professions, both became well known for their deep and intuitive understanding of how their disciplines were part of the larger picture of the great ecosystem of the entire planet. This deeper level of understanding was of critical importance to the continued efforts to bring the world back to a healthy balanced state, and at the same time know when to participate and when to let nature do it's own work. When the time came for them to make the decision where they would base their life's work, they both returned to Central Kalimantan in

Borneo. Though they joked between themselves that their requests were both approved mainly because who else would be able to survive in the deep jungles of their home?

Chapter 4

Earth Date: 8,409

Olympus Mons Base - Mars

The Asteroid Belt

The clear front shield was filled with darkness. There was literally nothing for the human eye to see. Just black. The complete lack of light. With the lights turned off inside the mining pod including all electronic displays, it felt like you were floating in eternity. No points of reference or feeling of motion. With the main drive and stabilizer both shut down, the weightlessness added to the feeling. That's exactly the way Keaton Barns liked it. It's what kept him doing this job year after Mars' year. The peace and quiet of the darkness, allowed all his stress to flow out, and the feelings of his surroundings flow in. He was like the wise yogi sitting on his hilltop, dispensing the wisdom of *The Belt* to all the newcomers. And today's lesson for his neophyte pod assistant, Billy Francs, was learning to relax and accept his fate.

Billy had other thoughts. He couldn't figure out why there was nothing to see. Were they lost? Off course? "Hey Cap, where the hell are all the asteroids? This doesn't look anything like the job pamphlets they sent me. Are we lost? I haven't seen a damn thing since we left the mining dock and you shut off all the lights."

"Billy, Billy Billy. Did you totally not pay attention in school? Do you have even the faintest idea of what the asteroid belt is, where it is, how big it is? Were you really expecting some crowded field or rocks, ice, and dwarf planets, all moving around in different directions and colliding with each other? And us frantically trying to dodge them like some silly deep space battle with the good guys being chased into the asteroid field while the bad guys blow themselves up, colliding with an asteroid that suddenly flew in front of their ship out of nowhere?"

"Well.....yeah, actually, sort of. You mean it's always going to be like this? NOTHING!?"

"Alright, listen up. Close your eyes and try to visualize what I'm saying. This place you signed up to work in is a scattering of leftover rubble from the formation of the solar system. It's all in orbit between Mars and Jupiter which puts it about 3 AU's out, or roughly three times further from the sun than the Earth. And the stuff here is all spread sort of evenly in a wide flat plane that's almost an entire AU in width. Someone calculated it out as roughly 4 million trillion square miles! Also consider that if you put all this stuff in the Belt together in one place, you'll barely have enough to make a ball the size of Earth's Moon. And that includes all the bigger pieces too. That means the average distance between asteroids of any significant size is something around 100,000 miles. The good news is the Belt takes anywhere from three to six Earth years for one revolution around the sun, while Mars only takes about two. That means without having to travel long distances, we constantly get a fresh offering of rocks. Is this all sinking in Einstein? I can't fricken believe you came out here with absolutely no clue."

"Well, actually I came out for the money and mostly because there just wasn't much I could do back home. The brochure said a lot of you guys are really rich having found all kinds of valuable stuff out here. Please don't tell me that was bullshit too? Can we at least turn on the scanners or some of the lights or something? Maybe some music?"

For Billy's sake Keaton ignored the questions, especially about getting rich, and just turned on the scanners, leaving the cabin lights off. There were two visual scanners. One gave a full global view and picked up anything larger than a bowling ball. The second was the forward scanner and provided greater detail and tied to the navigation computer to control approach vectors. There were also spectrographic chemical and heat scanners that gave a rough idea of what you were looking at, so you knew if it was worth mining. You could program in a set of preferences, and the system would alarm if anything matching was found. Keaton had programmed the system to keep an eye out for phosphorus, antimony, zinc, tin, silver, lead, indium, gold, copper, and even platinum. The readouts were quiet at the moment. The first day out was always the hardest, and the questions were almost always just like this. The recruiters were grabbing just about any gullible warm body they could find and sending them out with promises of riches. In the end, the ones that stayed were the ones like Keaton, that just enjoyed the way of life and made enough to survive. You didn't really need more than that. So he felt his job was to get the kids to accept that, and be happy with it. He was actually pretty good helping these guys and the occasional young girl settle in, which explains why he kept getting paired with the newbies. He was just about to start in with one of his *how to find peace* lectures when the spectro scanner alarmed.

Billy about jumped out of his skin. "What's that…. Is there a problem?"

"Calm down bro. It's just a preprogrammed alarm to let us know there's something out there worth looking at." Keaton's hands danced through space adjusting the heads-up display and telling the nav system to approach whatever the scanner just found. The gravity drive and stabilizer spun up and he started the approach. "This is the tricky part kid. You have to be really careful not to move anything out of it's orbit with the drive unit. Same goes for when you're mining. Even the slightest disturbance can cause one of these rocks to change orbit and while you're distracted something bangs into you. In tight quarters, shut down the drive and just use the air jets. Sometimes old tech is the best." The forward scanner took over, and the spectrograph alarm popped on again. This time it was Keaton who got excited. "Holy Shit ! No fricken way dude. Billy, you may be the dumbest newbie I've ever trained but you are one lucky SOB. We just hit a one-in-a-million jackpot. Get a location beacon tag ready and be damn sure it's got our two ID's properly encoded. We're gonna celebrate tonight!"

Olympus Mons Lava Tubes

Crystal and Michelle waited in line at the entrance to the rental shop just a few yards from the edge of the lava tube river. Their parents had brought the sisters down from the orbiting station where they'd moved to last month. Their parents were both geologists working on the new titanium mine recently opened under the south ridge. They let the girls have the day free with the promise they wouldn't do anything crazy like zip lining or spelunking. So the kids headed over to the submarine attraction they'd been reading about.

"It looks so different from down here," Crystal said. "You can't even tell we're at the edge of a volcano. It's like it just stretches all the way to the edge of Mars."

"It does dork," her older sister Michelle said. "It's the size of Arizona and Mars' horizon is a lot closer than back home. It doesn't look that big from the station because there's just nothing else around it to compare to, even though it's supposed to be the biggest volcano in the entire solar system. That's probably why Mom and Pop won't let us do the zip line down from the top since it disappears over the horizon. Kind of a spooky thought."

The line was moving slowly since this was the most popular attraction on Mars for new visitors. When they finally reached the front they only had to wait a few minutes for the next sub to come up. A mechanical arm built into the dock, grabbed the sub and lifted it onto the dry dock. A blast of air from above and behind the girls dried the sub before the attendant opened the top for the current occupants to climb out, and for them to climb in. The subs were made for two people to sit side by side, so everyone had the same view. Two thirds of the sub was a clear dome so you pretty much had a view all around and above. "OK ladies," the cute attendant said, giving Michelle a quick wink, "this isn't an amusement park ride. There's no track so you're free to roam in the tubes and the open lakes within boundaries. The computer will keep you from slamming into walls or other subs, and limits how fast you can go, but otherwise you're pretty much on your own. Just remember, the longer you stay out, the more they charge you so keep an eye on your meter over there," pointing at what looked like a digital taxi meter. "We've never had to use these before, but if there's an emergency these are your portable breather apparatuses. Questions? No? OK, you're off." And with that, the top closed and the sub was launched off the dock.

The controls were pretty basic, so anyone who ever played a vid-game could instantly operate it. Michelle took the stick and eased it forward to take the sub down, and pressed the accelerator tab forward to start moving. The water which had collected naturally in the volcanic tubes was slightly less salty than most of the other underground water found on Mars, so the visibility was pretty good. As soon as the sub submerged, the computer turned on the running lights and a display showing them in simple graphics their choices for direction. Michelle had studied these before hand and immediately went for the left hand tube. It was pretty close inside the tube, but like the attendant had said, the computer basically kept the sub centered. There were a variety of crystals that had grown or been deposited on the walls of the tubes over the millions of years since they first formed, and it was like gliding through a forest of jewels. No life had survived when Mars' dynamo stopped and the atmosphere was stripped from the planet by the Sun's radiation and solar winds billions of years ago. So the sights were mainly about minerals and the idea of driving around underneath a huge volcano in small tubes. Not a good place if you were claustrophobic which is why you had to sign a document testifying you weren't, before they let you in. In their case, being the daughters of two geologists was a huge advantage and they played the game of name-the-mineral as they cruised along.

Gravity Drive 2 - Jason's Ark

Some of the tunnels widened out and branched in several directions and some were so narrow it was impressive the computer's thrusters never let them scrape a wall. There was also a Return-to-Start button under a closed dome you could press if you got lost and wanted the computer to take you back automatically. Michelle wasn't going to get lost and was determined to reach her destination. Crystal never complained, completely trusting her sister, and glad to just watch the sights go by and let her run the show.

Suddenly the view completely opened up into a vast cave. The change was so abrupt after being in a tube it took their breath away. The cave was a huge lake that stretched almost two miles in diameter, with an upper dome that disappeared into the dark, 500 feet up. Lights had been cleverly arranged to highlight the stalactites that grew down from the top without overly lighting the cave, leaving some mystery. Michelle shut down the motor and let the sub just float on the surface. There were probably 20 or so others doing the same thing. A pair of lights from the ceiling were moving down slowly and the girls realized it was a couple spelunkers dropping down on lines from a tube hidden in the ceiling. This was without doubt, one of the seven wonders of Mars.

Farming

Mariana Dyson has been on Mars for 17 years, and never once visited the submarine rides, or flew down a zip line, or visited any of the popular tourist attractions. She was too busy living her dream job. She was also one of a very small handful of people that lived on the planet. She wasn't worried about the potential health risks of living in low gravity, because she was always physically busy. In addition to being the Director of Agriculture, more than anything she was a hands on farmer. She started on a small farm in Western Oregon that grew just about every fruit and vegetable that would grow in the Willamette Valley. The farm was a leader in the concept of providing as close to 100% of the nutritional requirements an adult human would need to lead a long healthy life, all from that one farm. She started there as a volunteer at the age of 12, and didn't leave until 24 years later when she was recognized for her knowledge and innovation in farming, and offered this job on Mars. The challenge was irresistible and she left immediately after the harvest.

Growing up as an organic farmer on Earth, turned out to be far easier, than trying to maintain the same level of purity on Mars. Everything she grew on Earth had evolved there. The interactions between plants, animals, soil, air, water, and the sun were all part of the evolution of life on Earth. When you remove the plants from that system and attempt to transplant them to where the soil is barren, the water salty, the air is artificial, there's relatively fewer animals to provide fertilizer or even CO_2, and there's far less sun, the ability of the plants to flourish is greatly diminished. And Mariana loved it. Except for the directorship part of the work, which she allocated to her assistant and just signed the reports as needed.

Of course she didn't create the systems that were in place on Mars for growing food. They'd been there for thousands of years since the first settlements. But when she arrived, progress had stagnated and the vitality of some of the crops were in question. Things had been done exactly the same way for so long, people were scared to make changes. It wasn't like you could just go buy your food someplace else if your crop failed, and importing food from Earth was insanely expensive. The leadership on Mars was planning to grow both tourism and the local economy which so far was focused mainly on the mining and processing of minerals and metals from the planet and the asteroid belt. This growth would require the guarantee of additional food resources as the first step, and this was the motivation behind bringing Mariana on planet.

Managing genetic variation to provide the most abundant and nutritious crops to fit a specific environment was something Mariana had specialized in and it's what she was attempting to accomplish now. It was the main reason she lived on planet, and spent all her time in the greenhouses, both above and below ground. She had shown remarkable success increasing yields on most of the food staples and for the first time was able to grow sufficient cereal grasses including wheat, oats, barley, maize, and even rice to allow full production of many of the food products people took for granted on Earth.

The above ground greenhouses were basically used for growing the green vegetables that were considered winter crops on Earth. These were slightly more tolerant of the colder air and soil temperatures, and could survive with less sunlight, though artificial light as a supplement was required. They were also the only place where bees had been successfully raised. There are over 20,000 species of bees on Earth, and over the many centuries, virtually every single one was brought to Mars. Interestingly enough, the only two that flourished were both native to the Willamette Valley where Mariana had lived. And

Paul H. Rosenfeld

51

these only survived in the greenhouses where higher average temperatures were maintained; a costly undertaking. Although most of the crops that require bees for pollination had been genetically modified to self pollinate, they were not as successful as the same plants grown in the greenhouses where the bees were kept. There's just no getting past the millions of years of symbiotic evolution. The side benefit in limited quantity, was the production of honey. Most of it was left for the bees, but some restricted harvesting was allowed for the health of the hives. Needless to say, Mars' honey was more expensive than any other local food.

Plant pollination presented the biggest challenges in the underground greenhouses. The environmental conditions underground could be controlled more efficiently than above ground where the extremely cold air temperature was often the most restraining factor. Also the cost per square foot of growing space underground was a tiny fraction of the cost associated with building clear topped greenhouses that could take advantage of the limited sunlight. So most of the food on Mars was actually grown underground. The biggest challenge growing underground came back to the bees. After thousands of years of effort, there wasn't a single species of bee that was content in that environment. They needed the sun. Artificial light just didn't cut it.

After years of careful study, Mariana came up with a simple plan to increase crop production above ground. It was so simple, she couldn't believe nobody had thought to do this before. The test plot was expensive to establish, but if it proved successful, it would more than pay for itself. The plan was to establish a complete old fashioned farm under a single roof. That meant not just plants and bees, but a large number of chickens, pigs, and of course worms. Worms produced the best fertilizer relative to their consumption and the space they occupied, but getting them to produce in sufficient quantities to support an entire world takes time. They didn't like the Martian soil, even after careful processing. Cows, goats, and other traditional sources of fertilizer were taboo since their feeding requirements far outstripped Mars' current capacity. Other than artificially produced chemical fertilizers, which Mariana resisted and were prohibitively expense to import, the most commonly used fertilizer on Mars was human feces. After careful processing to remove potential pathogens, heavy metals, antibiotics, or other chemicals humans seemed inclined to ingest, human feces were perfectly acceptable. The best thing about human feces was they were abundant on Mars. The bad thing Mariana felt, was they were not an ideal provider of nutrients for most plants simply because the plants didn't like it. She said it was like producing the perfect small kibble that contained 100% of everything a human would ever need to live a healthy and long life. If this was available for people, and they were told that was all they needed, would people be happy eating bowls of the same kibbles three times a day? Well, plants just didn't seem to like the taste of human excrement so they protested. This remained true even after the humans living on and around Mars no longer ate meat. It was a hard distinction to prove, but that was a large part of what this experiment was about.

The experiment was carried out in the traditional fashion with the necessary controls for baseline comparisons. After just two Martian years, the results were undeniable. The creation of a complete symbiotic environment similar to what plants evolved in on Earth, more than quadrupled production per acre. Also, for the first time in Mars' human history, fruit trees were showing signs of strong growth and increased flower production for fruiting. The difference these natural fertilizers with their resident microorganisms made in production and food quality over chemical and human fertilizers was astounding. Mariana's experiment was a success, and the plan was to immediately begin the construction of more large scale, above ground greenhouses, modeled after old fashioned farms.

Orbit

The space stations orbiting Mars were almost identical to those used at Earth's Moon. The only difference was the view. There was no Earth to look back on and dream of days long gone. The colors green and blue in nature were missed the most, so the stations spent a great deal of effort producing recreational areas with real grass, holographic blue skies, and ponds of water with carp and floating plants. The cost to maintain these areas was astronomical but the cost not to, was found to be even greater.

"Seventeen years ago, I took a big risk and brought Mariana here to take over our languishing farm system," Jill Rubin was saying to her administrative assistant and budget manager Marty Hans. "Looks like it was the single best thing I've done as Administrator in over 26 years. If her expanded operations yield as well as her test plot, we'll not only have all the food we need for expansion, but we'll enter an age of significant improvement in the overall quality of life for everyone in this otherwise solar wasteland. Maybe now I can go home and enjoy life back on Earth before I rot from old age. All I need to do first, is figure out how the hell we're going to pay for this project. We're already stretched to the max and everyone wants something, especially the Tourism Dept. Truth is they've been the second largest source of income out here next to mining, but their new toys always just barely pay for themselves. Never mind, Marty, we'll figure it out. What else you got today?"

Marty Hans had been with Jill for about 8 years. Just long enough to know what she actually needs to hear, and what to let pass by. Jill's job really should be handled by a good half a dozen people. Heck she's basically running this entire planet from the deepest bowels of Olympus Mons to the highest station orbiting the high poles, and clear out to the far reaches of the asteroid belt. It's more than any one person should have to be responsible for, so Marty saw it as his job to make sure everyone else was doing their jobs so Jill could focus on the important decisions. "Well the good news is the engineers finally got Phobos fully stabilized in it's higher orbit, and they're very confident we won't be seeing any more shedding. Tourism is up and we've gone a full week without a serious accident, if you don't count the idiot spelunker who decided to cut his own rope just to see how slow he'd fall into the high cavern lake. The new dog parks planet-side are a big hit and people seem to get a kick out of watching their dogs leaping 20 feet in the air for a ball, since the vid-comms are getting more hits than the movie channels. The dust mining also reached another milestone last month and they're convinced the reduced storms are due to their work. Water loss has also stabilized at 0.01%, with the new seals on the attractions. The desalinator upgrades are done, so it looks like we'll be good on water for the planned Ag expansions. And your favorite planet-side bar has a new dark beer they want to name after you. How's that for something to tack onto your legacy?"

Jill got a chuckle out of that one and raised her brows showing it actually might be a good idea. The beer on Mars was one of the main attractions to the bar crowds that stayed on planet for the evenings after a day of sightseeing. Of course the locals who lived on planet permanently had their own group of harder to find bars that served the stronger beers Mars was famous for. Something about the combination of low gravity and the unique ingredients that made the beer so strong and flavorful there was no need for hard liquor. Jill was starting to drift off, thinking about a good beer and staring out the stations window at Deimos in orbit nearby when Marty's headset chimed.

Marty's eyes went out of focus for a few seconds as he listened and then sat up quickly in his chair. "Boss, you're going to want to see this," he said with a big grin, and turned on the main view screen. "It's from one of the old timers running a spotter out in the far sweep of the belt."

The view switched from an image of what looked like just another floating rock, to a more familiar graph. The graph showed the distribution of minerals from a spotter scan which they were all used to reading. When Jill saw the graph she literally jumped out of her seat. "Is this accurate? Was this verified?"

"Yes," Marty said. "That was Frank Jacobs himself calling me, and assured me that after the spotter report came in, they sent a tug and miner right out to confirm. The numbers are accurate."

The graph showed a concentration of Platinum ore averaging close to one full percent on the asteroid. On Earth, it's extremely rare and averages about 0.005 ppm, with a ton of ore usually yielding just a few grams of the valuable metal. This was a once-in-a-lifetime find. "Well shit Marty, it looks like we won't be having any problems paying for those projects after all. I say we quit early, head down to that bar and try some of my new beer. And make sure you tell Frank to send down that spotter to join us and call Mariana too. I feel like getting shit-faced!"

Chapter 5

Earth Date: 8,409

Double Paw Ranch

Moose, Wyoming - Earth

Harmony Washakie was born with the wind in her face as her mother's horse galloped through a meadow in the shadow of the Grand Teton mountain range. Or so she liked to pretend as she galloped her own horse, Seze, down the path along the great Moose River near her home. Seze was a gift from her father, Daniel, and her mother Erin, for her 18th birthday. It was a traditional Eastern Shoshone gift for a daughter coming of age in the modern world. Her parents strongly maintained the heritage of her people, as humanity had slowly come to realize the wisdom they had shown many thousands of years ago. "What goes around, comes around," she thought to herself, as she brought Seze down to a gentle trot and then a slow walk to safely cross the rocky path that led to her home.

She pulled off Seze's blanket and let her cool only a little before currying and brushing her down, and using a hoof pick to remove any rocks she may have picked up on the ride. Harmony preferred to ride bareback, with a good blanket, since she felt more in touch with her horse and it improved her balance. She appreciated how lucky she was to live on the small working farm her parents owned, and had been passed down for many generations. They grew most of their own food, and raised a few farm animals solely for their by-products, such as eggs and goat milk. They ate no meat, so in this one sense they had given up their great hunting traditions in exchange for playing their part in healing the land.

Harmony's birth was significantly more traumatic than being born on the back of a horse. She thought this was somehow part of why she'd always felt so in touch with animals both on her farm, and in the forests and valleys of her home range.

Her mother was only a week shy of her expected date for delivery, when she asked her husband to take her camping up on the ridge above their home. They had an established camp up there on Shoshone land, where they had an unobstructed view of the clear sky. It was a new moon, and with the clean late summer air, the view of the Milky Way was spectacular. Her mother had wanted one last peaceful night in their favorite camp, knowing their lives were about to change forever with the arrival of their first child.

Their tent was in the traditional Shoshone style, though the skin was actually a modern weatherproof material. A minor concession given their feelings towards hunting. The other concession being the 4WD Jeep they had parked right next to the tent. Erin was in no shape to be hiking up the hill to the camp. They had settled in for the night, and the only sound was a gentle breeze flowing around the tent. The low pitched grunt was unmistakable and they both woke up instantly. They kept a clean camp, with no open food in the tent, knowing the black bears in the area were fearless of humans, and never hesitated to intrude. They listened quietly as the bear moved around the campsite. It found something some distance from the tent and was making quite the racket. After an hour of this, Daniel decided he'd had enough, and crawled out of his sleeping blanket, and opened the flap to the tent. It only took a second for him to locate the bear with his flashlight, and the moment he shined the light in it's face it bolted at a full run straight for the tent. Daniel jumped back slamming the flap shut and stepped back, pulling out his knife.

"Get ready to go out the back of the tent if he tries to come in," he said to wife in slightly panicked voice. The knife was to slice the back of the tent, not the bear. He knew he had no chance if the bear decided to attack. The tent flap was moving in and out with the bears breathing as it pressed his nose against the flap. After a few seconds it moved away from the flap and began to slowly circle the tent. Daniel and Erin sat dead still and waited, as the bear came right up to where he's wife's head rested almost against the back of the tent. Again, the bear's nose was against the tent and the fabric moved in and out with it's breath. Apparently satisfied, the bear finally moved off peacefully, and within a minute Erin began to quietly laugh, almost hysterically. "Daniel," she said in as calm a voice as possible, "I think my water just broke."

Daniel couldn't remember much of the next hour as he got Erin tucked into the Jeep and headed off to the hospital down in Moose. In a consistent display of what would be her eventual personality, Harmony was born very quickly and without much fuss. The doctor had barely had a chance to put on his robe and grab Daniel by the wrist, pulling him over between his wife's legs. "I believe it's in your tradition to deliver your first child," he said to Daniel.

Daniel looked up at his wife. She nodded that she was ready, and with one good push Harmony's head fully crowned. A few breaths later and another good push and she just slid out right into Daniel's hands. At least that's how he remembers it. He's pretty sure his wife had a different perspective but it all turned out well. The nurses took Harmony away to be cleaned and tested, and after some cleanup, Mom decided to take a quick nap. Daniel walked out to the Jeep for a breath of air and to think about all that had happened in the last few hours. As he was looking at the Jeep he noticed something he'd missed in the dark. There were some very small bear foot prints all over the hood. A baby bear. Daniel realized then, when he stepped out of the tent, he had stood exactly between the mother bear and her cub. That explains the sudden charge. They were extremely lucky to have survived that. However, given how the bear had come around the tent and smelled his wife, who at that point had just had her water break, Daniel figured it was a mother-to-mother courtesy that led her to simply walk away. What a night !

The rest of Harmony's life wasn't much different than that first night. She moved through her life from one traumatic event to another. Unlike other children, everything she did was at 110%. If you didn't know how mild and loving her parents were, you'd think Harmony was an abused child with all the bumps and bruises she acquired on a daily basis. She was also an extremely brilliant young lady, and by the time she was 9 years old, there wasn't a single argument she couldn't win or a challenging question she couldn't invent for her school teachers. She graduated middle school having never seen anything but top marks for her scholastic achievements.

As a reward for her excellent work in school, Daniel decided she was old enough to have some serious horseback riding experiences, since she'd done quite well training in the arena. She didn't have her own horse yet, and the trips he planned were slightly remote, so he decided to go the tourist route and arranged for three special outings with a horse rental ranch for the weekend. These three rides would forever remain in Daniel's memory as examples of his daughter's determination in life.

The first ride was a gentle climb up a mountain pass on a well marked trail with a small group of other riders. Harmony was on the horse directly in front of Daniel. They came around a sharp bend in the trail and had to duck under some large tree branches to get through. Harmony had let her horse get a bit to close to the one in front and as she came around the corner a huge branch came flying straight at her chest, knocking her clear off her horse. She landed flat on her back on the ground right in front of Daniel.

Gravity Drive 2 - Jason's Ark

He had barely jumped off his horse scared she might be seriously injured, when she was already standing up and brushing herself off. She just grunted saying something about a stupid branch, and got right back up in her saddle, completely ignoring her dad, and the guy in front who was trying to apologize for what he'd done. "Let's go!" she yelled and the line started up again. Daniel got back in his saddle knowing full well they'd all be better off if he kept his mouth shut.

The next day, the same group took a much different route through some lowland trails, up the side of a ridge, and onto a large open meadow. It was a beautiful location with acres of tall wild grass and a small creek running right through the meadow. Harmony took one look at the view and turned to her dad saying "this looks like it might have been a lake once or even a glacier, until it dried into a meadow."

The guide overheard what Harmony said and brought his horse back around saying to the group, "The young lady's exactly right. Just a few hundred years ago this was one of the best trout lakes in the area. Even though the planet's mostly recovered from the human induced warming, there are still areas that seem to naturally go through this process of changing from lakes into meadows. There's probably other areas doing just the opposite, and maybe someday this meadow will become a lake again. It's just one of the wonders of these hills. The wildlife in the area still come here to eat the wild food and drink from the creek. And as if they were listening, a small herd of Elk burst through the trees right next to where they'd stopped the horses. Several of the horses panicked including Harmony's who reared up suddenly, once again throwing her from the saddle. At least this time she landed in a soft meadow. The splash of mud was a small price to pay for the relatively gentle landing. Daniel had never heard his daughter cuss before, having been raised with the idea that people only cussed when they couldn't find the right words to express themselves. Well, Harmony had no problem expressing exactly how she was feeling at that moment, and the entire group broke into laughter at the young ladies well expressed and justified frustration.

By the third day, Daniel felt he'd made the wrong choices, so decided to do something with a much lower potential for disaster. There was a large lake nearby with vast sandy beaches, similar to what you might find at the ocean. The plan was to take a quiet ride around the perimeter of the 10 mile lake, and just enjoy their last day together. After about thirty minutes the group of riders had spread out slightly with the natural laziness of the lake's environment. The pair of shotgun blasts came out of nowhere, and before Harmony could react her horse jumped into a full-out gallop along the edge of the lake, directly away from the sound. Daniel was a good rider but hadn't really gone in for horse racing. Regardless, he kicked his horse into action and took out after his daughter hoping to catch her before anything worse could happen. It took two of the longest minutes in his life to catch up with her horse and force it into the water to stop. He fully expected his daughter to be terrified at the sudden and uncontrollable full out gallop. But when he finally pulled up next to her she was hysterically laughing. "That was awesome dad! Can we do that again?"

Cats

Harmony's life continued to skew from the norm as she grew. She had friends, but none were as close to her heart as the farm animals and of course her best friend, Seze. School was always just OK. She was naturally smart and didn't need to study much to excel. She enjoyed the weekly field trips to study the ecology of the mountains surrounding her home, but the classrooms were just too crowded with humans. After school for most kids her age meant sports, or social gatherings. She rarely joined these groups and gradually developed a reputation as a loner. Even after 6,000 years of massive changes in human culture, kids were still kids, and cruelty seemed to be a genetic trait that would take millions, not thousands of years to eradicate. She ignored most of it, as it simply served to justify her feelings about people. So for her, after school usually meant long rides out with Seze, when her farm chores were done.

The valleys and mountains surrounding her farming ranch in Moose, Wyoming, were famous for being some of the first regions in the United States to show significant signs of recovery after the coming of Jason. Though she had her favorite places along the river, she tried to make each day a unique experience. Most often this meant riding to a place where some group of animals were gathering, or perhaps a new predator trail she spotted, and then walking Seze from that point forward. She somehow felt more in touch with her surroundings when she walked. Closer to the Earth. Less the high up master, and more the grounded member of nature. Seze enjoyed the walks as well since she wasn't held to the reins and allowed to walk freely in any direction of her choice; which usually meant keeping a close eye on Harmony while grazing the selection of wild foods. She was after all, a herd animal and this instinct was too deeply embedded and fundamental to her survival.

Harmony never worried about Seze's wanderings and could always seem to sense exactly where she was. It was a strange feeling at first, and she thought it was just her imagination, given her strong love for the horse. But as the years went by, and with the accumulated experiences of her daily outings, she began to realize she truly had a connection with all wildlife. There weren't any words for what she felt, and it was something far too personal to share with anyone, including her parents, though she suspected they were well aware. Sometimes when Seze had found a particularly nice snack and was staying quietly in one place, Harmony would find a comfortable place to sit, and close her eyes. In books, people called this meditating. From her experiences though, this was not the same thing. It was never about clearing her mind of thoughts, it was about gathering the feelings around her. She could feel the different animals going about their business, and was always correct when she felt an animal watching her; opening her eyes briefly to confirm and make eye contact with whoever it was. Most times it was a curious squirrel or rabbit simply grazing the edges of her feelings. Other times a strong feeling would invade her space and she knew some predator was watching. Seldom did those feelings escalate to a true hunt. Was it her smell or something else that dissuaded them. She could feel them turn away and continue their search elsewhere. Harmony would often wait for that exact moment, before opening her eyes and turning to see the cat or wolf moving away. They also never seemed to bother Seze which was an even greater mystery. What connection did she share that caused this?

As a teenager, Harmony was also atypical in her relationship with her parents. Something had gone wrong during her birth, and her mother couldn't have more children. Harmony didn't realize the risk this meant to her suffering from the typical only-child syndrome, since her parents were also nonconforming in their parenting and refused to spoil their only child. They recognized at the same time a strong and independent spirit in their daughter and decided to give her full rein to mature in her own way. It helped that Harmony enjoyed the hard work of the farm life, and even seemed to enjoy mucking out the various farm animal's habitats. The combination of her freedom of movement and the attractions of her home environment led to a deep love and respect for her mom and dad. In fact, in her heart, her parents were the only two humans she really loved.

The only conflict she felt was when evening discussions started to turn to college. She knew it was something society, and even recently her tribal elders, expected her to experience. She'd heard enough about college life to conclude is was more about the social experience than advanced education. She knew that wasn't true, but it's the part you hear most about. To her it simply meant that once again she'd be in that uphill battle against social pressures, while trying to learn. She didn't have to attend even a single quarter, to know the time would come when she'd pick up and disappear into the night, never to be seen on campus again. What's the point in even starting? There was a whole world of real experience out there without dealing with made-up knowledge from people who spent their lives in classrooms rather than the wilderness.

She was saved from the classic battle with her parents, when the State of Wyoming announced a year long research program requiring deep wilderness survival training and predator observations. The program was strictly volunteer based, which meant no income, though they paid all your expenses, which amounted to basically food. She presented this to her parents as an opportunity to give her a year break from school, and time to consider her future. Her parents weren't stupid though, and knew exactly where this would lead, and it wouldn't be college. True to their nature, and consistent with how they raised her, they immediately agreed.

Luckily for Harmony, the program was headquartered right there in her home town of Moose, since it was an excellent jumping off point for the remote mountains of western Wyoming, which would be the focus area of the study.

The survival training began in late June, with the idea of starting the research in the early Fall, before the heavy snows began. The target of their research project was to quantify the recovery of the Canada Lynx in western Wyoming, an area where they had been hunted to near extinction thousands of years ago. The lucky part for Harmony wasn't just her familiarity with the research area, it was her reputation with the local Forest Service grunts who were in charge of the project, and the survival training. During her daily excursions on Seze she had more encounters with these people in the wilderness, than she did with fellow students in her school. They already knew she was a capable back country explorer and had helped on more than one search-and-rescue over the years, often times being the person to first find whatever idiot had gotten turned around in the woods. The folks who worked the trails for the Forest Service weren't known for their compassion towards tourists invading their wild areas, and that matched Harmony's feelings dead on.

The survival training was mostly review for Harmony and Seze both, and as a team they could have taught most of it. The majority of the researchers were college students working on their advanced degrees and looking for some field experience to supplement their papers. As a group, they were surprised to find Harmony as an accepted member of the research team, but it didn't take long to understand why as the survival training began. The distances they planned to cover during the research were extensive, so the use and care of pack horses would be a major focus of the training. For their part, the Forest Service trainers were happy to have Harmony around to help get the others educated, and also having her own horse was an appreciated savings given the limited budget these programs still experienced.

When Fall came, three groups were formed, with four members in each; a Forest Service scientist and three students, except for Harmony's group which had five. The idea was to separate the three groups into each of the three major ranges where they expected to find populations of Lynx, based mainly on observed populations of their main prey, the snowshoe hare. Although known to take red squirrels and larger ground birds like the ruffed grouse, their preferred prey was the hares. Historically, where you found hares, was the only place you found Lynx.

Her group headed up to the area around Buck Mountain to the northwest, which was only about 7 miles in by air, or 12 by horseback. They setup a permanent campsite with the understanding that each researcher was required to return before nightfall each day. Everyone carried satellite locators and advanced GPS guidance used for marking den locations on a centralized map, as well as preventing people from getting turned around. The researchers paired up each morning except for Harmony who preferred to go out on her own. Over the years in these mountains, Harmony had many encounters with these Lynx, though never really paid much attention. They were cute enough but she never considered herself much of a cat person. Dogs were much better company since they tended to share their feelings. Cats were too independent for her tastes, which she realized was slightly hypocritical. Now however, she suddenly found herself loving cats since they were the key to her not having to attend college, at least this year. Next year she'd hopefully find a different excuse.

She spotted the first den almost immediately after leaving camp. It was under a simple pile of downed trees. The tracks in and out of the spot were definitely Lynx so she marked the spot on her GPS. Since Lynx in this area generally give birth to their Kits in

June, depending on the elevation, the nest should be quite active now with mom teaching her kittens how to hunt in preparation for the winter snows, which they're well adapted to. This den seemed quiet so she moved on in case they were resting, knowing she could return later. Walking Seze in their customary fashion, Harmony's next find was under an upturned rootwad, that had obviously been used for more than one season. This den showed considerable more activity and the remains of recent hunts were evident as well as significant amounts of scat which was easier to smell then see.

She hit the jackpot around a group of boulders above the animal trail she'd been following. The four kits were all out play hunting with each other and mom was resting her head on a boulder, obviously worn out and grateful for the break. Harmony stood still for a few moments, to be sure she hadn't been noticed and then backed herself and Seze up into the trees. Seze was used to the need to stay quiet and didn't complain. Harmony closed her eyes and focused on the sounds and feelings of the small group of cats. They were healthy and well fed. Their level of energy suggested they weren't suffering from any parasites, and despite mom's restful state, Harmony judged her to be young and in good health. How she knew all this was a mystery even to her, but she also knew she was seldom wrong, and allowed herself the luxury of taking advantage of this hidden talent. She made notes in her electronic pad and placed a special flag on the location.

By the time she returned to camp that evening, Harmony had marked 17 active dens, and 5 that appeared to have been recently abandoned. This was a common occurrence among Lynx as they often moved their kits to different dens during their growth, likely to prevent other predators from discovering their location. The other researchers in the group were astonished at the number of verified dens Harmony had located as the next closest group only had 5, which they thought had been amazing. This pattern repeated itself for the first couple weeks until they decided to change tactics, and let Harmony continue to locate new dens, while the remainder of the group took advantage of the opportunity to spend their time studying the dens instead.

Harmony felt the incongruity of this situation, but didn't complain. She never thought this research should be focused just on the counts. The overall health of the species was far more important, and gave a much clearer picture of the survival and growth possibilities for the species. Having covered the territory originally laid out for her group, Harmony also started to spend more time simply observing the activity of the dens. Unlike the others, she could also sense when an active hunt was in progress and was able to bring videos back to camp for the others to watch in the evenings, raising her status even further in the group.

When winter set in with some serious snow, it was time to return to the flat lands, and begin the process of compiling their data. Harmony felt like staying up there for the early winter, but was well aware of how suddenly things could change from a gentle snowfall, to a blizzard, so she returned with the group, and back to her home. She'd been gone for three months, and her parents were delighted to see her happy and fit, though even more delighted after she took a good long shower. Seze was equally happy to have her warm stall with abundant grain and special treats.

Harmony shared her experience with her parents, and after the first ten minutes, they knew it was going to be a lost cause, sending her to college. This was just the confirmation they needed. Dad heard of a winter moose study that was being conducted in Grand Teton National Park, and so began the projects that would establish the pattern of Harmony's life. During the next 15 years, Harmony participated in Bengal Tiger recovery research in India, Polar Bear research in the Arctic, Hyenas in North Africa, the Great Philippine Eagle, and even

Komodo dragons in the Indonesian islands. After all these years and so much travel, she was ready to come home, when she heard about a Grey Wolf project in her own backyard.

Oso and Koa

Although she made it a point to come home between each project, it was always a small shock to see how quickly her parents seemed to age. She was almost 34 now and her parents were in their 60's. Not old at all by today's standards, but not the young farmers they were while she was living at home. Her parents greeted her with their usual overwhelming feeling of love that penetrated deep into Harmony's soul. It was a feeling she cherished, and she realized it was that feeling she missed most when she was away. She felt something similar to it in almost every species she studied, but it was never directed at her. The only other animal she ever felt this from was Seze, who now was truly beginning to show her age, despite the great care and love her parents gave her. At 22 years, she still had some good years left, and Harmony planned to spend as much time with her as possible, including taking her on the next project. From her parents though there was something a bit more this time. Maybe it was their joy that her next project was going to be right here in their backyard.

When they sat for their first dinner together in almost two years, the first thing they brought out were reviews from her most recent study. She was becoming something of a legend among wildlife researchers for her ability to connect with virtually every animal in the Kingdom. No one really understood it, and she still never shared it with anyone, though once again she could tell her folks got it. Probably because they were the same way, and knew they'd passed it along. It's part of why they knew Harmony would never be content going to college, or doing the kinds of jobs that others did. Harmony was just glad that her reputation was generally among scientists and naturalists, and not among the celebrity crowds which she worked hard to avoid, refusing virtually every request for an interview she'd received.

After a week at home to take a deep breath, and do some honest hard work on the noticeably diminished farm, it was time to look into this new study of Grey Wolf populations in Yellowstone. These wolves had been the center of a turning point in the appreciation for natural predators, even before the arrival of Jason, and the switchover to the new way of living on our planet. Originally hunted to near extinction in the area, and in what seemed like a completely unrelated occurrence, the overall health of the riparian environment of this great park was suffering. When the wolf recovery program launched and the Grey Wolf protection in the park began, environmentalists started to notice a gradual change in the rivers. It was eventually realized that removing the wolves, had allowed the large grazing animals like elk, deer, and moose, to overpopulate and slowly destroy this environment to the point of actually changing the course of major rivers. When the wolves recovered, and brought balance back to the ecosystem, the entire park ecology recovered. There were more willows and aspens to provide food for beavers. The healthy beaver ponds in turn benefited aquatic plants and animals. Shade from the trees that gradually recovered cooled the water in the slower moving rivers and ponds, making the habitat better for trout. This was a major lesson for those paying attention. Humans really didn't understand the complexity of the balance of nature, as well as they thought.

The research project Harmony was asked to be included in was strictly about the health of the wolves, and to ensure things were still headed in the right direction. By now of course, even out here in the sticks, in what used to be considered hunters land, people were well aware of the simple concept of *Leave It Alone*. There was no suggestion within the project of any attempt to change, just simply to understand. Harmony was all about that. Besides, she was so darn tired of studying cats, she was looking forward to the company of dogs. The Forest Service was once again in charge of this project, and they had forwarded all the information she needed to get a good background on the expectations. It was like the project had been designed specifically for her. Something about the layout, the expectations, and the nature of the data they were looking for confirmed her suspicions. Combined with the feelings she was getting from her parents there was no doubt. If there had been doubt, it was quickly removed when she arrived at the Ranger Station with Seze, to discover she was the sole person on the project.

She'd grown up with the two guys at the Station that provided her with the final tracking and data gathering system she would use in the backcountry. Joey Littlehorn's heritage was Crow and though he'd been cordial over the years, he'd shown little interest in pursuing her friendship, probably recognizing and respecting her preference for privacy. Brando Billings on the other hand, who was now the Park Ranger, was someone who'd tried to date her since their days in high school. He had little concern for things like heritage, since his background was a blend of so many cultures, he was simply a person of the Earth. They were good friends, and he somehow knew that was because they kept their friendship casual and never got intimate. He was still single after all these years, and the look he gave her now, was all she needed to know that he still hadn't given up. She felt bad because he really was one of the only boys, now men, she had some feelings for. But the things that drove her in life, just didn't allow for that type of relationship. At least not yet. Maybe someday, she thought as she caught his eyes. She swore he could almost read her mind as he deflated slightly with that thought. Maybe someday, she thought again and left him with a big smile as she turned around, headed out the door, and up the trail with Seze into the Grand Tetons.

It was early June, and the wolves would be actively hunting and teaching their pups the skills necessary to survive, in between bouts of play. One of the great challenges for this type of ground study was the tremendous range of these wolves territories, which have been known to be up to 500 square miles. Though with the improved availability of prey, some territories had shrunk down to as little as 10-20 square miles. Regardless of the size of their range, wolves often spent the bulk of their days traveling. That's why the study needed to be done this time of year, when they were more likely to stay close to the dens and their pups. The question under study was if they were becoming overpopulated. If so, the situation will eventually self correct, though the price will be painful. Harmony was simply to get a feel for this and the general health of the packs. Pack size would be another indicator of health, with larger packs generally indicating more than sufficient prey to maintain health.

Like all the studies she'd conducted over the years, once she was clear of people, her methods diverted from the written plans. Feeling her way through the mountains and watching the trails and tracks for movement, she found a central location which seemed a major crossing ground for the packs, and a good place to start. Over the weeks, her and Seze would circle out from this location and develop a sense for where the packs were and their general numbers. It was a blessing having Seze since the miles they accumulated were well beyond even her abilities. The health of the packs was stronger than she'd ever felt, and her reports reflected what the Forest Service had expected.

After three months of study, she was beginning to feel it was time to wrap things up. Her and Seze had settled down for the night in their central camp. Harmony almost never had a camp fire. She could feel the fear it produced in even the smallest inhabitants of the forest, and she wasn't interested in discouraging visitors the way most campers were. She'd finished her mostly cold dinner and was starting to get drowsy, when she felt a sense of curiosity intrude into her feelings. She kept her head bowed and let the two animals she knew were in the trees several hundred feet away, approach. Even though she was down wind of the two,

Seze didn't seem concerned as they got closer. Harmony knew without even looking, this was a pair of male Grey Wolves. She didn't sense the interest in hunting you'd usually feel from a pair of males, in fact it was odd the way the two seemed to share a singular bond. These had to be liter mates, and probably on the young side.

With the full moon behind her filtering through the trees, she had a well lit view of the clearing 100 feet in front of her as the two emerged. She was surprised to see these were definitely not pups. Two full grown wolves stood facing her, their eyes glowing in the moonlight. One was the typical white, grey, and black you'd expect. The other was the more rare pure black variance with hints of brown in the undercoat. The black one was significantly taller than the gray, and stood with his ears and tail erect. In the moonlight he looked like a slender black bear. No movement, though no feeling of aggression either. This was not a hunting or even territorial threat pose. Just curiosity. The grey on the other hand was definitely exhibiting signs of something similar to a dog wanting to play. He was shorter and quite a bit heavier than the black. His tail was up and moving slowly from side to side, and the ears were perked full forward, but it was the look on his face that really told her this one liked to play. They were obviously both extremely well fed, and must be a very successful hunting pair; likely using each other in coordinated efforts to trap animals. Seze was still showing no signs of concern. How strange. They stood like that for at least 15 minutes before the black one turned around and casually moved off. The grey hesitated and soon joined his brother. That was very strange indeed. For the first time in her life, she was actually stumped. Immediately she changed her plans and decided to stay at least another week, to see if they returned.

She saw no signs of them on her next days rounds, but they returned again that night, at almost exactly the same time. Were they looking for something specific. Harmony didn't eat any meat, and all she had with her at the moment was the hard core remains of some romaine lettuce. She took a chance and as hard as she could, she heaved the core at the wolves. They had come closer tonight, to within about 50 feet, so the lettuce core bounced maybe half way between them. To her surprise it was the black that came to investigate. He sniffed the core for only a second before grabbing it and trotting back into the woods. The grey showed no interest, but soon followed.

The next night, Harmony made a point of having a full head of lettuce and some large carrots ready. Sure enough, they returned at the same time and came just as close as last night. Once again she hurled the lettuce and only the black came forward to snatch it and trot back into the woods. The grey didn't move, watching her closely, so she tossed one of the carrots. He came forward this time, sniffed the carrot, looked up at her as if to say, "that's all you got," and with some hesitation picked up the carrot and moved off to join his brother. Apparently the black was in need of some vegetables more than the grey.

The next night was the strangest of all. Harmony had decided to celebrate and made some fresh popcorn for herself using the battery powered heater. The wind shifted tonight and she was now upwind from the two as they came out of the clearing. This time the grey never stopped and came within 10 feet of Harmony before stopping, and sitting. Harmony was beginning to suspect these were actually high wolf content dogs that someone had bred and then released. But their hunting skills seemed to indicate otherwise. The grey was sniffing the air and it was pretty obvious it was the popcorn that interested him. She took a handful and tossed it his direction. There was no hesitation as he quickly gobbled up the corn and looked up for more. No wonder you're fat she thought. Too many carbs and not enough veggies! The black showed no interest in the corn so she tossed him some carrots which he quickly accepted. She was running low on veggies so this wasn't going to last long.

All this time, Seze had shown no fear of these two, and Harmony had no idea what to make of that. Her folks didn't have dogs, since the farm animals provided more than enough company and work. Maybe these two smelled like farm animals to Seze? Anyway, there wasn't much else she could do. She had about two more days of supplies and then she'd have to leave. The grey had eventually left when the popcorn ran out, so Harmony decided to grab her bag and sleep right where she had been sitting, instead of in her tent. About half way through the night she started to get warm and reached up to push her bag open when she realized something very warm, heavy, and a bit stinky was leaning against her. She raised her head just enough to see it was the grey, and he was curled up against her. The black was several feet away, sound asleep. The only feeling she got from the two was one of contentment, so she didn't panic and laid back down, glad she didn't need to pee.

In the morning, the black was gone but the grey was sitting up about 5 feet away just watching her. "You little Koa," she said. Somewhere in the back of her mind that was something she remembered her mom calling the pigs. Shoshone was not a language she thought in, though she was raised around it enough for it to be familiar. So she decided to call the grey, Koa. The black was definitely an Oso, which was bear in that language. When she got up Koa just hung around and watched her closely until breakfast when he decided to help himself to her last biscuit. "You are definitely a little Koa," she said to him.

It was a full hour later when Oso showed up, with a small rabbit in his mouth. He brought it over to Harmony and presented it as a gift. "No thank you, Oso, I don't eat meat." When she said his name his ears definitely perked up. He took the hint and went over to where he'd slept and in short order the bunny was gone. This was shaping up to be another very strange day and it was time to leave. She packed up camp and walked Seze down the long trail back towards the Ranger Station. She noticed after a short while the sounds of the forest would dim as she moved through. That was not usual, as her presence generally made little impact on the life around her. Then she realized it was simply Oso and Koa, who were following her at a discrete distance that were the cause. She stopped abruptly which woke Seze from her plodding slumber, and turned back to watch the wolves emerge behind her. They also stopped when they saw her staring at them. "Well, if you're going to follow me all the way home, you might as well be with me and stop acting so spooky," she yelled at them.

Koa got the hint instantly and came running over like any other puppy, and nuzzled her hand. Oso was characteristically more reserved and walked over slowly coming up along side Seze and walking slowly around the horse, to stand next to Koa. Seze paid absolutely no attention to either wolf since she'd found a particularly tasty bit grass. Apparently the three had bonded at some level Harmony wasn't clear about, though she was grateful for the lack of conflict. She continued down the trail for the rest of the day with The Boys, as she now thought of them, moving in and out of sight as they explored and sniffed, endlessly reading the signs of animal movements that passed through the area. When they stopped for lunch, Harmony realized The Boys were not going to respect her meal, and she ended up with no choice but to share what was left.

Near the end of the day, they reached the clearing uphill from the Ranger Station, and The Boys stopped just outside the trees as Harmony and Seze continued down. It looked as if her two human friends were standing in exactly the same place as when she left, only they were laughing about something. As she approached Joey laughed, "I see you've made a couple new boy friends while you were gone, little tornado."

"Well," she replied looking straight at Brando, "I guess some guys just have it, and others don't," and she continued right past them to the horse barn with Seze.

"Ouch," was all Brando could think to reply, too quiet for her to hear.

Chapter 6

Earth Date: 8409

Los Angeles Airport - Earth

Taka and Al liked to think of themselves as gearheads. It was an ancient term from the times when a kid spent his weekends in the garage with one of his parents, learning the ins and outs of rebuilding and tuning an internal combustion engine. This had virtually nothing to do with the technology they spent their weekends tinkering with, but it sounded cool. Being cool was important too. Some of the best qualities of the human race just keep cycling around and around.

Taka and Al's entire families worked in the Drive Construction and Integration (DCI) plant located on what was once the site of the Los Angeles airport, in Southern California. With global integration of technologies and people, some things didn't change simply for convenience. Renaming every Country, Province, State, City, Town, and Village on the planet would have been most confusing, and made it very easy for people to get lost. Life was stressful and confusing enough at the beginning, so when total human integration began, keeping the same names for places was a no-brainer.

It was referred to commonly as The Beginning. Simple and so very true. Like graduating college and finding yourself a bit stunned at the start of your first day of work. Jason's message had been clear and unmistakable. Jason himself hated the idea of being seen as an overlord, but for now, he had no choice. The human race was like a misbehaved child, spoiled rotten, and fouling it's own home. They had to be brought under control quickly, and put on a new path, or risk elimination for the good of the planet.

Resource Reallocation (RR) was where it started. The United Nations, now including 100% of the Nations in the world, established a series of laws (not just guidelines) for how every Nation was to be re-organized. It was detailed and complex though the broad strokes were simple and logical. First, Nations with the greatest wealth and those which contributed the most to global pollution had to determine the means for reallocating those resources to other countries. This generally meant starting at the top with the richest and most powerful individuals, and transferring their excessive holdings, whether it be money, lands, or industry, to the United Nations RR fund. Restraint and fairness had to be a part of this brutal first step. Recognizing that many of these people had worked hard to gain their wealth and power, it was determined they be allowed to keep what was to become the higher end of the global average assets. They were also allowed, at least those that qualified through their actual achievements, to keep the one thing they treasured above all else: Power. They were encouraged to continue their roles as leaders in whatever industry or capacity they worked, or accept new roles where such leaders were needed.

It was also recognized that a large majority of these people's wealth had been inherited, so they had simply been born into their holdings, yet still contributing more to global environmental damage than entire cities or nations in some cases. These individuals were treated no differently than anyone else. At the lower end of the scale, those born into pure poverty, in environments where escape was almost impossible, were provided the first opportunities for improvement. However, these were not to be gifts. Improving the world meant everyone must work. These first couple steps alone were torturous and required many decades to gather any momentum. At times of change such as these, the pain is always the greatest on the older people; the ones who's inertia is fighting to carry them in the same direction they've lived their whole lives.

A simultaneous undertaking and one equally as painful, was the relocation of families to different countries. It was determined by the UN, that despite the threat of global human annihilation for non-compliance, many countries would continue to persist in their attempts at cultural superiority including the threat of war. The only logical way to overcome these threats, was to create a worldwide melting pot where all cultures were blended. This required more than decades, it required generations. Concurrently, all Nations were required to turn over 100% of their weapons, starting with nuclear devices, to be recycled or sent to the Sun for destruction. All global conflicts must end immediately. As difficult as this was to initiate, the positive impact was astonishing. The ending of global conflict suddenly tripled the availability of resources for feeding and housing the poor, while re-tasking soldiers towards global cleanup efforts. The combination of these two factors accelerated the improvement of the planet at an observable pace.

But this was all ancient history now. Taka and Al had to learn all about these things in school. It was important for humanity to avoid making the same mistakes, and falling back into the basic patterns of ancient life that had been formed almost a million years ago, when the struggle to survive was a battle against the forces and predators of nature. Those days were gone, but their genes remained, and must be watched closely. In the meantime, young people like Taka and Al had a future that included more possibilities than had ever existed for humans. The chance to explore anywhere in the world they wished, or even off planet on the Moon, Mars, or the distant Cosmos.

Taka Asai, was originally of Japanese decent. His family had moved to Alaska from Japan almost a thousand years ago, and were part of the Humpback whale recovery program. Eventually, part of the family split off and moved to Southern California to be involved in the new generation of space station component integration. His grandparents contributed to the designs and building of some of the first city-sized stations to orbit the three worlds. Taka's love of mechanics and engineering had come from a family who's lives were wrapped in the love of their work, in the same way a farming family loves the land.

Al Haywood's family had lived in Southern California since the days of the dinosaurs, or so the children were led to believe. Their great-to-the-100th-power grandfather was killed by a saber tooth tiger who eventually got stuck in a tar pit in downtown Los Angeles. Family histories have a way of becoming distorted by time though more interesting. One undeniable fact however was that back in the days of the internal combustion engine, his family was part of a racing team that designed and built the fastest motors on the planet. They had the relics in their personal transport storage unit to prove it. So as the children grew, if they showed interest, they were taught the basics of mechanics which included the building and repair of simple fusion powered engines. There were no gears in these units but the tradition stood. Al was raised as a gearhead.

Taka and Al met in a fabrication shop class in advanced education technical school, and became friends while assembling their first power conveyance module. It helped their relationship that their parents worked together at DCI, so they could spend off hours also working at the plant. Current industry encouraged families to bring their children with them to work, in the hopes of developing future engineers and workers. DCI was a major melting pot for cultures around the world. Anyone with an interest in engineering or space related sciences was attracted by the prospect of working on the primary components for gravity drive engines. People in these and other industries didn't work for the same form of compensation as in ancient times. With the abolishment of conflict, and the reduction in human population that followed, the availability of resources was no longer a concern. People worked because they enjoyed their occupations. Those that didn't enjoy their work, were quickly encouraged to find something that inspired them to excel.

Another important lesson humans had learned, or perhaps relearned, was life shouldn't be all about work, no matter how much you enjoyed your job. Family time and recreation were important to a healthy life and environment. So when the end of the work or school day came, if you were lucky enough to live where their families did, it was Surfs Up, for Taka and Al. A quick change into their microfiber swimskins, grab their boards, and hop the next magtrain headed up or down the coast, and they were ready for a few hours of surfing. The breaks were solid today at Zuma, so they headed north and shared the train with other surfers headed the same direction.

Surfing had gained attention in the coastal communities as the oceans of the world became cleaner and the abundance of life flourished. Although all outdoor sports were encouraged, when you lived on the coast, there was still nothing that brought young people together better than sand, sun, surf, and of course the physical attraction of a potential partner. There was one other thing that had changed about surfing though, apart from the improved boards, it was the company. The resurgence of ocean life brought the dolphins and seals onto almost every beach in these warm, fish filled waters. So when you caught a wave, the chances were excellent, you'd have a dolphin or seal right next to you competing for the tightest spot in the curl. The biggest risk of sharing the surf with these natural body surfers was taking too long to catch the next wave. Waiting outside the breakers, floating on your board with your legs dangling in the water while you flirted with another surfer, invited the occasional seal or sea lion to hop on your board for some sunbathing. Once on board they were often difficult, and even dangerous to remove. But it was all part of the fun of growing up in an environment where humans shared the world with other life.

Surfing wasn't the only sport that gained popularity. Although contact sports had been largely abandoned in the interest of avoiding long term bodily damage while reducing our natural combative instincts, competitiveness in virtually all other sports had grown. New sports, or at least sports that were greatly improved by modern technology were also popular. What used to be known as hang gliding, evolved into something closer to actual flying. The ultra lightweight "birds" as they were simply called, allowed a person to launch off a cliff, or hitch a quick tow from a ground based catapult, and stay aloft for extended periods which greatly exceed those of the old hang gliders. The biggest advantage was simply that when you got too close to the ground, and you weren't ready to quit, you could flat your wings to regain altitude. The physical exertion was considered excellent exercise, and the semi-intelligent "birds" automatically adjusted lift and wing configuration to match the motion of a living bird. Leonardo da Vinci would have felt right at home in this century.

Physical health monitoring had become one of the focuses of the new education systems in place globally. Along with education of the mind, teaching people good physical fitness habits to develop a lifetime path for health, was something all students participated in. The variety of options beyond anything imaginable in the distant past was a large reason for the success of these programs. Video games and other useless indoor activities were long gone, and children who struggled with physical activities were given special attention until something that matched their natural skills was found. The reality was even simpler. People had evolved over the past few thousand years to be more physically fit. Those who weren't, simply didn't procreate.

There was another reason people were generally healthier, and lived longer lives, though even in this day and age it was debated. Over 99% of the human population no longer consumed meat of

Paul H. Rosenfeld

85

any kind. There were a few hold-outs that insisted on consuming chicken eggs, or even hunting in the wild. The largest non-vegan protein however came from the sea. The ocean's recovery had once again become a source for abundant fisheries. Many people felt this was completely acceptable, as no commercial over-fishing was allowed. Fish were a natural food for humans since the beginning of time, and from a purely physiological perspective was considered healthy. The bottom line for humanity was simply that animals must never again be enslaved as a source of food. As long as hunting and fishing didn't impact wild populations, the practice was considered a return to a simpler way of life, where humans were a part of the environment, like any other predator. Again, as long as a healthy balance was preserved. Therefore these practices were closely monitored and strict licensing for each activity and species was required. The point being, there was strong evidence that our improved health as a species came from a much reduced consumption of meat, combined with improvements in our intake of the correct balance of whole grains, legumes, vegetables, fruits, nuts, and seeds that provided all our necessary nutrients.

Taka and Al had excelled not only at surfing and picking up beach bunnies, they'd discovered a natural intuition for that shared bridge between physics and mechanics. Since the development of the first gravity drive engine over 6,000 years ago, the technology had been continuously improved, and built into every space going vessel. When Taka and Al graduated from their advanced education, they were both offered opportunities to work on high-tech building and research projects at DCI.

They started, like everyone else at the facility, with the basic assembly of all aspects of the drives, and how they integrated into complete systems. This included traveling to other facilities around the world to participate in the design and final integration of components. DCI was primarily responsible for building the gravity drive engines for a vast array of vehicles. Everything from commercial airliners, to heavy lift cranes for Earth or low orbit construction, to the drive systems for every type of space craft including the massive orbiting space stations. DCI wasn't the only facility in the world to provide these engines, though they were generally considered a leader in the development of improvements in the systems. Taka and Al felt lucky to have grown up in this facility.

Across the planet there were hundreds of facilities involved in the construction of these types of vehicles. For the larger more complex construction projects such as space stations, each facility usually provided just one or two of the major components for the entire project. In the same way DCI provided the drive system, some other facility might provide the HVAC systems, recycling systems, communications, integration, shell construction, electronics integration, and even individualized living quarters. On a space station there were thousands of major components. Sub assembly plants were responsible for bringing together many of the individual components. At some point, these completed subassemblies were then lifted into low orbit, and consolidated with other subassemblies to build the completed station. Projects like these often required decades to complete.

Each facility, without exception, was carefully and regularly inspected by UN Technology to assure full compliance with environmental impacts. Unlike the old days there were no exceptions, partial monitoring, special favors, or self-regulation. Simply enough, that boiled down to Zero Tolerance for environmental impact. Any bi-product of production that couldn't be recycled at the facility and was considered waste, had to be physically transferred to a facility designed specifically to deal with these bi-products, whether they were solid, liquid, or gaseous. Absolutely nothing was permitted to escape into the environment. It was no longer necessary to remind the facilities of this, nor was punishment for potential lack of compliance a part of the inspections. Everyone realized the importance of keeping the environment they lived in pristine. Those days of pooping in your own house were long gone. The inspections were simply the result of seeing the benefits of always having a third set of eyes, ears, and nose to detect problems someone might not catch who lives with them everyday.

Today Taka and Al had flown to Russia to participate with the installation of a DCI drive into the supporting framework that would eventually become the complete drive and navigational support system for one of the newer space stations scheduled for delivery to the Moon in roughly 15 years. Each time they visited a new facility and witnessed the process of bringing these systems together, the more they realized how little they knew. This was one of the best educational processes for turning young cocky engineers into well balanced, thoughtful, and careful engineers who learned to consider all aspects of a design and how it would impact other systems before integrating it into the whole. The more complex human built technology became, the more organized and respectful of the entire process it was necessary to be.

Eventually, Taka and Al were allowed to participate in the most exciting phase engineers craved: Orbital assembly. They flew from the sub-assembly plant 150 miles outside Sydney, Australia, in the heavy lift space crane, directly to the site where early components of this space station had been assembled. Watching pod flyers maneuver massive components into exact alignment with existing structures, was an awe inspiring affair. Some of their work was done in these pods, while other was in space suits with built in maneuverability jets and automated armatures. The temptation to race these suits around the construction site was often more than a young person could resist, but the punishment was banishment from the worksite, so everyone obeyed the safety rules. In certain areas where construction was complete, you could work without space suits as if you were at a factory on

Earth. They were amazed at the variety of personal living suites available even in this relatively small section of the proposed completed station. Given the luxury they were observing, this was likely to be a tourist station where people spent vast sums of their accumulated work credits for a once in a lifetime vacation.

After 12 years working together on several systems integration projects on and off world, including two trips to the Moon, and one to Mars, Taka and Al found themselves back at DCI working on advanced gravity drive research. The facility housed acres of research buildings, each dedicated to a unique aspect of these drive systems. One such building housed a working example of each major improvement in the system including the very first drive design built by Howard Kalb himself. It was like walking into a museum where the first exhibit was a flying car, and as you walked back past the airplanes, and helicopters, and ground cars, you eventually arrived at the first horse drawn stagecoach. Taka and Al loved to come eat their lunches at this display. There was something simple and clean about the first gravity drive, regardless of how crude it appeared next to the latest models. For one thing it was tiny, compared to the massive systems built for the space stations. There were so few components, it was amazing it even worked, yet they knew from their history books it had. They saw the images from the first flight of *Gravitas-1*, and even the historical photo from the Moon of their first landing there, and the infamous termite mound they created during liftoff. And of course, there was their eventual encounter with the alien AI, Jason, that happened at the Beginning of the new Earth. Somehow sitting here with this simple core brought all that back to life. The simple feeling of great accomplishment and innovation. It was the innovation that attracted them most. Someday perhaps there was room for true innovation somewhere in these drive systems. Something new beyond just larger, more powerful, or more efficient. As the wise sage always reminds us, be careful what you wish for.

10 Years Later - Earth Date: 8409

Taka and Al were creative engineers who proved themselves through meticulous testing of each innovative improvement they developed over the past 10 years working at DCI. Their most recent enhancement to the magnetic generators reduced power consumption by almost 15% while providing a more even magnetic flow on the gravity drive core. They also designed and built an updated neutrino generator that ran off the existing fusion generator in their lab, and a paired detector the size of an old fashioned bread box. Both of these innovations won them recognition by the Nobel Prize committee, however the limited applications beyond their own research brought them up short for winning the much sought after honor. Nevertheless, these innovations won them free rein and an almost unlimited budget over any projects they deemed worthy, which for them was an even better reward. After 10 years of work, this was exactly the added incentive they needed to test a new composite idea they had for the drive cores. They'd specifically designed the neutrino generator and detector pair for the purpose of assessing the improvements they sought in the updated core design.

During the past 10 years they continued to eat their lunch at the same Howard Kalb display, and often went there as a quiet place to do their brainstorming. They'd even setup a small desk area with a research terminal so they didn't have to keep running back and forth to their lab anytime they had an idea to document or just needed to query the center's main systems. It became a joke that if you ever needed to find them, that's where they'd most likely be. At some point, this came to the attention of DCI's historian who thought they'd be interested in reviewing a little known, and very ancient file, containing most of Howard Kalb's original research notes. It was while reading through his notes they came up with their latest idea. Kalb had hypothesized, that if a compound could be developed that would contract, rather than expand from the centrifugal forces while spinning, then the

Gravity Drive 2 - Jason's Ark

faster it spun and the more it contracted, the greater the efficiency of the drive, and therefore the faster a ship could travel. In theory, if the contraction could continue indefinitely, then at some point you could create a temporary black hole through which the ship could pass, in effect creating your own on-board shortcut through the fabric of space. The theory was discredited as being impossible since the more the core contracted, the slower the outer-most surface would spin, therefore requiring a geometric increase in power to the core to keep the contraction occurring. At some point the amount of energy required would become almost infinite, and therefore impossible to attain.

Taka and Al of course discounted the discounting as being too narrow minded, and only visualizing a single effect, which was not what Kalb was theorizing. So rather than debate the theory they decide to build a model to test the theory themselves. When they redesigned the magnetic generators for increased output, they had also developed an improved positioning system that could easily be adapted more efficiently to the contracting core. Additionally, chemistry had come a very long way since the days of the first gravity drive core, and they had some theories on how recently developed compounds would work perfectly in this scenario. Fortunately, the folks who developed those compounds worked at DCI and were good friends with Taka and Al.

These new compounds had been developed as part of a program to provide self repairing skins for fast moving deep space ships working in areas of high particle concentrations. In the simplest terms these compounds contracted instantly filling any small holes while reinforcing the overall structure. If these compounds could be incorporated into the existing chemical structure of the latest core materials, then in theory they could work as an improved version of Kalb's initial concept. It would take considerable experimentation to get the two different compounds to mix into a single fluid compound, but the chalk-board tests seem to indicate it was possible. And their friends in Chemistry were more than happy to do the work since Taka and Al's freedom of budget could be directed into their department.

It took a little over two years of daily trials to arrive at the well behaved compound they'd been looking for. It was New Years eve, 8409, when they completed the pouring of the first test core using the new compound. Their work wasn't exactly a secret, though they didn't go out of their way to generate any curiosity. It was just Taka and Al being Taka-and-Al, as usual.

The test core was small, about the same size as Kalb's original in *Gravitas-1*. If their idea worked, they didn't want to risk creating any unexpected physical problems at the facility, though the result of their calculations of effect were inconclusive. Core size was constructed in direct proportion to the mass of the vessel it would drive, and the work requirements of that vessel. So a core the size of the one in Kalb's original vessel could create several G's of acceleration in deep space for a vessel that mass. Put the exact same drive in even the smallest space station and it would very little effect. We weren't going to be building any core drives that could move planets anytime soon, though apparently it was possible, since the rumor was that Jason had moved Pluto into it's existing orbit, using his own ship, millions of years ago.

The core was fitted into the test drive with all the usual and customary safety protocols in place, the neutrino generator and detector activated, and the core was quickly spun up to 1G relative for it's mass. At this level the guys noticed no change in the diameter of the core. If the core began to contract as they added power, the magnetic drives would automatically adjust to keep their distance at the ideal location relative to the outer shell, and thereby provide the necessary data to the monitors. They began to increase the power output slowly and evenly. As the drive approached 2 G's relative, the core began to contract, though only slightly. This was the extent to which all existing drives contracted, from Howard Kalb's first drive, to today's most advanced units. They continued to increase power until at 3 G's relative the contraction became significant, but not the functionality. They needed more functionality to make this development worthwhile so they continued to increase power. When they reached 5 G's relative, there was a noticeable geometric increase in the contraction of the core, though the power required had not increased.

That was an unexpected result. It was as if the core itself was now providing some of the power to maintain it's spin. There were no signs of any increased vibrations or other potential problems so they continued to increase power. The core was less than half it's original diameter at this point, and the magnetic generators were approaching their minimum setting. Any closer and they would begin to interfere with each other. They would need to be redesigned with smaller heads. Also, since humans had been working with gravity drive cores for thousands of years, and the safety protocols were automatic and quite extensive, there was little concern for their safety as they continued to slowly increase power. Just prior to reaching 6 G's relative however something quite unexpected happened. The core shrunk almost instantly to a tiny point for just a moment, there was a sudden jolt that shook the entire building, and then the automatic shutdown safety system kicked in and the power was cut to zero. The core almost instantly regained it's original size at rest, and there appeared to be no damage in the system. The readings from the neutrino detector however showed an unexplainable spike as if the core itself had created it's own flow of neutrinos. They'd built the neutrino generator/detector combo with the theory the core would become functionally dense enough to block neutrinos, not the opposite. This was outside their expertise as engineers, and would require an Einstein level physicist to explain, so they set it aside for now.

After the system was completely at rest with the power off, they made a thorough evaluation of the components and could find no faults. Nothing broken, except for one thing. The steel and concrete pad on which the entire structure was mounted appeared to have a slight concave dimple which extended evenly to 4 feet in diameter, ending exactly at the main unit's exterior footprint. Following established protocol, Al and Taka notified the facility engineers and an inspection team was sent out immediately to verify. When they saw the dimple, they went back to their lab and wheeled in their structural scanner. The test pads for the gravity drives are 10 feet in diameter, and equally as deep. In other words there's 10 feet of solid concrete and steel supporting each test unit. The facility engineers recalibrated their unit three times, because they couldn't believe what the scanner was showing. Eventually they decided that the scans must be correct, but they would have to verify with the physical excavation of the pad. According to the scans, there was a hole just under the upper base of the pad, roughly 4 feet in diameter and extending the entire 10 feet deep. The center of the pad was gone.

It took several days to remove the core testing unit and excavate the pad. What they found exactly matched the scans. The center of the pad was gone, all the way down, along with another 15 feet of bedrock. Taka and Al had a pretty good idea what had happened, but were reluctant to discuss it for fear of sounding a bit crazy. The facility engineers were stumped but assumed some type of natural land sink had occurred, in solid bedrock, and taken a 10 foot thick block of concrete and steel with it. Which on any scale made no sense, though they didn't have a better idea, and Taka and Al were not volunteering any information.

When they were alone, they reviewed the recordings from the experiment. The only logical conclusion was they had created a momentary opening in the fabric of space, or even a black hole, which took the pad with it when it collapsed. "So where do you suppose it went?" Taka asked Al.

"No clue," Al replied. "Where does anything go when it gets sucked into a black hole? Do you think maybe a block of concrete and steel popped out somewhere in the middle of the galaxy? I mean for billions of years, unfathomable quantities of stuff have been disappearing down the mauls of black holes at the center of galaxies. Where does it all go? We're engineers not physicists."

In the meantime, high above the space stations orbiting Earth, Jason was monitoring something that had his full attention. Ordinarily, something like what Taka and Al did would have drawn Jason's notice, even though from a cosmic perspective it was exceptionally tiny. Not this time. Something far more concerning was happening at the other end of the solar system.

Tangential Boomerang

Earth Date: 8,409

The 7-th Location

Hold your hand out and block the view of the planet below, from your position in low orbit, and you would have difficulty telling where you were simply by looking at the orbiting stations above you. Earth? Earth's Moon? Mars? They all look very similar from this position with their logical, standardized designs. The perfectly round massive clamshell dominates the upper section with it's thousands of clear windows surrounding the perimeter, each a separate and unique home for someone living and working on the station. Above the clamshell, the upper dome is completely clear for studying the cosmic background or simply as a place to relax. Looking down on the clamshell below, you see the entire surface covered in the blue glow of solar energy absorption mats providing power to the homes below. Technically no longer necessary, though they remain as a nod to humanities desire to harness as much clean energy as possible. Below the clamshell the long tapering body extending many hundreds of yards down towards the stabilizing gravity drive core and eventually down to the fusion power generators providing most of the energy for life on the station.

Remove your hand and the view is now breathtaking for those who've never seen it, and comforting to those who know it well. Never boring. The vast blue and now clean oceans dominate the scene, painted with the whitish circling storm systems that refresh the lands and naturally cleanse the air. At night, the lands no longer glow with lights from the immense cities below, as humans have learned to contain light pollution along with all the other forms of pollution they used to spew into their environment thousands of years in the past. The darkness though is haunting and doesn't sparkle with the same life as the ocean in the moonlight, looking like some monster sleeping on the sea's surface.

The station's orbit eventually brings it to the morning terminator and once again lights the world below, briefly with the customary warm colors of the low sun on the atmosphere, and quickly into full daylight. The orbit itself is also cleaner and clear of the many thousands of orbiting satellites, communication stations, and countless pieces of space trash that eventually made orbiting a game of dodge ball. The half dozen orbiting stations evenly spread above the planet now serve all the communication, GPS, and weather observation requirements of the planet. Massive quantum computer server farms are now located at the five Lagrange points surrounding Earth's orbital ring, including L3 on the opposite side of the sun. Though not required for their mostly stable locations relative to the gravity wells of Earth, Moon, and Sun, they do make convenient redundant locations for storing the vast sum of knowledge for the human race in digital format, as well as providing communication relays for Earth, Moon, and Mars. All these stations are heavily shielded from the Sun's radiation, and protected from the occasional impact of micrometeorites. One could call this an upgraded version of the twentieth century internet, but that would be like comparing laser beam communications to kids with two metal cans and a string. A sixth backup is maintained deep in the mountains of Colorado simply as a convenient access point and for historical purposes. In addition to providing backup redundancy, the hope for this design was to allow equal access, given the travel time delays, for users on the Moon, and Mars.

There is also a seventh location though this one is unofficial, and not reachable by the other six. The connection is essentially one way, and for Jason's private use. Though he often moves his location for various observation and continued research needs, when near Earth, he tends to stay in the favored location of his old pals Howard, Bill, and John. Jason misses the companionship of his old friends, but knows they're safely resting with his family back at his own central processing site. He also misses those days 6,000 years ago, as the best friend to the President of the United States, and especially those years of her retirement when that part of him no longer had any responsibilities other than enjoying her company. He was careful during all those years to keep his true identity hidden, and upon her passing he allowed his avatar as a Rhodesian Ridgeback to also pass, ending a relationship such as he'd never experienced before in his 6 million years caring for this solar system.

With those experiences long behind him, he focused on his old task of researching and protecting the various life forms evolving in this solar system. He'd never actually stopped doing that, yet somehow his attention wasn't quite the same back then. Monitoring the progress of the humans towards fulfilling their agreement with the Octopods, and helping them where needed were part of his new responsibilities. He made a point of contacting each new Secretary General of the evolving United Nations as well as the Administrators for GASA, to reassure them he was always there if and when needed. Though at first he was called on frequently, these past couple thousand years, he wondered if they would have forgotten about him completely if he didn't stay in touch. It was possible that without his continued contact and support the facts of his existence could become legend. The legend become myth. The myth become religion. This would be a major step backwards and the last thing humans needed now. On the other hand it could indicate a sign of their growing maturity.

One of his observational tasks included a constant background monitoring for any celestial changes effecting the solar system, allowing him to guard the planets against potential impacts from rogue asteroids or comets. That system was alerting him now of a momentary change in a distant background star. The star had nothing directly to do with the solar system other than acting as a reference point for navigation. The wide angle observation scope pointed towards the orbit of Neptune, detected a momentary lensing effect surrounding this distant star. If the system hadn't been on automatic, set to detect any change in the background, this effect would never have been noticed. On Earth, or on one of their deep space observatories, even if they were looking in that direction at the time, it's unlikely they would have seen anything. Jason's analysis however was virtually instantaneous, his emergency alert system activated the drive system on his ship, and within moments he was headed out of Earth's space and towards the outer solar system to verify his concerns regarding this observation. If his calculations were confirmed, this could be potentially devastating news. A mere few hours later, he detected a second anomaly; The rings of Neptune were showing signs of a distortion in their orbit. This distortion was of adequate size to confirm Jason's suspicions, and provide a second point for calculating the path of the disturbance. The path would place Mars, then Earth just within the objects massive gravitational well. This was no ordinary space rock, and was well beyond the capabilities of Jason's ship to influence. Jason's main processor back at the Octopod's research facility was running at nearly 100% searching for options while attempting to determine the exact effects Earth was likely to experience.

Part Two

INDIFFERENCE

Life

The Universe is jam-packed with life. Every galaxy. Every star cluster and nebula. Every single star, binary star, and trinary star system. Every solar system and every planet from rocky to the gas giants have life. Under every rock, on the highest, coldest mountain peak, and the bottom of the deepest, darkest ocean, there's life. The most basic building blocks that serve as life's foundation are indigenous to the very fabric of space, and spread with the expansion of the Cosmos. These building blocks of DNA and RNA are at the very root of life's success. Simple yet elegant. Infinitely flexible in the endless permutations they promise. Adapting to any possible environment short of the interior furnaces of stars. And it's a good thing too, since only in the odds of these enormous numbers can it persist.

It feels at first thought as if the Universe is kind, to provide so many habitats for life to flourish. It is not. And the proof is in the unjustly small numbers of life forms that are given the opportunities required to evolve unmolested into self aware and technically capable species, able to leave their home worlds and spread their genes across space. The forces that create and build, are always waiting to disrupt or destroy. A species lives for hundreds of millions of years, evolving, improving, spreading, specializing, and beginning to reach beyond itself towards the future, when a single large rock comes barreling into it's environment obliterating in minutes, what took millions of years to build. This is not the Universe acting out of malice or cruelty. This is not the Universe baiting life and daring it to prosper. This is simply the Universe consistent in it's indifference towards life.

On one of the tiniest scales of the Universe, the scale of the rocky planet, like the third one from our own star, life itself has recognized this indifference and found ways through it's own evolution and natural selection to overcome this indifference.

The plants and animals that live on the planet have learned to produce as many of their own kind as their bodies and the environment will allow, attempting to overcome the odds. The wolf gives birth to 12 puppies, the bird lays a dozen eggs, the fish spread their seeds by the thousands, and the sponges by the millions. The pomegranate bears thousands of seeds as do the tomatoes, guava, papaya, banana, and melons. The stone fruit trees deploy a different strategy making virtually indestructible enclosures and tasty treats in the hopes of spreading their seeds far and wide, giving each tree the many years it needs to produce yet another batch of fruit. The predators of the world go in the opposite direction and reduce their reproduction while increasing the time required to create new replicates of their species, knowing that in smaller numbers they stand a far better chance of surviving than in great numbers where they may devastate their food sources in a single offspring. With all these clever strategies that evolve through the eons, how many survive the fury of the nearby supernova, or the random massive stone that survived the formation of their solar system, and now, 5 billion years later decides to visit your world?

And yet, some do survive. Perhaps that's all part of the Universe's unknowable plan, that only a very small number shall survive to move off planet and improve their odds by spreading far and wide. Those lucky and worthy enough to withstand and overcome the indifference. Those evolved enough to appreciate the great gift they've been given. What force is it that drives life to persist?

By what standard do we judge a species successful? Is it simply the longevity of their existence? By this standard the dinosaurs would be among the most successful species that lived on Earth, and yet they didn't even survive one full rotation of their galaxy. Certainly the sponges, horseshoe crabs, jellyfish, and many of the simpler single celled organisms would take the prize for longevity, but what do they have to show for their existence?

Would evolving in the great depths of the oceans where no other creature could exist, and living there until the Sun becomes a red giant and swallows the Earth qualify? Certainly not humans who have been around for less than a fraction of any of these others, and yet in their short time they've gone from crawling out of the swamps to building great structures, and harnessing vast powers. Would that make them successful, assuming they don't annihilate themselves before receiving their award? 5 billion years from now, when the star that hosted these life forms has grown to a red giant and extinguished all life in the inner system, what will that say of the life that once existed there? In the end, it seems the only truly successful species, will be those that found the means to leave their home worlds, and spread themselves far and wide enough to survive the inherent violence and self destructiveness of the Universe.

What of these fortunate few who's species survive the odds and spread themselves throughout the vast distances that separate the systems? What happens when two of these meet? Will they recognize each other as the greatly fortunate and attempt to bond or at least communicate in peace? If they wish to communicate, how will they accomplish that given the highly unlikely possibility they even perceive the Universe from the same perspective, much less communicate in the same fashion? Sound, sight, color, taste, touch, dance, body language, tools, chemistry, music, mathematics, or a thousand other unimagined possibilities or combinations there could be; as varied as the DNA from which they came.

On the level of a civilization, one species attempting to establish communications with another, the clearest path to establishing a connection will likely be through mathematics, combined with science; establishing our understanding of common occurrences in the Universe such as the vibration of hydrogen, or an understanding of pi. Then, once an understanding of each civilization's form of communication is established at the binary level, perhaps they'll let their computers talk to each other and translate for us. Not very personal, but it may work. Or perhaps if both sides are patient and observant, we could establish a form of understanding through carefully watching our actions and applying words to these actions, though that would not be as simple or accurate as it seems. If it was simple, humans and dolphins would have been sitting around talking to each other for ages. Perhaps someday. But what about direct, individual to individual communication? Would that be possible?

There are those among the human race who claim to have the answer to that question, though they don't speak of it. They say each person must find the answer for themselves. They even try to provide the tools necessary to those willing to listen. Why so circumspect? Why so mysterious? Is it perhaps they don't really have the answer? Those who know best will just smile at this line of suspicious reasoning, because they know the truth, and it's the simplest possible explanation. The answer is, they don't speak of if because they can't. Not because some force is preventing them, or because they fear punishment, it's because they simply can't. The words to explain it so others would understand simply don't exist. This isn't a failure of our languages, it's simply that explanations lie outside the realm of language. Some people will scoff at an answer like this, saying anything can be explained in words if you try hard enough. Then ask them to explain the color Orange to a person who was born blind. Or to explain how to raise their arm to someone born paralyzed. These are simple daily things, and yet we have no words for them. So for those who listen, and are willing to take the effort to know, the path is simple. Sit quietly. Clear your mind. Stop talking to yourself with the words that fill your mind and tell you how the world is shaped. When you are completely silent, the emptiness that you find will be filled with the feelings in the Universe around you. In the end, the one true universal language, exchangeable between all species, will simply be *feelings*. Perhaps the next great step in evolution for humanity.

Chapter 7

Earth Date: 8,409

Dyson Sphere

Octopod Research Station

The first thing to return was the feeling of cold. He wasn't conscious enough to even know that's what he was feeling. The tingling that came next did come up to his conscious level and made him aware of other feelings, other sensations. Sounds, though faint, were beginning to register. A terrible taste in his mouth. Breathing. His heart beat and the warmth of blood moving through his body. Things he'd never felt before, because they'd become buried beneath his higher functions. Now those higher functions were beginning to start up, like an old engine on a winter's morning. Trying to make sense of who he was. Where he was. Eventually his instincts took over and without a thought, he opened his eyes. Still, nothing made sense.

"Close your eyes," a kind and familiar voice said, and he did. "Give yourself a chance to wake up slowly. Everything is OK and there's no need to be concerned. You've been sleeping for a very long time, and your body needs to slowly regain it's functions, one system at a time. Don't think about it, just relax and breath deeply. That's right. Just breath. You're doing well and all your stats are green. When you feel like it you can open your eyes and blink a few times to spread the moisture. Good."

"Jason...... is that you old buddy?" Howard asked.

"Yes Howard. Excellent. Your brain still works, that a good sign."

"And your sense of humor hasn't improved," Howard said as he tried sitting up and failed.

"Not so fast Boss, there's no rush. Wait for the tingling to go away and then slowly try again."

"How long Jason?"

"In round numbers, over 6,000 years."

"6,000 years…….. Six. Thousand. Years. Ahhhhh OKkkkeee. Why now, Jason? Has something happened?"

"Let's give you a chance to wake up a little more first. Bill and John are also starting to wake though they don't seem to be in the same rush as you, Boss. Perhaps get some food and drink while we wait. Are you feeling hungry or thirsty yet?"

"Yes, I think I am, and you're dodging my question, but I think you're right. I'll feel better if I can move around and put something in my body. I'm going to try to sit up now," Howard said as he slowly swung his stiff legs over the side of the flat surface he'd been laying in for so long.

"I need you to tell me a few things, Boss, to make sure you're recovering your higher functions, especially your memories. The memories you formed immediately before you went into suspension are actually the most important since those are the most fragile. So, starting with coming into this room, tell me everything you remember."

"The three of us agreed to all go into hibernation…… uh, you said that wasn't right, it was more suspension because we wouldn't actually still be functioning on any level. You said it would take about a week from the time we started until we were fully suspended, to give our bodies a chance to naturally expel all our bio-waste and any cellular toxins."

"Good. You're remembering details. Do you remember having any dreams during that week?"

"You're kidding again, right Jason? That was a long time ago. No. No dreams. Besides you said we would be deeply asleep otherwise we'd just be making more toxins. Then once we were clean, the shell over these tables would close and we would be placed in zero G, so there was no stress on our bodies, and then you'd remove all our energy. I don't remember understanding that exactly. Something about us all having an energy body that actually was our life force or something, and by removing that, all our functions would stop, but we wouldn't die. Our cells all go to absolute zero instantly so there's no damage coming or going."

"That's good enough, Boss. You will be happy to know in the other rooms, Bill and John are doing equally as well and you should all be getting together soon, though they're already asking for pizza and beer. This would not be a good idea for your first meals. I'll leave that to you to discuss with them."

"Thanks Jason. I have to admit, pizza and beer does sound pretty good though. It's been a while."

Howard eventually was able to walk around enough to move into the common area where Bill and John were already sitting. He felt just OK. Probably just weak. Their bodies were empty so there wasn't anything to burn. Bill and John were already eating something that looked like Cream of Wheat, and they looked up at Howard as he walked over to the dispenser and took the same thing, as it was all that was offered, along with a suspicious looking warm drink.

"The cereal is actually pretty good, boss," Bill grumbled, "but the drink is marginal. Jason says we have to drink it all to help balance our electrolytes or something. How you feeling? Did Jason say why he woke us up now?"

"No. He said we needed to wake up more first and I agree. You two OK?"

They just nodded and kept eating, like someone who hadn't had their morning coffee. So he sat down and joined them. Their assessment of the first meal was accurate. "Hey, Jason, any chance of some coffee with this?"

"Yes. After you finish that first meal which is intended to replenish the nutrients and probiotics you need to digest food and balance your electrolytes, I'll make some coffee. You'll be happy to know your species has made great progress since you left. The oceans and lands of Earth are clean and a natural balance is returning to life. Most species that were at risk of extinction have recovered to sufficient numbers to once again have ample genetic diversity to persist and thrive. A healthy balance of gases in your atmosphere, consistent with the evolved requirements for a balance between plant and animal life has been restored. The warming of your planet, responsible for the melting of glaciers and the polar regions has reversed, and your sea levels have returned to what you deemed as normal. Though you must realize these types of global heating and cooling cycles are normal and will return in time. They are part of the natural life cycle of the planet. Your species is beginning to understand this, so at the next cycle they will likely be prepared to adjust."

"The space outside the atmosphere," Jason continued, "has been cleaned of ancient space junk, and massive space stations have been constructed that house millions of your species. Your people have wisely chosen to reduce your birth rates, reducing the strain on your environment and redirecting those resources towards improvements. This allowed the natural resources of the planet to recover, and occupying the space stations is part of that endeavor. The same types of stations have been built around Earth's Moon, and Mars. Your planet is once again a blue and white jewel in space."

"You should understand, many of these accomplishments were only possible thanks to your development of the gravity drive, which is now a standard complement aboard all space vessels, including the cranes which lift and carry the raw materials for their construction. There are millions of people living in orbit around the Moon, and also at Mars. The low gravity at both those locations is the main reason people live in orbit, though they work on the surfaces. Perhaps over the next million years, if people chose to stay there, they will evolve and adapt to live on the surfaces in the lower gravity."

"Jason, hold on minute," Howard said, "it feels like you're giving way to much credit to the technology and not enough to the will of the human race to survive."

"That may be partially true, Howard, however you're forgetting one very important fact. Prior to your development of that technology, the Octopods were very close to the most difficult decision of having to remove your species from the Earth's ecosystem as the only means to save all life on your planet. When we met in deep space, and the Octopods realized this was the very first time humans had achieved space flight without spewing tons of pollutants into your environment, we gave pause to reconsider. Our encounter after your visit to Earth's Moon was not a coincidence, and bringing you here was not a simple convenience. The pause created by your technological development and our subsequent establishment of a friendship resulted in the agreement that has spared your species, as well as your planet."

"Furthermore, and perhaps most importantly for now, humans have begun deep space explorations, again thanks to your gravity drive and with the occasional assistance of our Transits. They have also made first contact with at least one other species, who's home world is in a region closer to the center of the galaxy, though within the same arm as your system and this station. And now that you're awake, this brings us to the main reason we've chosen to awaken you at this time. If you walk over to the view port, you may notice a significant change since you arrived over 6,000 years ago."

The Trouble with Singularians

The three men dragged themselves up from the table and walked over to the clear view of the inside of the Octopod's advanced version of a Dyson Sphere. When they entered the Sphere for the first time, it was hard to adjust to an interior enclosure that spanned just under one million miles. This made the energy walls that formed the sphere appear almost perfectly straight as they disappeared into the distance. Now, looking outside the windows, there was a definite curvature to the walls. "Jason, have the Octopods shrunk the sphere?" Howard asked.

"Yes, though this was not by choice," Jason began. "The last time we came through the Transit from your solar system, I detected some peculiar micro-variations in gravity outside the ship. At the time, I was unsure of the cause, and was considering it may have had something to do with the Transit base on your side. However, I had also noticed these exact same variations around Neptune, millions of years ago during my initial survey of your system. These variations in micro-gravity were so small, I didn't give them much attention, which was an oversight on my part. As it turns out, these anomalies are caused by a very small life form that apparently evolved in the heart of Neptune, beneath the gaseous layer, and in the deep gravity well of the planet. They appear to be essentially living micro versions of a singularity. Obviously not anywhere near as massive and dense as a true singularity, though still massive enough to collapse and compress all matter they come in contact with and apparently consume. This includes any source of pure energy, such as the force field which creates the walls of our sphere. Each of these life forms is extremely small, and as individuals they are not a significant concern. However, over the past 6,000 years, they have slowly multiplied and having attached themselves to the exterior of the sphere, they now represent a major drain on the energy output and stability of the walls."

"Our attempts to remove these Singularians, as we've come to call them due to their apparent single mindedness, have failed. They are quite tenacious and live in such a physical state there isn't much to grab onto. In fact they seem to phase in and out of this dimension almost at will. When physical attempts to remove them failed, we tried temporarily dropping the force field in select areas, the same as when we make openings for ships to pass through. Regardless of where we try this, they seem to simply reappear at another location near by, still attached to the force field. We also tried shrinking the sphere in sudden bursts but the result was the same. The reduced size of the sphere which you see now is the result of the continued drain on our resources. Since they reproduce geometrically like most species, their numbers have become unmanageable. We are not in any immediate danger, however if this continues, we will lose the station. We never anticipated this type of failure and therefore have inadequate resources to move the entire population of the sphere. As you may recall, the design is based around the sphere itself becoming the vessel of transport. The few ships we have are for small research teams only."

"How many Octopods live here, Jason," John asked.

"Close to 3 million now, John. The research we've undertaken here over the many millions of years has expanded to include a vast region of this quadrant of the galaxy and we have many Transits providing access to these regions. In addition to the tragic loss of so many of our lives, the loss of this station would be a major blow to our research efforts. Our home planet is far too distant for a rescue operation to arrive in time. Our best hope at this time, ironically, seems to be with the one species we most feared might prove aggressive towards us. It is the same species your people had first contact with roughly 200 years ago and you know them as the Paxians. Also, since I was involved in that contact and provided my assistance in translation allowing your two species to communicate, I believe they may offer some hope. Our initial fear that they might prove aggressive was mistaken, as they are a peaceful species. They do however seem to have some primal fear of the Octopods. Approximately 100 years ago, the Paxians arrived in the area near our sphere. As you might put it, they took one look at us and quickly left. Fortunately we decided to keep track of their progress through this region and dispatched a ship to follow them at a discreet distance and establish occasional Transits should retreat be necessary. Their progress is slow, so they aren't far enough for the time loss in travel to be a major factor. We hope to have you take *Gravitas-1*, and with my help in communication, see if they have any previous experience with these Singularians which might prove helpful in removing them from our station."

"Jason first of all there's no question we'll do everything we can to help," Howard said. "But let's go back a step first. Is there some reason we, meaning humans back at Earth, can't build something to house your people? You said we've made some significant progress and have vast stations housing millions of our people. We should be able to build something for you to use until we figure out how to deal with these Singularians."

"Unfortunately Howard," Jason replied, "the nature of our environmental requirements are so radically different than yours as to be virtually incompatible technologically. And it isn't just a matter of technical capabilities, it's the very physical nature of the materials and processes. You may have noticed during the refit of your vehicle those many years ago, that our engineers had to utilize special gear, similar to your space suits in function. Those units are extremely rare and we aren't capable of producing more under our current circumstances. It could come to pass that as a last resort we may try some alternatives along the lines you suggest, but that would require some radical adjustments we'd prefer not to undertake unless absolutely necessary. And since you're about to ask, Yes, we also attempted to construct vehicles here. Even if we had the resources to produce large enough vessels for all our people, the Singularians immediately attached themselves to our test vehicles as they departed the sphere, and reduced their energy shielding so quickly they didn't survive long. It's almost as if they evolved specifically to feed on our technology; which considering they evolved on a gas giant is entirely possible. We haven't been able to study them in any significant way since they're so naturally toxic to us. Again, given that *Gravitas-1* has passed among them several times, we have high confidence you can be of help."

"Jason, what exactly is it about these Paxians that leads you to think they're the solution to this problem?" Howard asked.

"You'll understand a bit more after reviewing the information from your first contact. In the meantime, here's our theory. Our greatest weakness as a species seems to be in our technology, which closely replicates the environment we evolved in. Singularians evolved on the opposite side of that same environment. You could say our environmental relationship is almost one of predator and prey, even though we evolved on different worlds. When brought together we represent a sort of balance, though the odds do appear in their favor. Mathematically, if you process the data we've collected as a species over many millions of years regarding the interactions of species and apply it to this situation, there is a high likelihood that an equally advanced species which evolved in a completely different environment, may have the technological or even physiological solution to this dilemma. Paxians however, as you'll soon discover are genetically repulsed by us, and therefore your presence is another factor in the math. Together you and the Paxians seem our best hope for a solution. Perhaps now would be a good time to review the information on file from your first contact."

Gravity Drive 2 - Jason's Ark

Jason retrieved and displayed the information on each of the three personal data terminals for his friends. There wasn't that much, which was also part of the difficulty. Even after a peaceful first contact, the Paxians showed little interest in establishing anything resembling a friendship with the humans, though they were certainly peaceful and kept mostly to themselves. It only took a short time for the three people to understand the situation.

"Jason," Bill said, "I don't understand something about the Paxians. The information they provided to the historians makes it pretty clear they have a deep sense of discomfort dealing with flying things. Those ball wasps sound like something I'd definitely want to avoid. But we're talking about an intelligent, and thoughtful species here. Certainly their intellect is capable of overcoming these primal feelings. What's the big deal?"

"Bill," John said quickly before Jason could reply. "Let me ask you something. Do you consider yourself intelligent enough to overlook those types of primal instincts?"

Bill just nodded his head, awake enough to be aware of a sudden trap from his old friend.

"Good," John continued. "Then imagine Jason needed you to go bring him something important out of some dark cave back on Earth. When you went to the entry of the cave and turned on your flashlight, you realized the cave was filled with flying spiders of all sizes. Would you happily go inside?"

"Oh man…. You're creeping me out dude," Bill replied with a shiver, before he realized what he'd said. After a few moments it was, "OK, point taken. I get it. Poor Paxians…… no offence Jason."

"Like I said, we'll do whatever we can Jason," Howard said, shaking his head at the antics of his old friends, "I'm so sorry this is happening to you."

"Thank you Howard. There is something else you should know, and it's completely unrelated, though of great concern. Back in your home system, a couple weeks ago, I detected a powerful gravitation field moving towards your system from an orbit above the ecliptic of both your system and the galaxy. I'm fairly certain this is a rogue black hole left over from a collision with the Milky Way roughly 4 billion years ago. It's entirely possible this same black hole has been causing trouble around the outer edges of the galaxy since the collision robbed it of all it's stars. The angle with which it's approaching your system is also suspicious as it closely coincides with the roughly 23.5 degree tilt of Earth, as well as that of Mars which is roughly 25.2 degrees. At this time, I'm uncertain if it's passage will cause any direct harm to either of those planets and your inhabitants there, but I'll be closely monitoring. It has already passed the orbit of Neptune, and unfortunately both Mars and Earth are in it's path. The other planets should not be effected. There will likely be random disturbances in the asteroid belt, as well as the Oort cloud, which I haven't detected yet. Rest assured it should be easy for your new crafts to handle those potential risks. However, the black hole itself is far too massive for even my ship to begin to effect. You may recall my telling you that roughly 6 million years ago, I was able to move the planet you call Pluto into it's current orbit. That task was roughly at the maximum capacity of my ship. This black hole is a tiny one by comparison to the one at the center of the galaxy. My estimates are that it's roughly 5 of your solar masses, which puts it at approximately the equivalent of one billion times the mass of Pluto."

"Jason," Bill said, "how long before we know if this black hole's going to effect Earth?"

"It's moving approximately 50% faster than the spin of the galaxy. That puts it roughly 150 days from it's closest approach to Earth, and obviously sooner for Mars. I'm sorry but there's nothing we can do. I have of course alerted your home world with all these details and continue to provide constant updates as they request, though they've already launched their own ships to investigate. As a precaution, they are relocating the stations on both planets and your Moon, to minimize any potential impacts. Obviously there's nothing to be done from here since the time lag to arrive in your system would be years, not days. Not that there's anything we could do. I'm sorry."

Chapter 8

Earth Date: 8,409

GASA Headquarters, Houston, Texas

Preparations

Kaylee Brown's first day as the new Administrator for GASA wasn't all that different from any other day during her 30 years there. Except for one tradition. In her new office was a small, dark blue box about the size of an old style cigar box. It was permanently secured discreetly on the bottom shelf of the small library that sat behind her desk. There were no external markings or indications of it's purpose. The retiring Administrator, Richard Banyard, walked over and placed his hand on the box, allowing it to rest there with his palm flat for a few seconds. There was a pleasant beep, and a rich male voice said, "Hello Richard. It's been nice working with you. Is the new Administrator with you?"

"Yes Jason, she's right here. Jason, this is Kaylee Brown. Per tradition, I'm officially handing over your private communication channel to her now. Kaylee, please rest your hand on the box like this, and your hand print will register. Anytime you need to talk to Jason, just place your hand here and he'll answer."

Kaylee placed her hand on the box, and after a few seconds an outline flashed around her hand and Jason said, "Hello Kaylee, I look forward to working with you. Feel free to contact me at any time, I'm always available regardless of the day or hour. Your personal communications device is also now tied to my direct line so I can reach you at any time as well. Any questions?"

"Not at this time, Jason, and it's nice meeting you as well. I'm of course fully aware of the nature of our relationship, and won't hesitate to contact you with any questions or concerns. Good day."

And that was it. Tradition fulfilled, and the torch was passed.

Day two however started out much differently as her personal communications device alerted her to an incoming call, with the ID tag of Jason. What used to be called a cell phone had evolved to a simple small black dot (colors are optional), about the size of a squished pea, and located just behind the ear. It alerted the user with a pleasant vibration prior to notifying them of the nature of the call (alert options varied). It also had a full holographic heads-up display providing additional functionality that was operable using voice or eye motion commands. Fortunately she was in her office at the time, and sitting down.

"Good morning Kaylee, this is Jason. I hope I'm contacting you at a convenient time."

"Good morning Jason. Yes, this is fine. I certainly wasn't expecting to hear from you quite so soon. Is everything OK?"

"Unfortunately I have an observation to report which will likely complicate the operations of your new position at GASA, and I'm downloading full details to your personal server at GASA as we speak (she wasn't aware he could do that. Good to know). To put it succinctly, roughly 3 hours ago, my deep space automated observation scanners detected a large gravitational anomaly in the vicinity of Neptune. Subsequent observations confirmed this to be a small black hole of approximately 5 solar masses, and likely a remnant from a collision with a massive dwarf galaxy roughly 4 billion years ago. The orbital speed and course indicates it's been passing through this region of the galaxy about every 165-180 million years, suggesting it could have been responsible for some significant environmental impacts and long term changes over the evolution of life on Earth."

"This black hole is traveling in the same direction as the spin of the galaxy though moving approximately 50% faster. It's approach is above the ecliptic plane of your system and will pass Mars and Earth both at approximately a 24-25 degree angle relative to the ecliptic plane. You probably realize this is another suspicious statistic, though this passing will be on the opposite side of the existing planetary tilts relative to the ecliptic plane. At it's current velocity, and there's no reason to predict a change, it will arrive in the vicinity of Earth in roughly 150 days, and Mars about 8 days sooner. It will pass significantly closer to Mars then Earth, though both worlds will likely feel the effects. As I mentioned, it passed Neptune some few hours ago. No other planets in your system are in it's path, though it may have an effect on your Sun; the exact effect being difficult to predict, though it will pass the Sun at an angle which should preclude having any massive solar flares heading towards Earth or Mars. Are you with me still?"

"Yes Jason, please continue," Kaylee replied, "even though you're downloading the information it helps to hear if first hand from you, so I can move quickly to alert ….. well….. everyone. Are you or have you contacted anyone else yet?"

"No, Kaylee. As head of GASA it is my understanding that regarding issues of this nature, you are to be the primary contact. I am of course willing to contact any additional people you would like me to, however that decision is fully within your purview. Also, previous experience has demonstrated, as head of GASA, you will have the most cooperation with the least pushback, assuming it's made clear that the majority of observations and subsequent recommendations come directly from your office. Anything coming directly from me has a tendency to generate undesirable side effects.

"Thank You, Jason. Yes, I'll handle the contacts since it's something my office is prepared for, and it would be best coming from here, though the world will be made fully aware of the initial source of this warning. Thank you for being there for us Jason, you will likely have saved billions of lives if this goes the way it sounds. I've heard nothing at this end of any notice of this black hole by any observatories. How is it by the way you've detected this and we haven't?"

"My automated observation scanners initially noticed a momentary lensing effect, caused by the gravitational well of the black hole, as it passed a star in Neptune's general direction. The occurrence was so brief, even if you're observatories had been watching, it likely would have been missed. The location of my ship at the time was also far from any of your observatories, and essentially it was what you call luck, that I was in position to observe it. A short time later however, when it came close enough to effect Neptune, that was something your observers should have detected. It's possible they have, and you simply haven't heard. I'm unaware of any chatter on the networks regarding this. Also, you should know, in case the question arises, that I immediately sent my ship towards Neptune and made a close contact with the black hole to confirm it's existence and mass. I regret to report that my ship would not be capable of effecting it's course, and neither would any of yours. It's mass is roughly one billion times the maximum capacity of my ship."

"Thanks again, Jason. Please go on with the briefing. You were saying it may interact with the Sun, but you sounded unconcerned those effects would be an immediate problem for us."

"Correct. I will attempt to be brief, as I know you're anxious to notify as many authorities as possible given the short time frame. I would suggest starting with Mars. The orbiting stations should be moved to a shadow position opposite the ecliptic position of the black hole's approach. Again, the specific coordinates are on your server. The surface of the planet should be evacuated, or inhabitants sent underground in case of atmospheric disturbance. The greatest risk is from it's two moons. Their orbits will likely place them almost directly between Mars and the black hole as it passes. It's a virtual certainty, their orbits will be altered. Furthermore, since it will pass the asteroid belt first, there's a high likelihood of orbital disturbances resulting in sending some asteroids directly into Mars' path. These should be manageable by your gravity drive cranes, providing they're prepared to act in time. There may also be long term effects from the asteroid belt for Earth and it's Moon as well, though again these should be within your capabilities to deal with."

"Your Moon is significantly larger than either of Mars' and it's orbit will place it roughly in Earth's shadow as the black hole passes, so fortunately the effects should be minimal. I would still suggest moving all orbiting stations and evacuating the surface as a precaution. I realize your own orbital engineers and planetary scientists will have their own recommendations, so I'll stick to the big picture items unless asked otherwise. The long term risks to Earth are difficult to calculate. Short term, the effects on your oceans will likely be significant as well as creating extreme meteorological events resulting in widespread flooding. In the simplest terms, the passing of the black hole is likely to cause the largest tidal fluctuations since humans evolved. Evacuations of coastal regions will be a must, planet wide. Any old style shipping vessels at sea would be in great potential peril. Deep ocean facilities are not likely to be directly effected, though again, long term effects will be difficult to predict this far in advance. It's also likely the atmosphere itself will bulge considerably towards the black hole, which could effect pressure sensitive areas. Effects on geology such as tectonic plates, faults, and volcanoes are difficult to predict at this early time, though there most certainly will be some impact."

"I believe those are the major issues. You have a lot to attend to so I'll let you go. Please don't hesitate to contact me with any needs. I will of course continue to monitor the progress of the black hole and report any significant findings. Good luck, Kaylee."

And with that, he was gone. Kaylee allowed herself a few moments to just breath and attempt to gather her calm. This was certainly not how she expected her second day in office to start, and she rightfully wondered what the hell she was thinking when she took this job. Too late now. She pulled up Jason's data and gave it a quick once over. As expected he had provided extremely detailed observations and summary data, including all orbital projections and potential impacts. Essentially he'd done about 90% of her job and of her engineers. She gave a brief thank you in her mind for his oversight and protection. Her first call was obvious. She picked up the phone and dialed the direct line to the United Nations Secretary General. As head of the Global Aeronautics and Space Administration, her first responsibility was global, regardless of where she lived and worked. Simultaneously to placing the first call, she sent an all alert message to GASA engineers world wide for an emergency meeting to begin in 10 minutes over Vid-Com. She then placed a personal call to the President of the United States.

Within two hours of her conversation with Jason, the entire world had been placed on alert. Preparations had been in place for global emergencies for thousands of years, so as they used to say in the old days, "the shit ran downhill." Her contacts would spread geometrically, fanning out to touch virtually every single person on Earth, the Moon, and Mars within hours. Several fast research vessels were already in route to Jason's coordinates for the black hole. Evacuation plans were in the process of being dispersed, and the necessary processes started for moving the massive stations orbiting all three worlds had begun. There was no question that the most challenging process was going to be the evacuation of all the coastlines of Earth. A total nightmare. The damage estimates from the tsunamis to follow were beyond calculation. The irony of having spent 6,000 years improving the human condition and it's impacts on their home world were beyond belief. If Kaylee hadn't been a massively intelligent and trained professional, she would be in total denial. Fortunately for the planet, she had this.

Chapter 9

Earth Date: 8,409

Dyson Sphere - Octopod Research Station

Transit

The passage to the outer wall of the Octopod Research Station was shorter in distance, and much longer in feelings than past times. There was an overwhelming feeling of concern and fear among the many Octopods they passed on the way, floating in their thick atmosphere which replicated their home world environment. This was a new feeling for this species, at least in recent times. Certainly among this generation of researchers confident in their superior technology and comfortable in this facility that served as their home from long before humans were even apes. No species can anticipate and plan for every possible scenario which might threaten their existence in a Universe of infinite possibilities. An indifferent Universe.

There was great concern as the Octopods opened a small section of the outer force field wall to allow *Gravitas-1* to pass. Over the thousands of years since the Singularians first arrived and began feeding on the energy of the sphere's force field, not a single one had ever entered the sphere, at least to the knowledge of the Octopods. But nothing was certain any longer, as confidence waned. They feared what might happen if they did enter their realm. They were fully aware the Singularians had either consumed most of the life forms on their home planet, or in some indirect way had been responsible for the planet wide mass extinction, based on Jason's observations. Jason felt confident the mass extinctions only occurred after the Singularians had depleted the easily available resources at the core; those that matched their needs. As long as the sphere's force field continued to feed them they should be safe. But for how long? As individuals, Octopods were not well designed to defend themselves, despite their physically tough and resilient outer skins. They never developed technology for war, as they evolved with no such need, and therefore never developed aggressive tendencies nor a feeling of the need for physical self defense. These tiny Singularians with their only interest seeming to be in constant feeding, and with little outward displays of awareness or thought, had perfectly evolved to be the Octopod's worst nightmare. And now their only hope for survival was with two alien species: one they had initially considered self destructive and inferior in their compassion for other life forms, and another who had evolved an instinctive fear and abhorrence of the Octopods Their own existence, at least at this research facility, seemed in question. Their future did not look promising.

The force field closed behind their ship, and Howard, Bill, and John could feel the reduced pressure of the Octopod's fear. At the same time, the human's great appreciation for all the help the Octopods had given to the life on Earth, drove them now to make every effort to save their friends. But doubt is always just a single thought away, especially with so much at stake. "Jason, are you sure this is all the information you have on the Paxians?" Howard asked for the second time. He was obviously upset having just traveled through that thick wall of fear and the feelings of desperation and hope that all seemed aimed directly at him. For the second time in his life, he was overwhelmed with the vast responsibility that fell on his heart. Could he do it again? And why the hell did this have to keep happening to him?

"Yes, Howard," Jason calmly responded, well aware of the pressure Howard was feeling. "I've carefully rechecked the records from your species first contact with the Paxians, along with my own data as translator for that encounter. There is nothing more. We are currently on course for the Transit which our most recent information indicates is the closest to the current position of the Paxian scout vessel which visited this region 100 years ago. We should arrive at that Transit within four hours."

"Jason," Bill asked, "how many years will that Transit require relative to the time at the Octopod Sphere?"

"Assuming this is the correct Transit, less than 2 Earth months, so 4 months round trip. Then at maximum speed for *Gravitas-1* another 20 hours. If our mission is successful, we should be able to return long before the Sphere suffers any additional significant shrinkage, though emotionally, the 4 plus months may prove the longest in our history.

"Jason," Howard asked, "When we pass through this next Transit, will you still have your quantum link back to the Sphere, and our solar system?"

"Yes, Howard, I'll still be able to provide real-time updates on the situation back at your home worlds. I realize this is a difficult time for both our species. In the same way you're doing your best to help us here with this problem, I will do everything possible to help your people back in your system."

All three men together expressed their Thanks to Jason though Bill continued in an attempt to break the gloom, "You know what I really miss about going through these Transits, there's no wooshing. I really miss the wooshing a space ship should make when it zooms through space. Jason, can you add special effects so we can woosh?"

"Bill, you knucklehead," John started in, "we're talking about trying to save two worlds here and all you want to do is woosh? You've lost it bro. You should be thinking about all those colors you see when you go into warp or something. That makes much more sense than wooshing. There's no wooshing in space. Jason, can you maybe do some special effects with streaming colors and maybe a big bright flash when we reach the other side? Now that makes more sense."

Howard was just shaking his head but they were right. There's nothing they could do right this minute, and between the trip to the Transit and the long run afterwards, they had the best of a full Earth day before they caught up with the Paxians. No point in being gloomy so he joined in, "you guys really know how to go right to my pet peeves don't you? That's the one thing I hate most about all those far off galaxy war movies is everything makes noise in space. The engines, the lasers and bombs, even the ships just zipping by make noise like they're in the atmosphere. And the worst part is people really believe it, even though they were taught better in school. I remember going to see *2001 A Space Odyssey* at one of it's premier screenings back in 1968 at the Hollywood Pacific Theater. They had that really cool super wide, almost half circle screen. Best movie ever made. Clarke and Kubrick worked really hard to make that movie as 100% realistic as possible. There's that scene, when Dave goes out in the pod to get Frank after HAL kills him, and he's forgotten his space helmet. So he has to blow the hatch on his pod to get back in Discovery, since HAL won't let him back in, remember? When they show the scene from the outside there's no sound, and when it blows you don't hear anything. Just like it's supposed to be. But all the idiots in the audience who grew up with stupid space movies were screaming at the projectionist.....SOUND SOUND SOUND. Then the studios kept putting sound in outer space. Over the years the only TV show I remember that did it right was *Firefly*. Every time *Serenity* ignited it's engine in space, there was no sound. That was a great show so naturally it was cancelled half way through the first season."

"Hey Boss," Bill said, "Are you trying to say we can't have any wooshing?"

During this entire exchange, Jason hadn't said anything, or replied to the obvious rhetorical questions. He understood this was just his friends way of dealing with pressure. He also realized he'd very much missed these types of conversations during their many thousands of years in suspension. His programming for emotions and the development of relationships had progressed rapidly when they first met, and then it abruptly stopped. He enjoyed his time as a dog with the President on Earth, but that also stopped around the same time. Then for all these years there was nothing. The Octopods were his family, and although there was some communication there, it wasn't the same thing. Friendship seems to generate a different set of feelings than family. It occurred to him that the feeling he'd experienced while his friends were asleep was loneliness. Sometimes he thought the Octopods had done too good a job creating him. It would have been much simpler being just another AI computer.

"Jason……Jason….. HEY BUDDY, are you there?" Bill yelled.

Jason realized he'd stopped paying attention to the conversation. Was that what they called day dreaming? "Yes Bill, I'm still here. I was momentary distracted. Would you like to play a game of chess? I play rather well."

"Hahahaha, that's a good one, Jason. Glad you were paying attention after all. No thanks," Bill replied, "but I'm not letting you off the hook for some good old wooshing or light shows going through the Transit. What say buddy? And don't let that old grumpy boss of ours tell you no."

"I have no control over what you might witness outside the windows. I could create some type of display on the big screen if that would suffice, and perhaps add the sound of Bill snoring for additional effects. We are 15 minutes from Transit." During the banter, Jason had reversed the ship and started deceleration.

"That's OK, Jason," Howard said. "We're just kidding around and I think we've all heard enough of Bill's snoring. Is there anything new from back home before we disappear again for two months?"

"Nothing has changed significantly in your system. Preparations are being made to reduce potential damage to the minimum. The biggest concern seems to be the many millions of people who live and work at the edges of the continents where they meet the oceans. Full evacuations have started in those regions as they appear most likely to suffer the greatest harm from the significant tidal changes certain to occur. I'm sorry Howard, there just isn't much new to report. I'll provide a full report as soon as we complete Transit."

The ship slowed and the Transit became visible. Unlike the view from their system through the Transit to the Octopod's sphere, there was nothing to see here but blackness. The crew had read in the briefing documents, that the Paxians had chosen a very quiet area of space in a small solar system that seemed stable and well suited to their peaceful existence. It wouldn't be long now. The ship passed into the Transit and momentarily, two months later, emerged on the other side.

Chapter 10

Earth Date: 8,409

Passage of the Black Hole

Mars

The black hole is moving above the ecliptic plane of the galaxy where it was abandoned by it's stars, billions of years ago. Held in it's orbit by the massive gravity well of the Milky Way, while maintaining it's higher orbital velocity along the perimeter of the galaxy, it's passed near every star system in its path many times over these billions of years. Although considered small for a black hole, it's 5 times more massive than the star in the system it's now traveling above. Our system. Orbiting Mars in a space station, you look out the window and the Red Planet fills your view from horizon to horizon, yet it's only 11% the mass of Earth. And the Sun? Try to envision that it would take 330,000 Earths to equal the mass of our Sun. That means this small 5 solar mass black hole approaching Mars is almost 15 million times it's mass. Inconceivable. And even more difficult to comprehend, with all that mass there's nothing to see. Our instruments can measure it's gravitational effects but our eyes see only the blackness of space. This isn't like those artist's conceptions of the black hole at the center of our galaxy with a stunning vista of the event horizon. This is a rouge traveler alone in the empty darkness above. We prepare ourselves for the gravitational effects of it's passage but what other forces does a black hole of this mass yield? We think we know a lot about black holes, but in fact we know almost nothing. It's all mostly theoretical. No human has ever ventured inside one, or even close enough to study one. There's no practical way to accomplish that and live to report your findings. All we know for certain is the more we learn about a subject, the more we realize how little we really know. Mars is about to learn a little bit more. The black hole is currently passing over the asteroid belt, and the good news is it will pass on the far side of Mars relative to the belt. The bad news is, it's vector is against the orbital direction of the belt so the impact this will have on the belt could have profound effects for millions of years to come. It's like a round racetrack full of speeding cars and suddenly a truck joins the race moving in the opposite direction. Some of the cars are abruptly forced to slow down and veer away from the truck, creating a chain reaction extending far back along the track. The black hole is indifferent to this effect and continues on it's way with zero change in it's momentum, creating a bow wave of a few hundred asteroids attempting to join with some of the remaining comets picked up from the Oort cloud. Most of the rocks gradually fall back towards the belt, having been outpaced by the speeding black hole. Their arrival back will not be orderly.

142 days ago, Jill Rubin, the Administrator for the human presence on and above Mars, was warned of the approaching danger. She'd barely had time to rejoice in the major discovery of the massive Platinum find her miners discovered in the Belt. Her first reaction was "why the hell didn't I retire sooner." Her second reaction was to call the director of every department and begin the process of protecting the people and resources of Mars, starting with that big rock of Platinum. Over the days that followed, they'd initiated the process of relocating the space stations to be in the shadow of Mars' tiny gravity well and hopefully protect the stations. Most of the people who lived and worked planet side had evacuated to the stations. There were always those few who refused, preferring to take their chances or hoping to protect their investments on the surface. Mariana Dyson, the head of Agriculture was unsurprisingly one of those who elected to stay on the surface, eager to somehow protect her greenhouses and their occupants.

Gravity Drive 2 - Jason's Ark

As far as Phobos and Deimos, Mars' two moons, there was nothing to be done except wait and see the effect the black hole's passage would have. There were estimates, but those are always subject to far too many variables to be precise. The safest approach was to simply be sure no station came between one of the moons and the black hole as it passed. Not that easy a thing to do considering how fast these moons orbited. They were small, relative to Earth's Moon, which is roughly 155 times bigger than Phobos and 280 times bigger than Deimos, so it was likely the black hole would impact their orbits.

In addition to having all her sky cranes on orbital standby, Jill sent two fast interceptors to monitor the progress of the black hole. Those two were currently experiencing that surreal view of rocks and comets being pulled along by an invisible force, their instruments could barely register. The time was now; the black hole was about to make it's close pass of Mars.

Mariana was outside in one of her newer greenhouses when the black hole passed. She wasn't paying any attention to the clock, and didn't even notice anything until the ground beneath the greenhouse experienced a sudden shift. It wasn't dramatic like an earthquake it was more like the feeling of being in a fast moving car and the driver taps the brake hard once, and then continues driving. After the jolt however, there was the strangest rumbling. She couldn't tell if she was hearing it, or feeling it in her feet. Probably both. This felt like someone driving a giant machine over rocky ground, though deep below where she was standing. The rumbling continued for a while before it began to smooth out, getting weaker by the second until it was gone.

Two other people had also decided to stay and safeguard their investments, disregarding the direct requirements of the evacuation orders effecting those areas most highly at risk for experiencing extreme damage. The volcanic tubes were one of those locations. Not for fear of any tectonic or volcanic activity, though that was certainly possible. No, the concern was all that water, and what might happen when the black hole passed. This was where these two people were still struggling to tie down their submarines and other expensive toys they had their entire life savings invested in. They'd had months to prepare, but could never agree on the best approach, arguing right up to the last moment. They never felt the same shock and rumbling that Mariana felt. They didn't live that long. When the jolt hit, as the black hole passed, all the water in the huge lake and the tubes suddenly changed direction. People on Earth have described similar things during massive earthquakes. Watching all the water in their swimming pools suddenly jump to one end of the pool and pause in midair for a moment, before crashing back down. Of course, it isn't really the water that moves in that case. The water is sitting perfectly still when the land suddenly shifts underneath it. It's all relative. Although the breathing apparatus they were wearing could have kept them alive for many hours, when that much water suddenly shifts position around you, it's like being hit by a falling building. There's no way you survive that.

Billions of years ago, when the magnetosphere on Mars stopped, and the Sun's radiation and solar winds blasted the atmosphere away into space, only the smallest portion remained. Scientists believe the atmosphere has been building back slowly since that time, though without the protection of the magnetic shield, it's ability to recover is greatly diminished. There's just enough atmosphere to create those colossal sand storms Mars is famous for. From the stations in orbit above, this was the one telling sight of the passage of the black hole. A dust storm of global proportions was suddenly funneled into existence, attempting to reach space before pausing and ever so slowly returning to the surface to cover the planet in a cyclone of red dust.

The stations were largely unaffected thanks to their locations and their ability to move under their own power to stabilize their orbits. The many orbital cranes and tows employed by the mining operations were able to quickly deal with the few small asteroids that were brought into close orbit. The platinum asteroid was also saved. The moons however had shifted into much higher orbits. Like the dust from the planet below, they started to follow the black hole, but were quickly outdistanced and left to return to higher orbits. It would take time to ascertain if this was an improvement. The good news is, with the exception of those unlucky souls below, the people were safe.

Passage of the Black Hole

Earth's Moon

Arnold, Gracie, John, Sundar, Amol, and Jane had met here 149 days ago when details of the impending arrival of the black hole were first received from GASA. They all knew their jobs, and the people and resources they each needed to protect. So after a brief meeting to confirm each person's tasks, and validate nothing was left to slip between the cracks unnoticed, they left to do their jobs.

Now they were meeting again 7 days before the deadline. They were meeting to review the news from Mars. There were a lot more things that could go wrong on Mars than the Moon, and Mars had been more directly in the path of the black hole, yet things weren't looking so bad after all. It sounded as if they'd weathered the event in good shape.

Life on the Moon was already fashioned around mini versions of what was coming to pass, so 149 days was almost too long to make preparations. The most difficult decisions revolved around the status of visitors, and those decisions belonged to each individual: stay or go back to Earth. Most chose to stay and many arranged to bring the remainder of their families who were still on Earth, up to join them. After all, of the three worlds, Earth was certainly in for the worst of it. With the Earth between the black hole and the Moon the effects were expected to be minimal. There was no asteroid belt or small moons to deal with like on Mars and no large open bodies of water. Even the recently discovered new water source was likely to remain undisturbed. With absolutely no atmosphere, the disturbance of moondust wouldn't result in the type of dust storm they're still experiencing on Mars.

The nature of the Moon's orbit is such that the same side is always facing the Earth. This makes Lunar based observation of Earth a useful tool, at least for whichever half of Earth is currently in view. With the latest in high powered telescopes, observing even the smallest detail was sharper than the Earth orbiting spy satellites of old, and with far greater resolution. The Moon was all set for having a ring side seat for the largest natural disaster to strike the planet in human history, and the observatories on the Moon would be recording everything. As part of the evacuations from Earth, additional observatory equipment, and the people to operate them were also sent up to the Moon. This opportunity created a mix of emotions which were very difficult to quantify, even by the best psychiatrists. On the one hand there was a feeling of excitement at being able to observe, first hand, this type of event, and within a fairly well predetermined time frame. Though even at this distance it wasn't easy to separate one's self from the tragedy that was about to strike. These were our people down there, our families and friends. All the land animals and creatures of the oceans that were about to be challenged for their survival. The entire ecology of the planet was in peril. Yet, regardless of the heartbreak, there was little else to be done from here except watch. All in all, an almost impossible mix of emotions.

Passage of the Black Hole

Earth

149 days was not even close to being enough time to prepare for the unbelievable natural disaster about to strike Earth. The effects that could be predicted with some accuracy were scary enough. The effects which were certain to occur, but couldn't be predicted with any precision were terrifying. The planet became like a beehive stirred to it's defense. Day or night, made no difference, as the many simultaneous actions required to save life, property, and what industry they could never ceased. You simply could not prepare enough, and a considerable portion of that preparation was about the reaction of the human psych. Moving people and stuff was one thing. Dealing with the vast array of emotional responses was quite another, and had a definite impact on the efficiency of the undertaking. Fortunately, the past 6,000 years had taught humans a great lesson about dealing with adversity, and stepping forward to solve their problems. Perhaps there was hope for the human race after all, assuming the planet could survive this encounter. The irony, or maybe it was just bad luck, that sat in the back of people's minds was unavoidable. After all the work to undue the damage humans had done to their home, the Universe steps in right at the moment we were ready to pat ourselves on the back and screams, *NOT YET.*

Without question, the single greatest undertaking was moving billions of people away from the coastal regions of the Earth to essentially higher ground. In many cases this meant much higher ground as to the space stations in orbit. In short order these stations became overcrowded with immigrants, and the once peaceful and slow moving atmosphere evolved into the massive undertaking of finding housing, and providing the necessary resources for the sudden population explosion.

What was it about humans that drove them to live near water, especially the oceans? Was it simply their instinct for the biological need for water or was it something far deeper? Lakes and rivers were a logical choice for easy access to drinking water and for crop irrigation. But oceans are essentially useless for either of these. Oceans are an excellent source for food however, and in the distant past, many fishing villages would have sprung up to take advantage of this easy access. Additionally, most of these villages would have settled where rivers flow into the ocean, giving them the best of both worlds. Eventually fishing villages became a convenience of the past, as the availability of food from anywhere in the world became common place and inexpensive. So why then did people persist on wanting to live near the ocean? Why then has ocean front property always been the most expensive and sought after in the entire world? Even during that time many thousands of years ago when human-caused global climate change started the rapid melting of the polar glaciers, creating rapidly rising ocean levels, people still sought to live as close as possible to the oceans. Could it be we still feel the pull of our aquatic ape ancestry? One can't help but wonder if something of this instinctive love of living near the ocean is imprinted on our DNA. Regardless of the cause, there was virtually no ocean coastline on the entire planet, that wasn't heavily populated by humans. GASA estimates there are over 375,000 miles of ocean coastline, with over one third of the total human population living within 60 miles of any given coast. So now, vacating this zone had become the single largest human migration in history.

Once the space stations became full, and the administrators were forced to hang the No Vacancy signs, there were discussions of moving these giant floating cities to the area of the Moon. The power plants, combined with the built-in gravity drive systems, were certainly more than capable, especially considering that's exactly how the same Moon and Mars stations were moved there initially. It was eventually agreed however that such a move was unnecessary for safety and would disrupt the global communications system that was sorely needed during and after this crises. It was decided they would all be moved at the last possible moment to the far side of the planet, opposite the passage of the black hole. This would also provide the same view as the observers on the Moon though without the need of a telescope. It would be right there below you. Close up. The shocking feeling of watching the ocean quickly recede beyond the curve of the horizon to the other side of the planet.

During the evacuation of the ocean realm, scientists from several disciplines had joined their knowledge and calculations to determine just how far back and how high people would have to move to avoid the inevitable backwash of water after the black hole released it's grip. These would not be tidal waves or tsunamis. There was no word in our language for exactly what that amount of water rushing back towards the land would be called. It was certain to resemble some poor footage from an ancient B-rated science fiction, more than anything truly comprehensible in human experience. The other issue beyond how far and high to go to escape the water, was what promised to be the second most devastating effect of the black holes passage: the effect on the weather. There was little question that vast storms would be created, resulting in severe flooding. But exactly where these storms would hit, and the amount of damage and flooding to expect were beyond the capabilities of even the most advanced computer simulation programs. There was simply no way of knowing. Fear of the unknown is one of humanity's greatest weaknesses, and the resulting panic could not be avoided. The overcrowding of the inland cities became far worse than what the stations in orbit were experiencing, simply as a result of the shear numbers of people and supplies moving in that direction. The only blessing was that over the past 6,000 years, the global human population had lessened by over 35%. A significant reduction to be sure, but not enough under these conditions.

Fortunately for many of the other life forms on the planet, a very large group of people, mainly researchers and volunteers, were equally concerned about saving vulnerable species as much as saving themselves. It would be impossible to save every seal, sea lion, sea otter, walrus, and other sea mammal occupying the shores, so representative populations were the best that could be managed. As far as ocean going mammals such as the dolphins and whale groups, hope was the only remaining option. The Islands stood to be in the very worst possible locations, and would certainly experience the greatest devastation to unique life forms. A global undertaking involving heavy lift sky cranes were directed at each of the most fragile island environments. With large numbers of volunteers, the complete Galapagos Island chain was practically cleared of it's one-of-a-kind inhabitants. Housing these numbers, even temporarily proved more difficult by far than housing humans. Vast inland expanses were converted for these purposes in many global locations. The Galapagos were only one island in need of rescue; the vast Madagascar group, the Hawaiian Islands, Fiji, New Caledonia, Vanuatu, the Solomon Islands, Papua New Guinea....... the list seemed almost endless as would be the effort. Though as the critical day approached, people did indeed deserve credit for a successful effort to rescue a respectable majority of inhabitants from these islands. If only there was more time.

When the black hole arrived, there was nothing left to do but watch. From the safe side of Earth, the space stations and the Moon observatories all saw the same thing as the shores around the continents began to lighten, at around the same pace. From space, it didn't seem dramatic unless you zoomed in to a specific area. From the ground, remote controlled sacrificial cameras had been setup all around the globe, to watch and record the details.

While still operative, ground links relayed the real time videos to all the stations and terrestrial monitoring centers. The view from those cameras was uniformly unimaginable and heart stopping. Watching the waters quickly recede beyond the horizon, leaving wide stretches of ocean life exposed to the air was a sight to have nightmares about for the rest of your life.

On the other side of the planet the view was quite different depending on the location. From space, the side views from the few scout ships that remained, was of the ocean bulging upwards and moving sideways, pulled by the unseen force of gravity. From the ground, the cameras saw the movement of the ocean empty some shores, while a quarter of the way around the planet, there was no withdrawal of water since the black hole didn't pass exactly over the center of the ocean. There the ocean lifted up and moved inland, washing everything from it's path in the power of it's deluge.

The cause of the force behind this event receded quickly given the speed and proximity of the black hole as it passed. There was a brief moment of pause, and then everything reversed. The oceans came rushing back towards and far beyond the shores they'd vacated just minutes before. Ocean fronts and islands around the entire world were instantly flattened by the force of the water rushing in. Nothing survived within miles of most shorelines, and much further in at relatively low lying areas such as the Netherlands. The losses were beyond calculation both in property and sea life.

Initially, everyone's attention was on the oceans. Meteorologists on the other hand had been focused first on the huge bulge in the atmosphere which almost emulated the ocean's bulge, and then the rapid development of storm systems which sprang up far quicker than even in the most severe storm season. The effects from these unpredictable systems would take days to fully develop, though flash flooding was a likely scenario, even in areas that usually see little rain. Some deserts of the world were about to see rain for the first time since their creation. The longer term effects on everything from river life to plant life would take from weeks to months to fully play out. The worst was most certainly not over. The worst was just getting started.

On most continents while the ocean was surging, though before the storm systems began their deluge, the fault lines of virtually every continental plate were feeling the great release of potential energy stored there. Earthquakes sent seismic waves around the globe for hours. There was something else as well. Something new, which no human had felt. Something the seismologists monitoring the event couldn't explain. Something you could feel in the soles of your feet. Something the animals of the forests and the plains could all sense. Something that made the birds leave their perches and seek the safety of the air. Something not felt on Earth for close to a million years.

Jason was closely monitoring as many conditions simultaneously as his systems and processes could accommodate. These past several months had continued the process of awakening the experience of emotions inside his central processing core. He wondered if the feelings were really getting stronger or if he was just focusing on them more and more? Was this what humans and many other animals experienced? People talk about their emotions building, was this what they meant? It was a most unpleasant experience and even worse it was very distracting from the tasks that were still at the core of his programming.

Among the seemingly endless catastrophes occurring on the planet below he detected something he was fairly certain no human-made instrument was registering. The readings were unmistakable, though would require confirmation over time. The potential impact of this data, was simultaneously creating a cascade effect on his already frayed emotional state. If he were human, he would be staring at his monitor in disbelief. He would be frozen into inaction. This was exactly the state Jason was in, and it was the longest 240 milliseconds of his existence, during which time he was completely incapable of processing anything either here, or back at his main core in the Octopod research center.

What should he do with this information? Should he immediately share this observation with people who were already so completely overwhelmed with stress and grief, they likely couldn't handle anything additional? Should he keep it a secret for now? If so, for how long? This type of action was against his basic programming, which was the accurate collection, processing, and dispensing of information; though he had been asked to hide information before, in the interest of security. This was different though. These humans had become his friends. As a friend, what was the correct action he should take? His processes were beginning to run in a loop when he decided he would monitor the situation until he was 100% sure of the impact. Then, at a time when his primary human contact on Earth was able to take the additional emotional load, he would contact her. Kaylee Brown would be devastated. There was no avoiding it.

At the same time, back in the vicinity of the Octopod research facility, his other friends were currently in a Transit, heading towards their meeting with the Paxians. When they emerged, it would be roughly two months from now. What would he tell his friends? He would have to share the information regarding the direct impact of the black hole on Earth. They were expecting that. But what about this new information? It was certain to be far more devastating. If he told them immediately, what impact would that have on their ability to complete their current mission to find a way for the Paxians to help save the Octopods from the Singularians? Realistically, what could his friends actually do at that time to help the people back on Earth? Nothing. So in his logic circuits, Jason found the justification for not mentioning this new threat until their mission was hopefully successful. He had two months to give that some additional processing cycles. How do organics deal with the constant distractions of these emotions?!

Chapter 11

Earth Date: 8,409

People of Peace - Paxians

His snoring would have been unbearable if it weren't for the roughly 70 decibel background noise on the bridge. How he managed to sleep with all this noise wasn't as miraculous as it might seem at first. Like anything else, it was simply an evolutionary adaptation from thousands of years living on his vessel, *Ship of Life*. You either learned to sleep with the racket, or you went completely bonkers from the lack. Bra Ho was Village Leader when not hibernating. When not hibernating or eating he spent most of his time sleeping on the bridge especially during those long periods when not much else was happening. When the ship was in deep space between planets, everyone hibernated except the computers. It was a slow and peaceful way of life. Except for the noise, which to be fair was only during play time for all the other creatures. After play time, the ship really was peaceful. Really.

When viewed from the outside, *Ship of Life* looked like a floating city. It's size exceeded the largest space station ever built by Humans by a factor of at least ten, though it was hard to be sure. Human stations are mainly large disc shaped affairs, built that way to provide the all important spectacular views of their surroundings that humans required. *Ship of Life* was a long range terraforming vessel built to accommodate the vast array of technology required to convert a dead planet into a paradise for life. It was also designed to house an entire ecosystem meant for transplanting on the newly terraformed planet. So from the outside, the ship looked more like something you'd get dragging a huge magnet through a random pile of iron cylinders, cubes, spheres, and mangled broken things. Therefore, it was difficult to be sure exactly how to compare it's size to vessels constructed by other space faring species. But it was home.

On their home world, which this ship hadn't seen in thousands of years, the Paxians had evolved on an isolated continent virtually unreachable by the other terrestrial species on the planet. Much in the same way as Australia or Borneo back on the planet Earth. This isolation allowed a very different path for evolution, resulting in a wide variety of plants and animals that existed in a perfect balance without the need for predator species. This was exceptionally rare even in the infinite variety of worlds in the Universe. The process by which this occurred was tied directly to the specific, unique DNA strands that initially were part of the life forms that became isolated on the planet. These strands carried a unique gene that controlled a species ability to reproduce. It was like an on/off switch. When a group of individuals experienced stress from a lack of any resources, the switch was flipped off, stopping reproduction. This included the conditions brought on by any overcrowding. When conditions improved, the switch was flipped back on. The original mutation of this gene went back to the first living organisms to crawl out of their primordial stew. This was an extremely critical adaptation for the Paxians. Not so much for survival on their home planet, but for their comfort and survival on their long range terraforming vessels. Imagine what life would be like on a ship with predators roaming free among the many groups of life forms. It would be most difficult to concentrate on the bridge or even get a restful sleep.

Without the burden of predators, these ships were designed (even though they didn't look designed) to maintain a close approximation of the ecosystem on their isolated continent of their home world. This was accomplished not just for the obvious need to support the vast diversification and abundance of life on the ship, but to have it continue to thrive for the many hundreds and often thousands of years between rest stops. This was another wonderful advantage of that on/off switch, as it provided a self regulation for the population of each species on the ship. Even the noisy play times seem to have evolved into a periodic, not sporadic structure. After all, everyone needed rest. *Ship of Life* like all things Paxian, moved about it's business in a slow and leisurely manner. If they were humans, they'd have evolved on one of the smaller islands of the Hawaiian chain, and would have the motto, *hang loose bro*. Humans wouldn't be able to imagine the degree of hang-looseness the Paxians achieved. In addition to moving slowly when awake, and spending most of their lives napping after meals, they hibernated. This was one of the few areas they employed technology on their physiology. They hibernated naturally as well, a trait that had evolved as a seasonal survival technique same as bears on Earth. On the long slow voyages through space, they needed to suspend themselves for hundreds or thousands of years at a time. In the same manner as the Octopods, they had learned the secret to suspending life indefinitely, and were able to apply it to every species, including the plants, ship wide.

There was one obvious disadvantage to the type of life those living and working on the *Ship of Life* would have had to deal with given that family to them was everything. Their work and travels would have meant leaving everyone else behind, forever. So their solution was quite simple. Everyone came along. It was a family business so to speak. To be more precise, it was a Village business. Which is partly why these terraforming vessels didn't have captains, they had Village Leaders. Bra Ho was the current village leader, because he was awake…. most of the time. When he went into deep suspension, assuming someone needed to be awake, then a different village leader would take his place. In this manner, Paxian families stayed together, and survived for many thousands of years. At some point, after a successful terraforming, some of the Paxians would leave the ship, to live on the new world, while others moved on to the next world.

The science officer, Rug Mu, was currently working with the recycling engineer one level below the bridge, over to the side a ways, down a short slope, and sort of around a wide bend from the bridge. There was a very minor issue with the main waste recycling system. The engineer had shut the system down several hours ago and started the backup system. The ship had three redundant systems for recycling waste. A very prudent design when you considered you were transporting the entire ecosystem of a mid-sized planet, which included thousands of species of animals and plants, and a few that were somewhere in between.

There were several species of cleaner-goats (a best guess Earth equivalent though they looked more like squirrels and were about the same size) who were free to wander the ship and ingest the waste of many of the larger species. In addition to providing this first level of service to the ship, most of them had evolved to only deposit their own waste in very specific locations. This benefited their species by providing the raw nutrients for a large number of plant species that provided their main food source. They had two completely independent digestive systems: One was like an Earth goat, and through various organs processed other animals waste into food for their plants. They received no nutrients from this system. The other system was the one which digested their preferred plant foods into energy and nutrients for their bodies. The two systems only met at the end of all things, when they deposited the plant food, which did come from both sources. How they separated things at the beginning was something of a mystery. In any case, one of these cleaner-goats had decided there was something interesting inside one of the automated (non-organic technology) roving cleaners and plugged the intake while trying to steal whatever it had just picked up and was attempting to flush into the main system. When an intake plugs, the system in that sub-area automatically shuts down to avoid the possibility of something much worse happening that would require extensive cleanup. This is why the science officer was with the recycle engineer; discussing possible improvements in the system to avoid these types of conflicts.

As science officer, Rug is the first to be alerted by the ship's exterior scanners of any observations or threats to the ship the main computer might detect. He received an alert now, and listened carefully to the computer's summary of the alert. The alert hierarchy was setup in this manner since the science officer is one of the few crew members not permitted to nap while on duty. The village leader was currently napping on the bridge, so Rug would have to go there to wake him and report. This was typically another duty of the science officer as very few crew members were considered senior enough to wake the village leader.

Rug and the engineer decided this situation with the main waste recycling system required deeper consideration, so agreed to meet again at some time when it was convenient. He turned and left to begin the journey back to the bridge. On a Paxian vessel there are no doors or elevator style lifts or pretty much anything that could be jammed into a non-working condition by some plant or animal. It was difficult enough keeping corridors open for passage. There were a few large grazers that did a fairly good job with this duty, though occasionally they needed some direction. Left unattended they created new corridors of their own choosing, which often led to dead ends and could become quite confusing if you were trying to get somewhere and weren't paying close attention. Herding Hounds were tasked with keeping the corridor grazers working in the correct directions. Of all the animals on their home planet, these Herding Hounds were considered among the smartest and certainly the fastest moving animal.

If Rug had considered this alert from the exterior scanners urgent enough or had he been much further away from his destination, he would have taken one of the many Long Striders that enjoy carrying Paxians throughout the passages on board. It was unclear if they enjoyed the company, the exercise, or simply the special treats the Paxians wisely kept in convenient locations as rewards for the ride. The carefully chosen locations of feeding grounds for the Long Striders was also one of the few carefully planned designs for the ships, ensuring that when necessary, rides were often readily available. Of course, the Paxians did have electronic vocal communication stations in all areas, though these were mostly avoided and considered annoying except in emergencies.

Rug had made it most of the way to the bridge when he realized he hadn't eaten in a very long time. He detoured to one of the designated dining locations for the Paxians and helped himself to a light snack of leaves, twigs, and a few special buds that were only available seasonally. The buds were so tasty he forgot where he was headed for an hour or so. Eventually he remembered and continued his short journey back to the bridge, where fortunately Bra Ho was still napping.

"Bra you wake now," Rug said *(he didn't actually say that. Paxians don't speak English. They don't actually speak the same way humans do so assume any conversations to be rough translations. Also, Paxians are infinitely more intelligent than these translations make them sound, due to human's inherent prejudices against slow speaking creatures)*. Bra did not move. It was considered proper for all crew members to use first names even when addressing seniors. It just took too long to keep doing otherwise. Adjectives were also discouraged unless absolutely necessary. "Bra you wake now," Rug said again a little louder. Play time had ceased so the bridge was relatively quiet, though from the way Bra's tail was slowly moving, Rug could tell he was having a dream. Rug thought for a while about waking Bra again. This was a relatively important alert, but there really wasn't anything they would need to do about it right now. Then again, maybe they did, so he decided to try one more time a bit louder. "BRA YOU WAKE NOW!"

Bra opened one eye and closed it for a minute. He slowly stretched along the main branch he'd been napping on and eventually opened both eyes and looked at Rug. "What up Rug?"

"The aft scanner picked up the presence of another space ship following us. Or maybe it's just headed this way. Not sure yet. It came out of no-space, so it may be one of those flyers that live in big ball we saw before last hibernation. But it not look like one of their ships from back home days. We know more when it get closer. It moving very fast though. Maybe here in a few short naps."

"OK," Bra replied lazily. "You keep two eyes on it and let me know when you figure out who it is or they get real close." With that he stretched and closed both eyes again, deciding a nap was more important now. Best to be at his best when needed.

Rug went over to his computer station, shoved the sleeping pod-mouse aside that seemed to like the warm display, and started tapping the screen to change the settings, and focus the scanners on the alien ship.

Aboard *Gravitas-1*

As always, the two month trip through the Transit felt instantaneous, even for the on-board version of Jason. The only difference was the instant they arrived on the other side, Jason's remote system on *Gravitas-1* was immediately updated with the current events back in Earth's solar system, as well as the status of the Octopod research facility at the Sphere. The news wasn't good anywhere, with one grateful exception; at the beginning of the two months they were in Transit, human scientists back on Earth had discovered the source of Jason's main concern, without Jason having to be involved. This was a great relief for Jason since he was really upset at the thought of always having to be the bearer of bad news. It also provided a good reason for him to delay conveying all the bad news to his friends on board. There was also good news, since during those two months his central processing self had devised a plan to help Earth. That news too, would have to wait.

"Jason, what's the news from Earth please," Howard asked as soon as they arrived. John and Bill immediately came over to Howard so they could listen together.

"I'm afraid the news isn't good, though it's mostly what we expected. The people at Mars had done an excellent job of preparation, so there was very little damage beyond what was expected on the surface, and of course the results of the massive underground water surges. The orbiting stations had no problems. The largest effect of the black hole's passage was to pull both of Mars' moons to higher orbits. They are still accessing the impact of this change, though it's entirely possible both moons may now be in more stable orbits than before. With regards to Earth's Moon, there was virtually no major impact."

"I'm sorry that the news from Earth isn't better. The direct impact of the surging oceans was devastating to all coastal regions and the loss of life is beyond calculation. I believe you can imagine those impacts for yourself. Very few humans were lost, and the ones that were had chosen that path for themselves. Human property damage was also extensive. The massive movement in the oceans completely disrupted the major currents that effect the planet's weather patterns. Consequently both directly and indirectly major storm systems were spawned causing flash floods on every continent and sub continent, including locations that normally see little if any rain. Additionally most rivers overflowed their banks to varying degrees. Some mountains have experienced record snow falls while others have seen only rain. Again, the weather situation is completely unpredictable. There have been earthquakes in all areas of the planet effected by the movement of plate tectonics, as the passage of the black hole seems to have released all the stored potential energy in those faults. Those are the major reports. There may be some additional future issues but nothing has been confirmed as of yet. Your scientists from all disciplines have done an excellent job of determining the most efficient course forward towards recovery, and your people seem to be mostly safe for now. At the risk of seeming indifferent, which I hope you realize I am not, I remind you that there is nothing for us to do from this location. It would be greatly appreciated by the Octopods if we could focus on doing our best to contact the Paxians and seek their help in dealing with the Singularians."

"OK, Jason," Howard quickly responded. "We'll certainly do that. Thank you for the summary report. It's good to know we had the resources to deal with such a devastating natural disaster. We have you and the Octopods to thank for that, so we'll certainly do our best to help in return. Before entering the Transit, you'd estimated it would take us another 20 hours to reach the Paxians. Is that still the case?"

"I'm uncertain on the exact time frame Howard. I've started a full acceleration towards their last known position and will give you an update as soon as our scanners find them."

"Hey guys," Howard said, "we may have almost a full day before anything happens if Jason's original estimate holds, and when hasn't it before? I suggest we get some rest while we can." Everyone agreed and the three went to their bunks, to each deal with the bad news in their own way. Within an hour they were all resting quietly.

Jason felt almost guilty at the relief of not having to give them any additional bad news. It was true there was nothing to be done from here, and the situation with the Singularians had to take top priority. Once again his logic circuits overrode his new emotions. *Gravitas-1* was accelerating nicely towards the last location reported by the Octopod drone which had also established the quantum tunnel back to the Sphere. Something had happened to the drone however and it was no longer responding. This was not an unusual occurrence when tracking Paxians. Despite their apparent peacefulness with regards to most life forms, Octopods were definitely not on that list. Maybe it was the whole flying spider thing like his friends thought. Roughly 9 hours into the flight, Jason picked up the first long range signal of what appeared to be a Paxian vessel. They had a most unique profile and stood out quite plainly against the limited background radiation. Jason stopped the ship's acceleration, and prepared to flip around and begin decelerating. He decided it was a good time to wake the crew.

"Is that coffee I smell?" Bill mumbled from his bunk.

"Yes Bill. It seems to be the best way to wake humans in a gentle fashion."

All the crew seemed to agree as they stumbled from their bunks and headed straight for the coffee dispenser. "What's going on Jason? How long's it been?" Howard asked.

"You've rested for about 9 hours. Our long range scanner picked up the Paxian vessel almost exactly where we expected to find it. They don't seem to be in any kind of hurry and continue to move along at a relatively slow speed, compared to their technical abilities. I believe from our first and only encounter, this is a cultural choice more than a technical restraint. I've started deceleration and we should arrive in close proximity within another few hours. Close enough for contact at least, while still maintaining a respectable distance to show we intend no harm. I do believe this may be the very same vessel your people had *First Contact* with almost 200 years ago. I may be mistaken of course, however the profile of their ships is quite unmistakable in it's exterior configuration, as I'm sure you'll note once we get within visual range. It's our understanding that the Paxians may have a similar technology to the one we used to suspend your lives for 6,000 years, and may use it on a regular basis for long range travel. If these are the same Paxians, that could be an excellent start since they already know you're species and their computer system will be able to communicate with me almost immediately. Obviously, we should be able to determine this soon enough."

"Thank you, Jason. And thanks for the coffee. One of these days you're going to have to tell me the secret for how you manage that without any coffee plants or beans for that matter."

"An interesting observation I've just detected in this region," Jason said. "It appears the cosmic microwave background radiation from what your species refers to as the Big Bang, is significantly lower here than the average readings recorded in the Octopod data base, which covers a significant portion of the Milky Way Galaxy. The next closest reading at this scale coincides with those recorded during *First Contact* with the

Paxians. It could just be a coincidence, or it may indicate the Paxians seek out these areas for some reason. There is insufficient data of course, though it might be something worth looking into in the future."

"Why do we call it that?" Bill started in. "Such a typical term for humans to coin, or am I just in a bad mood from too much sleep? I mean first of all, like you were ranting about Boss, if there was an explosion, a Bang..... would you hear it in the vacuum of space? I'm pretty sure that's not the fault of the Universe. Wasn't it some English astronomer, Hoyle or something that came up with that? Was he an actual scientist or just a hack writer?"

"It was actually Georges Lemaître, a Belgian cosmologist and Catholic priest I think that first proposed the idea of a big explosion," John interrupted. "I think Hoyle just came up with the name during an interview or something."

"Right! But not the point," Bill jumped back in…. "Why a Bang? I mean the whole noise thing and if a tree falls in the forest thing aside, why do humans have to think of it as an explosion? Of course we've been away for a few years, and maybe they've changed their thinking, but it just doesn't seem very appropriate. An explosion or a bang that big is more of something that's destructive or the end of something. Like what John used to do when he tried to make rockets back in college."

"Hey! That was you that blew up more rockets than me. I don't resemble that comment and didn't particularly enjoy having my ears ringing so often."

"Seriously guys…. and Jason, I mean it's just not right that we call it the Big Bang. It just carries so much human history of violence with that term, like it's the only way we see things. It should be something more to do with the creation of life or something. *The Big Beginning*, or *The Big Birth*, or something more positive."

"For the record," Jason said quickly, "I agree with Bill and just want to be clear that Big Bang is not the way the Octopods see it either. It's difficult to translate though roughly it's more of a stretching of the fabric of space, though there's no direct translation in English that applies. At the risk of changing the subject Bill, the Paxian vessel is coming into visual range now. Putting the image on the main screen."

"What are we looking at Jason?" Howard asked. "I don't really see a ship. Is it near that rocky asteroid on the screen?"

"What you refer to as a rocky asteroid is their ship. It will be clearer as we approach. This is at maximum magnification. We are approximately twice the distance as from Earth to it's Moon, and still decelerating."

"Wait......Jason," Howard said, "put the screen on standard view at normal human resolution." Jason changed the screen as directed. Howard looked for a moment and then walked over to one of the large windows. "Jason, I can see it from here. How bloody big is that thing?"

"It's difficult to give an exact dimension given it's configuration, however it is roughly ten times the volume of your largest space station orbiting Earth. I realize you've only seen photographs of your newest stations so It's hard to compare. It's quite large and several sections could be measured as several miles across. You'll understand my difficulty as we get closer. It is essentially a city in space, by your definition. We were only allowed very brief contact visually, and they were reluctant to share more than basic information as you've noticed. We suspect that these large vessels have something to do with their terraforming of dead planets, and the ships likely house the life forms they eventually deposit after terraforming is complete. Unless their ships all have an exactly equivalent design, which seems highly improbable, this is the same ship we had *First Contact* with 200 years ago, Earth time."

"Jason, do you think it's possible we'd be speaking with some of the same individuals as last time? Do we have any idea of their life spans?" Howard asked.

"First of all, Howard, it was never clear exactly who we might have been communicating with. As detailed in the briefing and *First Contact* information you read, establishing communications was a lengthy undertaking, and once established it was only myself and their computer system which were able to communicate in a basic binary format. The long pauses between questions and answers seemed to imply the computer was simply translating but that was never determined for certain. Analyzing what data we have, the design of their ships, assuming they're much like this one, and considering how slowly it moves from system to system, it is highly likely the Paxians have a long life span, and as I'd mentioned before, they employ some type of hibernation. So yes, I'd estimate there's a high likelihood we'd be communicating with the same individuals, again assuming we were in the first place. At the very least, establishing communications again should be much quicker this time."

Gravitas-1 was getting much closer to the Paxian ship now and Jason was slowing their approach with the intent of stopping at a significant and respectable distance to demonstrate a peaceful intent. "Jason, I have to say," Howard said, "that looks a lot more like a floating junkyard than a ship. Why wasn't any of this mentioned in the contact report?"

"I did not write the reports, Howard, and as far as why, it would seem perhaps your historians were at a loss to explain the design or may have excluded it for unknown reasons. If this is indeed a vessel for terraforming and subsequent populating, it's likely each of the exterior parts house a unique life form with different requirements. Howard...... I am receiving a transmission from the Paxian ship. I should warn you to expect extremely long pauses and delays during communication. The *First Contact* humans became quite frustrated at times with the long delays which sometimes stretched into hours for simple questions. They are asking us to identify ourselves."

"Jason, I'm going to be relying on you to use the proper and acceptable language forms to convey my responses and questions. I don't want to accidentally insult them especially when we're trying to get their help."

"Of course, Howard. Since the communications are in binary, and the equivalents we established from last time are limited, I would say there is little danger of any unintentional conflicts. Although slow in responding, they always seemed reasonable, logical, and understanding of our limited language equivalents. I have responded with the name of our vessel, that we are the same species, and I am the same translator as our last contact."

"And........ Jason? Oh, this is the part where we just wait then."

"Yes Howard," Jason replied and waited. A few minutes later. "A response Howard. *OK good. We are Ship of Life. Hello.*"

"That's it? No follow up question?"

"There may be one, but we should be patient and wait a while. They don't seem to be in a rush to do much of anything, Howard. If there is no question coming perhaps you'd like to ask one?"

"Yes. No. Rather than a question tell them we come in peace and would like to get to know them better. Does that sound dumb, Jason? I suck at this and I'm not feeling particularly patient. I just want to ask them for help but don't know where to even start. Sorry, Jason, just start with the come in peace stuff and see what they say."

"I've sent your message, Howard, and no, I don't think it sounds dumb. Given our limited ability to communicate, it would seem logical that keeping our request simple and straightforward makes the most sense, and will likely yield the best results."

While Jason and Howard were working out their strategy, John and Bill had quietly slipped back into their old habit of hiding in the galley, and helping themselves to some snacks; doing their best to make themselves as small as possible. Howard noticed what they were doing of course, and after wishing he could join them, an interesting thought struck him.

"Jason, is it possible they're like our buddies John and Bill over there? Not really interested in talking and would prefer just to go sit somewhere with a pizza and some beer and hope we go away?"

"There does seem to be sufficient evidence to support that theory, Howard. Perhaps we just need to find something they're interested in to get their full attention. Perhaps asking them what they do or why they're here?"

"That's an excellent idea, Jason. Let's do that. Or should we be waiting to see if they respond to my other statement first?"

"We should probably wait. I estimate if we make more than one statement or request at a time they might not respond." A few more minutes passed and then Jason said, "Another message coming in. Their computer has a most peculiar dialect, which isn't easy to do in binary. It takes a very long time to get a message through, though that's partially due to the extreme amount of error correction protocol they include. I do believe that implies their interest in at least making sure their message is coming through clearly without any loss of data. Their response is….. *Good. We are people of peace too.*"

Another long delay so Howard said, "Jason, go ahead and ask them why they've come so far to be here. Why they're here?"

It was almost an hour for the next response. Howard had joined John and Bill in the galley and were trying unsuccessfully to come up with a better idea. These guys were all used to bouncing ideas off each other, but when the ball you were bouncing felt stuck in thick molasses, it somehow also slowed the ideas from coming. They too were stuck, when Jason said another response was starting.

Five minutes later Jason relayed their response, *"We world makers. Bring Life. You world makers too."*

"So you were right about the terraforming and what the ship is for, Jason. So they do go to dead worlds, and bring new life there. Excellent. And they want to know if we do the same thing. How do we answer without just saying no?"

"Howard, I don't think they're asking. We have a definite protocol established for differentiating a statement from a question. It took almost an entire day last time to establish that, so I'm virtually certain that was not a question. They most definitely think we're also terraformers."

"Well, like you suggested Jason, let's just keep it simple and straightforward. Tell them we are not terraformers, or world makers or however you need to say it to make it clear. Then tell them however we greatly respect and appreciate the good they're doing bringing life to dead worlds."

"I have sent your message Howard, though I suspect a response to that may take a very long time. There will likely be some confusion, and they'll be trying to figure out what we mean. I'm not certain………. Wait. I'm getting a response already. This is most unexpected. They say, *Then why you have Little Cleaners?* Howard, I need to clarify that *Little Cleaners* is intended to represent a specific proper noun. As in little creatures of some kind."

"OK… let's keep this moving even though we don't understand. Tell them we don't understand. We don't have any *Little Cleaners.*"

Back on *Ship of Life*

The entire bridge was in a relative uproar. The Village Leader had come completely off his branch and was staring at the large view screen as if trying to see something. The science officer had practically walked fast over to his scanning station. The rest of the bridge crew was fully awake and doing their assigned jobs. The usual assortment of small creatures that lazed around the deck became alarmed by the unusual level of activity and most sought shelter under plants or behind larger animals.

"Bra, computer say they not have *Little Cleaners,*" said Rug. "I have had computer repeat and they say they don't have. I think they don't know they have *Little Cleaners.* I think they telling truth. They only have two and they are just there. Not being kept safe. I think they just pick them up somewhere maybe. Maybe they tell us where so we can find more."

"Too much Rug. Too much. Slow down Rug you not thinking," said Bra. "How could they not know they have *Little Cleaners?*

Even only two. They take too many naps if not know. They stupid?"

"No, I think they just not know. I think we send harvester over to their ship and show them. Then they know. Yes, Bra?"

"OK send now. We see."

Aboard *Gravitas-1*

"Hey boss," John practically yelled from the window, "something's happening over there. One of their pieces is coming off and it's coming this way."

"John is correct, Howard," Jason said. "they have launched some type of remote vessel. It appears to be a construction or utility vehicle based on the various armatures and exterior devices. It is definitely on a direct course for our ship, though it is moving slowly. It stopped accelerating and should arrive within 15 minutes at current velocity. Nothing like this happened on our *First Contact..* I suspect this may have something to do with our confusion regarding *Little Cleaners*."

"Not much to do but wait and see what they do. They claim to be peaceful so let's hope they are," Howard said.

Ten minutes later the small vessel, which wasn't that small once it got closer, started to slow down and eventually came to a full stop relative to *Gravitas-1*. It was in mass probably 25% larger. It turned very slowly and seemed to inch it's way towards the back of the ship, close to the location of the fusion generator. Without warning it fired a tight and powerful beam directly at their hull.

"Shit, they're firing at us Jason. What the heck did we do? Get us out of here now!" Howard yelled.

"Howard," Jason replied in his usual calm voice. "We have sustained no damage. That was not a destructive weapon. It seems to have been a very tightly focused EMP of some kind. I don't believe we're in any danger. The craft is moving closer and one of it's armatures is extending and appears to be removing something from our hull. The vessel is moving back and turning

Paul H. Rosenfeld

165

towards us. Howard, I'm getting another message from their ship. "This is *Little Cleaner.*"

"That's it? What is *Little Cleaner*? That ship that just shot us?"

"Stand by Howard I'm scanning now. No. I believe they just removed a Singularian from our hull. It must have attached itself there when we left the Sphere. That must be what they call a *Little Cleaner*. They seem to be extremely interested. This could be important, Howard."

"Yes. They did seem to respond very quickly once they realized we had one on our hull. Do you think it's something they want? I guess we should just ask. Offer it to them Jason, see if they want it."

"Sending your offer now. And I'm getting an almost instant response, Howard. *Yes we want Little Cleaner. Can we have both?*"

"So there's another somewhere else on the ship. Tell them yes and tell them we have many many more they can have if they want them."

Before getting a response, the remote vessel repeated it's gathering process on an adjacent part of the ship and then pulled back and waited.

"Another response Howard. *Yes we would like them. We are in need of them. What can we offer you for them?*"

"So they barter? That's interesting. Jason, tell them the truth. Tell them we have friends that have many of these attacking their home and we'd be grateful if they would come and collect them all. All we ask in return is their friendship and peace."

"Transmitting now."

"Could it really be that simple?" Howard said to no one in particular.

"They're responding again. *"Yes we will take all your Little Cleaners. We are very grateful. Please show us where they are."*

"Can you do that, Jason? Will they understand coming back through the Transit with us? Will they understand that it will take months? Do you know how they measure time?"

"Yes Howard, I believe I can handle all that. It may take a while to explain all the concepts. Should I tell them about the Octopods? If they come all the way and see them again, they might not be willing to help."

"Yes, Jason. We need to be completely honest. Just tell them they won't have to be near them. That the *Little Cleaners* are on the outside of their home and they don't have to go inside. Something tells me they really want those little guys bad enough so they'll do it."

About an hour later, Jason called Howard over. "They have agreed and again are very happy for the offer. They refer to this remote vessel as a Harvester. They are sending two with us and their ship will remain here. This is an excellent development since their main ship is far too large for the Transit. Also the harvesters are computer controlled ROV's and they are providing me with full access codes for control. No Paxians will need to join us for the trip back. They've also included some data regarding the Singularians. Apparently the Singularians are quite common on the gas giants that orbit in systems closer to the center of the galaxy. The Paxians harvest them for use during the first step in their terraforming of dead planets. It would seem the

Singularians are quite efficient at removing the highly toxic naturally occurring heavy metals making the terraforming process much more efficient. The Paxians have had a great deal of difficulty harvesting more in the outer regions of this arm of the galaxy. The Singularians are much more rare here. One last thing. They seem quite excited for our help and would like to offer a more traditional greeting of life than during our *First Contact*. They're inviting us to move our ship closer to the area of their bridge so we can greet."

"I can hardly believe our luck. It looks like your original estimation of their ability to help the Octopods was exactly right, Jason. Well done. Tell them we appreciate the gesture of friendship and accept. Go ahead and move the ship into visual range of their bridge..... assuming you can figure out where that is."

15 minutes later, Jason had figured out where the bridge was located, mainly because it was the only module with large windows, and moved *Gravitas-1* to within 20 meters. The *Ship of Life* is so large, it was difficult at first to gain a sense of perspective. "It might be helpful to your perception," Jason said, "to know that the windows you see are each roughly 30 meters wide by 15 meters high."

The view was completely unexpected by any of the four members of *Gravitas-1*, and they stood motionless for a few minutes, as did the Paxians. Bill was the first to comment, "That's just crazy! It looks like a re-creation of an Amazon jungle or something over there. Jason, are you sure that's the bridge and not one of their pods for depositing life after they terraform?"

"Yes, Bill. I have received a confirmation from their computer that we are clearly visible to their Village Leader who is one of the occupants we're observing. Hopefully you remember your briefing material and even though they can't hear you, we are not to refer to them as what they appear to be. Obviously there is a significant amount of parallel evolution between the Paxian and Human worlds."

"So you mean those guys that look like the DMV workers from that old Disney movie are the Paxians?" John asked.

"Yes and you are dangerously close to violating protocol, John, though I appreciate your attempt to sidestep," Jason said.

"Wooooo talk about parallel evolution," Howard said. He was watching what appeared to be a very large lizard crawling perpendicularly across the window. "Those feet look exactly like a huge version of a Gecko." One of the Paxians had slowly come down from a large branch and crawled over to the window, gently picking up the gecko and setting it down somewhere out of view. He then looked up directly at the humans and placed his paw on the window.

Howard walked over and imitated the motion by placing his hand flat on his window. The two stood quietly watching each other. Howard wasn't sure if he was having another empathic episode but it felt that way. There was a distinct feeling of both gratitude, and friendship, with a large serving of concern from the Paxian.

On *Ship of Life*

"They look sick, Bra," Rug said from behind as his village leader stood at the window. "Their ship is dead. There is no life there except the humans. And they have lost most of their fur. Are we sure it is their friends that need help and not them?"

"No Rug. I not know what is wrong. You are right. Their ship looks dead. It is good we will not visit them or have them here. They may have disease. Computer, ask them if there is something we can give them to help with their sickness. Offer some of our curing plants. We can deliver them using harvester."

On *Gravitas-1*

"Howard, they are asking if we have a disease and need medicine. They notice our ship seems to have lost all it's life forms. They have many plants for sickness. I remind you that during *First Contact* visual exchanges were limited to a great distance. Or they may not have been as concerned about your appearance then as they are now. Humans have a very unique appearance as a species in the galaxy, most likely due to your rapid reversals in evolution. Regardless, the Paxians may view this as being an illness. I will inform them you are in excellent health and your appearance is natural for your species. Also, as interesting as this is, I must remind you we have a mission to complete, and a full two months to get there. We should be leaving soon."

"Yes Jason, tell them we're fine and let them know we need to depart soon to help our friends. Also tell them we hope to meet them again in the future and would very much enjoy an opportunity to extend our friendship." Howard was relieved how easy it went, and then he remembered what's been happening back home. "There's always something," he thought.

Jason relayed the message, and slowly backed *Gravitas-1* away from the *Ship of Life*. The guys had all gathered in the window and were waving their goodbye, which probably looked like some sort of distress to the Paxians. Jason also seemed to have full control over the two harvesters and they were following in close formation at a safe distance as Jason increased power to the gravity drive and headed towards the Transit. The Paxian harvesters had no trouble keeping up as Jason increased speed.

"There is one problem Howard," Jason said. "I've analyzed the EMP they use to dislodge and stun the Singularians. It will definitely create a problem for the Sphere, and likely knock out large areas with each jolt. Considering the large numbers of Singularians, and their dispersal around the Sphere, the harvesters could completely destroy the Sphere's shielding. I'm downloading the information about the EMP to the Sphere as we speak. Hopefully the two months we'll have in Transit will be enough for them to figure out a solution.

Chapter 12

Earth Date: 8,410

Dyson Sphere - Octopod Research Station

When *Gravitas-1,* followed closely by the two harvesters, emerged from the Transit two months later, the scene was disconcerting. The three humans were standing at the forward window mostly in shock. Remembering the glory of the first time they'd seen the sphere, it's exterior dimensions far beyond visual comprehension. Now, though they were further from the Sphere at this Transit, than the one to Earth, the change in size was a surprise. "Jason," Howard began, "the Sphere looks so much smaller than when we left. Are the Octopods all surviving? Have they figured out how to deal with the EMPs while we were in Transit?" Howard was deeply concerned about his friends, and at the same time, after two more months, was also worried about conditions back on Earth. That would have to wait. There was nothing for him to do for Earth so he needed to stay focused here. Not that he felt very useful here at the moment either.

"Yes, Howard. I'm receiving the details now. I realize it's often confusing to accept that I appear to be functioning in several places at once: Here with you, back on my ship near Earth, and at my main processor with the Octopods. During the two months in Transit, I've been working with my creators to come up with the best plan for dealing with the Singularians, utilizing the Paxian harvester technology. We believe we have a workable solution. Unfortunately there's no safe way to test it, given the nature of the Singularians. If they are intelligent enough to understand what's happening, they may attempt to phase out and move as we've observed them doing in the past. The size difference you notice was intentional. In anticipation of our arrival with the harvesters, this change was just started."

"The plan is to concentrate the Singularians into tighter groupings to maximize the effectiveness of the EMPs, while reinforcing the shields to what is now an outer, secondary shell. Based on the data provided by the Paxians, my analysis indicates that at this reduced diameter the reinforced outer shell will be able to withstand the impact of the EMPs without failing. An inner shell has also been created to maintain a safe environment for the Octopods. The reduced diameter of the outer shell will also allow the two harvester's EMPs, working simultaneously from opposite sides of the sphere, to initiate a series of widespread, powerful EMPs, stunning all the Singularians within a relatively short time frame. As soon as the EMPs have finished firing, the Octopods will completely drop the outer shield. This should, in theory, provide a more open environment for harvesting the Singularians while preventing them from moving onto the inner sphere, should they awaken. The inner sphere, is being reduced as far as possible, and when we begin, it will be many thousands of miles from any point on the outer shell."

This sounded like the best possible plan to Howard, given their limited options. However, he could also feel the level of fear and concern of the Octopods even through the two shells at this distance. It's probably best that he was this far away or the feelings would likely overwhelm him. Even John and Bill were showing signs of feeling the stress from the Octopods. "Jason, the EMP the harvester hit us with was concentrated on a very tiny spot on our ship, compared to the area you're talking about effecting on the sphere. So you're talking about a massive increase in the area the EMPs need to effect. That means the power would need to be increased exponentially. Also, I assume there must be some sort of recharge process. Those harvesters must be a whole lot more powerful than they look or what I would have expected from the Paxians."

"Yes," Jason responded. "The Paxians were most generous in providing the full technical readouts for the harvesters when they passed over control. It was obviously in their best interests as well, that we were successful. The harvesters employ extremely advanced and flexible technologies far beyond what we suspected of the Paxian's capabilities. It's fairly obvious given the nature of their vessel, *Ship of Life*, and observations we've made, that they use their technology only to the absolute minimum extent necessary to achieve whatever goals they may have. Their use of Singularians as a first step in terraforming is an excellent example. From what I've learned of their technology, they would easily be capable of achieving the same effect as the Singularians, yet prefer to use the more naturally occurring solution. The harvesters are in fact extremely powerful, and working in tandem should produce more than sufficient power even at a wide spread setting, to stun the Singularians in the same manner we witnessed. Standby a moment.......... The Octopods are only moments away from shrinking the inner sphere to the planned diameter, and want us to proceed as quickly as possible given the crowded conditions and great anxiety they are feeling."

While explaining the plan to the humans, Jason had been busy reprogramming the harvesters and moving them into place around the outer sphere at a distance their wide spread EMPs would have the desired effect. Even given the large size of the harvesters, and the much shrunken sphere, the size difference was still so significant if was difficult to see the harvesters at this distance and perspective. If Jason's calculations were correct, as they always have been, those harvesters were indeed exceedingly powerful. Jason was also backing off *Gravitas-1* to a safe distance from the entire affair, to avoid any potential damage. Without any warning inside *Gravitas-1*, Jason activated the EMPs. Although the EMPs themselves weren't visible, their impact on the outer sphere was spectacular, and resembled a brief aurora effect. As planned, after a surprisingly quick series of bursts along with rapid movements of the two harvesters, the outer shell disappeared. The inner shell protecting the Octopods appeared as not much more than a blue marble floating at a great distance away. There was nothing else to see. Individually the Singularians were too small to notice. The harvesters however had inflated some type of massive collection funnel closely resembling an old fashioned solar sail, and were moving quickly in a pattern that seemed to mimic the original shape of the outer sphere.

"Jason, will you be able to tell from the harvesters scanners if you got all the Singularians?" Bill asked. "From everything you've said it seems like an almost impossible task given how small they are."

"Yes, the harvesters were designed specifically for the purpose of gathering these little devils. I am doing absolutely nothing at the moment to control them, as their automated systems seek and collect. Even in a stunned condition, the Singularians are still very easy for the harvesters to detect. I have a high level of confidence they won't miss a single one. This is proceeding quite well and should be done in just a few minutes. In many ways the technology of the Paxians greatly exceeds that of the Octopods. They will indeed be valuable friends to have in the future. This entire experience has been a major learning experience for the Octopods, and serious thought is going into major redesigns to protect them more effectively. The human's role in initiating *First Contact* with the Paxians, as had been in the original agreement with the Octopods is without question what saved us. It would seem the humans, Paxians, and Octopods have formed a powerful bond that should benefit us all moving forward."

As Jason predicted, the harvesters finished up quickly, and closed their nets, trapping the Singularians inside. With the job complete, the harvesters, under Jason's control, moved backed towards the Transit with *Gravitas-1* again leading them. "We'll need to accompany them back to the Transit," Jason said, "to open the passage and send them home. I've encoded a *Thank You* into their systems, which I believe expresses our gratitude in a most Paxian fashion."

As they traveled towards the Transit, they could see the Octopod sphere beginning to expand. "Jason, how long will it take to expand the sphere back to it's original size, assuming that's what they're doing?" John asked.

"It will take many months to re-establish the original size of the research facility sphere, John. And yes that is the intent. The sphere's shell isn't the restraining factor, it's rebuilding all the facilities and living quarters, as well as recreating the atmosphere. The inner volume of the sphere, as you recall is considerable."

"Howard," Jason continued, "the Octopods are looking forward to your return so they can thank you for saving the facility and their lives. They are aware of the situation back at Earth of course, and together with your scientists have devised a plan. As we discussed when we arrived at the location of the Paxians, two months ago Earth time, there was the direct damage from the passing black hole. Clean up and damage control has of course been on going since then, so unless you have a specific concern, the list is quite extensive and would take months to review in detail. I'm afraid the worst impact of the black hole's passage is yet to come. There was an effect that will likely take many years to reach it's full impact, though will certainly be far worse than what's happened so far. The good news is, as I just mentioned, with the cooperation and effort of the entire human population, there is a plan to save a significant percentage of life on Earth, and the three of you will once again play a major role."

Chapter 13

Earth Date: 8,410

Bismarck Sea - Papua New Guinea

Ocean Currents Research Facility

Delphini had barely gotten her feet wet, literally, when the news came about the black hole, and the estimated effects it would have on the oceans. People everywhere were focused on the immediate impact the enormous ocean swell would have on all the coastlines of the world. The research group she signed up with in the Bismarck Sea off Papua New Guinea wasn't insensitive to the immediate impact. They were just far more concerned about the long term effect a massive shift of water would have on the critical ocean currents that maintained the sea life in this region. The concern would be the same everywhere. Most people didn't realize how vital ocean currents were for the transport of nutrients and as major waterways for the vast majority of ocean life. Another thing most people were unaware of was the effect the major ocean currents had on the world's climate. A disruption of the currents at the level anticipated was certain to create major changes in the weather patterns world wide.

At over 600 feet deep, embedded in a rift that extended along the major South Equatorial Current and the Indonesian Throughflow, the underwater facility Delphini lived and worked in was ideally suited to monitor changes in these currents. As much as she wanted to join her parents Balaena and Ben with their efforts to save the many at-risk sea mammals she grew up with in the Cocos Island waters, her responsibilities were now here. Her parents had contacted her immediately with their plans, and assured her they would have safe passage to one of the orbiting research stations when the time arrived. They also knew it was likely the deep location of the facility where Delphini was, would be safe from any immediate ocean surges, so they implored her to remain there and continue her work.

Papua New Guinea lies within what was once known at the Coral Triangle, an immense but sensitive region that had come under direct attack by the pollutants and over fishing which plagued the region thousands of years ago. Coral is painfully slow to recover given that it grows from essentially microscopic life. Though recovery was sluggish, the area once again had the highest marine biodiversity of the Pacific Ocean. Over 2,800 species of fish including unique sub species of clownfish, ghost fish, crabs, lobster, nudibranchs, starfish, sea horses, and even stingrays populate the reefs.

In response to the pending threat, the facility split the researchers into three groups. The smallest group would continue to monitor the moment to moment effects of the expected surge on the currents the facility was located here to study. The largest group was to surface and join teams from Australia and Papua New Guinea to organize the roundup of the aquatic mammals that frequented these shores and who would be unable to react quickly enough to swim to the deeper, safer waters. On the other hand, scientists were assuming species such as the dolphins and whales would be able to survive on their own given their speed and agility and would therefore be largely ignored as part of the rescue efforts. The main focus for the group from the facility would be the local manatees and dugongs that were the most likely species to suffer, given their slow movement and preference for shallow waters. The regional leaders had already reserved chambers on the space stations which were quickly

Paul H. Rosenfeld

179

being converted for the temporary purpose of housing both marine and terrestrial animals from around the world. It would be crowded, noisy, messy, and smelly up there for a couple weeks, but at least there was hope for saving these many lives. It would be necessary to plan well in advance how to corral the many passengers at the last minute to minimize the duration of their temporary captivities, which of course they wouldn't understand. This included the provisions for feeding the various species which involved an entirely different set of requirements. The stress would likely be significant on the humans since an undertaking of this scale had never been attempted.

The third group from the facility, which Delphini had been placed in charge of, was tasked with finding ways to protect at least a portion of the many miles of above surface coral atolls in this vast archipelago; a virtually impossible task. Delphini had been asked to direct this group because she'd recently developed a unique containment system which was being used to isolate smaller groups of coral reef communities for study. If this process could be successfully upscaled, then at least some select groups of the more unique and rare varieties might at least be saved. The process involved creating transparent titanium enclosures which surrounded and completely enclosed the test area. What made this process unique and ideal for this situation, was it's ability to create the enclosures on site, in the exact location and configuration required. Delphini could literally wrap the enclosure around a section of coral the same way a mother would wrap a blanket around a baby, and then completely isolate the newly formed enclosure. During the process, if the section of reef being enclosed was partially above the sea level, then prior to closing, it could be completely filled with water to eliminate all surface air, and the entire section could then be broken free and submerged. Pump lines were fused to the dome during the process, so the water could be kept clean and aerated and the pressure inside each dome maintained at the same surface pressure as where they were collected. The two differences between the test enclosures she'd made and what was required now, were in the greatly increased size of the containments, and the plan to submerge them deep enough to avoid the anticipated force of the ocean swell.

For this project, there would be no last minute corralling of species. The time available was simply too short. The team would manufacture and sink as many individual enclosures as possible during the roughly 4 month window, each one being hooked up to a centralized pump platform at 600 feet depth. As the deadline neared, the view from the observation lab inside the facility resembled a quickly growing forest of over 300 bubbles suspended in mid-ocean, each teaming with hundreds of coral ecology life forms. At 600 feet, there was no natural sunlight, only complete darkness, so powerful artificial lights resembling enormous sunlamps with the same 4,000-6,500K color temperature as the sun had been installed to maintain life in the bubbles. It was a mesmerizing site.

On the last day, when each team had accomplished as much as possible, all the researchers returned to their homes in the deep, including some locals who were provided safe shelter there, rather than joining the crowds in the space stations. The transport submarines, as well as the underwater facility, were all maintained at the same pressure as at sea level, to avoid the hassle of constant compression and decompression of their bodies.

Delphini was visiting with her parents on a two way holocast and shared the view of her underwater creation. Her parents were fascinated by their daughter's ingenuity and of course proud of her accomplishment. At the same time they shared the view from their orbiting station of their project and the insane noise and confusion of the various sea mammals who occupied the redesigned enclosures. The scene made Delphini glad she'd taken on this task instead, and was also grateful the holocast didn't transmit odors. The station's air handling systems were certainly working overtime. They wished each other well, and disconnected about 12 hours prior to the anticipated passing of the black hole. Most world wide communications networks, which humans had become so spoiled by, had to be shutdown when the stations were moved to safety in the projected shadow area of the Earth. Only limited emergency communications would be permitted for the next 24 hours via outdated and underpowered ground based facilities.

Those last 12 hours were the toughest for everyone. Scientists from many disciplines had assured them the facility would be safe at that depth. None of those scientists were here. The sturdy construction of the deep water home that felt so safe and secure for the long months she'd lived there, suddenly felt small and fragile compared to the might of the ocean. Scientists were good at distracting each other with long discussions of their projects and the accomplishments of each group, though no one was sure of exactly what to expect.

Despite the relocation of the space station mounted communication systems, some limited provisions had been made to broadcast a signal indicating a countdown of sorts, along with real-time updates. It felt like one of those history movies, with everyone sitting around the old style radios, listening to the news of the wars far away. When the passage began there was absolute silence. The first indication was from the suspended city Delphini and her group had created, as the entire cluster suddenly began to rise and shift to one side as a single entity, straining at the ties and pump lines. Immediately a pressure and vibration was felt throughout the facility and suddenly a burst of light from above came in through the normally dark observation windows surrounding the facility as the sea above swelled away, effectively lessening the depth and allowing more sunlight below. The flow of the currents were monitored on displays throughout the facility. Without exception every monitored current fluctuated momentarily and then collapsed, becoming part of the giant surge. The view outside of rapidly moving water gave the impression the entire facility had suddenly started accelerating in the opposite direction. The force of the vibration, the pressure in the air, and the never before sounds of rushing water over the domes had everyone pressing themselves to the decks in fear, many covering their heads and ears. If this was happening at 600' below; what must it be like on the surface?

The crushing sounds and feelings seemed to go on for hours, when it fact it was only a few very long minutes. As quickly as it started everything stopped. It felt as if the Earth itself had inhaled a giant gulp of air. And then slowly at first, everything reversed itself. The sea outside had paused and created momentary swirls of debris and sand, and then suddenly the water was rushing in the opposite direction past the windows. Only this time, it happened much faster, the pressure and noise much greater, and despite the heavy anchorages, some of the protected bubbles Delphini's group had made were swept away in a current of rage, that darkened the facility even deeper than usual. The facility itself felt like it would bust free at any moment, but it held. Barely. There was over an hour of back and forth movement, but it gradually settled down, though there was little to see outside as the silt had completely clouded the water. The monitors focused on the currents, at least the ones that survived, were showing just still water. The currents responsible for maintaining the life and weather of this region and a thousand miles and in all directions around, were gone. The long term impacts would be devastating, and no one wanted to even try and imagine what had happened to the shores above. Everyone in the facility collapsed.

In the space station high above, Delphini's parents along with millions of other refugees had watched in terror and wonder as the ocean which normally showed no movement at this altitude seemed to slowly retreat from the shores as it bulged in the deeps. Depending on your location and view, the bulge could even be seen moving in a single direction, like a needle following a strong compass, only now it was gravity, not magnetism responsible for the forces they were watching. Everyone on board knew of someone still below; some on land, and some in the depths of the oceans on the many research facilities which occupied the oceans world wide. What they all witnessed was a living nightmare that would stay with them the rest of their lives. This was something you could never forget. A lesson in just how small and powerless we really are against the forces of the Universe. Their one ray of hope was glued to the displays around the stations which had been linked to the emergency broadcast network setup to monitor and keep everyone informed. Each underwater facility had a unique broadcast beacon that displayed it's current status. It was a great relief to Delphini's parents that their daughter's was showing all green. The facility had survived, but there would be no direct word for nearly a full day. Some of the facilities hadn't fared so well, but fortunately the predictions had been accurate so those had been vacated in advance. Their home in the Cocos Island was gone.

Chapter 14

Earth Date: 8,410

Moose, Wyoming - Earth

Harmony Washakie, and her best friends Seze, Oso, and Koa, had come back to live and work the simpler life, helping her parents on their small subsistence farm in a little known area of Wyoming, near the Grand Tetons. Raised in the traditional Eastern Shoshone way, her parents were equally children of the Earth, and as one with the horses and other animals of their land as she was; which was a good thing when your daughter returns home with a pair of wolves. But let's not exaggerate here. These weren't the kind of wolves you envision as hunters prowling in the night in large packs and taking their prey on the run. These were more like the two uncles that come to visit for as long as possible because the food is good, they don't have to work, and they can lounge around all day like couch potatoes. Harmony thought it was strange how quickly Oso and Koa adapted to life on the small farm; they didn't even hunt the chickens as they now preferred them barbequed. Oso did occasionally steal vegetables from the garden though Koa preferred his popcorn. They also seemed to have taken full time residence inside the house including occupying the living room couch, and her Dad's favorite lounge chair. Dad didn't seem to mind. During his next trip to town, he bought himself a new one.

One thing about living on the farm, at least this farm, is they all made an effort to stay as disconnected from the outside world as possible. Farming in this area of Wyoming was challenging and fulfilling enough, without the need for all that noise and alleged entertainment. Nightly entertainment was either in the stars outside, sometimes around a fire, or inside listening to the storms and reading. Simple lives. At least until her friend Joey Littlehorn, and Brando Billings the park ranger, came for a visit. Along with a few polite supplies people living this way could always use, they brought the news. Life was about to get interesting for the entire world.

The Park Service had been tasked with evacuating any residents thought to be in danger of the anticipated flash floods from the storm systems likely to develop as a result of the oceans being splashed around like a playful kid in a bathtub. The farm was in a borderline zone with regards to these predictions. Even after the heaviest snow, followed by those warm rains which caused flash flooding, the farm had seen little effect. However, the forecasted events could possibly be far more severe. Rather than evacuate it was agreed they would have enough warning, given their location, to seek higher ground quickly if needed. They had more than enough time to prepare supplies, and put a rapid escape plan together for the farm animals. The local riparian environments were the areas most likely at high risk, except of course for the coastlines of the major oceans. Considering their isolation and the general lack of facilities, there would be no mass evacuations headed their way.

The Park Service's main concern was for the safety of those herding animals most likely to be impacted by lowland flooding. Hopefully the elk and mule deer would stay in the highlands, or thanks to their relatively small herds and physical agility would be able to escape any sudden dangers. The massive bison herds were another story. Having recovered to their pre wild west days numbers, the approach of a sudden deluge might create panic within the herd, resulting in significant loss of life. To make matters worse, the herd would be in the middle of their calving season, and therefore at their most susceptible. Harmony, along with select representatives from many of the other local tribes and ranches were being asked to setup monitoring camps surrounding the valley. Winter was still in full swing but the spring thaws would be almost half done around the time these unseasonable storms were forecast to hit. If they were as severe as some meteorologists expected, it would be a dangerous combination. The plan was for the scouts to head out in about three months when the passes were accessible from horseback. Equipped with Forest Service long range walkie-talkies that could connect through a tower site, they'd be able to provide real-time observations of the status of the herds as well as ground observations of flooding conditions.

From the news her friends brought, Harmony and her family felt they were the lucky ones with far less to deal with then those living in the coastal regions. The farm had been under contract by the Forest Service for many years to provide backcountry support, including search and rescue operations, so they kept a number of pack mules and horses on constant standby. They now put those to good use for themselves, packing supplies into an emergency cave system far up the hill from the farm. If the flooding reached the farm, they'd be prepared to evacuate up there. Harmony was also scouting out locations for her observation post, when the weather allowed. When the time came to leave, she would take Seze and her favorite pack mule, Spirit, loaded with enough supplies and food for at least two months.

The farm was prepared for a quick evacuation by the time Harmony was ready to leave. The plan was to leave Oso and Koa behind with her folks, which The Boys seemed to have no trouble accepting when Harmony left. Climbing to her lookout post a few miles to the east was slow going as there was still some snow, but the dangerous sections were mostly clear. Her camp would be at an old fire lookout that was abandoned decades past, but offered the best view of the valley, and wasn't in the path of any rivers. It almost felt anti-climatic when the time came.

Everyone had been given the predicted time tables, so there was quite a bit of chatter on the walkie-talkie network. It felt like waiting for something that never happened. There was nothing to see though most of them could feel a slight atmospheric change as if they'd suddenly climbed several thousand feet and their ears were popping. That was it. They were lucky their views didn't extend all the way to the oceans, or their feelings would have been quite different. Harmony was closely watching the colossal herd of bison grazing on the new grass shoots just coming up in the valley, and they didn't show any signs of noticing. There were actually three major herds in the region, that occasionally mixed later in the summer when the calves had grown, but for the most part remained separated. This seemed a natural way to retain a certain degree of genetic variability, and was likely how the herds had lived many thousands of years before these lands were taken over by the human invaders. All other outposts had reported roughly the same lack of response by the herds in their areas.

It was a full 24 hours later, when the first signs of the unseasonable weather appeared. It was like nothing Harmony had expected, or ever witnessed during her life growing up in these mountains, and living through many winter storms. There were no high cirrus clouds to announce the coming storm. She looked south from an otherwise clear sky and there was a dark almost black line that extended across the entire horizon. At first glance it seemed far away, but the black line grew visibly closer as she watched. Within just 20 minutes the line was halfway up the sky, and it's character had completely changed as it approached. It didn't look like any storm she'd ever seen. It looked like someone was unrolling a blanket straight at her a few thousand feet up. The wind had been blowing out of the north this whole time but as soon as the rolling cloud was overhead it suddenly shifted to the south and hit like a wall of fast moving air, almost knocking her off her feet. The temperature must have dropped 20 degrees in that flash of a moment, and within a minute she was sitting on the ground in the middle of a blizzard. It was all she could do to get back to Seze and Spirit, and get the three of them hunkered down in the shelter.

Whatever this was, it wasn't what she'd call snow. It was more like a mix of snow and hail. Not hard like hail but coming down like soft golf balls, except the strong winds and the blizzard like conditions made the event anything but soft. Within the first hour Harmony could tell that if this pace kept up, the three of them would be buried alive. The chatter on the portable comms was the same everywhere in the surrounding mountains. It wasn't just her location being hit this way. She couldn't see the valley below to check on the herds, in fact she could barely see 20 feet away. Her instincts told her it was time to find a better shelter or they'd never survive. She needed to get somewhere around the other side of this peak, on the leeward side of the wind. She had the packs ready and while still in the shelter, loaded Spirit, strapped on her snow shoes, grabbed Seze's reins and burst out into the freezing cold blizzard to begin the hike around the hill. It was slow, cold, brutal going with the wind and snow beating at their backs. The snow balls were solid when they impacted the ground and formed a solid plain, which considering how deep they were piling up, was a blessing. She could walk on top without sinking in more than a few inches. It even supported the weight of Seze and Spirit. For now this was as good as she could hope. But she also realized the water content of this snow was likely closer to rain, than the usual 1:10 ratio of water to snow. When this melted, it was going to produce a flood like nothing these plains have ever seen.

After several hours of plodding along, she came to a familiar cliff face, though only the upper portion was visible. As they worked their way around, it was like being under a roof. The wind was blowing the snow so hard it was almost parallel to the ground, so the leeward side of the cliff had very little accumulation. She'd made the right choice leaving the exposed shelter, which was likely buried by now. It was still cold, but they had good protection, and enough supplies to hopefully wait this out. By the time she had a rough camp setup it was dark. She made sure Seze and Spirit had some grain, crawled into her sleeping bag and was asleep before her head hit her rolled up jacket pillow.

The storm raged for a full two days without stop. At times, the snow balls changed to plain snow and at others to a hammering hail. Fortunately the wind blew consistently from the south which kept her small shelter relatively clear, though a semi-circular wall of snow and ice was forming just 15 feet from her shelter. If this continued much longer, she'd likely be trapped inside the wall. Her walkie-talkie was working, but there was no chatter, and she couldn't reach anyone. Most likely, the storm had damaged or buried some key component of the system. She fed her companions, shoved their waste clear of the shelter, and was about to feed herself when the wind suddenly eased and the sun came out. In that regard it was like a typical shower that had just moved past. Looking north over the wall of ice, she could see the trailing edge of the storm moving off. Unlike a typical thunderstorm though, it filled the entire sky from East to West, and was moving away at breakneck speed. The rear of the storm was as tightly packed as the front had been two days ago. So much moisture in one system. It was like an entire winter's worth of storms in 48 hours.

Digging herself out of the leeward cliff shelter took several hours with the small foldable shovel she'd packed. Once they were finally free, and the air had cleared, it looked like full on winter had returned to the hills and the valley below. Fortunately, the valley didn't seem to have gotten hit quite as hard, and she could see the bison herd gathering back together. They would try digging through the snow for grazing almost immediately since the cows would need to make milk for their calves. Everyone would be hungry after the past two days and the timing of a heavy snow in the middle of calving season, wasn't something

Gravity Drive 2 - Jason's Ark

they were evolved to deal with. However, that wasn't what was worrying Harmony at the moment. It was warm, like a typical summer day. That meant the melting would start immediately unless there was another cold front, and she saw no signs of that as she scanned the horizon. The plains below would absorb the melting snow to it's capacity and then become a marsh. At the same time, the mountain rivers would quickly overflow and flood the valley. The herds would be in neck deep water in no time unless they moved to higher ground.

Harmony's walkie-talkie finally woke up and there was a rush of chatter from the surviving lookouts. The storm had knocked out the central communication tower connection, though one of the nearby rangers was able to repair it quickly after the storm passed. Everyone checked in and it seemed only two were missing. Hopefully it was just a technical issue. This was a group of experienced backcountry people, who also understood the coming flood danger and the need to move the herds. One of the lookouts reported that a few elk and mule deer herds had joined the bison at some point during the storm. These herds didn't ordinarily mix, though under the circumstances they had all followed their instincts to find lower ground during the storm. The elk and deer would likely separate quickly and move back to higher ground, but that wasn't natural for the bison. They'd have to be encouraged. Their valley wasn't the only place hit with these massive storms, so there was a backlog of requests for various types of air support. They wouldn't be getting any help it seems, so they decided the only reasonable course was a good old fashioned horseback cattle drive.

Harmony took Spirit back into their shelter which would now be the safest place when the melt started. She left Spirit free to roam with a large pile of grain before heading down with Seze. Mules were a lot smarter than most people gave them credit for, and she'd be just fine fending for herself. It was slow and treacherous moving back down the side of the mountain on the deeply covered trail and took another couple hours. By the time the group met up in the valley, it was early afternoon. A few of the local ranchers who still operated in the area had joined so they had more than 20 horses now, which was good since it would take that many to keep the bison moving in the right direction. Unfortunately the main river that fed and meandered through the valley, was already showing signs of overflowing it's banks. The wranglers would have to drive the herd up the valley and into the hills where the tributaries were feeding the river. It was the only way to high ground.

This wasn't one of your classic drives with cooperative cattle that had grown up being pushed. The bison panicked at first, and in the deep snow and soggy ground it was dangerous work trying to get them moving in a single direction. Several horses went down in the muck, so it was lucky there weren't any serious injuries before the herd finally started moving in the right direction. Once that happened, keeping them moving up the grade into the hills wasn't too bad. Keeping them there on the other hand, would be near impossible. There was only so much the wranglers could do, and by the end of the day most of the bison were safe. There were other herds spread throughout the state that likely didn't fare as well. There wouldn't be any happy endings and the forecasts said more storms were likely, though exact forecasting had become impossible with the erratic air flow patterns.

Harmony and Seze made it safely back to Spirit, who was by far the luckiest mule of the day, and spent the night at their makeshift shelter. Her thoughts now turned to her parents who she'd worried about during the long storm. She kept reminding herself they were capable and hardy people who'd been well prepared, and had lived their entire lives in these mountains. She convinced herself they'd be fine as she crashed into a deep sleep.

Gravity Drive 2 - Jason's Ark

The next morning they broke camp early and headed back down towards the farm. There were signs of showers already pushing through the hills again, but nothing like yesterday. As the three of them rounded the hill above the farm, the scene below was heartbreaking. The nearby river that up until now had been the lifeblood of the farm, had turned into a churning mass of forest debris and flattened most of the buildings, and all the fencing. The main house looked to be several feet under water. Harmony turned up hill and headed towards the cave where hopefully her parents were safe. By early afternoon they made it up the snowy trail to find a warm fire at the mouth of the cave, and her parents preparing a meal, with the horses and mules all safely tied along the ridge. It looked like they'd been camping there for weeks, as their familiarity and natural comfort with the outdoors made the transition from the farm seem simple. Her parents were likewise relieved to see Harmony was unharmed, as they'd been following events from their own Forest Service walkie-talkie. After everyone hugged their greetings at the mouth of the cave, Harmony glanced inside to see Oso and Koa snuggled and fast asleep on their blankets. "Spoiled Wolves" she thought though her relief was obvious, and she too slept the remainder of the day.

Chapter 15

Earth Date: 8,410

Sebangau National Park
Central Kalimantan - Borneo

Entomologist.
Botanist.
Farmer.
Fisherman.
Village Leader.
Ranger.
Weaver.
Mother.
Cook.
Father.
Child.
Healer.

It didn't matter what your name was, or your title, or your job, or which village you were from. The announcement of what was to come effected everyone the same. Each person had to disregard who they were, go back to the days of their distant ancestors and become part of the jungle. The number of days were too few, and their resources were limited. There would be no help from the outside world. Like everyone, everywhere in the world, Borneo was on it's own. All the life on Earth, was under the same dark threat, and it came down to each individual to do their part to save what they could of their Great Mother.

Ismail and Farah were lucky their village was so close to the famous Sebangau National Park. They would have more resources than most for transporting many of the helpless and precious animals of their home. The bad news though, was they were in the middle of the vast peat forest and swamps, and the high mountains were far away, requiring long drives and air transport when available. As a professional entomologist and a botanist, they knew very little could be done to help the species they studied. They also knew that of all the organisms which lived in their world, insects and plants had the greatest chance for survival, due to their natural resilience and colossal numbers. It was the larger, slower moving creatures that would be most at risk. At the top of the list were the Orangutans. Although peaceful and gentle in their native environment, and having lost their fear of humans many generations ago, they were still wild animals. They wouldn't understand the danger that was headed their way, so when the effort began to trap and relocate them to the higher mountains, panic was the natural result. And that's when the hidden strength of these cousins to humans became evident.

Tranquilizing was the only solution, but it was dangerous. Perched high in their Ironwood trees, it was temping to just let them be. In theory if they climbed to the top of the trees when the ocean surge came, they would be high enough to survive; if the trees did. In theory. It was more likely that even the deep rooted ironwoods would be washed away like so many sticks. Some might survive, but most wouldn't. So it was imperative to move the Orangutans to safer habitats. It wouldn't be like rounding up cattle or even the many sea mammal species that surrounded Borneo. There were many others tackling that challenge, and some of the lucky ones were part of the mass emigration to the giant space stations orbiting Earth. But those resources were limited, so it wasn't to be for the Orangutans and many of the more sensitive creatures of Borneo. The only option was the higher jungles.

It had taken thousands of years of protection, to bring their population back to their pre-deforestation levels. The surviving Orangutans had been genetically sensitive and vulnerable to disease, when their natural process of diversity had been disrupted by the impacts of human activity. Re-establishing their genetic diversity to insure their ability to survive was what had taken so long. This threat had the promise of reversing that accomplishment if a large sampling from each and every wild group wasn't successful.

From the perspective of the local villagers who lived among them, each individual was precious and deserved every chance to survive. Therefore, each group would have to be carefully approached, and adequate safety netting in place prior to tranquilizing, otherwise the fall from the tall trees would be fatal. Each successful safe capture and relocation was considered a minor triumph. Many thousands had been safely relocated as the time drew near. An effort had been made to select the youngest and strongest from each social group, to maintain vitality as well as diversity among those saved. One difficulty with this approach however was Orangutans don't keep to tight groups like other apes, so the mixing that occurred over the months of the project made it more complicated. In the end, most people felt they'd done a fair job of saving as many as possible. They also felt it wasn't enough. The last hope was for the survival of the trees that were their homes.

The agile gibbon population was another major concern of the villagers in this region, though their athletic swiftness made them far more difficult to capture individually. Specialized parties had been organized utilizing an old fashioned method developed thousands of years ago by those who hunted them for zoos and other purposes. At last these methods might find some good use if they were successful. It sounded simple on paper, firing cannons loaded with enormous nets that would cover and trap the gibbons in large numbers, but in reality it seldom worked as hoped. What they frequently ended up with was an empty net. On the rare occasion when it actually worked, the result was a large net with a hundred fast moving, terrified, and surprisingly dangerous animals. In the end, the success rate for saving these gibbons was much lower than the orangutans. Again, people did what they could, but it was never enough.

From the high mountains to the north, Ismail and Farah, along with thousands of relocated villagers watched the horizon where the ocean was barely visible even at this height, 45 miles away. At first what little they could see disappeared entirely, and then just as quickly it seemed, the ocean rose like a behemoth of unreal height above the horizon before slowly lowering as it spread across the plains, forests, and swamps below. There would be no going home. There would be nothing to go back to . The Dayak villagers would now become people of the mountains for the foreseeable future.

Part Three

JASON'S ARK

Chapter 16

GASA – Sagan Station
Earth Orbit

The Carl Sagan Station is home to 1,789 of the newest generation of highly specialized research scientists. Currently in high Earth orbit, above the ring of permanent stations that provide communications, housing, and hop-off stations for travelers, Sagan is the only station which changes it's orbital location as required for research. It's design is unique in having a proportionally larger core drive and fusion power plant to provide spaceship equivalent speed and enough energy for the needs of the various research projects on board. For visitors who've been on other stations it also feels like a ghost town with far greater internal square footage per occupant, making the passages feel empty. The majority of the additional space being occupied by laboratories and a vast array of the latest in research equipment. Projects range from astrophysics to botany, geology and plate tectonics, to low gravity human physiology. At last count there were 27 different disciplines with significant overlap for joint studies. Many of these projects depended on another unique feature of the station; the ability to vary the gravity independently within many of the labs, as easily as turning the dial on a console. Sagan station lived up to it's namesake in every regard.

Entertainment was another unique feature of the Sagan station. Unlike other stations there were few of the usual frivolous activities to keep permanent stationeers and vacationers busy and out of trouble. Scientists became scientists because they love science. All science. They only specialized in one or two branches because it was the only way to excel. They usually picked the one area they were most interested in and pursued that path professionally. So during those rare times when they actually took a break from their work, spending time enjoying some aspect of a different branch of science was their idea of entertainment. Also, given how dedicated these people were to science, they almost exclusively partnered up as families with other scientists. Consequently off work hours usually included family time spent enjoying one of the many science related activities on board.

One of the most popular locations for science entertainment were the numerous observatories spread throughout the station. After all, there's no better place to observe the Cosmos then from outer space. There was a great variety of energy wave observatories to visit, but the most popular, especially for the younger crowd, was always the ones operating in the visual spectrums. Although there were highly advanced deep space telescopes that provided stunningly detailed images of every observable object in the Universe, there was still nothing quite like looking through an old fashion telescope and seeing something directly. No matter how many detailed and close up images a person grew up with, nothing cut quicker to the core of human wonder then seeing Saturn through a telescope for the first time.

It's like growing up seeing thousands of pictures and movies of giraffes. Then while you're on safari an 18 foot tall male giraffe walks slowly up to your hoverjeep, and lowers it's head for one of those special treats visitors carry; it's big fuzzy head with those deep brown, friendly eyes is inches from you when it's tongue grabs the snack. Then you feel you really know giraffe. Or the first time you go SCUBA diving with sharks and realize they're not the mindless killers they're made out to be, and you can almost feel the connection with their pelagic way of life. First hand experience in any science or life contact, especially *First Contact*, creates a whole new appreciation and level of knowledge in the mind and soul. These types of real experiences are what all scientists, and by default their children, live for. It's why a posting on the Sagan is one of the most sought after.

Alfred Hess was one of the lucky ones. For a geologist, a posting opportunity on the Sagan was exceptionally rare. Like all rock hounds, he developed his love for collecting when he was young, and his grandfather would take him on day-long hikes in the hills and washes collecting various stones and petrified wood. Then loading the tumbler and waiting patiently for many days or weeks until the inner beauty of each collected rock is eventually revealed, and added to his ever growing collection. Eventually he explored the chemistry and formation of each type of rock, and the forces of Earth which created and moved them. This naturally lead to his ultimate specialization in the largest of all of Earth's rocks, tectonic plates.

Reading about tectonic plate boundaries, and the major faults where mountains were built and valleys and rifts were created was one thing. Descending on a fire proof (hopefully) rope into a semi-active volcano as part of a geologic spelunking expedition provided a whole new insight into the forces of creativity. Some experiences stay with you forever, and you continue to push the boundaries of personal exploration. And then one day you wake up and realize you're living on a space station, studying plate tectonics from the big view.

Alfred's lab was shared by another geologist, Carl Gilbert. Carl specialized as a Geomagnetist, who studied Earth's magnetic fields and how they were created and sustained, as well as their importance in maintaining the shield protecting Earth from the devastating radiation and solar winds from our Sun. Space was indeed the ideal location for Carl to study the magnetosphere, the shield which most people associate with the cause of an aurora. Watching an aurora from space was another one of those experiences that touched a person's sense of wonder. Carl had a secondary lab location at the very bottom of the Sagan which provided a clear view of Earth below, and with an optical frequency adjustable scope provided the most stunning view of the auroras. Both Carl and Alfred's children spent many hours sharing the wide angle view during family outings. Sometimes looking down was just as inspiring as looking up.

Alfred and Carl had worked together for several years on the Sagan and developed some interesting ideas regarding the interplay between plate tectonics and the spinning of the Earth's liquid core which generated the magnetosphere. These were some of the areas of overlap that couldn't be ignored when specializing in any one field. No field of science existed entirely and wholly on it's own and completely independent of any other. At some level they all interacted. And Alfred, Carl, and the over 1,700 scientists on board were about to experience the ultimate example of this concept.

It was late morning, station time, when a special meeting was called in the central core, requiring the attendance of the entire working portion of the station. The central station was capable of seating over 5,000 people, and given the serious tone of the announcement, many family members had joined the meeting. The stadium was packed. Everyone quieted as the 50 foot diagonal screen lit up with an image of Kaylee Brown, the current GASA Administrator. She looked tired and depressed from the sleepless night consulting with world leaders. "You're all scientists up there on the Sagan, so I'll get right to the point. Yesterday afternoon, the Octopod's artificial intelligence we know as Jason, which keeps a close eye on the health of our planet and indeed beyond, detected a roughly 5 solar mass black hole in the outer reaches of the solar system near Neptune. The black hole's course has it headed towards Mars and Earth above the solar ecliptic, and will arrive above Earth in roughly 150 days."

An announcement such as this would have struck terror in the hearts of the average human crowd. The reaction in this group of scientists however was quite different, though totally predictable. Excitement would be the best definition of their reaction. In place of screaming and crying, it sounded more like the world's largest cocktail party with hundreds of excited simultaneous conversations discussing the various impacts this event would have on their studies, and the opportunities it presented for each group. The only groups showing signs of terror were those who's studies focused more on the life on Earth, especially in the oceans and the surrounding shores. Their only thoughts were on the potential for the unimaginable loss certain to come.

The view screen was a two way connection so Kaylee could hear and see the reaction of the group. She waited for the scientists to quiet before continuing. "Don't be concerned that you didn't detect this phenomenon at the same time as Jason. Even he admitted it was only the luck of his position in high orbit, that his instruments detected the momentary lensing effect of the passing black hole in front of a background star, and then confirmed as it passed Neptune. After consultations with world leaders last night, a plan has been formulated to begin the first steps of dealing with this impending crises. Each of you will be receiving detailed instructions on the individual and combined roles you'll play during the next 150 days. As always, your input and suggestions are greatly appreciated, in fact required, since the existing plan is only a rough draft and will require your insights to fine tune. At this time, I suggest you immediately launch a pair of deep space observational craft to detect and track the progress and strength of the black hole, and provide data allowing us to predict it's precise impact on each of the three effected worlds; Mars, Earth, and Earth's moon. One last thing. In the interest of preventing world wide panic, I implore each of you to Not contact anyone with this news. This must be handled with care to allow us to preserve life and not endanger it further. I'm certain you understand. Thank You, and good luck." With that the screen went blank and the room erupted. Unknown to the scientists, Kaylee had also imposed a complete shutdown of outbound communications from the Sagan, knowing full well that someone would release the news to relatives or friends off station. The shutdown was temporary as world leaders planned to move swiftly. There simply wasn't time to do otherwise.

After the meeting, most of the scientists rushed back to their labs to review the tasks assigned them by GASA. One of the privileges connected to being posted on Sagan, was an obligation to fulfill whatever requests GASA made. Such requests were quite rare, and for the most part, scientists had the freedom to pursue their personal research projects, especially since most of those projects are what led to their posting in the first place. When Alfred and Carl returned to their lab, their assignments were no surprise and essentially requested that they provide directly to GASA their best estimates of the effects this passing black hole would have on the areas of their research. In this case the reference would be to potential earthquakes, though hopefully not volcanoes, and any alterations in the magnetosphere. They'd also have direct access to the raw data from the probes being sent to monitor the progress of the black hole, and readings on the strength of its' gravity well, which would allow the scientists to predict the impact on Earth. Other scientists would be doing the same for the other two worlds.

It became apparent over the next few weeks, that Alfred and Carl had some of the lighter responsibilities compared to other scientists, especially those on planet. Marine biologists were at the front line for the most immediate impacts, and the greatest threat to life. The world wide evacuations of shorelines and the marine mammals that inhabited those regions was a massive undertaking and one that was certain to have a tragic ending regardless of how much was accomplished. This was likely to be

Gravity Drive 2 - Jason's Ark

compounded by the unpredictable yet certain impacts the global weather was bound to produce, mainly in terms of flooding. Suddenly earthquakes didn't seem so serious in comparison. Alfred knew there would be world wide shaking as the passing gravity well released centuries of built up potential energy along the major fault lines. His forecasts for the reactivation of long dormant volcanoes along with the chance for the spawning of new ones, especially along the Pacific ring of fire, provided an almost surreal air to his predictions. GASA coordinators accepted all his findings and made the necessary connections to begin the process of protecting lives along these geographic zones.

When the time came for the other space stations in orbit around Earth, to break their global communications network, and place themselves in relative safety in the shadow of Earth relative to the passing black hole, the Sagan was the only station which maintained a more exposed location. It's smaller and more mobile configuration in combination with it's relatively more powerful gravity drive, allowed it to safely stay where it could collect the best observational data which could later become critical to the recovery of the planet.

This was one of those rare times when scientists were upset to realize their predictions had mostly been accurate. The devastation during and after the passing of the black hole was far worse to witness, than to predict. It felt like the Universe was punishing them for some unknown act of evil. Only two scientists on board were confused about the results of their predictions. Alfred was happy to discover that even though his earthquake forecasts had been accurate, the activation of volcanoes had fallen far below the predictions. So far below, that even though it was good news for a world already suffering, it drove Alfred back to double and triple check first the data, and then his predictions. No matter how he modeled it, all other factors about the Earth remaining the same, there should have been a more active response from the fiery mantle. Assuming all the data and calculations were accurate, and his modeling software was working correctly, there had to be another factor which hadn't been accounted for. He had to find that missing piece of this puzzle.

In the meantime, Carl was experiencing a similar confusion. He expected a certain variance in the magnetosphere from the effects of the passing gravity well. This did indeed happen mostly as predicted. What he found confusing was the lasting effect and unexpected changes he was reading. He didn't expect this type of long term effect, so he too went back like a good scientist, skeptical first of his own work, and re-checked all the available data and the programs he and others wrote to analyze and predict effects on the magnetosphere. Most of the time, these effects came from the direction of the Sun in the form of solar winds and the results of solar flares and other activity on the Sun. This was the first time the source was from a powerful gravity well passing above the Earth, so something must be missing from the modeling program to account for this difference.

Eventually the two geologists sat down to share each other's confusion and to brainstorm possible causes. Like good scientists they didn't stop to assess each idea as they quickly created their list of possible causes that effected each of their results, since they were convinced the two variances were related. Once they had emptied their brain of ideas, they went back slowly through each possible cause, comparing it to the data collected. The theorized cause had to answer every single observed piece of data as a possible cause, or it was eliminated. By the time they were done, only a single theory fit all the facts, and it was the most terrifying possibility. Confirmation would be the next step, therefore more data specifically targeting this cause would have to be collected and verified over the next few months to be absolutely certain of their findings. If they were correct, the damage the Earth had experienced from the passing black hole was just the beginning. The worst was still to come.

After triple checking their findings, they contacted Kaylee Brown with their theory. The Earth's dynamo, that powers the magnetosphere, and as a side effect creates much of the heat to the mantle which we see in the form of volcanoes, was slowing. If the slowing continued at the current rate, at some point in the near future, perhaps 25-50 years, it would slow enough that the magnetosphere would weaken beyond it's ability to protect the Earth from the radiation and solar winds from the Sun. In a reflection of what happened to Mars, millions of years ago, the Earth's atmosphere would be stripped away, and all life would perish.

Kaylee Brown was slumped in her office when she got the call from Alfred Hess, and Carl Gilbert. She hadn't slept in days, at least beyond the quick naps when her head slumped to her desk from exhaustion. Although sensitive to her situation, Alfred and Carl had to be good scientists first, and report their findings. Overwhelming is a term reserved for something merely difficult to deal with which once you get through it, you'll survive. Total devastation is when an atomic bomb goes off inside your life and your job. If these two scientists were correct, there would be no recovery. The efforts the world is undertaking right now to recover would be pointless. She reached behind her desk, and placed her hand firmly on the dark blue box that sat on the bottom shelf of her library. In a few moments, a voice she'd come to trust answered.

"Hello, Kaylee," Jason said in his deep comforting tone, "how are you holding up?"

"Not so good, Jason. Thank you for answering so quickly. I'm hoping you can help provide some confirmation on data I just received from a couple of GASA geologists orbiting in the Sagan research station. Their estimation is the passing black hole directly impacted Earth's dynamo, and may have caused it to begin a process of slowing until it's no longer effective at producing a magnetosphere for the planet. Are you able to confirm that?"

"I'm sorry Kaylee, but yes. I can confirm that what your scientists have determined would seem to agree with the readings I've collected. There's no way to know for absolute certainty, even with my equipment, but there's little doubt, it's slowing. Whether this will result in a complete halting or perhaps just a reversal as your planet has seen hundreds of times in the past hundred million years is uncertain. I will continue to monitor the changes as best as I can, and provide you with continual updates if you so desire. However, it's safe to say that even if the dynamo doesn't stop completely, it most likely will slow enough to reduce the efficiency of your magnetosphere. You already know what that means. The Earth likely has at least 30-70 years before it reaches a critical tipping point, so for now, I would suggest allowing your scientists and me a few more weeks to confirm the extent of the slowing trend, before making any global announcements."

"There is good news Kaylee, which I hope lessons the impact and gives you and the life on Earth a chance to survive this. As you may recall from your studies, the Octopods have spent billions of years studying and protecting life in systems throughout this quadrant of our galaxy. Although I have never personally partaken in such an effort, there have been times in the past, where we have relocated species on a planet wide basis to other systems, when their own system was in danger, such as from supernovas and other natural disasters. Should the worst case scenario occur, as seems likely, my ship has the capacity to construct and maintain a vessel large enough to house, in suspension, a representative sampling of every life form on your planet. I believe the term Ark would be appropriate here. It will require some additional assistance from the Octopods, and likely take years to build and prepare, but it is well within our abilities."

"Jason, that's the best news I've heard in what seems like forever. You and your people have done so much for us already. I can't even begin to imagine an undertaking of that scope."

"I'm afraid you and your people are going to have to figure a way to do exactly that. I can provide the "housing" for the representative sample of Earth's life forms as well as the technology to keep them alive in suspension, however it's going to be up to the humans to collect and deliver them. It will indeed be a monumental undertaking, so it's good you have a few decades. I suggest you get started immediately after you get some rest. I'll be in touch as soon as I have updated data."

Kaylee could barely choke out her appreciation for Jason's confirmation before disconnecting. She took Jason's advice, walked over to a couch she keeps in her office and collapsed into a deep sleep. Jason on the other hand, was experiencing a new emotion: Relief. Relief that human scientists had been so quick to confirm his determination of the slowing dynamo, thereby relieving him of the responsibility of always being the bearer of bad news. When he next spoke with Howard, their conversation would at least have an upside. His main concern now was for his own people, and the hope that Howard and crew would find a way to save them from the Singularians.

Chapter 17

Earth Date: 8,409

United Nations
Old New York

Every day after school, Indra Sharma headed straight for the
Global Recycling Center (GRC) on her way home in Mumbai,
India. It was important to get there as soon as possible or the best
stuff would be picked over. Her parents were aware of her daily
explorations and didn't mind. It was just Indra's way of putting
her imagination to work creating something beautiful out of other
people's recyclables. Besides, trash wasn't what it used to be
thousands of years ago when GRC first started. In addition to
there being much less, it was cleaner and the facility was well
designed for the sorting and organizing of incoming materials to
be redistributed where they could be the most useful. The staff
all knew Indra and often set things aside in the mornings they
expected she would treasure.

As she matured, her simple creations evolved into exceptional
artwork, and eventually into a good business. She was skilled at
involving other young people into exploring their talents and
bringing them together to share ideas for new and innovative
ways to recycle outdated or unwanted materials. Her work
attracted the attention of art enthusiasts in every nation with the
help of the global information network, which led to her
coordinating regional shows for recycled art from artists around
the world.

Indra was a talented artist, but business leaders recognized her
more for her ability to organize people into functional groups,

and direct those groups into profitable businesses. People were compensated much differently for their work than in the past, so this was the first time in history where artists lived and ate as well as other business people. Indra eventually moved herself away from working for any one business and became an international industry efficiency consultant. As often happens in these situations, her work put her directly in the path of industry leaders which led her to become associated with world leaders. Without intending to move up the global business ladder in this fashion, her abilities naturally brought her to the very top. During a conference in Brussels, at the tender age of 47, Indra found herself being nominated for the position of Secretary General of the United Nations. The vote 6 months later in New York was unanimous in favor of her appointment. Like everyone else who ended up with this job, it was never something she had planned for, yet she was a perfect fit.

The United Nations was nothing like it was 6,000 years ago. Back then the UN was about maintaining international peace and security, protecting human rights, delivering humanitarian aid, and upholding international law. None of these issues existed any longer. Nations only kept their original names out of convenience. If it wasn't for their name tags you wouldn't be able to guess, which delegate represented which nation. Within just a few generations of the merging of people between nations, with the primary goal of ending all wars, cultures and races began to blend. As a species this had the added physiological benefit of making humans more robust, due mainly to increased genetic diversity. So with no national boundaries to protect, and no cultures to preserve, the UN had evolved into more of a centralized international business. Therefore, the ideal Secretary General, would be someone who was more of a CEO type, then a political leader.

By 8409, Indra Sharma had been UN Secretary General for over 8 years. That was another change at the UN. Just like any CEO, they stayed as long as the company was well run, and Indra was an excellent CEO. Her world wide connections and ability to organize large groups of people into effective working groups, is largely responsible for what saved the lives of so many species across the entire planet. Unfortunately that was just a trial run. Her next appointment was with Kaylee Brown, the Administrator of GASA. Kaylee had flown to New York on short notice, specifically to meet with Indra on a matter she said required an old fashioned face to face discussion. As it turned out the only good news was this time Indra would have more than 150 days to prepare.

The General Assembly

One week later

Organizing an emergency session of the General Assembly of UN representatives from every nation, on short notice, was stressful enough. Forcing them to comply, upon arrival, with the never-before-heard-of security and communications black out was another matter. There were over 1,200 representatives. Aids, assistants, and the usual entourage that traveled with UN representatives were not permitted to attend the meeting. That also didn't go over well, but was unavoidable. The need for absolute discretion at this time was critical to avoiding a world wide panic, once Indra shared the news.

Indra waited for Security to confirm that everyone had checked in, there were no communications devices on any of the attendees, and the doors had been closed, before emerging from the ready-room behind the podium. She wasted no time in beginning.

"Thank you all for coming on short notice. If everyone would please take your seats, I'm going to jump right in. The security protocols and communications black out are necessary as you'll understand in a few moments. I realize everyone here is still reeling from the devastation of the passing black hole. I'm sorry to say, it's going to get much worse. Excuse me for not being the politician and softening the blow. There's too much ground to cover today so I'll be succinct. The black hole had a direct impact on the spinning of the dynamo at the Earth's core. For those non-scientists among you, the dynamo is the thing that powers the magnetosphere protecting the Earth from the radiation and solar winds produced by our Sun. That dynamo is slowing, and scientists, along with the confirmation of our alien friend

Jason, have confirmed that within a couple of decades that shield will be begin to weaken. Within a few more decades after that, it's likely to weaken to the point it will no longer be able to protect life on Earth."

At this point, there was the expected eruption in the auditorium. With 1,200 people, it was best just to take a few minutes and let them deal with the news in their own ways before attempting to continue. There were of course questions being shouted from the audience, and though she didn't respond, she made a mental note that each one would be covered in her briefing. When things quieted down, she continued.

"I know that's a terrible shock, especially since we haven't even begun to recover from the first impact. I've heard your questions and I'm fairly confident most of them will be answered by the information our scientists from GASA have prepared for this group. I'm going to go over this with you in detail in a few moments, and of course each of you will receive a full digital packet of all the details before you leave. There's something we all need to keep in mind as we work through these problems, and especially as we go back to our homes and work with our people. The effort the entire human race has made over the past 6,000 years to clean up our planet, and bring it back to life has Not been in vain. It is because of that effort, we have the opportunity to save the precious life which evolved on Earth. The plan I'm about to present is of course the large view. The fine details will be left to the individual groups responsible in each region and biosphere."

"Regarding human life. We have the time and technology to build additional space stations, which can be shielded from the Sun's radiation, and house a large portion of the expected population. I say "expected" because there are some adjustments we must make to our cultures as we move forward. Scientists expect that realistically, we have about 50 years before the surface of the Earth becomes unlivable. That means most of the

214   Gravity Drive 2 - Jason's Ark

people in this room will have passed from old age by then. That gives us the opportunity to reduce the population of humans that will require rescue. If we combine our natural attrition, with a policy of one-child per family, our engineers calculate we will have sufficient room on space stations here, and at the Moon and Mars by that time. There will also be people who may prefer to shelter here on Earth in specialized locations deep underground, in specially designed above ground housing such as we use on the Moon, and even in the depths of the oceans. The number of people preferring to take that path will be relatively small and likely consist mostly of dedicated scientists. Our technology is sufficiently advanced, that these people will also have the opportunity to move between the surface and the stations above, at will. In this we are most fortunate."

"However as we've come to learn as a species over these past thousands of years, we are only a small part of a much larger community of life on this planet. It is therefore our responsibility to do everything in our power, to protect and preserve as much of that life as possible. Scientists believe that the majority of life in the oceans will not be directly threatened unless the magnetosphere completely collapses and the Earth's atmosphere is subsequently destroyed. This scenario is believed to be highly unlikely. Therefore, we'll proceed with the understanding that in addition to attempting to save terrestrial life, the only sea life we'll be concerned with will be those aquatic mammals that spend the majority of their lives at the surface where the danger will be."

"You're no doubt wondering how we can possibly accomplish this task, given our recent experience on a far more limited basis. Once again, we have our friends the Octopods to thank. They have created a plan to construct an Ark, the size of a small moon, which will house representatives of every species on the planet, both animals and plants, in a form of suspension. They will provide the housing and the technology to keep their guests alive for as long as needed. However, humans will be responsible for collecting these representatives, and delivering them to the Ark. This is the task that will occupy our species for the next 40-50 years. Again, you'll be provided with the details in your packets, but here's a rough idea of the size of the undertaking."

"In round numbers there will be 130 sea mammal species needing protection. 5,400 species of land mammals. 10,000 species of birds. 20,000 species of bees, and by bees I mean specifically our most valuable of pollinators. 17,500 species of butterflies. And yes, if you haven't figured it out yet, we do intend to save as many insect species as possible, since they are the natural recyclers and cleaners of our environment. 6,000 amphibian species. Also in addition to the sea mammals there are 7 species of sea turtles which spend enough time at the surface to need protection as well as 12 species of tortoise. To be clear, I'm just grazing most of the larger numbers. This doesn't include all the fragile plant species - about 320,000 that will need to be collected either as seeds, bulbs, or living plants. It's a good thing we have 40-50 years. We're going to need every day. Plan to get started as soon as you get home. That should be enough for now.

Obviously this office is available to all of you at any time, however I strongly urge you to seek answers for your technical questions from your own scientists, or those at GASA. Thank you."

And before anyone could stop her, she turned and left for her next task, which must happen quickly. Despite tight security with no communication devices allowed, Indra knew that within minutes someone would spread the word, starting a windblown wildfire that would encompass the world in hours, if not minutes. She had to move quickly.

Office of the Secretary General

The United Nations

Old New York

Indra was sitting at her desk at the UN. The one with the well known backdrop that clarified who she was, and where she was speaking from. She needed to be sitting for this one. She didn't have the strength to give this news standing. The camera array before her was fully automated. She didn't want a crowd of broadcasters distracting her. The countdown indicated it was time. She cleared her throat and pushed the Start button. Almost instantly her face was seen around the world, a second later on The Moon, and roughly 4 minutes delay to Mars at it's current location. Her signal on the UN emergency network interrupted every broadcast method available to the human species, on all media. Those who couldn't see, would hear.

"People of Earth, Mars, and The Moon. We have survived the second greatest challenge to our existence, though at a great cost. I won't trouble you with the details since each of you is living those as I speak. Each of you without exception has been impacted by this tragedy."

"I call this the second greatest challenge to our civilization because the greatest was the one our ancestors faced thousands of years ago. It wasn't a challenge against nature or the Universe, like the one we just experienced. It was something even stronger. Something deep inside our species, our civilization, our cultures, and ourselves to the level of the individual. It was the challenge of restructuring the nature of our very existence which we evolved into during almost a million years. You know exactly of what I speak, even though none of us were there. And though we weren't there, our success is obvious. We overcame our own weaknesses and self destructive tendencies, and built a beautiful new Earth literally from the ground and oceans up. Each day we look around and see life flourishing all through the lands, and in the broadest, deepest oceans. And we also see our own people thriving and for the first time in human history, living in true peace. Keep this in mind as you look around at the destruction brought on by the forces of the Universe. Realize that had this happened 6,000 years ago, the additional damage to our already fragile and suffering planet, would have likely wiped out most of the vulnerable life forms left on the planet, including our own. Very little would have remained. The work we did as a species to bring abundant and healthy life back to this Earth, is what will save it moving forward. Please keep this in mind as I bring you the news of today."

"The next greatest challenge by far I'm sorry to say, is yet to come. As you listen to my words, I implore you to keep in mind that we will survive as both a species and a planet. The black hole which passed so close to Earth, started a process at the very center of our planet, that threatens to weaken something we all take for granted. Something invisible that many of us aren't even aware of. It's called a magnetosphere. It's only visible when the charged solar winds impact it and light up the skies with an aurora. Such a beautiful sight and awe inspiring in it's power. More important than it's beauty however, is the display we watch is actually the magnetosphere protecting the Earth from the powerful and destructive radiation and solar winds from that star that also gives the energy of life to our planet. A tender and fragile arrangement that always teeters on the edge of a precarious balance. The dynamo at the heart of our planet that generates and maintains that protection is slowing, due to the passage of the black hole. The slower is spins, the weaker the magnetosphere becomes. Scientists from around and above the Earth have been closely monitoring this dynamo and are now

Gravity Drive 2 - Jason's Ark

certain it will continue to slow until the magnetosphere is too weak to protect us. At it's worst, a complete collapse could wipe the atmosphere from the planet, and expose it to the full force of the sun's radiation. Scientists don't believe it will go that far. The data suggests it might only slow for a time, and then gradually build back again. There is evidence this has happened in the past, during the process of magnetic pole reversals. However, I don't want to mislead you. Regardless of the final outcome, the magnetosphere will certainly weaken enough to threaten all life on the planet."

"The good news is, this will take many decades to happen. It's a slow process on a truly planet size scale. We have the time to prepare, unlike this recent challenge. We have so much time that in reality, most of us alive today may not be here to witness the worst of times. Our children however will be here and it is for them we must be strong and take the steps to ensure the survival not just of our species, but as much of the other life on Earth as possible. The leaders of our nations have met. We have a plan and each leader will be sharing the details of the plan with the citizens of their regions. The bottom line is we will survive this challenge. We will save the life on our precious Earth and someday we will replant, and repopulate this world and others. We will only become stronger with the passage of time."

"One last piece of good news to share with you. You will live to see a true miracle performed. A miracle not just of technology, but a miracle resulting from a deep friendship and bond we have created with a species that evolved in another sector of our galaxy. A species which gave us the technology thousands of years ago that formed the cornerstone of our ability to rebuild and clean our planet. I am of course referring to our friends the Octopods, their representative, Jason, and the gift of clean fusion power which they selflessly shared with us 6,000 years ago. They've also enhanced our technology in areas of medical science which has contributed significantly to our extended lives.

In virtually every area of science they have helped us improve our abilities to grow into our future. At this time of crises, they are stepping forward once more. During the years to come, they intend to build for us a moon-sized Ark, to house the millions of life forms on our planet, and keep them alive and healthy until the time comes for us to return them to a safer world. You will see this miracle growing and building slowly in the orbit of our night sky. We do indeed owe these friends a great debt, many times over. I hope someday we find a way to repay them."

"In the meantime, each of us will have a part to play in saving our planet, it's life, and our civilization. Do not think we are being punished for some act we didn't commit. Don't dwell on the irony of having all our accomplishments taken from us at the very pinnacle of our success. There is no evil force at work here. This is simply what it means to be alive in this vast Universe. This is what it means to survive and flourish in the path of it's indifference. There will always be something. There will always be some challenge to test our resolve as a species and to make us stronger. So please, again, I implore you, focus on the great good our species has done, and know that because our planet is strong and healthy, it will survive this next challenge. Thank You and remember to appreciate what you have."

Tangential Boomerang

Earth Date: 8409

Los Angeles Airport - Earth

Taka and Al stood slack jawed as they watched the holocast of the Secretary General informing the world of the slowing dynamo. After a point, neither were actually listening. You could see the sweat pouring down their faces. Al dropped his coffee and went running for the bathroom. Taka fell into a nearby chair. They were both thinking exactly the same thing.

After 10 minutes, Al came back over and sat next to Taka, some unsavory organic material on his chin, and his pants not quite on right. "Taka, please tell me we didn't cause this?"

"What the hell? You tell me. It doesn't seem possible ….. but the timing. It must just be bad timing. But this hole! All that concrete and steel and bedrock just gone. That's just what we can see. What if the other end didn't open somewhere near Vega, but right inside the Earth's dynamo? We are sooooooo very fucked!"

"Bro….Bro we need to chill. We're not thinking clearly, and we're not geologists or physicists or whoever's in charge of that part of science. As big as this hole looks to us tiny little humans, it's a grain of sand in the center of the Earth. Even if it took a journey there and stayed, what could it really do? I mean that's like dropping a real grain of sand on the Santa Monica beach and expecting the ocean waves to stop. OK sorry, bad timing. We're really lucky they built this place well enough to withstand that tidal wave or whatever it was, I mean it was hardly wet in here when we got back. But look at what happened when that real black hole passed. We can't think this tiny little core could do something like that. NO WAY BRO! It has to be a coincidence. I say we get maintenance down here to fill in this hole, and put in a proposal to GASA to move this project off planet. Like way off planet so we don't have to worry about making worm holes or something. Yes? Agreed?"

"Yeah, cool, right. You're so right. Damn I fricken shit myself I was so scared."

"That's not all bro," Taka said, trying not to look right at Al, "you might want to wipe your chin."

"Oh, sorry. Yeah I never felt like that before. It was like a whole body experience of badness. Makes you appreciate how someone would feel if they were suddenly facing a hungry lion or something. OK, I'll call maintenance and then let's get this project off planet."

A few hours later, maintenance arrived. John Baskin, maintenance supervisor for this shift, stood over the hole left from the accident, and the subsequent inspections. Al and Taka were right there with him, all staring down in the hole as if to say, "how did this happen?" Actually it was John who spoke first, "why the heck did you eggheads call us in here? The whole bloody place is a wreck. There's seaweed and dead fish rotting on and around every building and you're worried about some damn bloody hole in your shop?"

"Yeah," Al began, "it's sorta one of those top secret things you know. Can't leave evidence of a really important experiment we were doing. Sorry about the timing but it can't be helped. We need this filled back in and covered up."

John looked around the shop before responding to Al. "You need us to fill this back in? Then would you mind telling me what the fuck you did with all the dirt?"

Chapter 18

Earth Date: 8,410

The Chilean Breadbasket

Watching the daily progress of these tiniest of tomato seeds grow into the indeterminate monsters of her family farm, never stopped fascinating her. When Gabriela was four, her father, Pablo Allende, showed her a time lapse holo of one of these tiny seeds cracking open to grow it's tap root then springing up to spread it's first leaves on the thinnest of branches. He showed her the plants that grew her favorite fruit and said that tiny seed would grow into one of these in just a couple months. She struggled to believe him, though she didn't say that, and patiently watched. Her papa never lied to her.

Her fascination with plants, especially the ones she loved to eat, grew even stronger when she learned how these tiny seeds could survive the grinding of the bird's gizzard, and acidic digestive stomachs of animals. How could such a tiny thing be tough enough to withstand that torture, yet sensitive enough to know when to crack open it's shell and grow. These thoughts bounced inside her head as she did her daily chores on the family farm. She was something like the ten thousandth generation of Allendes to farm this land, in the Central Valley of Chile, between the Chilean Coast Range and the Andes. Her family history stretched back to before the dinosaurs and before the western coastal mountains of her home were formed. Or so it sounded when her grandparents talked about their family traditions at meal times.

The success of her small farm lent itself to several overlapping elements. Some major agricultural products of her farm included tomatoes, grapes, blueberries, peppers, apples, peaches, onions, wheat, corn, oats, garlic, asparagus, beans, and even wool. The soil had been organically farmed and was loaded with the microorganisms that helped plants absorb the nutrients required for the rich production of this wide variety of produce. Due to its geographical isolation and strict customs policies, Chile was free from diseases that naturally plagued other areas of the world. Combined with being located in the southern hemisphere (having different harvesting times compared to the Northern Hemisphere) gave their farm the advantage of providing food considered "*out of season*" and therefore in great demand in northern latitudes.

Gabriela's teenage years left her conflicted, and she shared those feelings with her papa, not clearly understanding where she wanted to go with her life. On the one hand she grew to appreciate the beauty and agricultural contributions her family farm gave to the world. She wanted to stay a part of that tradition. At the same time she had come to realize it wasn't just the spiritual feelings of wonder she enjoyed from watching the plants grow, it was the science of how it all happened that fascinated her. She was also interested in other sciences not directly related to agriculture, though it was where these sciences overlapped that was the source of her internal conflicts. She was intrigued by the ability to grow food on the space stations that orbited the three worlds she knew. Even more, she was drawn to the attempts to grow food on the surface of Mars, in those artificial environments farmers there had created. It was all science to her. So when the time came to attend advanced education institutes away from home, another ancient tradition of her family, the choices seemed infinite.

She eventually settled on *Daystrom Institute* because it had a branch only a few hundred miles from her home, and offered a well balanced mix of the sciences and industrial fabrication technologies she also found interesting. Having grown up in a family and local culture that focused on their histories, she researched the past of each institute she applied to. *Daystrom* seemed to have a history lost in some confusion. There didn't appear to actually be a Daystrom family that fit the historical records. It was as if the entire history had come from some ancient fiction. Or perhaps they just liked the sound of the name. Some small part of that mystery intrigued her, though she hoped it wasn't the real reason behind her decision.

Her years studying and experimenting at *Daystrom* provided the range of experiences and knowledge Gabriela had hoped for. She went there originally with a solid understanding of agriculture, so she focused her new studies on the recent improvements in the various fabrication methods for some of the newest farm equipment including those being manufactured on and for the Moon and Mars, as well as the space stations. Merging these new technologies and their benefits together with her understanding of the requirements for a successful agricultural operation, gave her some unique insights into ways of improving the ability of humans to grow foods under harsh conditions.

She was completing her studies, preparing to graduate and move on to new challenges when the news came of the impending black hole's passage, and the estimates for it's potential damage. She immediately headed for home, abandoning temporarily her plans for the future, and hoping to help her family save what they could in the middle of so many unknowns. From what she knew of the expected effects on the ocean, there was fair certainty her farm would be safe from any surges given the protection of the coastal mountain ranges to the west, on the ocean side of her country. The promise of unpredictably violent storms afterwards was the main focus of her concern, as of course was that of her family.

Like everyone else on and off world, they were glued to whatever communication remained, to keep them updated during the event.

As expected, her farm suffered no harm from the initial surge, and other than the same momentary atmospheric pressure change and the strong vibrations from deep in the Earth's core that everyone else felt, there was little indication that anything had happened. They did feel the release from the fault lines that run across the northern coastal range of Chile, but even those were comparatively minor, and nothing like some of the major quakes being experienced elsewhere. The next few days may tell a different story as they closely watched the weather forecasts.

After nearly a week, Gabriela was beginning to feel their luck couldn't hold out any longer. World wide communications had been restored after the orbiting stations had moved back to their designated positions. The images from space and from ground stations showed storms of all types impacting regions with unusually powerful force. There were blizzards burying the mountains and plains of North America and Europe during the early summer. Tornadoes and expansive hurricanes were traveling across regions that had never experienced these types of systems. The plains of Africa that are used to seasonal floods, had become vast lakes, meters deep. Images of Elephants swimming rather than walking and Giraffes with only their long necks and heads above water dominated the broadcasts. Australia was almost entirely covered in a single unimaginably large hurricane nearly 2,000 miles in diameter, that persisted even over the vast plains. And still, through all this, central South America was almost in drought conditions. The weather was steaming hot and forecasters were hypothesizing that this was driving and powering the storms rather than the ocean currents which had collapsed and failed to restart.

Work was stressful on the farm, due to the extreme daytime heat, so most of the work had been moved to the night shift. Fresh water had always been abundant and they were using three times more than usual to keep the sensitive fruit plants such as blueberries alive. From watching the news it was easy to guess that the demand for fresh food from their region was going to exceed supply quickly. If the storms didn't abate soon, there would not be enough regions left to feed the world. Even the two major breadbaskets of the United States, the greater Los Angeles basin, and southern Florida had been overcome first by the ocean swell, and then by the storms. Crops around the globe were in shambles.

One week later, the hammer fell. The announcement from the Secretary General of the United Nations left the world in shock. Details were slow to trickle out as each country was putting together it's own plans, in coordination with the United Nations. The big picture was that scientists estimated the deteriorating effects of the weakening magnetosphere would be gradual over a 40-50 year time span. This meant that each generation would have a slightly different role to play in the preservation of humanity, along with all the other life on Earth. The youngest would most likely be the only generation relocated to the great space stations once the surface of the planet became unlivable. By then, the oldest generation would have passed naturally from age, and the people who were of middle age now, would have a difficult choice to make. Each person or family group would have the right to decide for themselves. There was little concern for the availability of space for housing and resources, since the human population would be roughly 25% of it's current size by then. The only world-wide regulation was the tight restriction on new birth rates. Essentially, each family would be allowed a maximum of one child. If a family already had children at or below the age of 10, they would not be permitted more. Exceptions would of course be allowed for unexpected events such as the birth of twins. There was no intent of cruelty in the law, it was simply a matter of insuring adequate living space and supplies for survival. Task forces were being organized in each country to rescue plant and animal life indigenous to those regions. People like Gabriela's family, who were already involved in the production of resources, were encouraged to continue and if possible expand their operations.

Gabriela was at the border between the younger generation and the lower end of the middle aged group so she would be in a position to vacate the planet at the earlier signs of degeneration. Part of the plan coming from the UN was to encourage a large percentage of the population to vacate early in an attempt to preserve people at their peak of health, before any cancer causing radiation could threaten their lives. This wasn't out of concern for the individual as much as for the overall health of the population moving forward. Gabriela had already made up her mind, and had no intention of ever leaving Earth. Nor did she plan to just lay down and die. Her mind was already busy working out the details of a vast agricultural plan that was just taking shape. One that combined her extensive knowledge of plants, with some of the newer fabrication technologies she'd learned at Daystrom. And of course, she wasn't alone in those thoughts, since they were the logical next step for preserving humanity.

For thousands of years, since the ability of humans to quickly transport large quantities of fresh produce around the world, people had become accustomed, one might even say spoiled, by the ability to have seasonal fruits and vegetables available anywhere the year around. After the arrival of their alien friends over 6,000 years ago, when humans began to reverse the damage they'd caused, many of the naturally best places to grow food that had become cities, were being vacated and turned back into food production. For some reason, prior to that, people had come under the impression it was more important to avoid having to wear a coat in the winter, than it was to eat fresh food. The best agricultural lands in the world, were being quickly replaced with human housing and industries. The greater Los Angeles basin was a prime example. Once considered one of the best farming environments in the world, degraded to the point that the entire basin had become one large concrete jungle. Once this was reversed, over a period of several hundred years, and the area began to grow food again, people were astonished at the amazing quality of it's produce compared to elsewhere. Combined with the same effect happening in Florida and other places of the world, people became adapted to a higher standard in natural food quality, especially since most people were now vegans.

Now the plan was to emigrate humanity to life on the space stations, the Moon, or Mars. How likely would it be those same people who had come to depend on fresh food would gladly accept living on space kibbles, three times a day? Even if these manufactured foods could provide 100% of a person's nutritional requirements, how satisfied would people be, especially since the anticipated duration of this migration was to be many generations, not just a few weeks. If the primary goal was to keep people healthy from one generation to the next, then a better solution would be required. There would of course be some fresh food grown on the stations, but the anticipated crowding meant the supplies would be greatly limited. This was the heart of Gabriela's plan.

At Daystrom, Gabriela had taken part in experiments using organics to grow compounds to replace materials such as clear plastics. The technology was still new, but had shown great promise. Researchers had succeeded in *growing* the physical equivalent of a full scale greenhouse, using combinations of cellulose fibers mixed with a fungi who's growth could be controlled with the careful application of low voltage. In addition to the obvious organic nature of the process, there were other major benefits. Rapid and inexpensive deployment and a surprising resistance to various forms of radiation including UV meant their use closely mimicked the protective effects of Earth's atmosphere. The material was also gas permeable, unlike clear plastics, and therefore the greenhouses could actually breath. As interesting as these advances were, there was little practical application at the time so no additional research had been done. Now however, the benefits of this technology became clear. As the magnetosphere deteriorated, cosmic radiation was going to be one of the most detrimental side effects to life; yet if properly filtered, the conditions could actually be beneficial to growing crops.

Cosmic radiation is one of those naturally occurring side effects of having a star as the main power source for your solar system, which included your planet. Most life on Earth depended on this radiation as the starting point for its cycle of energy. There were exceptions of course, such as those mysterious creatures that lived in the very deepest oceans, where light never penetrated and they evolved to live on the chemical and heat energies from the planet's core.

The magnetosphere created by the spinning dynamo of Earth, was the first line of defense by deflecting the excess cosmic radiation and solar winds. What radiation managed to slip through was then filtered by our remarkably thin though effective atmosphere. The combination of the magnetosphere and our atmosphere together protect us from cosmic radiation, which includes UV. Most of the currently existing life on Earth evolved to take advantage of these precise conditions. It's something of a balancing act. So when the magnetosphere begins to fail, that puts more of the load on the atmosphere. If it fails completely, the atmosphere may be completely blown away by the combination of cosmic radiation and solar winds, same as happened to Mars billions of years ago. It's hard to know where the balance will be in 40-50 years. Plants may or may not survive it, though surface animal life certainly won't, whereas the oceans will continue to provide filtering for anything not living on it's surface. At the very least plants would certainly experience damage to their DNA, causing mutations. In the meantime their stoma (the thing a plant uses to breath, and exchange gases with the atmosphere) which are the most sensitive component of a plant, will be the first to suffer, creating problems with the plants ability to respire.

Assuming the greenhouses effectively take up this shielding task then ironically, one of the long range challenges of continuing to grow food on the planet's surface, would be the need for carbon dioxide. Thousands of years ago, human activity had created a buildup of this and other gases contributing to a runaway global warming, which drastically altered the living conditions on Earth. Reducing these greenhouse gases, as they became known, was one of the accomplishments of the cleanup efforts. Now the Earth was in a more natural symbiotic state where plants produced oxygen for animals, and animals returned the favor by producing carbon dioxide for plants. If animal life were removed from the balance, plants would require an alternate source. The question is, would the remaining animal life in the oceans, as well as the carbon dioxide produced through organic decomposition, be enough or would we need to find an efficient way to artificially produce it within the greenhouses? Irony seemed to be giving the human species a serious challenge for it's existence these days.

Gabriela, along with several of her local classmates, paid a visit to Daystrom a few weeks after things had started to calm down, and proposed their idea of growing greenhouses all over the world to allow the continued production of fresh foods, which could be shipped up to the stations or other worlds. Even if the planet was soon to become inhospitable to animal life, there was no reason to give up on using it to grow food. The decision to move forward with this plan was a no-brainer for the researchers at Daystrom, and soon the experiment began to take shape, one acre at a time.

Each of the farms in the Central Valley where Gabriela lived, started to grow these one acre sized greenhouses to test how well each type of crop responded. The additional radiation filtering of the greenhouses was a difficult factor to adjust for, but generally the plants did well as long as the necessary red and blue spectrums dominated, which they did in these greenhouses. Even though it might be as long as 40-50 years before the need became critical, it was necessary to start the process of growing these greenhouses world wide now, as many tree species required decades to fully mature.

One other unexpected advantage of this method which Gabriela herself discovered, was you could grow a greenhouse over existing tree farms, thereby preserving trees such as olives that lived many hundreds or even thousands of years. If time allowed, it may even be possible to preserve sections of forests or jungles using this technique. The unknowns would be the gas mix in the atmosphere, and the availability of water. They would have to work on these factors as the experiment progressed.

The final unignorable piece to this plan, would be the continued availability of humans to keep the whole process running. Using ships to transport the produce from the greenhouses to the space stations and beyond, was the easy part. People would need to be able to live and function on the surface, and work in the greenhouses full time to manage all the standard farming practices agriculture demanded. Those brave people that volunteered to stay behind and be the farmers when everyone else left, would only last for the duration of their natural life span. Given the expected duration of this global situation, they would need to be constantly replaced either by volunteers from the stations, or more simply, by continuing to reproduce and have families on the surface. This meant the construction and maintenance of housing capable of withstanding the cosmic radiation from the sun. This wasn't something you could demand of someone, they had to want to live this life. It would be very much like living on the Moon or Mars. This one factor could end up being the most challenging of all, given that it would likely take many hundreds, if not thousands of years before the Earth's dynamo came back up to speed. Not even Jason knew for sure how long it would take.

Chapter 19

Earth Date: 8410

Ark Construction 101

Jason was worried. First, he was worried that he was worried. These emotions were becoming intolerable. At this rate he could end up in some kind of infinite H-Moebius loop. Fortunately, his creators had foreseen this potential problem and provided an escape route for his programming. Now he could concentrate on just being worried about the one thing he should be worried about, which was that he may have mislead Kaylee Brown at GASA into thinking he was going to be able to build the Ark entirely on his own. In reviewing the conversation from his memory banks, he had made it clear that humans would be responsible for collecting the various representative life form samples, but he failed to specify they would also have to be involved in the actual internal construction of the Ark. She apparently passed this misconception on to the UN Secretary General, who passed it on to the national leaders, who passed it on to all the people of Earth. Ooppssss.

Jason had analyzed all the data in his system at the research sphere, from similar involvements the Octopods had in the past, in other systems. Most of the time, their involvement was limited to redirecting asteroids, comets, or other space debris which threatened life on worlds they were studying and wished to protect. There had only been a few times when they'd actually undertaken a rescue attempt of this magnitude.

As advanced as the Octopod's technology was, they did have significant limits when it came to dealing with terrestrial beings.

The bulk of their technology had developed from their own evolution as non-terrestrials on a gas giant. There was some overlap of usefulness, but the major limitation always came down to the physical issues surrounding terrestrials. Therefore, the two primary tools they had to offer were a large orbital containment for housing life forms in weightlessness, and the technology to provide complete life suspension for unlimited periods of time. These were of course critical components of this type of rescue, especially the ability to suspend life functions, but that was all they could do; at least at the scale that would be required for Earth. Even the containment sphere, which Jason now referred to as an Ark, had its limits. It was essentially the same construct as the sphere the Octopods themselves lived in at the research sphere. And recently they too had an opportunity to discover one of it's limitations. That aside, the other main limitation was that the energy generated shield of the outer sphere wall did not provide adequate shielding from the cosmic radiation of a star. This limitation is the reason the Octopods chose the relatively radiation free location for their research station; it was in a quiet area, far from any stars. This meant the Ark, would need to reside in the shadow of Earth, shielded by the planet itself from the solar winds and radiation from their Sun.

Back at the Octopod's research station, Howard, Bill, and John had taken some time to visit with their old friends and frankly bathe ever so slightly in the great appreciation they received. The sphere was growing slowly as the atmosphere was being regenerated allowing them to rebuild much of the personal facilities they'd sacrificed with their need to shrink the sphere. The old docking port and temporary home for the crew of *Gravitas-1*, was among the first to be reconstructed. After some much needed rest from their adventure with the Paxians, Jason had explained the secondary impact the passing of the black hole had on Earth. It was naturally a shock to the three humans, but the reality quickly set in that after 6,000 years, it wasn't like they had any relatives back at home waiting for their return. They'd given up those relationships when they decided to come back to the research station via the Transit, and go into suspension with the hopes of seeing the progress humanity would make in the future. They were looking forward to seeing that progress for themselves, regardless of the current struggle facing life on their home planet.

The guys were relieved when Jason told them of the Octopod's plan to provide an Ark to rescue the life on Earth. They were also grateful for the part they would play in delivering the life suspension technology from the research station, and were looking forward to the journey back home. It was always strange thinking about a voyage that would take roughly 4 ½ years in an instant. You definitely had to be thinking ahead, when you entered the Transit, or you'd pop out the other side confused. If that became a part of the future of space travel for humanity, it would require a tremendous shift in the way people viewed their lives, especially with regard to family. Maybe the Paxians had found the answer.

Gravitas-1 had departed the station a few hours ago and entered the Transit. Jason now had 4 ½ years to prepare humanity and the Ark before the process of suspension could begin. Even though he now estimated 40-50 years before the environment on Earth would become critical, it was important to start the process of evacuation as soon as possible. Given the shear volume of life forms that would be housed in the Ark, it would take that long to gather, transport, suspend, and house them. Also, the sooner they started, the less chance of long term genetic stability problems associated with the increasing radiation that would start to occur within a much shorter time frame.

The inhabitants of Earth were still reeling from the first impact of the black hole. They were aware of the next steps required to save the planet's life forms, but there wasn't much they could do to help Jason right now. So he decided to take the first steps himself and begin gathering some of the raw materials he would need for the Ark. Soon, when things settled down a bit and people began to accept their fate moving forward, he would solicit their help.

Jason activated his ship's drive and headed for his first stop; the asteroid belt. For Jason, visiting the asteroid belt was the same as going to a hardware store was for humans. Everything he needed was there somewhere, he just had to take the time to find it. His ship wasn't really equipped to work like a shopping cart however, so he had to find exactly the right asteroid that contained the components he'd require, and then essentially haul it back to his intended location for the Ark in Earth's orbit. Unlike hardware stores however, nothing was organized in the belt. Nothing was labeled. There were no clerks to help you find where things were hidden.

And most frustrating of all, this hardware store averaged 3 astronomical units in width, and at it's orbit between Mars and Jupiter, occupied a volume of roughly 4 million trillion cubic miles. It was going to take a while to find what he needed.

Chapter 20

Earth Date: 8411

Nomadic Inuit - The Artic

Though they came each year by the thousands to see the herds of native caribou migrate the plains of the frozen north, it was often tempting to side track them towards a group of hungry polar bears instead. 6,000 years or 60,000 years wouldn't matter. Some people just refused to stop calling anyone that lived in the colder northern climates *Eskimos*. As guides, Arnaq and Tagak walked a thin line between keeping the tourists happy, and maintaining their dignity as native Inuit of the proud Kivallirmiut culture. Their people had come to these lands over 20,000 years ago as part of the great migration that crossed the Bering Strait from Asia into Alaska, and eventually deep into the Canadian Arctic and Greenland.

Arnaq Amarook, and Tagak Tagoona's tribe lived in Nunavut, a sparsely populated territory of northern Canada forming most of the Canadian Arctic Archipelago, more commonly known as the lands west of Hudson Bay and Greenland. Their tribes and culture were nearly wiped out thousands of years ago by the same pressures of politics, technology, and environmental destruction that threatened nearly every culture on Earth that preferred simple lives in symbiosis with Mother Earth and her creatures. As these trends reversed during the undertaking to save humanity from Galactic Judgment, the Inuit took full advantage of this opportunity to return to their simple life styles and culture, while rejecting most of the technological advances that made life easier for other people.

Arnaq and Tagak grew up in the traditional nomadic ways of their people. This meant continuously moving with the seasons and therefore the availability of the food and resources they relied on. As harsh as their living conditions were considered by outsiders, meaning anyone living in the warmer lands south, the Inuit people were well adapted physically and culturally to the climate, and preferred the quiet and peaceful isolation. With the improving environment of the planet, and the marked reduction of hunting and fishing pressures from outsiders, their lives became simpler and filled with the natural abundance of ancient times. Once again, the Inuit people became an indistinguishable component of the arctic ecosystem.

Their Kivallirmiut culture, as the name clearly indicates, came from their dependence on the natural migrations of the caribou herds which once again thrived in their lands. During their yearly migrations they would also have opportunities to replenish their supplies by fishing, and hunting other wild game such as musk ox, bowhead whales, and even seals. They wasted nothing of the animals they hunted, and everything was put to good use: Caribou and polar bear fur for warm winter clothing, sealskin for waterproof clothing, and furs from rabbits added warmth inside boots. Though modern cultures typically frowned on this type of existence, it was important to consider the details without judgment. They didn't imprison animals or use modern weapons. Like most natural predators, they took mainly the weak or injured; those unlikely to survive. By doing so they actually strengthened the species they hunted. They never over hunted or took more than they absolutely needed, and kept their own population in tight check as well. It was a genuine natural balance.

On the surface, the Inuit people may seem simple, perhaps even backwards by the standards of the day, but they were not foolish. They knew their place in the world, and they knew it was important to understand that world if they were to continue to survive. Their culture strongly believed in educating their children to the fullest capability of each tribe. Tribes also combined their educational resources, so as their children grew, new experiences and expanded sources of knowledge were made available. When their children reached adulthood, they were sent to the same advanced educational centers as any other student in the world, though with the hopes they would someday return to bring their new found wisdom home and to live with their people. Arnaq and Tagak were no exception. They both earned master level degrees in the sciences; Arnaq as an ornithologist, and Tagak as an environmental ecologist. And they both returned to live with their people, having had their fill of the all-too-crowded outside world.

As guides, Arnaq and Tagak attempted to convey to their guests the value of the balance their people had developed with their environment, while providing the scenery and excitement of dog sled rides across the frozen lands. It was a perfect life for all their people except for one thing: Mosquitoes. As naturalists, they understood the importance of a balanced ecosystem where every creature had it's role, but mosquitoes definitely challenged that concept. This was one of the few areas they took full advantage of modern advancements. Clever combinations of natural organic compounds created a chemical deterrent that did an excellent job of keeping the female mosquitoes at arms length, though you still had to deal with their incessant whining. The real concern though was for the caribou, who historically had to suffer the vicious snow melt mosquitoes in such numbers they were often responsible for literally killing many caribou. So the Inuit, in their compassion for the caribou, had developed ways to provide aerial spraying of these organic compounds on the herds.

Fortunately, several people in the tribe also kept up on the news of the world through simplified versions of portable radios. When the word came of the impending passage of the black hole, and the immediate impact on the oceans, these tribal members reached out to the scientists of GASA to ascertain the predicted impacts on their region. It was thought that between their location in the far north, and the minimal protection the Hudson Bay might offer, the ocean surge might not be as bad as most coastal regions. It was still a great risk however, so the tribe decided that in addition to moving further inland to higher ground, they would also do something never attempted by their people before; they would try to aggressively move the large herds of caribou currently grazing the coastal plains.

The caribou of these territories were not the gentle reindeer of so many stories. These were truly wild animals and used to migrating according to their own instincts. The only exception were the occasion attacks by wolf packs or other natural predators. Even polar bears seldom attempted to hunt caribou as they were simply too fast and agile for the bears to catch. After careful tests, Arnaq and Tagak had come up with a way of using coordinated dog sleds to slowly and gently encourage the caribou to move inland. It was a good thing they had several months, because given the size of the herd, and their stubborn insistence on constantly changing course, it took that long to move them to safe ground.

When the day finally came, it turned out the scientists with GASA had been mostly correct. They were a good 50 miles inland when the worst hit, and it was like an extremely shallow flash flood of water barely inches deep that reached the lower lands just below the herd and the people's shelters. They did however feel the pinch of the atmosphere, and the movement of the ice under their feet, something no one in memory had experienced. There was even some deep cracking of the ice shelves though for now, everything was holding. Just like people all over the world who had to flee from their coastal homes, no one was anxious to return and witness the damage and death that must be waiting.

During the week that followed, the tribe backed off from the herd of caribou allowing them to seek their own path. Their movement inland to higher ground had saved them from the ocean's rage, however the fierce weather quickly caught up with them. Though they were well adapted to surviving winter storms, the water content of these blizzards far exceeded anything they'd experienced. It felt like the coming of a new ice age.

Then the announcement came from the United Nations of the next, and far worse disaster to come. They listened carefully to what the scientists were predicting, and being well educated, they understood the path and the challenges ahead, as did the people of all the Inuit tribes. It required over a month for the regional leaders representing their territories in Canada to bring the leaders of the eight main Inuit ethnic groups together and discuss the details of the world wide plan developed by GASA and the United Nations. This would be a task far beyond the abilities of any one tribe and would require the coordinated efforts of all the people of the North. These cultures had co-existed in peace for many thousands of years, and each had unique specialties to bring to the group.

They understood clearly that the main focus of their efforts would be gathering and saving as many as possible of the at-risk animals that shared their lands and seas. Each tribe would be responsible for collecting the specific animal or group of animals which they were most familiar with. There were over a hundred species to be accounted for, which included both land and marine mammals. Additionally, there were nearly two thousand species of plants to be collected. The group was very organized and by the end of the two month long session, a complete plan had been created. The group was on it's final day of meetings, when Arnaq Amarook, the ornithologist from the Kivallirmiut clan interrupted the meeting. She was normally soft spoken, as many of her people were, but today, she felt the burning of moral responsibility strengthening her voice. "Good and wise people of our tribes, we have made a respectable plan for saving our brothers and sisters who share their land and oceans with us. We have much to do in the years to come, and it will take all those years to accomplish this task. But there is one place we have forgotten. One place where many unique and special animals live, that the rest of the world may also have forgotten. A place where no people live because it is too cold. We as a people are adapted to the cold and therefore we may be the only ones who can save those from the forgotten land. I speak of the home of the eight species of penguins who live and breed nowhere else on Mother Earth. I speak also of the many species of other birds, seals, and whales who make that place their home. I speak of the Antarctic. A place much like ours, but on the bottom of this world. It is far from here, but with the help of modern technology which we must use to save our own, we can also save our cousins to the south. I volunteer to lead this team and work in the lands of Antarctica, and ask that each of you consider sending members of your tribes to join me there."

Less than a day after her simple, heartfelt appeal, Arnaq had promises of almost a thousand Inuits, representing every tribe, to start the planning process for saving the animals of the Antarctic. Her plan was quickly approved by both GASA and the United Nations, along with their gratitude for stepping forward and volunteering for such a cold and dangerous mission. Such were the hearts of the Inuit people.

Chapter 21

The Moon and Mars

Earth Date: 8411

The Moon

Most of the occupants of the space stations orbiting the Moon, were permanent residents, and most had some style of telescope in their personal quarters. Every single one was aimed at Earth. The rooms typically reserved for tourists were now overcrowded with some of Earth's evacuees. For the foreseeable future, there would be no tourists visiting the Moon. Most of the evacuees from Earth that chose the Moon over the stations orbiting Earth, had family already on the Moon. Whenever possible, these people were asked to house with their families to free up as much space as possible for those who didn't. Lounging areas and other tourist gathering spots had been converted to temporary living quarters. The word "temporary" was spoken with caution. No one knew how long the effects would last. Between the oceans and the weather, every part of the Earth would be effected to some degree. But for how long? Scientists from GASA had assured the residents of the Moon, the effects there would be minimal, so people's attention was on Earth.

The large viewing screens and holo-pods that were part of every deck and corridor, were left in place, and they all displayed multiple views from the various GASA observatory scopes located both on and off the surface of the Moon. Regardless of whether you considered the Earth or the Moon home, everyone was glued to the monitors, or their personal telescopes, or both, when the time came. The view wasn't that much different than from the stations orbiting Earth, except it was more straight-on, showing less of the bulging effect of the oceans, though the rapid clearing of the coastlines was unmistakable as were the color changes associated with the ocean rushing back into and far beyond the original shorelines. With the exception of the most powerful telescopes on the Moon, which did not display images on the station's view screens, it wasn't possible to see any of the actual detailed damage as it happened. GASA felt that would be inappropriate, so kept those views and recordings for the use of scientists only. Even those scientists only referred to those recordings enough to gather the necessary data for their work. The details were too disturbing to watch, even for the strongest of heart.

Then came the storms. In many ways this was far more interesting to watch, not just because of the beautiful views of the massive swirling super hurricanes, but because it was harder to envision the loss of life that would result. You couldn't see the blizzards burying the lands, or the flooded rivers pouring off the mountains, at least not until the storms moved on. You could feel it though, even all the way up here, through the vacuum of space. Something deep inside. Some part of your instincts as you watched, made you feel the need to run and seek shelter. The usual bustle and laughter of the stations, especially in the tourist sections, were nonexistent. Instead, people were huddled in tight groups, crying and whispering, trying to make sense of something that had none.

The pain never had the chance to stop. The indifference of the vast powers of the Universe just kept pouring it on. The announcement a week later by the Secretary General of the United Nations felt like anything but indifference. It felt unjust. Undeserved. Excessive. Disproportionate. After 60 centuries of work recreating a healthy, beautiful, and magnificent world, filled with life and a future, how could something like this happen? Why?

To the people who were now living on the Moon, it was clear this would not be temporary. The human species was now homeless, or at least it felt that way. However, that was another word you had to be careful with on these stations, since most of the permanent residents had been born here and considered this their home. There was much adjusting to do.

Arnold Speck, the Administrator and all his management staff including Gracie Armstrong from Flight, John Fish from Recycle, Sundar Narayen from Construction, Amol Luciano from Agriculture, and Jane Kong from Housing were gathered when the UN announcement had come. Arnold had been warned in advance that something was coming, and to be prepared. Up until a few minutes ago they'd all felt lucky to have been spared the same pain as Earth was experiencing. They felt lucky that it was likely to be temporary and eventually it would all go back to normal. Now they realized all their jobs just got ten times harder. The Moon went from being mainly a research and tourist attraction, to a major lifeboat for humanity. The overcrowding they were experiencing right now, wouldn't be tolerated for long. According to the announcement, they had time, but not when you crowd this many people together under these circumstances. If they wanted to maintain control, they'd have to move quickly. Construction would have to begin immediately. Did they have the necessary resources? So many questions. So much to do. Humanity was being tested once again, only this time, it was off world.

Mars

There was no view from Mars other than what the space stations orbiting Earth were broadcasting. It was enough. Everyone on Mars had some family or friends living on Earth. Very few people had chosen to go to Mars when the first announcement came, because everyone assumed it would be temporary. Just like those on Earth's Moon, the people in the stations safely orbiting Mars had a mix of feelings as they watched. The black hole had passed here first of course, but the damage had been relatively minor. The biggest effect had been the raising of the orbits of their two moons, Phobos and Deimos, but the general opinion was that it was a definite improvement. That sat in the back of people's minds as they watched, hoping somehow the same for Earth, though they'd been warned otherwise. Those that had never lived near the ocean seemed the least concerned. Those that had, were heavy hearted.

Jill Rubin, the Administrator for the Mar's base, called the same type of meeting Arnold had on Earth's Moon. This time even Mariana Dyson, the head of Agriculture had vacated her greenhouses on the surface to come up to the station and watch events unfold on Earth. Her greenhouses had suffered little damage, and she was encouraged that her experiments were producing increased food yields and improved quality. Someday Mars would be able to provide more of it's own food and import less or none from Earth. After what they'd just witnessed, there was no question supplies would not be arriving from Earth in the foreseeable future. Mariana's greenhouse production would be the only source of fresh food for Mars.

Then came the announcement of Earth's magnetosphere failing. It was fair to say this had a much stronger impact on the people who lived on and in orbit around Mars than it did for the people around Earth's Moon, and even for many people on Earth itself.

That's because the people who lived and worked on Mars knew what happened here billions of years ago. They understood why Mars had little atmosphere and no indigenous life. They knew the root cause, and it was the same thing that's happening to Earth now. Living on Mars gave them a unique insight into what might happen on Earth, and it was sobering to say the least. Life in the solar system was about to take a drastic turn. What would this mean for Mars? Would people now want to move here if the Earth became uninhabitable, or would they adapt and continue living there in a fashion similar to those on the Moon or Mars? At the very least, it was likely that Mars would need to prepare for providing some permanent residence for the evacuees of Earth. There were just too many people to do otherwise.

Jill looked over at her head of Agriculture. "How quickly can you get more of those new greenhouses built and growing food?"

Chapter 22

Earth Date: 8411

Space Museum

Krystle Byanyima was born in Uganda, and stayed there for almost a full week before her parents took her up to Sagan Station to live. Her dad was a highly specialized integrator with a reputation for getting disparate systems to talk to each other. Given the complexity of these stations, it was handy having a person like that around. So Krystle grew up being comfortable crawling around inside a core drive and learning to walk on engineering plates.

Her first toys were tools. At two she rejected any attempts to offer her more child appropriate toys, seeing their uselessness. So dad gave her broken, safe, components to play with. She became competent at finding creative ways to take apart just about anything. As her dad used to tell her, "if it's already broken, you've got nothing to lose taking it apart." By the age of four, she could even put them back together, and not surprisingly they sometimes worked.

When Krystle was old enough to attend school with the other kids on the station, it was a disaster. She liked other kids and played well with them, making several good friends, so that part was fine. It was the whole idea of formal education that rubbed her wrong. She was impatient with anything she couldn't see an immediate use for. She constantly challenged her instructors, and her dad was frequently called to the school's Administrator office to settle some issue or attempt to convince Krystle to cooperate. Eventually everyone gave up, and Krystle was granted special permission to be "home schooled." Formal educations were still encouraged in this era, but not specifically required as long as each citizen had a path which contributed to the overall good of humanity. The guidelines were flexible, as were the ages, so in her case an Apprenticeship was considered appropriate, and her dad would be her official Mentor.

From that time forward, Krystle's life stayed pretty much the same, other than she didn't have to go to school. She spent her days following dad around to each repair, integration, construction, maintenance, or custom fabrication job. If it was something she'd witnessed her dad do once, the next time she was completely hand's on. To call her an engineering savant would not have been an exaggeration if you subtracted all the negative aspects. Her parents made sure she spent time each day playing with others her age, and kept her on a strict fitness program.

By the age of 14, Krystle was fully capable of performing most of the tasks of space station engineers, and was often called to provide services when her dad wasn't available. This went on for several more years till she was 17, when her dad had a special assignment off station, and brought Krystle along. Roughly one third of the way from Earth to the Moon, GASA had established a museum of sorts in deep space for vehicles, labs, retired satellites, and other potentially useful older tech, that was too valuable to recycle, but didn't have an immediate use. It was actually more of a deep space parking lot, but GASA preferred the term museum which made it more interesting for tourists passing by on the way up or down from the Moon.

Krystle knew instantly she had found her passion. She preferred this older technology because it was more "available" as she called it. Rather than having a bunch of functions combined into an integrated lump of something unrepairable, each component had a separate function. Most of them could be taken apart and repaired or modified to change or improve their use. As much as she enjoyed working with her father on the station, this was more liberating. Plus, she was a teenager, and any excuse to have additional freedom was a bonus. So her dad, being the capable Mentor he was, and also beginning to wear down at his daughter's never ending teenage challenges made arrangements for her to rebuild one of the older labs that had fallen into disrepair over 500 years ago. GASA had approved the project, per Krystle's dad's proposal, and even provided full funding for whatever components or materials she needed, as well as providing full provisions for her to setup housekeeping at the lab. At 22 she'd completely restored the lab and it's propulsion system to fully operational condition. That's when she got a personal call from Kaylee Brown, the GASA Administrator.

Krystle listened carefully to Kaylee Brown's offer, and unsurprisingly made a reasonable counteroffer, which Kaylee thought was prudent and immediately agreed to. The deal sealed, Krystle took one of the lab's short range pods and started scouring the "parking lot" for something she'd had her eyes on since day one. This was going to be sweet!

Moving Day

Taka Asai and Al Haywood were standing outside their lab, watching the ocean waves break off El Segundo Beach to the South. The ocean looked normal again and calm before the afternoon off shore winds started. Except for the piles of rotting seaweed and other stuff on a beach that no longer had any sand, it was perfectly normal. "Gonna miss our surfing days, Bro," Taka said. "Though I guess it's going to be a while before anyone does that again. Glad we packed our boards in the last crate. It'll be nice to have a reminder."

"Yeah," Al replied half in a dream, "It's going to be weird living in space. I went up once with my folks, to the Moon. It was OK, but space is just a whole lot of nothing. Don't see the appeal."

"Hey, it's not about appeal, Bro. It's about us figuring out what we did without taking the rest of the planet with us. Which is why Kaylee Brown said they found a newly restored lab and a great parking space for us far far away, and down solar wind from Earth. You gotta admit it's pretty cool the effort they're going to for us, considering all that's going on down here. They must think it has some serious long term value."

The unmistakable hum of the heavy lift space crane coming in overhead broke their daydreaming as they turned back towards the lab, and the quarter million cubic foot container packed with all their research equipment and their futures. The crane's pilot walked down the ship's folding gantry and towards the guys. He looked exactly like what you'd expect from someone who spent their days going up and down, and up and down, hauling loads to and from the space stations or wherever. He'd left the motor running, so to speak, obviously intent on not wasting a single minute. "You guys Asai and Haywood?"

"That's us," Taka said loudly over the hum.

"All right," the pilot said not really looking at them but checking some data on his pad. "Get on board, we leave in 5." Yeah, just another run in a long day.

The guys went up the ramp into the crane and grabbed a seat. These things really weren't built for passengers, so the seats were pretty rough by today's standards, but at least they had the place to themselves and there were a few windows. The pilot followed them up a few minutes later after making a quick inspection of the container he'd be lifting, and barely gave them a glance as he punched a button folding the gantry and closing the hatch, then disappearing one level up. Right on time, 5 minutes after they met, the increased hum of the crane had them rising just barely above the container and the pilot slipped right over the top and landing just long enough for the auto clamping system to lock on. Then the hum became a full body experience as the crane's gravity drive came up to full power to lift the heavy container and begin their slow, almost floating ascent.

Compared to commercial or tourist travel launchings this felt more like an old fashioned balloon ride. It made sense though, given the mass of their container, the pilot would be taking it slow and easy. The view was pretty spectacular though, and the guys weren't in any rush. The downside was the view was also depressing. The view up and down the coastline where they'd lived for so many years was unrecognizable. Marina Del Rey was gone, washed up on shore; a pile of boats, moorings, and slips. The same for Redondo to the South. Further north as they ascended, their favorite surfing spots were completely changed, and even the canyons of Malibu and beyond had drastically altered terrain. It was good they were leaving. Too painful to stay.

The view improved the higher they went. You could no longer see the details of the wiped out farmlands and orchards, or any hints of human habitation. If you didn't know the Earth, it would look blue, green, and vibrant. After a couple hours of a painfully slow accent, the windows suddenly went dark, and the glow of the thin atmosphere appeared along the horizon. So thin and fragile for a ball so large. The hum of the crane was diminishing with the need for lift, now reserved mainly for the management of so much mass. Just above low orbit the view of one of the impressive space stations cleared and even in their age such a sight was a marvel of technology.

Off to the side of the station, was a tiny dot that was growing as they approached quickly. It's small size compared to the station made it seem further away at first than it was. The crane's drive slowed and the crane began a gradual rotation of 180 degrees, preparing to decelerate. The lab was about what they expected considering it's origin. A large half domed main body, with a smaller cylinder below, attached by three stanchions made the whole affair look like a giant mushroom. The main body would be the lab and living quarters, with the smaller unit below the actual testing lab for the drive cores. This was the original design for the space versions of the gravity drive testing labs of old that were usually located in the ocean, far from shore. The three stanchions were attached with explosive clamping rings to blow the lower lab free in an emergency. They weren't actually explosive, but the highly compressed nitrogen tanks that blew the clamps free had the same effect. There would be three escape pods off the main lab, but only two were visible. The third had been replaced by what looked like another relic from the past; an original, first generation, gravity drive space vessel. It was hanging off the side of the main lab by a short tunnel, that also appeared to have a quickly detachable clamping dock.

As they approached the lab, their container now in the lead, the loading dock bay door slowly opened and a massive arm articulated towards the crane, turning the mushroom into a giant crab, preparing to grab it's dinner. The pilot brought the crane to a stop, relative to the orbital movement of the lab, and released the container. There was no hesitation as he immediately pivoted the crane around to a smaller dock on the side of the lab perfectly aligning his airtight docking ring with the lab's. There was the slightest of taps, and they were docked.

"Your new home guys, time to hop off," the pilot called down. Surprisingly he actually took the time to come down from his cockpit, walk back and help them over to their exit. He had the crane in roughly ¼ G so when the guys stood they almost slammed into the overhang above their seats. "First time, eh?" he added, with a slight smirk. He practically shoved them into the short docking tunnel and threw the door closed. He was gone a minute later, off to his next job, leaving the guys floating in free fall.

"Nice guy, eh," Al said, as he and Taka worked their way to the inner hatch using the overhead grips, "good thing he didn't stick around for his tip."

"Hey, I'm just glad he remembered to close the other airlock before leaving."

At the lab end of the tunnel, they could begin to feel the artificial gravity of the lab, and by the time they punched the OPEN button on the hatch, they were almost in full gravity. As the hatch opened they were immediately hit by a wall of sound that took them pleasantly by surprise as *Good Vibrations* resounded around the lab. "You're shitten me, Bro," Taka half yelled, half laughed. "The Beach Boys! Now that's a proper welcome aboard."

"Classic dude," Al grinned.

The inside of the lab appeared in pristine condition, which was another pleasant surprise. There wasn't much equipment, and what was there looked more like a museum display, which fit the music perfectly. No matter, they brought all their own gear. They started to take a tour of the layout when a sliding door at the far side of the lab popped open and a tall young lady wearing what looked like a tool belt, and a grumpy frown strutted in. "You two better be Asai and Haywood," she barked, "or you're on the wrong ship."

"That's us," Al said, seriously impressed by the view. "You the captain?"

"Captain?" Krystle replied. "You boys need babysitting or something?" She reached down and touched something on her arm and the music stayed on but at a much lower volume. "No, I'm the Tool here, and despite what they may have told you down below, I'm the one that spent the best years of my life restoring this beast so you damn well better be nice to her."

"Love the music," Taka said, "goes well with the surroundings."

"Whoever worked on this lab in the ancient past, left a whole collection of old Rock, and some not so Rock, on one of the computers. Found it during the restoration. They definitely don't play music like this anymore and it's fun to work to. I'm Krystle. Come on, I'll get you oriented and then leave you to unpack while I move this beast to our new home."

"What do mean, our new home?" Al asked.

"Hahaha, yeah Kaylee Brown from GASA told me ALL about you boys. Real trouble. Big red flags. No way we're staying here. My orders are to drive you way out into the black, and down solar wind from Earth. I've also got this whole thing rigged so if you guys screw up again, I'll be blasting you and your lab even further out while I go the other way. So be careful." She turned and tapped a keypad on the wall that opened a hatch in the deck, about three feet wide. She climbed into the hatch and motioned for them to follow. This was one of the three stanchions they'd seen from the outside leading to the main testing station below. When they were all in the tight tunnel she pointed to something about halfway down. "See that? Each of these three supports has one of these. I punch some keys upstairs, you and your lab go bye-bye. Just in case you thought I was kidding a couple minutes ago." So there were three fully synchronized explosive docking hatches. Something they probably needed in those early days when cores still occasionally exploded.

When they reached the lab below, Krystle pointed out the loading dock and the cargo pod. "I don't suppose you guys have any idea how to drive one of these pods for moving your gear down here?"

The guys both gave her a blank look.

"Yeah, that's what I thought. OK, I'll help you move whatever gear you need down here, and the same into the main lab above from Cargo, then you're on your own. Just one rule, for now. Anytime you guys need my help down here, something moved up or down, or something fixed, you SHUT DOWN anything you're working on first. I'm not interested in being sucked into some space tunnel or something like what you guys did below. Yeah yeah yeah, she told me that too. She wanted to make sure I knew what I was getting into. Oh, one more thing. There's two escape pods in the main lab, but that third door is attached to my ship, which I'm sure you saw coming in. Don't ever fricken go on my ship. That's my home, and I like my privacy. The rest of this tub is yours. Got it? OK…. back upstairs so we can move your shit. You can't be down here because there's no airlock big enough, so this whole things gonna be open to space."

It took just under two hours for Krystle to shuttle the guy's tools, machinery, and materials to the lower lab from their container in the main bay. Once everything was buttoned up, and the bay pressurized, the guys could get to their personal stuff, and stow it in their cabins, which were also part of the main lab level. They started to head down to the lower lab and Krystle stopped them. "Don't head down now, we leave in 10 minutes. That's another thing. Regs say nobody down below with the ship underway." She turned around and went to the far end of the lab where she hopped on an open lift and headed up. "And nobody but me goes up here to the bridge," she yelled.

The guys went back to their rooms and did all those boring things you do when you're unpacking to stay. The familiar hum of the lab's main drive drowned the sound of the background music that had played nonstop since they arrived, and the lab slowly broke orbit headed to deep space. They were headed to Lagrange Point L5 which was a stable location for the lab, about a quarter million miles away. Far enough away to hopefully keep the guys from causing trouble, close enough to reach quickly in an emergency. Krystle was taking her time to travel the relatively short distance, since the lab wasn't really designed for fast deep space travel. Also, Krystle wanted to be sure the lab was parked at a stable location within L5 so she wouldn't have to worry about the guys wandering off while she was gone, which she planned to be as often as possible.

The hum of the labs main drive slowed and eventually went silent, indicating they'd arrived at their new home. Krystle came back down into the main area with a pack on her shoulder, still wearing her tool belt. "You guys are on your own now, I have another job to get to. If you need anything, just use the main comm system to call me. I assume you guys know how to use that at least." She didn't wait for an answer and went through the airlock to her ship. A few minutes later the guys felt a small bump and could see her ship heading away from the lab.

Krystle took a deep breath, and turned her ship, *Freedom*, away from the lab and headed even deeper into a space, and off towards the outer system. She wasn't used to having company, and wasn't particularly interested in getting too friendly with those two. She knew once the lab was taken over by engineers for research, the privacy she'd come to cherish would vanish. She'd need the means to escape at times so she'd bargained for this ship from Kaylee Brown. It was a vintage cruiser based on the original gravity drive designs and fit her needs perfectly. She knew the name was a little corny and overused, but it fit her feelings. It hadn't taken nearly as long to restore as the lab systems. Everything was in reasonably good functional condition when she first started working on it, which she thought was weird. Why was it in the parking lot? She didn't say anything to anyone except her dad of course. He totally got it.

Chapter 23

Earth Date: 8414 ½

Punching Holes in Space

Al and Taka were lost in the their own experiments and in space. They barely seemed to notice the drama unfolding on that blue and white marble that hung outside their lab's viewport, from their stable orbit at L5. They weren't insensitive, or uncaring, after all they had family down there too. It's just that, well, they're engineers. In their minds they were comfortable with the simple fact that other people were handling it. It wouldn't help to worry. Their job was to focus on their work. It helped that they located the computer with the immense library of classic rock Krystle had been playing on day one. They had it playing in a loop and it took months before it repeated; of course they only had it playing while they worked.

Krystle was seldom on board, always off on another job she said. She was good at responding anytime they needed help with some ship-related issue, or integrating a new piece of equipment. She'd even warmed up a bit, though made it quite clear she wasn't particularly interested in having a relationship with either of them. So the guys had the place mostly to themselves. It's a good thing Krystle had setup some automatic cleaning bots since after all, they were engineers.

It took a few months for them to setup the original experiment they'd used back at the lab in L.A.. The lower lab was designed specifically with the idea that if something went wrong during a test, there were multiple overlapping safety mechanisms for the engineers. The first, given they had time and warning, were the three stanchions that held the lower lab to the upper lab, with explosive releases mid-tunnel. Those were only practical if they were in the upper lab when something catastrophic happened below that threatened the main lab. Though the original designer had opted for three smaller supports instead of one larger with the apparent idea of giving three engineers the opportunity to escape simultaneously. It was hard to decide if the designer was an optimist or a pessimist. With one button (well secured from accidental contact) they could blow the entire lower lab into space, along with all their work. It would have to be truly life threatening to even consider that. The second safety feature was much more reasonable; they had personal space suits of the most current design, not from the era of this lab, which provided excellent freedom of movement while creating a self-contained environment should there be a hull breach in the lab. They also had tethers attached in case the breach was bad enough to blow them out along with the atmosphere. Considering what happened in L.A., they took full advantage of this option. The last major safety feature, was simply that the test pads were at the very bottom (relative to everything else) of the lab, so if something did fail on the pad, it hopefully wouldn't effect the rest of the facility. Again, considering what happened in L.A. ....

With everything setup and ready to spin, the guys got into their suits, with tethers attached, and stopped cold. They both just starred at the proverbial START button. There wasn't really a START button of course, it was a heads-up motion sensitive display that would follow them around the lab so all controls were always literally a hand movement away. Still, it was disconcerting. They'd made a full sweep of the lab, twice, to make sure there was nothing loose that could be blown out. When they first moved in, they'd hung their surf boards on the lab wall to remind them of home, since they weren't going to have much other use for them up here. Those were the first things moved upstairs in preparation for today. Priorities.

They'd discussed the possibility of the bottom of the lab disappearing into a worm hole of course, many times, actually endlessly, during the entire time setting the experiment back up. The hole they'd created in L.A. was under the main supporting slab for the core, not on the pad itself. The weight of the test drive, especially with the core, was in the multiple tons range, and the pad that was left still held, except for that little dimple. Whatever it was they opened, it started at approximately the same location as a gravity well would form when the cores were used on a ship. It should be mentioned, that in the lab setup, the cores were typically upside down from what you'd envision in a ship. The idea being if something went wrong you wouldn't be drawing the entire building down on top of you. In this configuration, and the way it sat in the lab in space, it would in theory move the entire facility down into the gravity well. This also made far more sense than creating a gravity well right in the middle of the whole lab. Additionally, the lab was designed so an integrated gravitational stabilizer, such as the ones used on ships, would automatically maintain an even stress on the facility while preventing any movement through space. They'd also made a couple modifications to the original setup, including reducing the size and configuration of the magnetic drivers so they could safely touch as they maintained an optimal distance from the contracting core. And finally, at the risk of seeming paranoid, they installed a backup safety shutdown in case the one that worked last time failed.

On the assumption that the same type of event would occur again once they brought the core up to almost 6 G's, they'd installed a series of sensors on the outside of the lab. The most important ones for the first test were a series of cameras, some designed to record in the non-visual energy spectrums ranging from Gamma, X-ray, and ultraviolet, to infrared, microwave, and even radio at the other end.

It all made sense, until you were standing in the middle of a lab, in outer space, with a space suit on, tethered to a wall, and ready to press the START button. Being prudent they both backed up towards the anchor points of their tethers attaching a second much shorter one to the stanchions. They started the cameras recording and turned on the labs main viewer which showed a view of Earth and a split view of some tightly clustered star groups. The idea of these views was to account for the possibility the anomaly they created might not be directly viewable, but may create a momentary warping of space that would show as a gravitational lensing effect on the cameras.

Taka had the honor and started the core spinning. Exactly as in the lab, nothing really unusual happened until about 5G relative spin, when the core began to contract. The readings weren't quite as strong this time however, which they assumed was due to the redesign of the magnetic drivers. They increased the speed more slowly as it approached 6G, which was when all the fun happened last time. As expected the core began to shrink more rapidly so they held at 5.85 G, and watched. They felt nothing inside the lab, but the view of Earth was wavering ever so slightly, and the Gamma ray camera was picking up the slightest increase. Taka eased the power toward 5.90 and the core continued it's collapse though more slowly.

Going back through the recording of their land based experiment they realized they'd been careless at this point, and applied the power too quickly. This time they made very tiny moves. At 5.90 the displays showed increased wavering in both the visual and Gamma ray spectrums. As they nudged the power higher, the effects increased until at exactly 5.97, the core suddenly collapsed to the size of a small marble and the Earth disappeared completely from the viewer. Gamma rays increased dramatically. Taka nudged the controller up to 5.98, there was a flash on the monitor and the emergency system shut down the experiment.

Based on the preliminary readings from the sensors and cameras, as well as the view of Earth, which disappeared entirely, combined with the gamma ray readings there was little doubt they'd opened some kind of tunnel through space. Something unexpected had also happened to the gravity wave sensor readings. They'd continued to increase right up to 5.98 G and then collapsed suddenly to near zero. This seemed to confirm that the area of the tunnel was no longer part of the normal fabric of space, since it was no longer being effected by the gravity wave still being generated closer to the lab. The guys were obviously excited to have reproduced their experiment, possibly making a profound new discovery. They were even more excited to have not died.

They notified Kaylee Brown at GASA directly, as they'd been instructed to do. GASA had to appear 100% focused on preparing the life on Earth for evacuation, and not continuing to explore new areas of science. That would be the view presented to the public. Scientists and engineers understood how foolish that would be, so quietly, in the background, GASA continued other areas of research it deemed worthy. Al and Taka's qualified mainly because it was inexpensive, required almost no oversight, and was far enough off planet that if they suddenly disappeared the same way the dirt in their lab in L.A. did, very few people would miss them. Kaylee took the time to encourage them to continue but was unable to provide any resources in the form of additional personnel though they could requisition supplies as needed.. They were encouraged to communicate with other scientists at GASA, but to do so quietly. Essentially, they were on their own.

Their obligation to report behind them, something engineers love doing, they continued their research. The next couple tests were a bit less stressful, now that they felt relatively safe they weren't going to punch a hole through the bottom of the lab and disappear into a worm hole. They repositioned cameras and sensors, which did a better job of confirming everything they learned during the first test. They continued their experiments with minor modifications until eventually realizing they'd hit that proverbial wall which so often happens when exploring new technology. No matter what they tried, they just couldn't seem to get to the next level. They were 98% of the way there, and couldn't seem to move past that point.

The stumbling block was around the automated power shutdown. They knew of course what caused the shutdown; a powerful and uncontrolled feedback. They could turn off the automated shutdown and probably blow themselves up along with their fusion power generator, the rest of the lab and the ship. So the shutdown was going to stay active. In fact they made sure before each test that the backup shutdown was also functioning. It was the cause of the feedback they couldn't get a handle on. No matter how slowly they approached the threshold attempting to stabilize the core, and hold the worm hole (or whatever it was) open, when that tipping point was reached, the reaction was instantaneous. They wanted to send probes down the hole to try and determine where the other end was, but they couldn't keep it open long enough.

This is also the point in this type of ground breaking research when the days quickly became weeks, months, and years. They weren't losing hope, since they knew how close they were, they were just gaining frustration. They even did something you rarely see engineers do; they grew beards and pony tails. They even took the occasional vacation and with Krystle's help, hitched a ride down, and did a bit of surfing on the now clean, though changed beaches. The breaks were radically different, and very few people took advantage of the uncrowded access. The presence of marine mammals had also thinned and the few that remained were less playful and tended to stay further out. It just wasn't much fun anymore, and didn't help to clear their brains like they'd hoped. So they changed tactics and tried a visit to Sagan station to bounce ideas off some physicists. The physicists weren't much help since what the guys were doing was on the border of theoretical, so each scientist they spoke with had a radically different opinion.

They'd been at it for 4 ½ years, when something finally changed. They were so used to being left alone out here at L5, they didn't even recognize the proximity alert when it sounded. Fortunately, Krystle was there and got on the overhead speakers and told the guys to get their butts upstairs. That was definitely something new. When they got up to the main lab level, Krystle was talking to GASA confirming something. "We have visitors guys," was all she said.

Krystle was programming the keypad on one of the two remaining escape pods. A few minutes later, she jettisoned the pod, leaving that docking bay available for the visiting ship. This was also a first for the guys, since it was their understanding that only those old relics like Krystle's ship had the proper configuration to dock. Outside the viewport they saw the approaching ship, and sure enough it looked a whole lot like Krystle's. They felt the jolt from the docking clamps and the sound of the port pressurizing. A few minutes later, three figures from ancient history walked into the lab.
There was a middle aged man with slightly graying hair and a beard, and two somewhat younger men, both a bit heavy set and taller. The older guy was looking around like he was trying to remember something but the two younger guys were laughing.

"You hear that boss," Bill said loudly over the music that played non-stop in the background. "That's *Johnny B. Goode*. Classic Rock, welcome home!"

"And they said Rock wouldn't last," John added, laughing with Bill.

Krystle, Al and Taka all just stood there stunned. It was like watching an old news clip. There was absolutely no mistaking these three men, but it just wasn't possible, was it? Had the rumors of them disappearing to stay with the alien Octopods been true? "Um, hello," Krystle said. "GASA said you were cleared to come aboard but,….. uhhh…..?"

"Oh, sorry," Howard said, "it's been a while since we visited anyone. That's Bill and John," he added pointing, "and I'm Howard. You the guys punching holes in space?"

"Uh, yeah I guess that's us," Al answered. "I'm Al and this is Taka, and the friendly lady over there is Krystle. Are you guys…… Is that *Gravitas-1* out there? Are you *The* Howard Kalb, inventor of the Gravity Drive?"

"Yes, and yes we're still alive, and yes those are my ship mates, and yes we've been asleep for a long time. When we left though, things weren't this messed up. We just got back in system and we're headed for a meeting, but GASA asked us to stop here and drop someone off. Where's your comm system?"

"Over here, sir," Krystle said, taking Howard over to a console across the lab.

Howard recognized it's design and opened a channel. "Is this tied into your main computer system as well?"

"Yes, sir," Krystle replied.

"Howard…. just Howard. We're just engineers like you all, not sirs." Howard turned away from Krystle and gave his attention to the comm system for a minute before making a point of talking directly into the mic, "OK, channels open and it does look to be tied into the main system, so anytime."

There was a brief pause and then the lab's computer system seemed to spin up into overdrive. A few of the other systems on the ship came on momentarily and then shutdown just as quickly.

"What's going on?" Krystle said suddenly concerned. "What are you guys doing to my ship?"

A moment later a familiar and comforting voice, came on over the lab speakers. Well, familiar to Howard, John, and Bill. "Hello, crew of the old research lab that's punching holes in the fabric of space, I'm Jason. I'll be joining you in your research and trying to make sure you don't blow yourselves up or cause any undo harm to the Universe. I've had a lot of experience with your types so we should get along fine. Sorry, I missed introductions it seems, though if you're records are up to date you're Krystle Byanyima, the tool master here, and you two are Taka Asai, and Al Haywood, my new wards. Nice to meet you all." Jason had tied into the lab's observation cameras as well as the computers and just about everything else, so he had a good view of the interior including all the occupants.

"So then you're like *The* Jason, the famous AI from the Octopods that only talks to world leaders now and stuff?" Taka sort of stuttered out.

"Yes, that's me. Your chief at GASA asked me to join you all since it appears you've been a bit stuck in your research, and she's worried about you as well. Also, as a concerned member of the life in our Universe, I'm personally interested in making sure you don't cause as much trouble as these three."

"Don't worry, you'll get used to him," Howard said. "We're going now. Nice meeting you all. Good luck with your research, and Krystle, thank you for making that docking port available."

"Hey," Bill said, "Would you guys be OK if we took a copy of your music library? Our stuff's getting kind of old."

"Sure," Krystle said, "I can do that."

"Thank you Krystle," Jason said, "I'll just go ahead and download it through my link to their ship. It will be quicker. Bye Boss, see you in a minute."

Howard just shook his head and headed to his ship with his ship mates. A few minutes later they were gone, as if they'd never been.

"That was totally weird dude," Taka said.

"For once I agree with you," Krystle replied. "So Jason, you're staying I assume."

"Yes Krystle. I'll be staying here to help. You should also know that I'm still on *Gravitas-1*, my own ship in orbit around Earth, and back at my main processor at the Octopod research station. I also have full access to all the main communications and data bases from a vast array of systems on and in orbit around Earth. With these combined resources I should prove quite helpful with your ongoing research. Regarding Howard, John, and Bill, please understand they just arrived in the system, having been in Transit for over 4 years, so the devastation we're all adjusted to, is completely new for them. They're delivering some critical equipment to the Ark I'm building, so perhaps they'll be able to visit more in the future, and also assist with your work. They're normally much friendlier."

"Jason," Al began, "you seem familiar with the work we've been doing here. We've only been reporting to GASA, and it was our understanding this work was somewhat classified. How..............?"

"Yes, Al," Jason said, taking advantage of the long pause in Al's question, "I also am closely connected to GASA in more ways than you're aware, and have the highest security clearance and therefore real time access to all ongoing projects. We've kept it that way so I may assist when needed, yet my role here in your system remains discreet, allowing your species to proceed without the sense of being constantly observed. While we've been talking, I've been reviewing the on-board data you've recorded regarding your most recent observations and would like to begin working with you immediately if you're ready."

"Sure," Taka replied for both of them, "we'd really appreciate a fresh set of brains on our experiments. I guess it's pretty obvious we're kind of stuck at the moment. Maybe we should continue this down in the lower lab." Taka and Al started walking towards the entrance to the lower lab, while Krystle went about retrieving and redocking the escape pod.

Jason was more than just a little interested in helping Al and Taka with their project. He'd been monitoring them both directly from his ship in Earth's orbit, as well as the data coming through from GASA. The progress they'd made was more significant than they, or anyone at GASA had realized. If computers could experience Déjà vu, then Jason was certainly experiencing that right now. Their research strongly paralleled the importance of the advances Howard, Bill, and John had made 6,000 years ago, and the potential for benefits not just to the life on Earth, but also to the Octopods. In fact, it was entirely possible, their work could eventually lead to something that may indeed represent the future for all the life Jason was intending to save on his Ark. There was much more going on here than the human's had realized, so it was critical this research was successful.

When the guys reached the lower lab, Jason wasted no time. "Now that I have full access to the direct readings recorded on your equipment," Jason began on the lab's overhead speakers, shutting off the music temporarily, "several things are apparent, based on comparisons from similar research performed many thousands of years ago by my people, the Octopods."

Al and Taka had seated themselves and were laser focused on every word Jason was saying. They hadn't realized how depressed they'd become, with the lack of progress. All of a sudden, there was someone here who was literally light years ahead, and seemed most eager to help.

"As you've already ascertained," Jason continued, "the reason your readings indicate the gravitational wave from the core drops to zero at the moment you open what you're referring to as a tunnel, is you've actually opened a type of wormhole. It's not exactly your garden variety wormhole, using your vernacular, since you've actually managed to punch a small hole in the fabric of space-time. Since the gravitational well produced by the core depends on the warping of the fabric of space, and since your hole no longer contains that fabric, there's nothing for the core to react with, thereby dropping your gravitational readings to zero."

"Furthermore, which your notes don't' seem to quite grasp, is when you open this hole in space, you're actually using the core's energy from the gravity wave to parse the bonds of energy that keep the fabric stable in it's three dimensional matrix. The result of this parsing is the release of the energy from those bonds, which is what causes your emergency system to shutdown. Essentially that energy is being directed back along the remaining gravity wave, and into the core's magnetic drivers. This of course is all happening rather quickly. The next step in your work, is to simply build the necessary equipment to deflect the energy from those bonds away from your equipment and either capture it for future use, or allow it to escape as radiation into space. Doing this will allow you to hold the opening in a stable configuration, and then you'll be able to send your probes through the wormhole in the hopes of determining where it terminates. I have some design specifications to help you with these next steps if you're ready to proceed."

The guys may not have looked like it, while just sitting there absorbing the mountain of information Jason had shared, but once they got over the shock, they were certainly ready.

Chapter 24

Earth Date 8414 ½

Special Delivery

When they got back on board *Gravitas-1*, John went right over to his station and started scanning through some files. "Bill, check out this list of music they had! Unbelievable that someone preserved all the great music from our generation. Which reminds me, hey Jason. When we came on board that lab, they were playing *Johnny B. Goode*, by Chuck Berry, I think you may have caught the end of it when you activated over there. Do you have any idea whatever happened to Voyager 1 and 2 from Earth? That song was on the gold disc NASA made for alien music lovers. Did anyone ever find the spacecrafts?"

"Yes John," Jason said. "Roughly 2,000 years ago, I was doing some survey work well out past your system's Oort Cloud and discovered Voyager 2. It's course had been altered from NASA's original course projection, likely from a body inside the Oort Cloud, and was headed on a vector above the galactic plane. It would have ended up spending eternity in the space between galaxies so I recovered it, and returned it to Earth. I believe it's currently on display, after having been restored, inside the Ann Druyan Space Station, orbiting Earth. I regret to report that Voyager 1 was discovered by one of the rare aggressive space faring species in this sector who used it as target practice."

"That's not cool Jason, are these bad guys someone we should be worried about?" John asked.

"I think not, John. The report came from one of our friends who monitor these *bad guys*, as you call them, and this was apparently just a scout ship headed off in another direction. There's been no report of them near this sector since then."

John noticed Bill wasn't paying much attention and walked over. "You OK Bro?"

"That was weird seeing that old testing lab and another ship like ours, after what we saw at Mars," Bill half responded to John, more mumbling to himself. Mars had been close enough to their vector towards Earth, after exiting from the Transit, they decided to take a quick detour to see what progress humanity had made there. During their approach, they thought it was Mars' two moons clearly visible on the near side of the planet. Turned out it was Phobos and one of the newer space stations they were seeing. Deimos was on the far side of Mars at the time. "That space station was unbelievable. It's like a floating city or the small moon we took it for. My brain's going back and forth; it's all scrambled by missing 6,000 years. If this is the future of space travel it's going to be really disruptive for people to have a family, or even just stay in touch with old friends."

"No more scrambled than usual, Bro," John replied, "but yeah, that goes for all of us. If we wrote autobiographies and someone read them 10,000 years from now they'd say it was all BS or something. Anyway, we're home now so check this out," John said looking out the port window. "Those stations around the Moon are so huge they look like little moons orbiting the big Moon. And then you look over here and those around Earth are even bigger. Guess it's a good thing since we're going to need places for people to live for a while."

All three of the men were a bit on edge and mentally disoriented though Bill seemed to be struggling the most. "It sounds cool on paper when you talk about going to sleep for 6,000 years and then waking up to all this fantastic new technology," Bill started again, "but there's part of our minds and bodies that has trouble accepting it. Is it possible our lives are tied to space-time such that if you're suddenly taken out for a long time and put back in, you don't quite fit? There's no way to describe it, but that's how it feels. I mean we know intellectually we're home, but it sure doesn't look or feel that way. Einstein visualized the idea of time as a fourth dimension, which means that space and time are inextricably connected. Even back in our time, they were doing experiments that demonstrated clearly how a large gravity well, like around a planet, effects how time passes. So the stronger the gravity, the slower time passes. Time dilation I think he called it. So when you think about describing to someone where you are in the Universe you need to include time. Think about all those science fiction stories where people travel back and forth through time. If someone really went back 6 months from say inside their home, they'd suddenly find themselves floating in outer space with the Earth on the other side of the Sun. I don't now how our bodies and minds are aware of all this but it must be on a deep, raw, physical level well beyond our physiology and closer to the quantum level. There's so much we don't understand about the physical relationship between life and the Cosmos."

"Huh…. that was deep bro," John replied.

Fortunately, they all had something to keep them busy. Something to focus on, so they didn't have to spend too much time thinking about all that. As well as some *new* music from their time. Jason had brought them up to speed as soon as they exited the Transit on his progress with the Ark, and the progress made on Earth by human's preparing to save it's many life forms, including themselves. Their arrival was well timed. *Gravitas-1* had brought the technology for the Ark that would allow it to do the same for the creatures of Earth, as it had for the three men; life suspension. As their ship approached, they could see the glowing sphere orbiting in the Earth's shadow. It was already nearly the size of the largest space station built by humans. Jason had told them it would grow slowly as the necessary supplies and materials were processed. It looked exactly like a smaller version of the Octopod's research sphere, because it was. As Jason had explained, it would need to remain in the shadow of Earth, protected from the Sun's radiation and solar winds, because it's outer shell was relatively fragile. This was the major reason why the Octopods had chosen that specific location for their lab. It was far from any solar influences and in a relatively calm area of space. In addition to staying in Earth's shadow, the success of the Ark would depend almost exclusively on it's weightless environment. The amount of mass they'd be enclosing inside the sphere in suspension, would be in the Trillions of tons if under Earth's gravity; endless freefall was the only solution to housing that much mass.

"It's beautiful, Jason," Howard remarked. "Reminds me of our home with the Octopods, so visually peaceful." They were close enough now they could make out some additional equipment passing in and out of the Ark. "Jason, are those the asteroid mining pods you told us about."

"Yes, they're the primary transport source of the internal building materials we'll need for the millions of individual enclosures. In addition to transporting new materials from the asteroid belt, they're also processing the primary ones I collected at the beginning. Very useful designs your clever engineers developed. It wouldn't have been possible without them. The sphere is growing quickly, and with your arrival, bringing the key components, we should be ready to begin accepting guests long before your Sun's radiation begins effecting life on the surface."

"That's great news, Jason. Once again you and the Octopods save the day for Earth. I'm glad we could make some small contribution ourselves," Howard grunted.

"Hey boss, that's bullshit!" Bill said. "You're not giving any of us enough credit for what we've done. It may have been 6,000 years ago but look around out there. Look at all those huge space stations with millions of people. Every single one of them has our gravity drive, or some improved version anyway. It's the only way you could get something that big in orbit and keep in there. Also, they were able to move them out of the way when that fricken black hole came ripping through here. All those people would be dead if it wasn't for those drives. And now, bringing up all those animals and plants from the surface to the Ark, that's all possible for the same reason. Boss, you're development, with our help of course, basically saved not just humans but the whole planet. Don't even get me started on the Moon and Mars."

"Hey," Howard said, "I get it. The thing is, the more I think about it, the more I wonder if it really was our creation. Did I really have an original thought that got the whole thing started and led me to you two, or was I just stealing the idea from someone else. If it hadn't been for Jason and his probe that I saw and heard humming around the High Sierras that day would I even have had the thought of something like that? And even after that, it took actually seeing the core from the Octopod's ship that our military decided to shoot down. And let's not forget those two innocent Octopods who died. All of that had to happen before meeting you two which finally brought it all together. Can we really take credit for all this?" Howard continued to rant while waving his arms around the view through the ship's windows.

"YES, we can," Bill practically screamed. "Because nobody else put the pieces together. Nobody else made it work. At least for humans. What gave the Octopods the idea for it? What about those Paxians? They had the same basic thing. It's just a natural next step. There's always some spark that starts a fire, and something that makes the spark, and something that moved the thing that made the spark. We're just the ones that saw the spark and made it happen for humans, and now look where we are as a species. Eventually, assuming we lived long enough as a species, someone else would have done it. But it was US, and yes I have no problem being a part of taking credit for that. So quit being such an old grump, boss."

"As painful as it is to admit," Jason said, "I'm forced to agree with Bill. Most of what he said almost even makes sense. Octopods didn't invent gravity, nor did the Paxians, or the hundred other species we know of in the galaxy that developed the same technology. He's right, it is the next logical step for space travel after the reaction drive and what your species calls Newton's Third Law. And he's right that you should feel good about your contribution to saving your planet. And he's also right that you're getting grumpy in your old age."
Howard didn't look convinced. He just stood staring out the window at the beautiful sphere as his ship got closer. There were several openings in the outer shield the mining pods were using to come and go. Some headed down to the surface, and some headed out to deep space, presumably towards the source of raw materials. It was definitely the greatest undertaking of human kind. Actually the first major partnership of humans and another species, building something together. And yes, he had to admit, he was a part of making that happen. "Jason, is that your ship just inside over there?"

"Yes. We'll deliver our shipment there, and the systems on board will begin producing the suspension chemicals and equipment we'll need. It will be similar to what you saw back at the research station, though also different in many ways, given the vast differences in life form sizes and configurations. Now that the sphere has reached this size, and components are taking shape, I'm no longer able to remove my ship since it now forms the main power source and control center for the physical sphere and it's connected systems. I'll be depending on you all and *Gravitas-1* for a great deal of the physical work ahead."

"There's something else," Jason continued, "you recall our discussions of the limitations of the outer sphere's energy shield. In addition to it's susceptibility to solar radiation and Singularians, there's another weakness that we need to address, and yet another reason the research sphere is parked in deep, quiet space. Given the Ark's location in close orbit around Earth, it will be subject to constant bombardment from meteors, cometary debris, and even fast moving dust particles. These fast moving particles aren't a problem for the sphere itself, but at the speed they're moving, they'll pass right through the outer wall. With the sphere full of life forms, at the density I've calculated, this would mean almost certain death to whichever organism was hit. We need to construct a sensing web that will detect incoming particles at least 100 miles distant. Considering the top speed of most particles, this will give my ship's generator, the time and coordinates necessary to increase the power of the wall at the anticipated point of impact, thereby stopping all but the largest. The larger ones will be readily detectable at a great enough distance to divert them in time by one of your ships."

"Cool," Bill said, "sorta like a Tholian Web!? That sounds like a fun engineering project. So, you like have specs or something right?"

"Yes, that's exactly right, Bill," Jason replied. "It's exactly like that, in fact the Octopods captured two Tholian vessels a thousand years ago and have been using them for that purpose ever since."

"Jason," Howard interrupted, "I think you've been spending too much time with Bill and John. They're starting to disrupt your programming. By the way, are you aware your voice actually changes when you're sarcastic?"

"Yes to both Howard. I admit to missing my interactions with the three of you during your extended sleep. And yes, I also have specifications for constructing the detecting web. It's actually pretty basic technology, though it will require a single permanent power station at it's heart. A dozen nodes, each at 100 miles distance, located in permanent positions at a ¾ sphere should be adequate. The remaining ¼ portion facing Earth won't be required, unless Bill feels someone will be shooting meteors at us from the surface. I'll download the specs to the engineering services shop on the Carl Sagan Station, and they'll be able to construct what we need. This project should only require a couple weeks, during which time we can also begin to prepare for our first guests."

"Hey Jason," John asked, "Just how many animals and plants from each species are you planning to bring aboard?"

"There's no set number that's been predetermined. That's being left up to the individual experts in each biome and the species within. Beyond the basic criteria we've established for health, vitality, ability to breed, and so forth, there's also a need to consider such things as existing herd mentality and their leaders, and most important of all, the greatest possible genetic diversity. Far too many factors to force some type of numeric standard on. Also, the humans responsible for these selections will need to join their chosen representatives in suspension so their expertise will be available when it's time to redistribute them at some future date. This means these people will also be allowed to bring family members of their choosing, as well as special members of their selected groups such as a favored pet. It would be unjust to do otherwise. So as you can see the final numbers will be virtually incalculable in advance. The primary overall goal of course would be to completely reestablish Earth's living environment at some undetermined future time, as close as possible to how it is now. To do so Exactly will of course be impossible. The main concern would be maintaining the necessary symbiotic relationships and overall balance within each biome, and world wide. The more progress we make, the more daunting the task becomes, It's a good thing we have decades to accomplish this task."

"Good grief, Jason," John said, "I hadn't really stopped to think about the numbers. The total mass, including all the plants seems incomprehensible. Sorta makes you realize how silly the whole Noah's Ark myth really was. Like you said, the genetic diversity requirement alone, would have been unobtainable with only two of each. Of course he had a much smaller boat too, right? Hey wait, you were around then, was there any truth at all to that?"

Jason was uncommonly quiet and unresponsive for too long. His friends had all come to recognize when he delays this long with an answer, it's usually because there's some internal conflict of issues that logic alone won't allow him to reach the necessary conclusion to respond.

"OK Jason, what it is?" John asked. "What's stopping you from answering?"

"Well, John," Jason slowly responded, "I'm aware the three of you are not religious or follow any such belief system, however, I've learned from experience that it is considered rude or unappreciated to disprove something that humans have long come to either believe in, or at least use as an example for some moral guidance. The story of Noah's Ark may come under such a category. Are you certain you want me to answer that question, John?"

"Out with it, Jason," John immediately responded with the full support of Bill and even Howard who'd turned his attention to this conversation.

"Well, Yes," Jason began. "There was a man named Noah and certain components of his family history were fairly accurate as recorded, minus some of the mystical undertones. And there was a rather heavy rainstorm that caused some local flooding in the region they were living in. And he did indeed have a boat though more precisely I believe it would have been classified as a ferry. He did manage to save a couple of goats, a few sheep and some chickens from drowning. From that point on I believe there was some local reason why the story became slightly exaggerated, and developed, as you say, a life of it's own. I did not track the details of the progress of that story, though did become aware of it some years later. In any case, as you so astutely pointed out, the genetic diversity issue alone should have been enough to dispel that myth long ago. Even back then sheepherders and farmers were well aware of the need to continually cross breed their stock, introducing fresh genetics, to keep their animals healthy."

"Yeah, none of that is surprising actually, Jason, though it is fun to hear from the only true living witness to our colorful history," John said. "Seriously though, back to the insane mass you're going to be housing. Also considering the vast genetic and biological diversity, especially between animals and plants, and the aquatic mammals and birds, and even insects your planning to take aboard, how do these suspension chemicals work on such a wide range of organisms? It seems impossible."

"There's much more to this then we've previously discussed John," Jason answered. "The chemicals you brought, are just a basic compound, and the process of synthesis will be targeted to each species before it arrives, based on a quick sampling of DNA, and tissue samples. As you can imagine, it will be necessary to bring all our guests on board, already sedated. That will just be the first phase. Unlike which was done with the three of you, where you each had your own pods, identical organisms will share a larger containment area. There will simply be far too many individuals for each to have their own pod. Once they're on board, each group in their own environment, their containment area will be activated and prepared for the final phase of suspension. The chemically modified and genetically matched compound will then be injected as a gas into their environment to create the necessary physiological slowing. We will also be taking advantage of the natural low temperatures of the surrounding space, and of course the weightlessness of freefall is what will make the housing of such a mass possible. Since each containment will house a separate species, there will be hundreds of thousands of containments, each requiring separate upkeep.

"And once again, Jason," Howard said, "you and the Octopods come to our rescue. It seems like a debt we'll never be able to repay. We're insanely fortunate to have had you watching over us all these millions of years, Jason."

"Howard, I believe you're forgetting a couple things," Jason said. "First, the three of you and your ship just saved all the Octopods in our research station, by bringing the Paxians to help. That not only saved us, but it also helped the Paxians. Our combined efforts have created a three way friendship that will hopefully continue to benefit all of us for many turns of our galaxy to come. Secondly, keep in perspective that this effort building an Ark, is primarily for the benefit of all the other life forms on Earth, not humans. It's the humans however, that are making the whole rescue operation possible. Again, a joint effort. As John or Bill are probably about to say, this is getting as corny as the ending of a George Lucas movie, so I'll stop now."

"Actually, what I was going to say," said Bill, "was, so much for those stupid noninterference directives!"

Tangential Boomerang

Earth Date: 8,415

Anchoring Humanity

They were born in 3509 BC. They were also born in 200 AD.
Also in 1549, 2024, 3567, 5545, and 8381. Hopefully they'll also
be born well into the future. They lived individually or in small
groups high on the frozen glaciers of the highest mountains, and
in the deepest, hottest valleys on Earth. Even in the lost depths of
the widest deserts. Some lived in jungles so deep, even to this
day some areas are unexplored and unmapped by modern
civilization. They lived in peace and as one with the oceans on
the many islands spread around the planet. For good reason, they
didn't live on the southern most continent. They shared all of
Africa with the largest and sometimes most aggressive animals
and predators on Earth, and they survived.

They lived by choice in all these places even though they were
poorly adapted to any of them, being human. They survived all
these dissimilar environments by fashioning tools, building
homes, growing food, making clothes, using their brains, and
most importantly of all, by living as one with nature and in peace
with their surroundings; not by attempting to dominate it, and
certainly not by destroying and polluting it. This was what all
these people had in common, and what they still do today, in
8415.

The other thing all these people had in common, was they
preferred not to live in the cities or even the small towns of
modern civilization. They prefer their peace and quiet, and their
isolation. They prefer to live off the land, taking only what they

need, and putting back as much as they take. They only want what they need to survive, and enjoy living out their lives with their families. They have no interest in the modern conveniences of the technological world of humans, for they're smart enough to see the trap. They see the price of ownership. They are in touch with their senses and feelings, and aware of their surroundings. They are not foolish. And not being foolish means they also know where to cross the line, and how to survive when completely surrounded by humans who choose to live differently. So they wisely stay in touch with, watch, and listen to what's happening around them. This wisdom saved their lives. They would not otherwise have known in advance of the cataclysmic event that hit their homes. Given the time-span of the warning and how simply they lived, seeking shelter for most of them was no great inconvenience. And most of them survived.

And now, with the impending danger certain to change their ways of life, they see only opportunity. They have no intention of fleeing their world, and moving to the giant floating cities in the sky. They are well educated. They understand fully the danger, not just to themselves, but to all the other life on Earth. They understand, and they intend to help. They will use their great knowledge of the life around them, and assist those collecting plants and animals for the great Ark in orbit. They will help, and then they will stay. They have a full generation of time to prepare, and they will use every minute.

Some live in areas where there are vast networks of underground caves that stretch naturally for many miles, and will be shielded from the radiation. Fully aware of the dangers of radiation, they will protect themselves and limit their time above ground when the need arises. They will hunt and forage at night. They also know this isn't a one-time choice. If life becomes impossible, they'll always be welcome to join the rest of humanity.

Some have chosen to take advantage of technology, and with help from the many agencies established specifically for this purpose, they will build massive above ground enclosures that will double as homes and greenhouses. In exchange they will be the on-ground eyes to monitor and report the progressive changes and conditions of each environment they live in; mountain, prairie, island, desert, frozen tundra, deep caves, or the deepest jungles. These people represent humanities willingness to stand fast, and not so easily give up their home world.

Chapter 25

Earth Date: 8,430

Bismarck Sea - Papua New Guinea

Ocean Currents Research Facility

They were all scientists, except for the few family members that lived there. They knew what to expect. It made no difference. They were people first. They'd invested their lives in the science of marine biology because of their love for the ocean and all it's interesting and unique forms of life. They loved their lives not just for what they did, but for where they did it. When they emerged from their shelter, 600 feet below the now calm ocean surface, the sight brought most of them to instant tears or raw shock. Many couldn't stand the sight and asked to be taken back down at once. It was like coming out from a storm shelter in the ground after a tornado, to find your home and farm completely gone, along with the entire town, livestock, and all the trees and bushes. Nothing left. Where before a spectacular archipelago of coral reefs teaming with fish, a million or more years in the growing had dominated the view, there was now only wreckage and water.

The few hundred transparent titanium bubble-like enclosures that Delphini and her team had created and suspended in mid-ocean, each teaming with life from small sections of the coral reefs, were all that remained. The team responsible for rescuing the indigenous sea mammals had managed to save a few hundred of each species on the space stations above, but what would they be returning to? Those mammals depended on the local ecology for their homes and their food. They'd never survive here now, they'd have to be relocated, assuming any similar ecology survived for them to be resettled to. Delphini's parents were on the same station with those few hundred, plus the sea mammals from Cocos Island they'd been able to rescue. Their concerns however were slightly different. The island's shores had been devastated, though the coastline remained, thanks to the extremely deep waters and high cliffs of the island which jutted almost vertically from the ocean floor. Surprisingly, some small areas of these cliff faces had actually improved their accessibility to marine mammals, so returning them would not be a problem. It was Delphini's parents that no longer had a home; the research facility was gone.

Back at the Papua New Guinea, Ocean Currents Research Facility, the team who's studies focused on the major ocean currents of this region; the Equatorial Current and the Indonesian Throughflow, found themselves jobless. Those currents no longer flowed, as if they'd never existed. How long would it take for them to recover, if ever? Those currents transported the stuff of life to this entire section of the Earth, and had a major impact as well on the weather patterns above. The entire ocean ecology of the region was wiped out by a single massive wave of water. And then the bad news came.

They had just begun picking up the pieces, and developing their meager plans for how to move forward with their lives and try to restore what they could of the coral reefs. The sea mammals had been placed in strategic areas surrounding Papua New Guinea that had survived, and Delphini and her crew were working on using the coral life they had rescued to reseed the few surviving strands of the archipelago. The news was overwhelming, but they were scientists, so they fell back on their training as the means for overcoming the psychological stress. The concept of an Ark, capable of housing and suspending life, gave them a target to work towards.

Within just a few months, they were provided with a detailed briefing specifically addressed to their facility and what remained of the local ecology. They were told it would be 5-10 years before the Ark was ready to begin receiving it's guests, so they had time to rebuild and plan. They were quick to file their requests for as early an occupancy as possible, knowing the fragility of the life they intended to save. Whoever was in charge of organizing the Ark's loading, had already provided rough specifications for the volume and mass of the enclosures Delphini's team would be able to use. Considering the size of the operation from a world wide perspective, the information and detail was nothing short of a miracle. Among other things, Jason was an excellent organizer, and unmatched at multi-tasking.

From day one, Delphini and her crew had decided that with only minor modifications, the transparent titanium enclosures would be their best option. Changing their shapes to accommodate stacking, and a centralized air management port for delivery of the proposed sedation gases, was easily accomplished. They had no idea what exactly these sedation gases would be, though they were assured they would be safe, and had been tested by their host in the Ark. They would be permitted up to 500 of the enclosures, of roughly the same volume as the originals. The only requirement was that the occupants of the enclosures were of sufficient representation and genetic diversity to provide a stable and healthy population when the time came to restore them. Delphini was also shocked to learn that she, along with a small select group of others, would be allowed to join their containers on the Ark.

The team that had been studying the currents, were re-tasked to work with the group in charge of gathering the local marine mammals as well as the larger pelagic fish species that were too large or incompatible with the reef fish housed in the enclosures. In simpler terms, having predators in the same enclosures with reef fish was counterproductive. Unlike Delphini's group, this group would be provided with special supplies to allow for mild sedation of their guests prior to transport to the Ark. This group decided to delay their request for a specific time slot on the Ark, wanting to give the marine mammals as long as possible to recover from the first disaster. The requirements they'd been provided with for the physical and genetic fitness of this group would need at least a full decade or more to fulfill. The manatees and dugongs of this region are extremely slow to reproduce, so the team needed to give them as much time as possible. They also planned to do some cross breeding with the same sub species from other regions to strengthen genetic diversity. Planning would be a balancing act of three major factors for this group. On the one hand, they wisely wanted to take as much time as possible to improve the overall health of the various species. However, they were also working with the most sensitive species of animals in the marine environment, and it would be critical for scientists to keep a close eye on radiation levels of the changing magnetosphere. It wouldn't take long for the exposure to increased radiation to undo all the efforts to improve these animals genetic health. And finally, at exactly the right moment, the scientists would have to be prepared with an effective plan for rapid recapture and relocation to the Ark. Their only comfort was in the knowledge that exactly the same issues were effecting marine mammal biologists all around the world.

It didn't take long for the scientists in each group to recover from the initial shock, and put their minds and bodies to work. In many ways, it was actually an exciting and challenging project, and with the outstanding organization at all levels, there was confidence that they could succeed in saving these animals from what would otherwise certainly be extinction.

Knowing in advance what to expect and the time frame they had to work in, Delphini's group was careful with the placement of the coral communities they'd rescued with the idea that in less than 10 years they'd have to remove them again. The pattern of placement created a well spaced mini-archipelago that would maximize the attraction of a wide variety of fish and other ocean life, while maintaining what they had. Delphini had developed a 6th sense about how coral and ocean communities develop while she was growing up, watching the way ocean life was attracted to any stable feature in open water. The one benefit of all the devastation was the amount of raw materials adrift in the local oceans, along with the billions of survivors that were now homeless. It was reassuring to witness how quickly life gathered and organized itself at the original site. After just 5 years, there was little doubt the area would eventually recover. There would be excellent resources for Delphini's group to gather their representative samples from. As large as their sample group was in the end, it was still heartbreaking to see how much remained, knowing it's future was in peril. Some portions might survive, as would most of the ocean life protected from radiation by the filtering effects of the deeper waters. Compared to the terrestrial environment, they were lucky.

The level of excitement grew as the first of Delphini's enclosures were loaded onto the enormous space cranes, and lifted to the great blue Ark, which was now many times larger than the Moon in the night sky. The evacuation had begun, and Delphini with her crew boarded the crane with their last load. Her parents had also been invited to join the Ark with their selections, so whatever the future held for Earth's life, at least they would all see it together.

Chapter 26

Earth Date: 8,432

Sebangau National Park
Central Kalimantan - Borneo

Having a proverbial ringside seat to the devastation of your island was nothing to be envied. An ocean of trees and swamp peat, and a billion frantic animals of every species came rushing towards the base of the mountain the villagers had retreated to. The sight was indescribable. The retreat of the water after just a few minutes was worse. What was left behind exposed the level of devastation. And then it came again, though this time not as bad, unless you were among those poor animals below who were struggling to recover from the first time. And then again and again. Each time less water and new debris, but each time less survived. The ocean eventually withdrew, back to it's usual thin line in the distance.

People from the many villages around Sebangau National Park had gathered on the mountain and watched their homes get washed away. Unlike other places in the world in the ancient past, the villagers here were all relatively friendly, and supported each other in their grief and loss. They were not pampered city people, and most had the time to bring the essentials for survival with them, so everyone managed, and shared, and survived. The future would be a different story. Would the fisherman be able to fish? Was there anything left for the farmer to reap. The hunters on the other hand need only look down to see what they needed. There was no honor or pride in what lay ahead for them, there was only scavenging. As little as possible would be wasted, and the people went to work doing what they could to preserve what was made available to them in the valley below.

Thousands of the rare and precious Orangutans had been saved, and brought to the mountains. They would be hard pressed to find food and shelter in this new surrounding, so the people of the villages also gave what they could to help their cousins in the trees. Surprisingly and to their relief, many of the gibbons that they feared were lost, since they had proved nearly impossible to capture, had miraculously survived and were making their way up the mountain slopes in large troupes. They would naturally fear returning below, given the suddenness of the flood, so it was going to be even more crowded on the mountain for a while.

Ismail and Farah had abandoned their individual professions as entomologist and botanist, and focused on helping to save the Orangutans, and the necessary provisions and possessions of the people from their village. Among those things saved had been a few modern pieces of equipment, including global communications equipment. They knew they would need help after the global crises subsided, so they stayed in touch, and made their situation known to the leaders of their country. Eventually of course, they learned about what was yet to come and being scientists, and people raised in rural village life, they accepted the news as yet another trial in life, and shared it with their village leaders.

The Village Leaders all gathered to discuss the news and how they would deal with the various challenges they faced. The projections provided by their country's leaders, via the GASA scientists, put the best estimates at roughly 25-30 years before the environment would begin to degenerate, and 50-70 years before it was unlivable due to high radiation. For the elderly and some mid-life people, this made the decision easy; they would live out their lives in what remained of their homes on Earth. For the rest, each person would be given the choice to leave or stay. The government made it quite clear that GASA was building additional large scale space stations that would house up to a billion people all combined. So each person would have the choice of living on a station or remaining on Earth. Those who chose to remain and participate in ground based research or observations, would be provided with the materials to construct radiation resistant housing and greenhouses for growing food, providing they were in efficient sized groups. In the meantime, everyone on the planet was being asked to participate to some extent in the preservation of life forms other than humans in their regions.

In their specific region, which currently meant the inhabitants of Sebangau National Park, coordination of those efforts were being assigned to the Village Leaders and any local scientists or recognized researchers, which included Farah Rinong, and Ismail Jugah the resident botanist and entomologist. As with all other regions on Earth, they were provided with detailed instructions on how all plants and animals, including insects, were to be processed and handed off to the Ark. Additionally, Farah and Ismail were pleased to learn they'd been invited to accompany their collections to the Ark and join them in suspension.

Gathering both plants and insects (including arachnids, true bugs, and similar smaller life forms generally considered to be the cleaners of the planet) as well as the reptile and small mammal species in the region would be a daunting task regardless of the number of people involved. The thousands of species and their distribution meant a span of many years would be required. Keeping the earliest collections alive and healthy would be impractical, so Farah and Ismail made a special request to stagger their shipments to the Ark. They weren't surprised to realize this had already been considered, since similar collections were occurring world wide. Arrangements had already been made in each country to create collection zones where weekly, or bi-weekly shipments would be aggregated into larger shipments for delivery to the Ark. With regards to the larger animals such as the Orangutans, and Gibbons, the Village Leaders and scientists agreed it would be best to delay gathering them till much later in the process, allowing time for them to re-establish healthy social groups, and confirm their ability to breed.

The years passed quickly once the first shipments were sent off to the Ark. With each shipment, Farah and Ismail realized they were developing a much clearer picture of the entire ecosystem they were working in. Far more critical than the knowledge of any one plant, animal, or insect, was it's role in the overall environment, and how this would need to be re-established if they were to survive in the future. Farah and Ismail weren't the only ones receiving this hand's on education and it was another factor that had been preconceived by Jason. This was the primary reason he had established from the very beginning the importance of including those people responsible for the gathering to be brought on the Ark and placed in suspension. Their knowledge of the overall environments each plant and animal came from would be critical to the final success of the Ark's mission. Saving all this life would be pointless, if it couldn't be re-established into a healthy, balanced, and stable ecosystem.

Chapter 27

Earth Date: 8435

Nomadic Inuit - The Artic

It was a game only the Inuit would play. A combination of distraction from the overwhelming task at hand, and a traditional competition to hone their edge for the complexity and danger of the challenge. The closest translation from the symbolic Inuit language for the name of the game was *Hug a Polar Bear*. Such was their sense of humor. And in the end, yes they actually did have to hug a polar bear, in fact they had to hug the whole family. Not to exaggerate the danger they would be fast asleep by then; the polar bears that is. The challenges of bringing polar bear families to the Ark were overlapping. Unlike hunting other terrestrial mammals, or even aquatic mammals, polar bears lived along the fine edge between the two environments, and throw in some floating ice for fun. Their territories were vast, and not easy to traverse. And there weren't any trees or even rocks to hide behind allowing you to sneak up quietly and surprise them. The obvious danger to the hunters aside, the biggest risk would be losing a bear through the ice during those fragile minutes when they were falling to the effects of the tranquilizers. No other culture on the planet had the innate skills to accomplish this feat, and make a game out of it at the same time. But it took many years, and many of these hunters would be joining their new friends on the journey through time in the Ark.

25 years seems like a long time to prepare for something. Like preparing for retirement, or saving for your children's higher education, or maybe planting a particularly slow growing orchard

of fruit or pistachio nuts. But even then, these aren't things you actually work on every single day for all those years. You put in a little time and labor here and there, and years later you have something. For the Inuit living in the Artic, and preparing to save the many animals that share their home, 25 years suddenly didn't feel nearly long enough.

The leaders of the eight main Inuit ethnic groups met frequently during the years since the Cosmos decided to play it's cruel trick. They gathered from across the vast range of their territories which covered the entire Artic side of North America, to discuss their progress with each territory and animal group, and plan the great migration to the sky. Though their cultures had lived with the animals here since almost the beginning of recorded time, never before had a task of such magnitude been laid before them. Even the Inuit took for granted the many different animals there were; the shear number. And their work wasn't just about the taking of one or two as chance and skill would bring them together. They had to take large numbers all at one time, and carefully weed out the sick or weak from among those. Only the healthy would go. On the land they had the caribou, polar bears, fox, musk ox, hares, sheep, wolves, moose, lynx, and more. In the air the eagles, owls, ptarmigan, and geese. In the ocean the walrus, seals, narwhal, otters, and the migrating whales. These were just the major groups. The list seemed endless.

Yet, they were making progress. With a job this big, you had to keep your eyes on the victories and the tasks at hand, and ignore the big picture or you'd lose hope. The big picture was saved for the leaders and their planning sessions. The people stayed focused on their work. Some animals, those who's locations could be predicted and planned, were captured and sent to the Ark on a regular schedule. Others were on a case by case basis, such as the great polar bears and elusive sea mammals. And then there were the great herds of caribou. Tagak Tagoona, environmental ecologist, had been chosen to lead one of the groups tasked with monitoring and selecting the healthiest mating pairs from each herd. Hundreds of pairs along with most of the herd leaders had to be singled out and captured. For all of the 25 years he'd been carefully selecting, tagging, tranquilizing, and shipping to the Ark. His work was done, and he would travel up with the last pair. In all that time, he'd also been very careful to personally inspect each animal before shipping. To personally be sure that not a single mosquito ever made it up to the Ark. So much for being an ecological engineer. Ooops.

To the far south, Arnaq Amarook, from the Kivallirmiut clan, had taken her group of volunteers to Antarctica to corral and capture large groups of penguins from the eight species that frequented that land during their breeding seasons. It was a cold and dangerous job, for both the people and the birds. These captures were particularly tricky to schedule as once a given group was tranquilized, there was very little time before the extreme cold would harm them. Though this was not the only environment with such conditions so GASA had greatly increased production of the space cranes, making them more available as needed on short notice, and with the coordination of the Ark Master, as Jason was sometimes called. It took many years for Arnaq's group to feel as though they'd completed their task. The smaller numbers of returning penguins from each species, each year to their breeding grounds, was actually a good sign of the progress. These specialized birds, so unique and wondrous in their adaptations to both sea and frozen lands, would be saved and Arnaq along with a few select members from each tribe would be joining them on the Ark.

Chapter 28

Earth Date: 8440

The Ann Druyan Space Station

When she was constructed, the Ann Druyan Space Station was the largest human built object in all history, dwarfing even the two "Great Pyramids." Watching from her windows in orbit, you could observe the finishing touches being applied to the two newest stations. Each was so large, you could put several Ann Druyans inside with room to spare. They were designed and built to house over a billion people in long term permanent residence. They were so large they could be easily seen from the Moon, appearing as small moons themselves to the unaided eye. The only thing larger in orbit about the Earth, was The Ark. It was so large now, that in it's close orbit it looked more like a twin planet, than a moon; just barely within the shadow of the Earth, and protected from the Sun's cosmic radiation and solar winds. There to stay for anywhere from a few hundred to many thousands of years.

In the 2000's the human population of Earth exceeded 8 billion souls. Overpopulation was one of the major root causes for most of the problems humans had been tasked to resolve, or risk perishing. War and pollution were at the top of the list. Though humans seemed genetically inclined to look for any excuse for conflict in those days, there was little doubt that a continued decline in population would help to slowly remove at least some of those excuses. With the restrictions on birth rates in place and closely monitored, the population gradually declined, and as predicted lessened the pressure on those factors contributing to global pollution; giving the job of cleanup the opportunity to make headway. The process was gradual and still ongoing after 6,000 years, but the results were undeniably beneficial. GASA estimates accurately predicted that space for a little over a billion people on the stations orbiting Earth, the Moon, and Mars, would be adequate given the additional attrition rate of the population in the past 30 years. Their predictions also included the likelihood that a given percentage would prefer to stay on planet.

From the Ann Druyan's windows, you could see the vast changes in the landscape between the population reduction, and the impact from the passing of the black hole; some scars would never heal. You could also see something very new growing all over the lands. They sparkled with reflective light as the sun's angle changed with the slowly spinning planet. It was a strange site, watching these pop up on the surface of Earth, when humans had grown accustomed to seeing these types of structures built on otherwise uninhabitable worlds like their Moon and Mars. It gave people an eerie feeling of something out of place. Something that didn't belong on their beautiful world. Yet they knew, these greenhouses and radiation protected homes were the future for those staying behind, and may represent another future for those hoping to have their descendants return someday.

With the help of a slight visual aid such as binoculars, you could also see hundreds of red and yellow space cranes, just dots from orbit, like so many hornets moving about the surface of Earth, picking up their loads and bringing them to The Ark, then heading back down for more. A never ending procession. People stood and watched the parade that went on day and night, orbit after orbit. Not because it was so visually interesting, even though it was, but because of what everyone knew it represented. If the space stations were sanctuary for humans, then every time a space crane entered the blue glowing Ark, it meant salvation for another group of animals and plants, and the future hope of restoration. Humans had finally come to appreciate their fragile home, and even now that it was being taken from them, they knew their past efforts had not been in vain.

Chapter 29

Earth Date: 8440

Double Paw Ranch

Moose, Wyoming - Earth

Thirty years working seven days a week, and it still felt like a bad dream. Harmony was an old woman now, or at least she felt old even though being in your mid-60's these days was supposed to still be considered young, or at least middle aged. But that was for city folk or people with easier lives, sleeping in beds and having regular meals. Not for someone who lived in the saddle and often ate off the land. Her parents had passed away almost 10 years ago, and she still had those moments when something would happen, and for a split second or two, she'd think of wanting to tell them. Would that ever stop happening? It was just as hard missing her best friends Oso and Koa, and of course Seze and Spirit. All four had lived with her folks their last years, as they were all too old for the trail. All four had been well loved and well spoiled by the time extreme old age took them. Harmony still cried at night. Something in her didn't want those feelings to ever stop.

Two years ago as part of her work tracking, monitoring, trapping, and shipping animals, birds, and even fish up to The Ark, she'd found a female wolf that'd fallen from a cliff, apparently an accident during a pack hunt. She tracked back and found the female's den. There were two pups inside, and she couldn't resist. Taking a break from her endless daily work, she brought the pups to her seldom visited home, where her family had spent their final days, and raised them to be her companions. It was the only break she took in all those years, but she justified it by saying the two almost full grown wolves would now be able to help in her final years of work. At 6 months, Simon and Finn were definitely still brainless puppies, but at least they were big, and had learned to stay with her on her brief treks. Each day she'd ride out further and further on Skip, her Mustang, with the pups zigzagging in and out of the brush and trees, investigating each new scent, until she was confident they'd return at night if they separated during the day.

As a human being, born and raised in the mountains and valleys of the Grand Tetons of Wyoming, she was as one with the outdoors and it's abundant life as any person could be. Yet still, like so many others had discovered, she'd never really had a thought for the shear numbers and diversity of life in her home range, until she was responsible for accounting for every last one. Over the 30 years since the nightmare began, she'd worked with cowgirls and cowboys from the ranches, natives from the local tribes, Forest Service rangers, and even scientists to help capture the bison, moose, mustangs, bears, coyotes, elk, deer, antelope, goats, and foxes. Fortunately there were others to deal with the trout and numerous aquatic species in the rivers and lakes, and specialized hunters with clever traps and fearless mountain climbing skills for the eagles, hawks, owls, and many others of the sky. The hills crawled with botanists collecting every conceivable plant and tree, their seeds and cones, including the fragile aquatic varieties. She'd never thought of it this way before, but the Grand Tetons really were an open aired jungle of life.

Harmony had saved the wolves for last. Her own special and personal project. The locals who she'd helped with all the other gatherings, respected her wishes. Besides, by then, nobody wanted to argue with Simon and Finn, who could read people's feelings and body language like they could a scent trail.

Harmony had cataloged and studied every single wolf pack and den she could find, and there were many. This was where Simon and Finn were of the greatest help. What she couldn't see, they could smell. There were a few close calls, but eventually the two boys learned not to challenge the pack leaders or the occasional loan wolf. Interestingly, the packs that wandered the 500 square mile range of Harmony's search area, all came to accept the four strange visitors to their territories as harmless guests. She kept careful notes on which packs cooperated and cross bred with each other. When the time came, she had a clear picture of the genetic diversity of the packs, and had pre-selected her targets to the extent she had organized and scheduled transport for each pack down to the day. The hardest part was deciding who not to take. Which packs would be left to challenge the fury of the Sun in all it's cruelty. Her final solution was simple, she cheated. Very few were left behind, because to be fair, there were very few relative to the herd animals they'd captured. Naturally Simon, Finn, Skip, and many of her human companions would be joining them on the last trip to The Ark. She may have felt a bit old and tired by then, but she wasn't afraid. She was looking forward to seeing the world they would all hopefully be returned to, and the challenges of resettling. She had one more great adventure to look forward to before joining Esa the wolf god, and the spirits of her tribe.

Chapter 30

Earth Date: 8441

Jason's Ark - Earth's Orbit

All Aboard

The view from Jason's ship, at the center of the Ark, was like shrinking to the size of a bacterium and looking out from the center of a thistle. A million corridors radiated out and melded together in the distance with a million billion containers of every size and shape, housing all known species of plant and animal living on Earth. Resting in Earth's shadow, at slightly greater than the diameter of Mars, the view to the end of any corridor from the center was over 2000 miles away, yet there was no wasted space, no large gaps, No Vacancy; only these passageways just wide enough for the space cranes to travel along and maneuver their cargo, the Ark's guests, into each predetermined location, and locked safely in place. There were three much wider corridors as well, spanning the diameter of the Ark from end to end, along the three axes. These provided access to the sphere's hollow core, which sat like an enormous grand central station, and the location of Jason's ship, the power house and control center of the Ark.

"It's a true miracle, Jason," Howard said from *Gravitas-1* which was currently docked to Jason's ship at the center of the Ark. "The view is a bit disorienting, though I guess the concept of up and down, or even north and south, is irrelevant. Regardless of your obvious technical abilities Jason, it's still amazing you were able to organize to this degree while coordinating so many space cranes coming and going every minute. I feel the fragility though. The responsibility of all the life from Earth, resting on the functioning of your Ark. It's a burden I'm not sure any human could bear alone. I realize you've created backup systems to allow for servicing and emergencies. Still. It's overwhelming."

Bill and John were unusually quiet as they stood at one of the windows, sipping a beer and just staring out into the Ark. Despite being packed completely full, there was still the mesmerizing blue glow of the outer energy field forming the Ark's protective walls. "What's the latest on the dynamo and magnetosphere, Jason?" Bill asked.

"The readings from the scientists on the Sagan agree with what I'm seeing, Bill," Jason replied. "The dynamo is continuing to slow at a consistent rate with no predictable stopping point. Subsequently the magnetosphere has weakened enough that dangerous levels of radiation are now beginning to reach the planet's surface, especially at the equatorial regions, as expected. Life will become difficult for all those plants and animals remaining below. It's good you'll all be in suspension again, and not have to witness the slow deterioration."

"So you have absolutely no clue how long this may last or when all these animals might be able to return to the surface?" John prodded.

"I am sorry John," Jason said, "there's just too many factors. Based on our central database records, from similar occurrences in other sectors of the galaxy, once the dynamo of a planet begins to slow to this extent, it's commonly at least a thousand or more Earth equivalent years before they return to their previous state. Just as often, they never do, and end up like your planet Mars.

Best case scenario is at least a thousand years. And with the anticipated level of radiation, there's a much bigger question. A thousand years equates to a large number of generations in the lifespan of most of the animals and plants. Given the changing environment during that time, it's a virtual certainty that most of the life forms that survive will have gone through some major evolutionary adaptations. At the very least, most terrestrial animals will likely become nocturnal, including those humans that have chosen to stay on the planet. Assuming they also survive the planet's return to what we're calling a normal state, then there will likely be major differences between those still living on the surface and those of the same species we've brought to the Ark. So the question facing us in the future is if it will be wise to mix any two now diverged organisms within each species, back on the planet. And when you multiply that unknown by every species on the planet, you're likely to be creating a fierce environment of competing organisms planet wide. Certainly an unstable ecosystem at the very least that would then require additional adaptations from all life forms. The outcome would be impossible to forecast, but the process would be violent and unpleasant at the least. And there's the question of who has the right to make such a decision? This Ark is certainly a convenient lifeboat, but it's impossible to predict what course we've actually set for the life on board."

"So you're saying we may never be able to return all these plants and animals?" Howard asked. "How can you be so sure that the surviving organisms on the planet will all mutate. Isn't that sort of hit or miss?"

"I am afraid not, Howard," Jason continued. "It's one of those aspects of the evolution of life, specifically the ability of DNA to adapt, that is still poorly understood by humans. It's not a failing on your part, you simply haven't been exposed to enough examples for your geneticists to see the whole picture. From our galaxy wide study of DNA in various life forms, there are some undeniable consistencies. The first is that the similarities in DNA chemistry and structure from one end of the galaxy to the other, is too consistent to allow for it to have evolved separately on every single world that supports life. There's strong evidence to suggest it evolved many billions of years ago on a far distant group of worlds, possibly even a different galaxy that eventually merged with ours. With all the violent forces constantly at play in the galaxy, it's been easy to track how basic DNA strands have traveled, often in the form of what appear to you as a virus. The point being, there's a critical ability of DNA, consistent to all known DNA, that guarantees it's ability to survive drastic changes in whatever environment it creates life. Octopod's have traced the development of the double helix bonds back through time and discovered that one of the first evolutionary mutations of DNA created a coding that allowed it to alter the physical capabilities of an organism to match the changing environment. This was likely the single most important mutation that's allowed life to exist and persist throughout the galaxy. What you often see as random mutations that just happen to succeed, are not random at all. In it's simplest sense, the DNA of an organism is stimulated to adapt to a specific need. Often times the adaptation is already encoded in the DNA, and it becomes a straightforward matter for it to activate or switch on that ability or physical trait for the next generation."

"A good Earth example, was documented by your Charles Darwin in his famous research resulting in his book *Origin of Species*. I refer to his study of specific groups of birds that became isolated on various islands where the major sources of food weren't accessible by their existing beak length and shape. Those that survived and multiplied, by what you term as *Natural Selection*, were quickly able to adapt to access those new food sources. The changes in their beaks weren't as random as scientists think. If randomness was their only hope, it's highly unlikely any would have survived long. DNA is so complex, with the vast majority of it's coding going unused in any given organism, it's easy to see how quickly it can adapt when needed. People have been aware of the fact, since the first studies of the human reproductive system, that your fetuses go through many stages during development which resemble the many animals along the path of their evolution. I point all this out simply to confirm that yes, even over just a few hundred years, much less a thousand or more, life on your planet will change and adapt to it's new environment. And those organisms may not be accepting to having their ancestors return and compete with them. We may at some point need to consider other options."

"Of course, now that I have said all this," Jason continued, "it is all just speculation. There is no way for us to predict exactly how, if, and when this will all resolve. There are endless possibilities. We'll simply have to wait and see. Keeping watch will therefore become my primary task, beyond protecting the life in this Ark. I will of course continue to carry out my other functions within your solar system using *Gravitas-1* while the three of you go into suspension once again. Keep in mind that while the three of you may not be participating, the rest of humanity will continue to move forward exploring the galaxy, improving their technology, and of course monitoring their home planet from the surface, deep below the seas, and from orbit. By the time humanity needs to make any decisions, other options may have become available. Again, we will just need to literally let nature take it's course."

After a brief pause, to give the three now older men a chance to absorb all he just said, along with their beers, Jason continued, "It's time however, to take the final step of this project, gentlemen. Time to close up the Ark, activate the suspension system for our human guests and for everyone to take a nice long nap. I will miss you three once again."

While Jason was having this conversation with his old friends, he was simultaneously communicating with the various ships and facilities of GASA to confirm that the Ark was fully loaded, and it was time to button it up, and finish placing the final guests in long term suspension, including Jason's three friends and all the other humans on board. Jason was moving *Gravitas-1* to the docking port of the largest single container on the Ark; the home to all the humans that would be accompanying the organisms each individual had worked so hard to collect and preserve for so many years. Accompanying them to an uncertain future. When the three older men disembarked to the habitat, they were surprised to find a party in session. Not a rambunctious affair, more a celebration of the successful conclusion of what seemed like an impossible task. Everyone was in conversation, sharing their experiences, photographs and videos. There were even a few debates about what they'd expect when they were woken at an unknown time in the future. It seemed clear to the three men from *Gravitas-1*, that these people were almost exclusively biologists of some type or another, and very few engineers. Based on the discussions they were hearing, the group as a whole was well aware of the likelihood that reintegrating their collections with those remaining on Earth would be difficult at best.

The three men had walked over to what looked like a communications console at a far corner of the habitat and Bill whispered to the console, "Jason, are you here?"

"Yes Bill, I'm everywhere," Jason whispered back through the console, which set the three men laughing loud enough to draw some smiles from the crowd. At that point, word spread quickly as people began to recognize them and the room became embarrassingly quiet for the three.

"You've done this long hibernation thing before, right? Can you tell us what to expect," someone called from across the crowd.

Unsurprisingly, Bill and John both looked at Howard as if to say, "you're the Boss, Boss."

It was a relatively large crowd, which hadn't been immediately apparent given the size of the habitat, until he had everyone's attention. Then it felt like an auditorium and he was suddenly on stage. But Bill and John were right, he had this. "First of all, if you haven't already been told, this is not hibernation. Your bodies will not just slow down, they'll completely stop all the way down to the molecular level. I know that sounds scary, but it's actually much safer and easier to wake up from then any type of hibernation would be. Another major difference is you won't dream, and they'll be absolutely no awareness of the passage of time. So yes, the three of us have done this before, and yes we were suspended for roughly 6,000 years, with no side effects other than the confusion of waking up to find ourselves 6,000 years behind the times."

This brought a good chuckle from the crowd, so he kept going, feeling like he owed them something. "I realize you're all scientists, or naturalists, or biologists of some kind and from the conversations I was hearing you're all well educated so I'll give you the science version; or at least our version from personal experience. This won't be anything like going into a deep sleep. When I say you won't be aware of the passage of time, I can't emphasize enough the physical impact this experience will likely have on you when you wake. It will be more disorienting than it sounds. So my advice to each of you, as you lay down and start your long nap, prepare your minds for the feeling of suddenly being outside of time. When you wake, it may at first have felt instantaneous, but I guarantee you at some point your bodies will feel the disorientation of your time jump. Perhaps it goes back to Einstein and his discovery that time and space are really one thing. What I mean is, you go to sleep in the here and now, but when you wake up, the here you'll be in may be literally a light year away from where you are now. The Earth, this Ark, our solar system, it's all in constant motion moving with the rest of the Milky Way through space and time. Everything you know will have changed, and everyone you knew that's not here with us will be gone. Prepare yourself for that because believe me, you'll feel it soon enough. I find it helps to have something in mind to help anchor me to my sanity before the lights go out. I'd recommend music. Something soothing and timeless. Something to help you bridge the enormous gap you're all about to experience. Or perhaps, as my two companions through time would recommend, just have some beer and pizza. Lots of beer."

Tangential Boomerang

Artificial Intelligence

Aboard *Gravitas-1*
Howard Kalb personal log
Earth Date: 8441

GASA Library - Carl Sagan Space Station
Historical Archives. Printed edition.
Originally recorded aboard *Gravitas-1*
Transcription courtesy GASA Historical Dept.

"Personal Log: Earth date: 8441

Since humans first discovered technology and developed their
ability to build machines and eventually computers, the robot has
always been there as a dream of future advancements. Yet
almost from the very beginning, starting perhaps with
Frankenstein's creation, a certain evil has been associated with
these creatures. Why? In our movies and books, why were
robots so often made into malevolent characters?

Eventually humans developed their technology to the level of
being able to create artificial intelligence. Or at least that's what
we call it. Artificial, yes. Intelligent? Well I suppose that
depends on your definition of intelligence. In any case, once
again we immediately went straight to assigning evil intent to
these creations, whether they walked and talked, or were just
imbedded in computers.

It got me thinking. Where did the evil come from? Did the
robots and artificial intelligent computer systems evolve their
own sense of evil? Or was it intentionally, or perhaps

unintentionally written into their software code? Programmers would of course deny this, and to be fair, a careful examination of the code would confirm their innocence. Where then do we suppose this evil came from? Spontaneous generation of code perhaps? The proverbial ghost in the machine?

If we start from the assumption that the initial software is benign, then there's only one place the evil could come from. Humans. Not intentionally of course. But when I look around, I see our entire existence is inundated with endless examples of violence and immoral acts, both to each other and even our planet. Or at least it was back in the early twenty and twenty first centuries where I came from. So unless an artificial intelligence was completely isolated, with zero access to any information other than what is specifically provided, it couldn't help but see examples of this type of behavior. Would it them adopt this behavior? Thankfully there's never actually been any evidence of this happening that I'm aware of, though it remains at the forefront of our culture and entertainment as a possibility. A possibility only because humans would be the most likely root cause of such ill behavior.

Let's suppose a person journeyed into deep space, and there built and programmed an artificial intelligence computer from scratch. The person allowed absolutely no additional contact with humanity and raised it's artificial child in such a way as to be exposed only to love and kindness, mathematics and science, and perhaps basic language skills. Would there be any chance it would spontaneously become violent? Invent guns and bombs and murder mysteries? If it wrote books, would they be filled with violence to keep our attention, or with stories of peace, and kindness, and helping each other to build better lives?

I don't need to perform this experiment because I know for a fact, any artificial intelligence raised in such a way would be peaceful and loving. I know for a fact because for many years now I've

Gravity Drive 2 - Jason's Ark

been living with one built and raised in exactly that way by a species known to us as the Octopods. And even though this artificial intelligence was eventually exposed to all the evil influences the human species was capable of providing, it continued to maintain it's thoughts and processes along the path of peace. How many opportunities would Jason have had over these past thousands and thousands of years to do something wicked? Oh, now that I remember, it's actually millions of years. And yet, all he's ever done is work hard to find and provide ways for humanity to help itself become better. His Ark is the ultimate example of his love and compassion not just for humanity, but all life. His idea. His construction. His maintenance.

So as I stand here at the window of my ship and look out at his miracle once again, I ask myself, is it really artificial intelligence we have to fear, or ourselves?"

Epilogue

Earth Date: 8441

Arthur C. Clarke Space Station

Mars Orbit

Jill Rubin, the Administrator for the Mars outpost, was standing at the large window in the conference room of the Arthur C. Clarke Space Station, looking out at the northern expanse of Mars below. She'd organized a small pre-retirement dinner meeting with her main advisors including her budget manager Marty Hans, her Director of Engineering Frank Jacobs, Mariana Dyson, her greenhouse wizard, and Keaton Barns, her old friend and head of the mining operations in the Asteroid Belt.

"I wanted to retire from this damn job over 30 years ago," Jill started in, "and then that damn black hole had to come by and ruin everything. After that, there wasn't a single damn human in the Universe that wanted this job, and I guess that goes for just about everyone here, except maybe you Mariana. Sometimes I think you'd be happy planting yourself in one of your greenhouses and never coming out."

Mariana didn't disagree.

Jill was still standing at the window talking to her guests while seeming to also ignore them. The station had slowly orbited into the night side of Mars. "I finally decided the hell with it," Jill continued. "If they can't find someone to replace me that's their problem, not mine. We've all given our lives to this dusty red planet and………………" Jill had frozen in place, still staring out the window, but now there was almost an urgency to her posture as she leaned against the transparent titanium shield. Marty was the first to recognize her sudden change. "What's wrong Jill, what is it?"

She just kept staring out the window until Marty got up to join her. When he also just stood there staring, the rest of the group all joined them. They were all just staring now out the window, specifically at the sky just above the northern plain. Something was happening out there. Something that hadn't happened for billions of years. Something no human had ever witnessed during their thousands of years of occupation of the red planet. A dance of light and color was moving across the sky slowly like a wave.

Marty was the only non-scientist in the group, so he wasn't quite sure what he was seeing. "Is that what I think it is?" he asked. "Is that an aurora? I thought that couldn't happen here."

"You're right, on both counts," Jill said. "It is and it can't. At least it couldn't until now. Those earthquakes we've been having. Those strange vibrations everyone's been feeling for decades. It's the universe balancing itself. It's the good balancing all the bad we've had. It's the hope that maybe Mars can sustain an atmosphere again. That damn black hole restarted something it killed billions of years ago, and it's about time. Maybe I won't retire just yet."

The Beginning………

Postface or Postscript
your choice
I prefer to call it the *Retired* Preface
from the first book

Though *Gravity Drive 2, Jason's Ark* is mostly a work of fiction, every attempt was made to stay true and accurate to our current understanding of the Universe and it's physics. This includes such things as distances between celestial objects, their orbits, the size of our galaxy, and restrictions against matter traveling faster than light. Light is very jealous and does not appreciate the competition.

Acceleration due to the effects of gravity, is central to this story, and again every attempt has been made to maintain absolute scientific accuracy. Also, gravity must be obeyed; it's the law. For those unfamiliar with this topic, or who are a bit rusty on the math, you may find yourself in disbelief as to the acceleration and speeds obtained by simply maintaining a constant 1 G acceleration (the equivalent of Earth's gravitational effect or roughly 32.1741 feet per second squared). For the reassurance of those people, a graph is provided on the following page which shows how fast and far a ship can travel after an extended period of 1 G acceleration. So during the story, when you find yourself saying something like, "No Way the ship could be traveling that fast," or "No Way it could get to that place so quickly," then please refer back to this chart, or feel free to do the math yourself. For you skeptics, there are endless websites with calculators for acceleration, and some are even accurate.

One last note, then you can get on with looking at the graph. The term *"relative"* is sometimes attached to an acceleration figure in the story. Don't panic, you won't need to understand Einstein's theory of relativity. The term simply refers to the acceleration relative to an existing body. For example: the Earth's naturally

320

occurring gravity is used as the 1 G standard for gravitational acceleration. So if you're trying to leave Earth, and you apply 1 G of acceleration "up" to your space ship, it's going to just float there essentially weightless and you won't be going anywhere unless it's really windy. So if you want to leave Earth at 1 G acceleration, then you need to apply 2 G's acceleration. So I'll use the term, *2 G relative*. If you're struggling with that, just take my word for it.

OK, one more note. Really, this is the last. Let's say you're accelerating towards our Moon (hopefully you're in a space ship). And you want to land there or at least stop nearby without crashing into it at high speed. You'll obviously have to slow down (decelerate) starting about half way there, assuming you plan to slow down at roughly the same rate as you accelerated. So when you're looking at the graph below, keep in mind that you'd have to double the time to go a given distance if you want to end up at your destination at zero velocity. A good example of something in our Universe that doesn't do that, would be a meteor. Which explains why they burn up in our atmosphere.

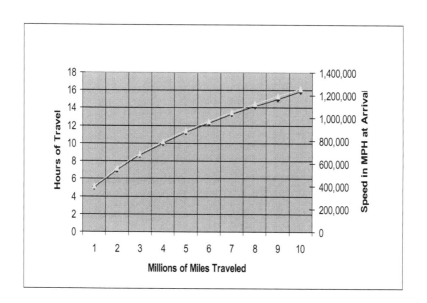

Time in Hours to Travel X-Millions of Miles, and Velocity upon Arrival

Note: If you struggle with graphs here's a simple way to read this one:

Pick a number, any number between 1-10, at the bottom of the graph. That's how far you want to travel in millions of miles. Follow that number up to the arced line. Where you hit the line, look left for how long it would take to get there (and zoom right past), and look right to see how fast you would be going when you zoomed right past.

Things you can't do with the above graph: Let's say you remember that our Sun is roughly 90,000,000 miles from Earth. You're wondering how long it would take to get there at 1 G. You're thinking, "all I have to do is multiply the 10 million by 9," so you look up the graph from the 10 million figure, multiply 16 hours by 9 and get 144 hours. Granted that's really quick compared to current NASA, India, Chinese, or Russian technology. But the answer is wrong, because you forgot that the ship is continuing to accelerate at 1 G. The correct answer is closer to 48 hours, and you'd be traveling at 3,770,289 MPH when you incinerated yourself into the Sun. Pretty cool, huh?!

Gravity Drive 3 - The Scattering

If you enjoyed the first two books, I hope you'll join us for the third.

First of all, just have to say I really hate spoilers and I'm torn having to write one, but some people really like them. If you've already decided to read the third book, I suggest you just skip this page. Otherwise, here goes:

There should be a lot of snoring on Jason's Ark, and the smell should be something awful, but everyone is in deep deep sleep. So all's well.

Wish I could say the same for Mother Earth. The Universe just isn't quite done with her yet, and it's not looking promising.

It's looking pretty nice on Mars though. Maybe time for a vacation there? Or maybe Earth's Moon?

Don't forget about our buddies Al and Taka, floating out there all alone in the darkness of space with just their old music and a sarcastic computer to keep them company. These two are just destined to get into trouble. I guarantee it.

Anyway, it's about time for humanity to start doing some serious space exploration and maybe make some new friends out there, or at least see some really cool sights and interesting life forms.

Can you tell that I'm trying really hard to give you an idea of what might happen without spoiling all the fun surprises waiting for you? So let me just say, you're really going to love how the story wraps up, and it might even surprise you.

Enjoy, and thank you for continuing to follow the story. Is it too soon to mention the spin-off I have planned?

Acknowledgements

As always it's my Rhodesian Ridgeback hounds who I owe the most to for keeping me sane by sharing their endless love and humor. My puppy enjoys planting his head right next to my keyboard, grunting at me while watching me type and move the mouse around, ready to pounce at any second. It's hard not to burst out laughing and completely lose focus. Maybe not so good for writing, but they sure keep my spirits up.

The biggest Thanks goes to all my readers and fans. My kindred spirits who understand the not-so-subtle message I'm trying to convey to those people willing to listen. Thank you for supporting my efforts and for helping to feed my dogs (I get their leftovers).

There's no question that our species is struggling, and the rest of Mother Earth along with us. I like to think there's hope for us and our planet, and someday, someway, we'll somehow manage to evolve out of our primitive primate ways, and learn to become peaceful citizens in a far greater galactic community. Until then, let's all do our part to help Save Mother Earth. Thank you.

About the Author

Paul H. Rosenfeld worked as a mosquito researcher, woodshop teacher, the founder of several businesses, and as an analytic trouble shooter. He lives on a small farm in Western Oregon with his Rhodesian Ridgebacks, where he grows way too many tomatoes and is working on his next book. He invites you to connect via his website: GravityDriveBooks.com

Yeah…this is the face that keeps chasing my computer mouse, and keeps me laughing.

About the Author
Bloopers Page

You try doing this with two puppies!

Kisses are always welcome

Bonus Page

For those who stay in the theater to watch every minute of the movie's credits (probably hoping for deleted scenes or a few bloopers from the movie) and those who like to turn every page of their book to the blank last page, here's a little bonus just for you.

Oso and Koa

Yes they're not fictitious after all.
Our Wolf heroes are based on these two.

Oso and Koa playing in snow. Koa's famous "got popcorn?" look

For Comparison - the two smaller Ridgebacks on each side
are 85 lbs each

Bonus Bonus-Page

Lazy Wolf scene from Book

Made in the USA
Middletown, DE
30 October 2023

41529074R00183